HAWK

HAWK

JAMES PATTERSON

AND

GABRIELLE CHARBONNET

JIMMY PATTERSON BOOKS
LITTLE, BROWN AND COMPANY
New York Boston London

Copyright © 2020 James Patterson
Excerpt from *City of the Dead* © 2021 James Patterson

JIMMY Patterson Books / Little, Brown and Company

Hachette Book Group
1290 Avenue of the Americas, New York, NY 10104
JimmyPatterson.org

Paperback Edition: August 2021
First Hardcover Edition: July 2020

JIMMY Patterson Books is an imprint of Little, Brown and Company, a division of Hachette Book Group, Inc. The Little, Brown name and logo are trademarks of Hachette Book Group, Inc. The JIMMY Patterson Books® name and logo are trademarks of JBP Business, LLC.

The publisher is not responsible for websites (or their content) that are not owned by the publisher.

The Hachette Speakers Bureau provides a wide range of authors for speaking events. To find out more, go to hachettespeakersbureau.com or call (866) 376-6591.

Library of Congress Cataloging-in-Publication Data
Names: Patterson, James, 1947- author.
Title: Hawk / James Patterson.
Description: First edition. | New York: JIMMY Patterson Books, 2020. | Audience: Ages 14-18. | Audience: Grades 7-9. | Summary: Maximum Ride's seventeen-year-old daughter, Hawk, is living under the radar in post-apocalyptic New York City until a destiny that is perilously close to her mother's forces her to take flight.
Identifiers: LCCN 2020005643 (print) | LCCN 2020005644 (ebook) | ISBN 9780316494403 (hardcover) | ISBN 9780316289221 (trade paperback) | ISBN 9780316494410 (ebook other)
Subjects: CYAC: Adventure and adventurers—Fiction. | Science fiction.
Classification: LCC PZ7.P27653 Haw 2020 (print) | LCC PZ7.P27653 (ebook) | DDC [Fic]—dc23
LC record available at https://lccn.loc.gov/2020005643
LC ebook record available at https://lccn.loc.gov/2020005644

Printing 1, 2021

LSC-C

HAWK

PROLOGUE

I solemnly promise this one thing to myself: I swear that this is the last day, absolutely the *very* last day, I will *ever* wait for those heartless bastards: my parents.

I leaned back against the corner of this building, the fading gray stucco chipped and pitted and slowly coming off. Five years ago it had been a bank; now there were no banks anywhere. I don't know why. Now the only things this building is good for are squatters, who'd broken in through the heavy glass door; looters, who'd taken anything of value from it; and me. I used it to prop myself up during my daily pointless wait. Today I was extra mad at myself for being the gullible smack that I am. We're talking way gullible. Why else would I be *here*?

"Hawk." The ragged homeless woman shot me a quick worried glance as she hobbled down the street with surprising speed.

I nodded at her. "Smiley." So-called because she'd lost a lot of her teeth. You hang out on a street corner long enough, you get to know the natives. I'd been hanging out here every day—we're talking *every single fricking day*—for *ten years*.

Every day at five o'clock, whether it's raining, blistering hot, freezing, snowing, wind blowing, whatever. Every day from five to five thirty. I was here.

And, like, *why?* Such a good question. One that I ask myself a hundred times every day, when I pretend not to notice what time it is, when really, it's ticking in my head, down to the minute. Like a bomb I keep playing with, every day, one that I actually want to explode. Because if it did, maybe this time, I really wouldn't go.

So why do I keep doing it?

The answer's always the same: because they asked me to. My parents.

And you know, I can remember just about every face I've ever seen. I'm like a *super recognizer.* I should work for the government, I'm not kidding. Not this government, obvs. But *some* government, somewhere. Anyhow, a million faces, good, bad, and ugly locked away in my mind-vault, and yet...

Yet I don't remember them. Mom and Dad. I remember my father's hands, standing me on this street corner. For some reason I feel like we were afraid. I could feel a tremor in his fingers, tight in mine. I think I remember this so clearly because my hands were clean and haven't been since then. One of them said, "It's five o'clock now. Stay here for half an hour, till your watch says five thirty. A friend of ours will come get you—or we'll be back. Promise."

I don't remember the voice, whether it was soft and warm, or harsh, or desperate, or whispered. I don't even know if it was my mom or dad that said it.

I lost my watch years ago. Actually, it got broken in a fight.

Along with my nose, that time. Other things have been broken and bruised since then, and I've got the scars to prove it. The one thing that hasn't broken yet is my spirit. But a few more days of keeping this lonely watch on this crap corner might do it.

My parents' muted voices, the fogged-out faces—that was *ten years ago*. No friend ever came. My parents never came back. Remembering that makes me laugh at myself.

What kind of a pathetic idiot waits on the same corner every day from five to five thirty for their whole life? Or at least ten years of it? The biggest idiot in the world.

This was the last, very, very last time.

PART ONE

PART ONE

CHAPTER 1

5:12. *Splat!* I winced and jerked as something wet and gushy exploded on the wall right next to my head. *Ick!* I wiped rotten... *onion?* off my forehead, its sharp, rancid odor making my nostrils twitch and my eyes tear up.

Oh, goddamnit, not today...

Instinctively I dropped into a crouch just as a bullet ricocheted off the wall where my head had been.

I immediately straightened, eyes easily finding Tony Two-Toes and Racelli.

"This is our corner, bitch," Racelli said. "You keep trespassing."

"Yeah, girls are annoying like that, right?" I asked, sounding bored.

Whoosh! Tony Two-Toes swung his gun butt right at my head with enough force to crack my skull, if he'd managed to make contact. Instead, I leaned way to my right and the gun smashed into the building wall, cracking old plaster and stone and sending chips flying.

"The thing about you," I said, "is you're so goddamn *slow.*"

With that I jumped straight up into the air, nine, ten feet, then pivoted and pushed my feet off the building, sending me out into the middle of the street. From there I took a run at Racelli, landing with a big leap, my worn-out boots almost touching his extremely expensive sneakers—stolen, no doubt. I chopped the back of his knee with the flat of my hand and his muscles gave out under the pressure. He buckled, and I grabbed the gun from him. Backing up quickly, I flicked the safety off and waved the gun at each of them.

"Careful, shit-heels. Do not piss me off today," I snarled. "And if you're going to throw food at me, make it something fresh. I prefer apples."

Racelli lunged for me. Moving as fast as only I can, I chucked him under the chin with the gun butt, knocking him on his ass again. Tony raised his gun to shoot, so I aimed and blew his hat off. He yelped and looked back for it, giving me time to adjust my aim.

"Sorry, Tony," I said, right before I shot his gun out of his hand. "I don't think you can be trusted with that." This time he screamed, looking at his hand, which was running red. The gun lay on the concrete, surrounded by bright red drops that almost looked like rain...except they weren't.

Charging him, I kicked his gun off the pavement and down a sewer grate while he held his hand and screamed at me.

"I didn't make you Tony One-Finger, did I?" I asked. Then—too soon—I tossed Racelli's gun down the sewer grate also, feeling like I was a fecking boss. Tony took advantage of that to roar and punch me in the jaw, snapping my head sideways. Tendons in my neck cracked, and there were black spots in my vision. I didn't have time to get out of the way when he pulled his arm back to hit me again, but Ridley had seen what was happening and she swooped down.

Her wings beat the air as she dropped onto Tony's head, her long, razor-sharp talons raking his skin. Twin rivers of blood flowed into his eyes, blocking his view as he shrieked and tried to punch her. She flitted gracefully out of reach, her cold black eyes now focused on Racelli, who had run over to us. He retreated a few steps as Tony doubled over, wailing and holding his scalp as more of his blood fell onto the concrete to pool with the earlier drops.

"You're gonna regret tossing my gun," Racelli said meanly.

My eyebrows rose. "I doubt it."

He made a quick move at me, but Ridley hunched her shoulders as if preparing to strike.

Racelli looked at Tony, then at Ridley, then at me. Without even telling Tony good-bye, he turned and walked away. Walked, not ran. But walked fast. Tony, swearing to rain hell down on Ridley and me, hobbled after him, leaving a trail of red as he cradled his injured hand to his chest.

Ridley floated down and landed on my shoulder, careful not to grip me too hard. She brushed her hard beak gently against my hair, trying to smooth away the endless tangles. I put my hand up and stroked her warm brown wing, crooning to her.

"That silly Tony," I told her in a baby voice. "Doesn't he know we're *already* in hell? We *live* here, man." It was 5:18.

CHAPTER 2

5:20. When I was sure those two berks were gone, I leaned against the building again. I was sure this wall had a Hawk-shaped indentation in it from ten years of me keeping a stupid promise. I tried to settle in just right, find the position that dug into the familiar ache of my back, maybe bring a little relief while I put in the last ten minutes of my watch. My tongue probed at my teeth to see if Tony's punch had knocked anything loose. *One molar might be a little wiggly, and there's an ache in my jaw, but I totally came out of that tangle on top.*

Ridley perched on my shoulder, preening herself and my hair at the same time. Absently I stroked her breast feathers, enjoying her warm, five-pound weight, the quick, gentle movements of her beak. The same beak that could rip a rat or a person to shreds was also precise enough to pick ticks off her feathers and dirt out of my mohawk.

With no warning, as usual, the Voxvoce suddenly blared throughout the city. People stopped in their tracks, some sinking to the ground, holding their ears. Ridley gave a high-pitched whine, and I clamped one hand around her silky head, shielding her ear holes as best I could. Then I closed my eyes and escaped within myself, away from the Voxvoce and the twisted, corrupt government who used it to control its people.

It ricocheted off buildings, filling the air and making my teeth ring. Even my eyeballs felt like they were vibrating in my skull as Ridley curled closer to me, looking for shelter from an enemy she couldn't see and didn't understand.

5:24. Finally, it ended—it had been about a minute and a half this time. Sometimes it was longer, sometimes shorter, but the sound always had the ability to make kids cry, terrify animals and make birds drop from the sky, make grown men sink to their knees and women cringe against buildings, silent tears streaking their cheeks.

It was super-effective. I pictured catching the bastards who'd come up with the idea of the Voxvoce, and the bastards who had created it, and locking them all in a room with it playing 24/7. They'd be writhing like worms within minutes, vomiting and crying and screaming for mercy. I would have no mercy.

They always killed it right when you thought you were about to lose your mind, go totally insane and shove something sharp into your ear just to make it stop. The bastards were smarter than that, though; they turned the noise off before you hit that point, and instead you were just thankful that it ended. I'd actually seen people thank them for stopping, like they forgot it's the bastards that started it in the first place.

5:25. Everyone knew this was my corner—which was why so many thugs tried to take it from me. For a half hour every day, I people watched, usually with Ridley on my shoulder, which kept some of the rougher elements away. The smarter ones, anyway. There were certainly some dumb ones walking around with Ridley-induced scars on their faces. This city was a nightmare. What kind of parents would leave a little kid on her own in a nightmare place like this with only a raptor to protect her? I looked around. Every person here was packing, the outlines of their guns plain against their clothes. I'd seen kids as young as six with their own handguns, scaled down to fit their smaller hands and weaker grips.

5:27. Besides all the freaking gun-carriers, there were the Opes. Opes were scary, even to me, almost. Every once in a while you saw one who was a relatively cheerful addict, maybe someone with money and a sure supply. Much more often Opes were ragged, desperate, dirty, and lost. At a certain point they forgot to eat, forgot to do anything except find drugs. They were bony, with sharp cheekbones and elbows, scarred skin, rotted teeth, and hair that looked like it had been stapled to their heads in sad clumps.

An Ope was lurching toward me now, singing under her breath, dragging one foot, sticklike fingers twirling in hair dirtier and more tangled than mine, which is saying something. I carefully looked away, just another drug-free kid with a large hawk on her shoulder. She paused when she saw me, but I refused to meet her eyes, and finally she loped past, almost stumbling at the curb.

When she was gone, I grinned a little and rubbed Ridley's head. The Ope had been wearing a Max T-shirt—filthy and full of holes, but still. I loved Maximum Ride, though I didn't really know who or what she was. Maybe a comic book character? Maybe a movie star or something, I don't know. Just every now and then I saw her picture on a T-shirt or a book cover or a billboard, and I liked the way she looked: god-awful fierce and determined as hell. No one to mess with. I'd named my bird after her: Ridley is like Ride, with an *ly*.

And it was 6:00. I was out.

CHAPTER 3

"Attention, citizens!" The familiar, oily voice boomed all around me. The huge vidscreens designed to reach every last corner of this city glowed with the image of the governor, McCallum. If he had a first name, I'd never heard it. All I knew was that he'd been yelling his word salad at us for as long as I could remember. The Voxvoce had been his idea, I was sure of it.

"Citizens!" he shouted again, his wide, fleshy face forming the words as if a puppeteer were controlling him. Hell, maybe one was. I'd believe anything about McCallum. "Remember that here you are free!!! Free to get jobs, free to take care of your own stuff, free to quit sponging off the government! Act like the adults you pretend to be! And, Opes—there's nothing wrong with you! You're just seeing the world a different way! But you gotta support yourselves, you know? Everyone has to mind their own garden, their own weeds! You don't want crabgrass in your garden, do you?"

Several Opes pawing through garbage across the street looked up, then hunched their shoulders again, pushing trash aside.

God. McCallum was such a fecking shit-heel. Who in this city has a damn garden? I mean, I can't stand the Opes—nobody can. But he didn't have to yell at them like that in public. I mean, he yelled at everybody. But he seemed to single out the Opes.

"He's such a dick," I told Ridley, and she shook out her feathers, obvs totally agreeing with me. I smiled as I remembered the Ope wearing a Max T-shirt. I had three of them myself, swiped from someone's street table. Sure, the seller had yelled at me, said she'd sic her brothers on me, that she had a gun and would take me out the next time she saw me.

Really, lady? You're gonna get upset about losing a couple shirts that you got off the back of a truck? Yeah? C'mon. And you got a gun? Hell, I figured. Babies around here come out of their moms dragging a pistol after them.

I used to have a gun myself, a Barracuda. I'd gotten it years ago, and in my fifteen years I'd only ever killed one person. At that thought, I stuck my tongue hard against the tooth Tony had knocked loose, letting the pain distract me. I didn't need to think about that person now, and I didn't want to carry a gun anymore. I had bigger concerns.

Now I needed to get home to my kids.

CHAPTER 4

I take different routes home through the City of the Dead. They call it that because, a couple years before I was dumped here like trash, everyone who lived within like a mile all got sick and died. A couple of the Oldies told me about it—it was horrible, and to this day no one knows what happened. But they all just up and died. Over the years, other people moved into the empty apartments, like a free move-in day. All you've got to do is carry out the dead, and it's yours.

So everyone here is from somewhere else, and the City of the Dead has filled up with Opes, Oldies, Rebs, Freaks, and Tourists. I like the Rebs. They've never messed with me. They plastered colorful posters around, advertising their particular gangs: Smothered, SlavesNoMore, Freedom…there were a couple others. Of course it was pointless, rebelling against McCallum. I didn't know how they'd managed to string two thoughts together to make these posters, what with the Voxvoce and the Proclamations and the Emergencies. But they had, and I liked looking at the posters stuck to the walls of burned-out buildings. A little bit of color never hurt anybody, and sometimes I tore them down, took them home to help teach my kids how to read.

It was the Tourists who were the worst. There weren't many—fewer every year. They came here from non–Cities of the Dead and looked at us like we were slime molds. Like, Look, honey, there's an Ope getting beat up! Take a picture! Once I saw Smiley actually posing for someone, showing off her empty gums in exchange for a handful of coins. It pissed me off—not at her—a girl's gotta do what she's got to do. But if I ever saw that Tourist again, I'd show them what a mouth with teeth in it is for.

Sometimes if I'm standing at my corner they'll offer me money, like I was begging. I'd love to make them swallow it. Instead I grit my teeth and take it, shoving it deep in my pocket. Because money is money. Money means food, medicine, favors. I couldn't afford to throw it back at them.

A couple years ago this shiny clean Tourist came up to me and I waited for him to hold out some onesie coins. He didn't.

"You're what they call an Ope, aren't you?" he'd whispered, pulling a baggie of blue powder out of his jacket pocket. "Tell you what—we go into this alley over here and you let me do anything I want, and I'll give you…half this bag. You'd like that, wouldn't you? Half a bag of dope? Just for you?" He smiled encouragingly, trying to screw a thirteen-year-old kid.

I'd broken his jaw.

While he was writhing on the ground, some Opes had run up and mugged him, taking everything, including his car keys. I'd almost laughed myself sick.

Maybe Tourists shouldn't come here. Or maybe I should leave. But I can't. I promised.

CHAPTER 5

"Hawk!"

Night was falling. In the City of the Dead it was more like heavy, greasy clouds looming down from the sky, wiping out the stars, dulling the moon. I was tired and wanted to go home, but I knew that voice.

"Pietro," I said as he came up to me.

Ridley gave a huff and took off into the night. I'm pretty much the only person she likes.

"How ya been?" He looked like he really cared. Some people asked just because they wanted you to ask back, and are too busy answering with a long sob story that they never notice you didn't actually ask.

"I'm always fine, Pietro," I said. We'd been pals when we were like seven, eight years old, but then his father had forbidden him to play with the riffraff and told him to stick to his own kind. His own kind being from the Six.

In our city, only that barking, false-fronted rager McCallum was more important than the Six. The Six were the gangs who ran this city, and not in a kindly, thoughtful way, either. They'd carved out their territories and set up their own leaders. Pietro was a prince; his father was Giacomo Pater. Their gang was One of Six, and I lived in their territory.

Two of Six were the McLeods. Three of Six were the Harrises. Four of Six were the Stolks, Five of Six were the Diazes, and Six of Six were the Chungs. They made life fun around here, and by *fun* I meant violent and scary.

"What brings you down to the dirt, Pietro?" I asked.

His handsome face suddenly hardened, and he gestured behind me with one hand.

"That piece of trash over there," he said. I turned to see another prince, tall and pale with thick, shiny, red-brown hair and a face that was all angles. He came out of an alley like he'd been waiting on somebody. I could only hope it was Pietro he was looking for, and not me.

"Chung?" I guessed.

"Yep," he bit out and spit on the sidewalk.

"Okay, what about him?" I asked.

Pietro frowned. "They tried to open a business two blocks into our territory. The Chungs are trying to muscle in, and my father wants to send a clear message. So he called for a duel."

Duels happened pretty often, but not all in the same territory. They were exciting as hell—if you didn't care that one of your friends might be about to die.

"Do you have to?" I asked.

He nodded, looking unhappy. Suddenly he looked into my eyes and took my hand. "Hawk, I wish—"

"Duel!" someone shouted, and instantly the crowd picked up the chant, making it impossible for either Pietro or the Chung prince to back down now. I saw one of Giacomo's henchmen edging out of the crowd, standing in the street with his arms folded. Likewise, one of the Chung henchmen stood on the opposite side of the street, the gold symbol of the Chung clan embroidered on his blue silk jogging suit.

Pietro dropped my hand and walked to the middle of the street.

There were rules about duels, even if there weren't many rules about anything else. 1) Whoever *called* the duel shot second. 2) They had to use single-fire handguns. 3) They had to bring a second, someone who would carry their body home if they died. 4) It had to be a public place, with plenty of witnesses.

So here they were. I was one of the plenty of witnesses. My stomach twisted and my mouth was suddenly dry. I was about to watch Pietro get a bullet in the head.

We hadn't been close in years, but he'd been my best friend for a while. We'd played "hide from the plague people" together. We'd played "behind enemy lines" and "lava floor." We'd practiced stealing from street markets together. Together we had collected trash and sorted it and sold it to the trash peddlers. And here I was about to watch him catch a bullet just because that's how things were done in the City of the Dead when you were a prince of the Paters, a One.

I wanted to tell him it didn't have to be this way, but there were too many people and the chant had begun to die down, the crowd aware that they were going to get what they wanted. If I stood in the way of that, I'd risk being hurt myself. I stepped to the side, giving Pietro a nod for good luck.

"Begin!" shouted Pietro's second.

Pietro and the Chung prince stood back-to-back. Pietro was trembling slightly, so slightly that probably no one saw it but me. His face was set, his mouth pressed into a firm line.

"Count off!" the Chung second yelled.

"One!" "Two!" "Three!" The boys counted their paces as they walked away from each other, taking big steps.

The streetlamps came on, casting a sickening orange glow over all of us. Pietro looked even worse in the light, his skin a harsh color as he paced off with the shouts. I was starting to get mad. This was so freaking stupid! This was just gangs flexing their muscles! Was Giacomo really willing to sacrifice his son over a couple blocks of territory? There was no way a Chung would deliberately miss a Pater! I pictured myself storming up to Pietro's big house and yelling at Giacomo.

Then I pictured one of their soldiers throwing my body over the wall into the city dump, Ridley soaring over my body for days as she waited for me to get up. I swallowed hard, my fists clenched.

The two princes pivoted and faced each other.

"I'm glad they pick each other off every so often," a woman next to me said. In general I agreed with her—the fewer gangsters, the better. But this was Pietro, and whatever he was destined to become in his family, there'd been a time when he was a fun, good-natured kid.

The Chung prince raised his gun, pointing it directly at Pietro. Pietro wasn't that far away; it was a shot I could make easily. Laser aimers weren't allowed, of course. Maybe the Chung prince had bad eyesight? No—he would have had it fixed by now. They had that kind of money, and as much as the princes were used to settle their fathers' scores, they'd want to make sure they had every possible edge.

Pietro stood without flinching, even as the Chung prince fired. Then he jerked to one side, his hand clapped against his head. I almost screamed his name but covered my mouth.

He was still standing. Dark red blood ran through his fingers and splattered on the street. Slowly he straightened, shook the blood off his hand, and wiped it on his maroon Pater uniform.

Please don't kill him, I thought, as if my thoughts could influence Pietro. Please don't kill the Chung dude. Don't become the killer your dad wants you to be. Just injure him a little, like he did you, and you'll both save face. Please.

Pietro raised his gun. I held my breath. The Chung prince's chest heaved as he tried to control his breathing. His arm hung limply at his side, the gun shaking in his grip as he waited for a bullet. Running would be a disgrace, and so he stood, waiting to die.

Please, I thought.

Pietro fired. The Chung prince whipped backward as the bullet struck his arm. The crowd was so still that we could all heard the clink of the bullet as it hit the wall behind him. Someone cheered, and then we all cheered. Pietro had shot the Chung prince in the arm; the bullet had gone cleanly through. It would be an easy recovery.

Beaming, I yelled Pietro's name. I saw the Pater henchman spit on the ground in disgust. I guessed Giacomo wouldn't be too happy, but I was proud of Pietro for making his own decision. The Chung henchman was walking toward his prince. The Pater henchman left Pietro's side and also walked toward the Chung prince. Before anyone could react, he grabbed the Chung prince with big, meaty hands, and snapped his head around. We all heard the loud crack of bones breaking, saw the light leave his dark eyes, saw him crumple to the ground, dead. He was still smiling from relief at living through the duel. Several of the Chung footmen started toward the Pater goon, but the Chung henchman stopped them.

"It is over!" he said, but he was obviously furious at the Pater killer.

I stopped in my tracks, my own smile disappearing. The crowd cheered even louder. A duel was one thing; a flat-out murder another. This was enough excitement for days.

Pietro looked at me, saw my expression. "I didn't do that! I didn't want that to happen!" he yelled.

I turned and walked away, disgusted with all of the Six. He might not have wanted the prince dead, but he had still been a part of this. Everyone in the Six families was as bad as the rest, including Pietro. He was a full-blooded Pater now.

CHAPTER 6

Okay, the show was over. Time to get home. As I walked past a vegetable stand, the woman threw a bunch of rejects into the gutter. Me and a bunch of Opes fell on them, and I snagged some sprouting carrots and a plastic bag of not quite rotten apples. I put them in my backpack. The sooner I was away from this street—this corner—the better. Obviously my parents hadn't come. They were either dead or had long forgotten me. This was the last day I would waste like this.

Hearing footsteps behind me, I glanced over my shoulder and groaned quietly to myself. I was being followed.

I sped up a bit—enough excitement already—but a sneaky look back showed me that it was two men, strangers. Great.

I knew this city. I'd been exploring it since I was five years old. I knew every abandoned building in the City of the Dead, every sewer, every tunnel, every escape route. And the closest one was four blocks away. I sped up more, now able to hear the men's eager mutterings. I could stay and fight, of course, but I just wanted to get home. Plus, I'd been collecting food all day and now had about twenty pounds of nutrition in my backpack.

I was just tired of this shit. Girls out on their own faced a different kind of danger than boys, and trying to explain I was just getting food for my kids wouldn't earn me any mercy.

I crossed the next street fast, dodging through the pedicabs, occasional cars, trucks, and bicycles and getting honked at, yelled at, sworn at, and flipped off. I gained twenty yards. I needed to turn at the end of this block, but they were trotting now.

I broke into a run, and so did they. I did a fast left turn and really started running, backpack thumping against me as I went. We were just two blocks off the main street and it was already completely dead back here; people who couldn't afford the main drag didn't get streetlights. I passed several Opes, talking to themselves, curled up in doorways.

I turned right at the next corner, and crossing this street was easy because it was barely more than a garbage alley. Two kilometers upwind was the prison. Three kilometers as the crow flies, southeast, was the city hospice and the factory where they made the dope for the Opes.

I just had to make it to the last building on this block.

"Girl, wait!" one of the men yelled.

Sure! Why not! That's a great idea!

With a sudden screech, Ridley swept down and did a power dive on the two men. They ducked and swore, one of them taking out a gun and shooting. Ridley turned sideways and swooped out of reach.

Then I was at the building, rushing into the darkness, swerving to avoid once-ornate columns and chunks of ceiling. The men were right behind me. I was breathing hard, sweating, and starting to think about plan B in case this one didn't work. Pushing through a fire-exit door, I grabbed the stairway handrail and headed up two steps at a time. I had passed the second story before the door banged open. There was some muffled discussion, then they started up the stairs after me.

Well, *I* knew which treads were rusted out and when to let go of the handrail because it had come loose. I was faster than them, even with a twenty-pound backpack. I was on the fourth floor before they'd gotten to the second, and I rounded the sixth floor when they had barely made it to third.

My heart was pounding in my throat—despite my grade-A fighting skills, I didn't want to deal with two determined men with guns. First thing a girl learns on the street is that when men are after you, being fast is your best bet because you're usually not going to be stronger, and if they've got guns, the game's already over.

Eighth floor. My feet were slamming down on the rusted metal treads, my calf muscles screaming from the strain. From long practice I automatically jumped over ones that weren't safe. A yell below told me one of the men hadn't been so lucky. I thought of the rusted metal scraping against skin, maybe puncturing, getting caught up in some muscle.

Finally, finally, the tenth floor. I burst through the metal door and rushed out onto the roof, starting to pant, my hair plastered to my head with sweat. The men were at least five stories below.

I climbed up on the roof ledge, looking down at the City of the Dead. Whatever my parents had intended, this was my city now.

Ridley was swirling in circles above me with a hurry-up expression in her eyes. Smiling at her, I threw back my poncho and extended my wings, almost groaning with pleasure at finally being able to stretch them out. The constant ache between my shoulder blades released with them. Tip to tip, they were almost four meters across, but I might grow some more.

I jumped off the roof and felt my wings fill with air. As always it was an amazing feeling—the feeling of being free and strong in a city where no one wanted you to be. Laughing, I swooped away from where the men struggled on the stairway, far below me. They might give up; they might make it to the roof to find that I was somehow just gone. They might assume that like so many others, I'd taken a long, last leap down to the pavement below. Anyway, I never needed to think about them again. I rose above the greasy mix of fog and clouds that blotted out the moon, breathing in cold, clean air. Ridley looped in big arcs around me as if I were slowing her down.

"Get stuffed, Ridley!" I yelled, laughing to feel so free above the City of the Dead. Even if it was just for a little while.

CHAPTER 7

I soared upward, moving my wings strongly, feeling their power as I worked out the kinks I got from keeping them hidden all day. This was—just so great. It was cool and dry and quiet up here. Down below was always warmish, always wettish, noisy, crowded, dangerous. Everything below was old and rotting; everything above fresh and new.

But up here—no one up here but us birds.

I flew higher and higher until the air thinned and it became harder to breathe. From up here I could barely see the City of the Dead—it was hidden by the ever-present mucky clouds. I couldn't see anything else, either. For a good twenty, thirty kilometers, I saw land—bare, rocky, treeless land. No other cities, no other lights, no other clumps of clouds where another city might be hidden beneath. No escape.

Ridley matched me stroke for stroke, obviously enjoying stretching her wings, too. I called to her, "Better be getting home. The kids'll be getting hungry."

As if we were connected by a string, we coasted in a huge circle, curving downward. We closed our eyes as we went through the clouds, then saw that we were over the factory that made dope for the Opes. There was a line of them waiting now outside the door, but it was too late for them to get anything tonight. They would camp until morning, a long line of huddled, miserable people who would stand through falling rain, pelting snow, or blistering heat. Anything to get their next fix.

We headed north to the McCallum Complex. It was big, covering several city blocks and surrounded by three-and-a-half-meter cinder-block walls topped by razor wire. Which was nothing to me, of course. Ridley flitted down to clamp her talons around a streetlight—I usually didn't take her indoors.

The McCallum Complex had even more vidscreens than the city did—everywhere I looked, he was onscreen, smiling or angry or teasing or silly. I didn't know why he was everywhere, I didn't know why his name was on everything—McCallum Incarceration, McCallum Laboratories, McCallum Children's Home.

I waited till the yard outside the Children's Home was empty, then gently let my wings slow till I came down in the deep shadows behind the trash dumpsters. Sighing, I folded them, hot from exercise, back under my poncho.

Even before I got to the double glass doors, the kids had pushed them open and were running to me.

"Hawk!" "Hawk!" "Hawk!"

"Hey, hey, hey, wait a sec," I commanded, unhooking hands from my backpack. "This is it, and we have to share it. Let's get inside." These were the people I lived with. Not so much my friends as my kids. I was the only one of them who could leave, who could bring back food. I was the only one whose experiment had worked.

My wings. I'd guessed I was either a genetic freak, or that I'd been experimented on, had wings grafted on. It was probably why my parents had dumped me here. Who'd want a freak for a kid? Anyway, my wings worked great, and I was glad to have them. Some of the kids, my fellow lab rats, hadn't been so lucky.

"Okay, Clete, this is for you," I said, divvying up the bits of food I'd snagged during the day. Clete came forward slowly and awkwardly—in the last two years, he'd suddenly grown three-quarters of a meter and was now about two meters tall. Too bad his weight hadn't kept up with him. He looked like a tall, camel-colored drinking straw.

He was my age but seemed younger and had come here when he was still an Ope. I'd seen him OD and almost die at least twice. Now, though, he was pretty okay. I mean, okay for him. I don't know if the dope did it to him or if he was born that way, but he sort of had trouble dealing with people. Even us, sometimes. We'd all learned not to sneak up on him and to be patient while he talked because he had trouble getting words out sometimes. He got upset super easily and just wanted things to be the same all the time. On the other hand, you could give him any two numbers, no matter how big, and he could multiply them or subtract them or anything, like lightning. He knew how computers worked, more than any of us. He read stuff, like news and science books. "Thanks," he said, shuffling off to eat it.

I looked at Moke, the only lab rat who was older than me. "He okay today?" I murmured, making sure Clete couldn't hear.

Moke nodded and took the food I held out. Most people are

shorter than me, but Moke and I saw eye to eye (and Clete was twelve centimeters taller). "Or as okay as that freak can be," he said, not bothering to lower his voice. Clete looked up but kept eating, slurping a bit.

Moke was *pretty* normal; he'd never been an Ope, and he didn't have wings or anything else. It's just—he was bluish. His skin was sort of blue, his hair sort of a dark brown-blue, the whites of his eyes were the blues of his eyes—you get the picture. Something about them trying to meld his DNA with silver? The metal? Why? Who would think that was a good idea? A moron! Anyway, Moke was kind of blue. So him calling Clete a freak was lame, at best.

Rain smiled one of her fast, distant smiles, holding out her hands. "We already ate in the cafeteria," she said, pulling back so my hand wouldn't touch hers. "It was gross."

"Duh," I said, and deliberately took her arm, sliding my hand down until I clasped hers firmly. Rain cringed as if it caused her pain. "Rain," I said, and waited until her brown eyes looked into my black ones. "You are beautiful," I said, and she jerked her hand away.

"Stop it," she muttered, and grabbed her portion of my take. Stalking to one corner of the room, she sat with her back to me and everyone else.

I did think Rain was beautiful. She just—looked like rain. Once Clete had mumbled something about her getting caught outside in acid rain, but I didn't know the whole story. She had puffy hair almost as dark as mine and dark skin that looked like a watercolor picture that had gotten rained on—kind of melty. There were long drips in some places and spots and flecks. She'd broken the only mirror we'd had and usually wore a gray hoodie pulled low over her face.

"Hi, Hawk," Calypso said cheerfully, sitting on the table next to me.

"Hey, sweetie," I said, and split the last of the food with her.

She bit into a bruised apple and crunched. I followed suit, testing my newly loose tooth against the apple.

"What did you do while I was gone?" I asked.

"Hid," she said matter-of-factly.

I nodded. That was what most of the lab rats did, most days.

Calypso was around eight, I thought, and had been dumped here in the Children's Home when she was maybe three? She'd been wearing a diaper and a dirty T-shirt that had a picture of a sunset and the word *Calypso* on it. I'd been taking care of her ever since. I gave her another apple and she ate it, expertly avoiding the bruise.

Moke always said that Calypso looked like a match, right before you light it. She had curly, bright red hair, really white skin, freckles, and green eyes. I'd taught her to read and write her letters, and Clete was still teaching her numbers. Moke let her tag along when he snuck into the abandoned gym between here and McCallum Incarceration. He said she could climb anything and lift almost as much weight as he could, and he was almost twice as tall and three times as heavy, at least.

"Want me to check your back?" I asked, and she nodded. I got closer and pulled out the neck of her shirt. Peering down, I saw her small black antennas, four of them, arranged in two neat rows against her white, white skin. I reached a few fingers down and stroked them lightly.

"Can you feel that?" I asked.

"Yeah. I can feel more and more," she said, rummaging in my backpack for something else to eat.

"Okay, they're about maybe fifteen centimeters long now?" I said. "Should we cut little holes in the back of your shirts, or do you want them more protected? Gotta say, you're lookin' a little insecty."

Calypso grinned, liking the idea. "I want them to be more protected," she decided.

"Good enough," I said, and jumped off the table to throw our trash away.

Take that, I thought, pretending I was throwing away my parents. These lab rats are my family now.

CHAPTER 8

"Victory! We have victory!" McCallum shouted at us from at least four screens.

"Yay," Moke said sarcastically.

"Stay still," I said, holding the clippers away until he quit moving.

It was family haircut night—we all kept it pretty short. Why? Because we were on the edge of fashion? No. Because of lice. We lived next door to a *prison,* and the less hair you had, the better.

"My citizens," McCallum said, "today we have achieved a goal I've been working toward for two years! In a brilliant sting operation devised by myself, our own CD Police Officers have apprehended the worst of the worst."

"Oh, he was squawking about this earlier," Clete said. Sometimes he talked out loud, but not aimed at anyone, you know? Not looking at anyone. We didn't know how to respond sometimes. "They caught some huge criminal."

I looked up. "One of the Six?"

"No," said Clete, facing the wall, rocking slightly on his

feet. "Someone else. He killed a bunch of kids and some other stuff."

"Whoa," I said, pushing Moke out of the chair.

"They're bringing him here," Calypso said suddenly, her eyes bright. She looked off in the distance and held up one finger.

Twenty seconds later we heard the whining sirens of cop cars. A minute after that their flashing green and yellow lights flashed across our faces.

"How bad *is* this guy?" I wondered out loud.

"This is the worst, biggest criminal we've ever caught!" McCallum shouted, almost like he was answering me specifically. "He's going into our maximum-security lockdown at McCallum Incarceration. We do prison right!"

"Huh," I said, mystified. "And he's not one of the Six. Amazing."

"They're in the courtyard," Moke said, and we all ran to the big windows overlooking what passed as our play yard.

A green police van, siren and lights still going, stopped and two cops got out. They unlocked the van and yanked out their prisoner.

"He's gonna be a troll," Rain said, watching from under her hood. "Guy like that...he just sounds nasty."

Suddenly I gasped. "Ridley!" My hawk had just come down and landed on the creep's shoulder! She'd never done that to anyone but me. "Oh, my god, she's gonna take his eyes out!" I predicted with excitement.

"Go, Ridley, go!" I shouted, urging my bird on. I knew I sounded just like the crowd the other night, excited at the idea of blood. But this guy had killed kids. He deserved whatever he got.

But Ridley didn't attack. She pushed her beak through his black hair, then took off into the night. My mouth open, I watched as the worst of the worst turned around. Of course he could see us—we were standing in front of big, brilliantly lit windows. Quickly I pushed my lab rats aside and flicked our lights off.

"Why'd you do that?" Clete asked.

I shrugged. "Better for them not to see us, no?"

Since Ridley had left, the horrible murderer had been staring right at us, like he was memorizing our faces. Like we would be his next victims. A shiver ran down my backbone and I realized the covert feathers at the top of my shoulders were bristling. I stepped farther backward into the darkness.

Still the murderer seemed to see right through everything, right through me. The guards prodded him along, and the gate to the long walkway leading to the prison opened on the other side of our play yard. True, we had never used the play yard much—it was a quarter of an acre of depressed grass and eager weeds, but who had thought it would be good to put a prison right on the other side? A MORON.

Until he had to turn and go through the tall iron gates, the murderer seemed to keep his black eyes on me intently. Was he looking at my black mohawk, the ring in my nose, the feathers tattooed above my eyebrows? I didn't look that unusual—lots of kids looked like me. Without the actual wings, I mean. Which were hidden.

And me—I couldn't look away from his angular, strikingly

handsome face. He was the furthest thing from a troll, despite his evilness. My feathers were bristling, my wings itching to expand, and my breath was coming faster, almost like my body was responding to him.

What was the deal between this horrible killer—and me?

CHAPTER 9

My gang was talking about the murderer like it was the most exciting thing that had ever happened. Maybe it was. But I felt uneasy, maybe a little afraid, and I didn't want to show it.

"It's time, Hawk," Clete said in my general direction. He tapped the watch on his wrist, the watch I'd stolen for him. He was intense about time and schedules.

"Right, right," I said, and took off my poncho. Everyone here was a freak—my wings didn't make anyone blink.

"Will you be gone long, Hawk?" Calypso asked.

I pushed my fingers through her short red curls. "Depends on how much laundry there is, kid," I said.

"K," she said.

The manager of the Children's Home—a woman named Stella Bundy—had put us to work a couple years ago, once she realized there were some freakish misfit kids still living in the McCallum Children's Home. She couldn't turn us out into the street 'cause then McCallum couldn't claim a charity Children's Home as one of his good deeds, but I bet she thought about it. Instead, they came up with the next best thing—free child labor. During the day, Clete fixed the office computers and phones and stuff. Moke did like plumbing and electricity. I could never be found, for some reason ☺. During the night Moke sometimes helped out in the gym when the prisoners were allowed to use the equipment. I wondered if the prison manager would let the new murderer use the gym.

Anyway, at night Clete and I did laundry in the huge industrial machines.

When we were all together, Clete faded into the background, but when it was just me and him, he never shut up.

"I'm really close, Hawk," he said happily, enjoying our time together, as usual.

"Oh yeah?" I said automatically, dumping bins of laundry into a wheeled cart. Most of the laundry was from the prison, and most nights we saw bloody sheets, jumpsuits, towels. Everything in this city has blood on it, from the sidewalks to the washrags.

"Yeah," Clete said. "I had to install some updates at the offices and it was takin' forever so I was workin' on my own stuff an' I mean, Hawk, I swear I'm close."

"Close to what?" I could work without thinking. I could usually talk to Clete without thinking, because he didn't require a lot of interaction. I'd heard it all a million times before: He was close to a breakthrough. He was about to change the world, and no matter how many times he failed, he kept trying. I kept listening because I thought he really might change the world. Someday.

"It'll be an app," Clete said, lowering his voice. "If I install it on the office computers, it'll start replicating and infiltrating other computers. Hawk—it'll change everything."

I gave him an absent smile. "Yeah?"

"Yeah! It'll totally change the balance of power, for one thing," he said. "Everyone could have power, not just McCallum. I hate McCallum and his Voxvoce. It's awful. It hurts my ears."

"I know, bud," I said, adding extra bleach to this load. This was his biggest idea yet, and while I loved hearing about it, it felt like a daydream. Kind of like mine, about my parents coming back to my corner to get me. It's hard to get excited about something you know is never gonna happen.

"Yeah. I'm close."

The other workers, mostly Opes hired by the day, shuffled in and started mechanically picking up mops and brooms, then shuffled out again as if they hadn't seen us. That made sense, since we weren't two giant bags of dope.

"Another thing," Clete said later. We stood opposite each other at one of the large folding tables, each with baskets full of towels. Usually we raced to see who could get them all folded fastest, just about the only entertainment around here that didn't involve something illegal or somebody getting hurt.

"Okay, go!" I said, and we started folding.

"I heard about these really cool experiments, over in the Labs," Clete said, expertly folding towels in seconds like a machine.

"Really?" I said, looking at him. This was different. Anytime I heard the word *experiment,* my ears perked right up.

"They're messing with memories," he said. "Like, memories are stored in your DNA, right? It depends on how the chemicals are laid down, first you got the glutamate activating the neurotransmitters—"

"Cut to the chase," I said gently.

"Yeah, yeah, yeah," he said. "Anyway, so they're taking murderers and trying to erase the memories of the bad things they've done, to help them rehabilitate. If they wipe out just those memories—"

"Is it working?" I asked, eyeing his pile of towels. Clete was getting involved in his story, and if I could keep him talking, I might win our little competition.

He shrugged. "It might, someday. Right now it's hard for them to just choose a few memories to erase. A couple lifers got wiped completely."

I slammed my hand down on the empty table. "Done!"

Clete's face fell a little bit, but he perked right back up. "Count!" He demanded. "I know I did more than you."

I rolled my eyes. "Fine," I said, as I touch-counted my towels. "What do you mean, wiped completely?"

"Like they don't know their own names, completely," Clete said, his own fingers flying through his pile. "Seventy-eight!"

I was still counting. "Oh, my god—seventy-seven!" I hated to admit it, but Clete beamed. He didn't win often. Suddenly his smile disappeared and he clapped his hands over his ears, sinking to the ground. The Voxvoce had started, was filling this room, this building, this *city* with unbearable, painful, eardrum-breaking noise. I went away inside myself till it was over, a pleasant daydream like Clete's, where he saves the world with his app. *I guess I'm selfish, but I don't want to save the world. All I want is my parents back.*

If they could erase memories, could they also *uncover* memories? It killed me that out of all the stupid info my brain had chosen to squirrel carefully away, it had somehow let all the memories of my parents slip through its coils. When my parents had left me I'd been old enough to understand instructions. Understand promises. Old enough to understand that Ridley was a friend, not a pet. But I couldn't remember anything before the day they'd stood me on that street corner. Couldn't remember their faces. Their names. What they'd smelled like.

Clete stood, shaking his head, which told me the Voxvoce was over. "God!" he said, massaging his ears. "It's so horrible! McCallum is such an asshole! My program is gonna change all that."

"Change McCallum?" I asked. "No one's ever seen him. For all we know he's a hand puppet. There's no way to get close to him."

We pushed through the doors and started heading back to the Children's Home. This was the creepiest part—this long, poorly lit hallway back home. It was late now—I was beat and it was hard to stay alert. This hallway ran along the back of prisoner cells, and every once in a while, one of them would tap on the high, narrow windows and startle the crap out of me. Usually this was followed by a laugh, or suggestions that made my ears burn.

Suddenly I heard the whoosh of—wings? I spun around, but Ridley wasn't inside, wasn't in this hall. I walked faster.

"The way to get closer to McCallum is through...computer lines," Clete said serenely.

But I was hardly listening. What if...what if they'd already experimented with erasing memories? What if they'd experimented on me?

CHAPTER 10

We all slept jumbled together in what had once been a large closet. Over the years I'd collected sleeping bags, blankets, tablecloths, pillows, you name it. If it was relatively soft, it was in this closet, and we slept in and around and on it, our body heat pooling together to keep us warm, breath mixing as we slept in a pile, like a litter of puppies.

Our common room, where we did everything else, was basically a big, depressing space with a couple tables, a bunch of chairs, and some broken furniture that the orderlies had stashed here. The walls had once been white, probably, but now were tinged with yellow and almost gray with years of dirt and dust. There were splashes of dark brown that might have once been red, but I tried not to think about that.

That night, my dreams were horrible. I was fighting my way through the clouds over the City of the Dead, voices filling my ears. Unseen hands grabbed at me, snatching feathers from my wings.

I bolted upright, damp with sweat, still twitching from my nightmares. A thin, pale strip of light at the bottom of the door showed me the sun was up, so I extricated myself from various lab rats, easing my arm out from Calypso and untangling my legs from Clete's, and tiptoed out. In the common room the sun looked like it was leaking through the dirty windows. I remembered last night, standing there, watching the new prisoner. The worst of the worst. Feeling like he'd been trying to pry into my brain.

That had been super creepy. I hoped they were keeping him locked up tight.

It was when we were scavenging leftovers for breakfast that Calypso suddenly looked at me, her eyes round. "Soldiers," she said.

Soldiers meant one thing: they were coming to get us.

"Okay, guys, scatter," I ordered.

And just like rats, they did.

Moke pulled a bookcase away from a wall to reveal the hole we'd chipped out of the cinder blocks. He shooed Calypso and Rain through it and pushed the bookcase back. That small space was full now, so he climbed up on the table, jumped, and pushed one of the big ceiling tiles out of place. Another jump and he was through and setting the tile back down.

The sound of marching feet was loud now, and I watched as Clete went back in our nest, pulled some bedding aside, and opened a trapdoor in the floor. He crawled through and closed it, pulling on a thread so that bedding would cover it again.

Two seconds later one of our doors opened with a clang, hitting the wall behind it. Four soldiers stood there, hands clutching automatic rifles.

"Hey," I said calmly, and popped the rest of my peanut

butter cracker in my mouth. "I didn't know there was a parade today."

A man wearing the black lab coat of a doctor stepped around the soldiers.

"Where is everyone?" he asked, and I shrugged. "Don't just stand there," he snapped at the soldiers. "I know there's some kids left around here. Search the place!"

I stood and casually started drifting toward the doors to the outside. They were here because we were lab rats, after all. Some experiments were better done on kids instead of prisoners or some poor Ope. Sometimes they needed a healthy body in order to get the results they wanted. The McCallum Children's Home used to have more than five of us in it—years ago there had been maybe twenty-five or thirty. In twos and threes, kids had been taken away by one doctor or another. Usually they didn't come back. The few who did come back were in bad shape and didn't last long.

Which is why we had come up with a bunch of escape routes—the three the kids were using this time weren't the only ones.

The soldiers clumped around and I tried not to laugh as they looked under tables, in shelves, behind broken furniture, like maybe we thought it was a game, like hide-and-seek. We knew better. It might be a game, but if you were found, you died.

One soldier, a mean-looking woman with scars on her face, went into our sleeping closet and kicked at piles of stuff, stabbing the end of her rifle down into the pillows and sleeping bags. Like maybe they were hiding by lying really flat in the one place that made sense.

"Where are they?" the doctor asked me angrily.

"Who?" I said, rocking back on my heels. Any second I was going to have to bolt—there was no way the doctor was getting between me and the door.

The doctor nodded to the soldiers. "Take this one, then search outside."

That was my cue. I spun and bolted through the heavy glass door, hearing pounding boots behind me.

"Get her!" the doctor howled, and I raced for the one tree in the yard, a decrepit wreck that was going to fall over any day now. I leaped up into its brittle branches and climbed till I could spring on top of the twelve-foot concrete wall, this one place where I'd cut the razor wire. Bullets sprayed around me, taking out stone chips as I dropped lightly down outside.

"Open the gate, you idiots!" the doctor shouted, and almost instantly I heard the rusty, scraping whine of the metal gate being pulled to one side. I was halfway down the block by then but could still hear the soldiers running after me. A quick left, and then the old, broken sewer grate was right there. I slid sideways feet first, fitting neatly through the narrow opening, then braced myself for what I knew was a ten-foot drop.

Silently I chuckled as the boots above slowed in confusion. I didn't wait around, but headed quietly down the dark tunnel, a tunnel I knew as well as my own black eyes.

CHAPTER 11

There were hundreds—maybe thousands—of kilometers of sewer tunnels beneath the City of the Dead. I'd been down every one. Despite all the crazy people on the surface, I was the only bird-kid I'd ever seen. So I'd made sure that no one but the lab rats saw me fly.

It had been a lot easier to map the tunnels when I was smaller. Now I was fifteen, almost two meters tall, and my wingspan was just about four meters wide. Only the biggest, main tunnels were wide enough for me to still fly through them. But running was almost as easy as flying, and I could still cover a lot of ground fast, even if my shoes did get all kinds of stuff on them that I'd rather not think about.

In less than fifteen minutes I was right beneath my corner. When I realized that I had instinctively come here I punched the wall, my knuckles coming back smeared with mold and dirt. I'd been coming here so long my feet took me whether I wanted to or not, whether I was aboveground or below, muscle memory so ingrained I didn't have a choice. I had promised myself I would never come back, yet here I was.

But I had promised them, too.

Anyway. More important stuff to worry about: there were a lot of abandoned buildings in the wheezing, dying downtown of the City of the Dead. I liked to explore them, steal what I could, sell it on the street to buy food for the kids. There were also huge trash heaps to go through, people to spy on—my days were just packed.

But then it would come time for me to be on my corner. Again. Giving the ghosts of the past their half hour. So stupid.

"Ask yourself, what have I done to make my community better?" McCallum was booming on a vidscreen when I surfaced. "In the City of the Dead, you are given everything you need for success! But what are you doing to earn your success?" As usual his voice was much too loud, inescapable, his broad face pixelated like he gave off interference himself.

By late that afternoon I had done a lot to earn my success. The morning had been great—I'd broken into a forgotten locker near one of the old, unused underground train tracks. Got all kinds of neat shit. I'd taken it to market square and sold all of it. Bought food. Now it was just about time for my vigil. Even though I'd said I wasn't doing it anymore, my body took me there anyway. How could I fight that? Might as well be there for the usual time. If nothing else, I could scope out the people. Sometimes it helped to know what people needed, to better judge what I should steal. I might even see Pietro.

But no, I shook my head. I didn't want to think about Pietro and the dead Chung prince, lying broken on the sidewalk, even though he had survived the duel. I sighed, scratching at a flea bite on the back of my knee. At least I had Ridley to keep me company.

"Got any money?" The Ope's dirty, desperate face came at me from a shadow.

"Nope," I said. "You want a banana?"

The Ope's eyes turned crafty and I instantly realized that she would take the banana and sell it to another Ope, then save the pennies for her next fix.

"Yes," she said eagerly, holding out two shaking, freckled hands.

I held it out of reach. "You can have it if you eat it right now, in front of me," I said. "Otherwise go bug someone else."

The Ope frowned, thinking, then held out her hands. I gave her the banana. Once she started eating it, she wolfed it down, cheeks puffing out. I gave her some stale bread and she ate that, too.

"Is that a chicken?" she asked with a full mouth, pointing at Ridley on my shoulder. "You gonna eat him?"

Ridley squawked indignantly as I tried not to laugh.

"Not a chicken," I said, feeling her talons cling a bit too hard. "Not gonna eat her."

"We live in the best city anywhere!" McCallum shouted as the Ope shuffled away. "But I can't make it the best all by myself!" His unnaturally white smile stretched across the vid-screens. "What are you bringing to the table? Why do you deserve the space you're in?"

The space I'm in, ha. Not only did I deserve it, but I couldn't freaking get away from it. It's like my parents willed that corner to me, or something.

"Freakin' nut," I muttered, heading toward the next street,

the main street. As usual, Ridley took off to do an overview of the street from above. I knew she'd join me later.

At my corner a big, muscle-y guy was waiting for me. He was twitchy, jacked up, his fingers tapping the wall behind him. He knew it was my corner. Hell, everyone did. But everyone likes to pick on Hawk.

I could just do a U-ie, fade into the crowd, slip into an empty building, jump off the roof, and head home. That would make sense. It was the only thing that would make sense.

Rolling my eyes, I kept walking, aware of a few regulars on the street stopping their convos, looking up, waiting to see the fight. This guy had probably been paid to be there, to fight me. He was bigger than Clete, and Clete was dang big. I was close enough now to judge his pale skin, the grayish circles under his eyes. He was an Ope. He needed money. Someone had def set this up.

I was able to get real close while he was scanning the crowd in the other direction. I don't believe in fighting fair, so I trotted up to him, pulled my fist back, and then—*wham!*—punched him in the side of his head. He staggered, almost losing his balance. I stayed close and snap-kicked the side of his knee, knocking him to the ground, where he lay looking up at me, confused and mad. The whole thing had taken six seconds.

"You bitch!" he sputtered, getting clumsily to his feet.

"Stay down," I warned him, but he didn't listen. Like an angry bear he hulked toward me, his large, meaty hands curled into bricklike fists. I'm tall but super thin and really fast. It was easy for me to duck his wide swing, but he couldn't stop and he punched through the air and right into the concrete wall. I heard his grunt of pain.

Jumping high, I wheeled around and kicked his head, knocking that into the wall, too. He sank down again, blinking.

"I'm not afraid of you!" he snarled, rubbing his temple.

"I don't know why not," I said. "I just kicked your ass."

He started to get to his feet, and I backed up in case he swung again. "I just don't want to hurt Pietro's girlfriend," he said tauntingly.

I frowned. "I'm not anyone's girlfriend!" Just for that, he got a left uppercut punch that snapped his jaw shut and made the back of his head hit the wall. Again. Then I socked him in his gut. He hadn't had time to tighten his abs so his breath left him in a painful whoosh. This time he staggered around the corner, leaving my spot free at last—the spot I didn't even really want but kept coming back to, like a trained dog.

And my day went way downhill from there.

CHAPTER 12

Every time I took my place on my corner, a new wave of embarrassment and rage washed over me. Fury at my parents for abandoning me, of course, but an even hotter anger at myself for being stupid and gullible *every day for ten years*. I would never forgive them. I could never forgive myself.

The minutes passed with miserable slowness. I tried to distract myself by people watching—there was always some drama going on. Up the street, two women with rival plastic-goods stands were shrieking and hitting each other with toy umbrellas, rain boots, packages of cups.

Every so often an Ope came up to me, begged for money. Sometimes they took the food I offered—crackers, corn nuts, some kind of jerky that might be real meat—and ate it in front of me. Mostly they refused and went on begging. Whatever. I'd always give food to people, but if they didn't want it, it just meant more for us.

I smiled, thinking about the haul I'd made this morning. Had I already checked every underground train stop, along all the lines? Probably not. I tended to stick to sewer pipes and mechanical access tunnels. I'd been down all the underground train lines—I was sure of that—but hadn't fully explored them. They hadn't been used in so long that some of them were collapsing. Once I'd been in one, trying to check out its abandoned stops, when I heard a rumbling. I looked up to see a heavy chunk of plaster ceiling drop down on an Ope, knocking him across the third rail. Amazingly the third rail was still alive and the tunnel had filled with the Ope's agonized screams and the gross smell of burning flesh. He'd popped like a tick, and I got out of there.

So I hadn't checked them out as thoroughly as I probably should—the memory of that smell kept me away. I was mulling this over when I became aware that people in the street looked agitated, ducking back into their street stalls, disappearing down side streets, jumping inside and slamming their doors shut. Straightening up, I scanned the street, listening to the cries, the harsh whispers of warning.

Soon I saw why: A bunch of Chung thugs were ransacking the street, knocking over stalls and tables, breaking glasses at a tea pub. If anyone was in their way, the thugs knocked them down, felling grown-ups with one punch, kicking kids to the side. They left behind them a street of destruction and a lot of bruised and bleeding people, the ones that weren't quick enough to get out of the way or hadn't paid attention to the changing mood on the street. I stepped onto the boarded-up stoop of the building on my corner, totally out of their way. My fists automatically clenched, my feathers bristled.

I counted at least eight of them, male and female, all pretty young. They had razored haircuts and tattoos and other body mods, like stubs of horns put under the skin of their foreheads, twenty rings in one ear, piercings through upper lips, eyebrows, the septums of their noses. I looked like a cuddly kitten next to them.

They stopped not far from me and made a circle, their backs to one another.

"We're looking for witnesses!" a guy bellowed.

"One of our own was murdered yesterday!" The woman's bleached-blond hair contrasted oddly with her smooth tan face. "We know some of you must have seen it!"

Murder. They weren't going to pretend that the duel had been fair, weren't going to slide back into the shadows and accept defeat. That meant trouble for Pietro and the Sixes. Big time.

I thought back to when one of the Pater henchmen had snapped the Chung prince's neck, after Pietro had spared him. Had that been only *yesterday*?

One of the Chungs' people took out a semiautomatic pistol and shot it into the air. People scattered. I calculated the angle of the bullet and followed its trajectory downward. It fell against a window, breaking the glass. When I looked up again, one of the Chung soldiers was looking right at me.

I glanced away quickly, trying to seem unconcerned, but he was headed my way. I could run, but unlike most regular people and Opes, these guys were probably genetically enhanced as much as they were physically altered. The Chungs took security very seriously.

"You," the guy said, pointing his gun at me. "You're a street rat. Is this your corner? Did you see it?"

A woman came up next to him, her long black hair hanging down in two braids tied with silk ribbons to match the Chung uniform. "Don't make us cut it out of you," she said, pulling out an eight-inch hunting knife, the kind used to skin deer or wild pigs. "My name is Ki-Iseul. It was my brother, Prince Chul-Gun, who died yesterday. You will tell us what you know." Her voice was icy and a bit raw, as if she had been crying.

"I don't know anything," I said firmly. "I didn't see it."

"Grab her!" ordered Ki-Iseul.

CHAPTER 13

I jumped up, but from a still, standing position managed to get only about two meters high. Hands clamped onto my ankles, dragging me down to the waiting group. When I landed, many arms grabbed me. I twisted free, punching, kicking, knocking heads together, but as soon as I downed one, two more would take his place. Someone cracked my head with the butt of her pistol and I saw stars but didn't fall over.

At eight against one, it took them more than five minutes to subdue me, twisting my arms behind my back, grabbing my feet so I couldn't move. Then Ki-Iseul leaned over me with her knife.

"Tell me what happened yesterday," she said in a voice like razor blades.

"I didn't see anything!" I insisted. "Gunfights happen every day here—how was I supposed to know which one was extra special?"

We both realized my mistake at the same time. Ki-Iseul's brown eyes narrowed, and her lips pressed into a line so tight that they lost color. "I never said it was a gunfight," she said.

Crap. Crappity crap-crap. I forced myself to shrug, or shrug as much as I could, considering there were seven people holding me down. "I was guessing," I said. "There's lots of gunfights— it's an easy way to die."

I could see her weighing my words. This would be a perfect time for the Voxvoce to strike—the Chungs were probably as susceptible to it as most people. *Come on, McCallum!* I thought. *Show your paranoia!*

Someone really tall moved in back of the thugs holding me. It was the guy from earlier, the one whose butt I'd kicked when he was on my corner. Now he looked at me and gave me a mean, snide smile.

"She's the Pater prince's girlfriend," he offered, and I immediately tried to break free again, yanking my arms and legs.

Ki-Iseul looked at me with loathing.

"I'm not anyone's girlfriend!" I spat, silently promising myself that I would kill that guy as soon as I could.

"Let's let the Paters know that we will surely avenge my brother," the princess said. She nodded to one of the Chung soldiers. "Mark her!"

Two people held my head while I bucked as hard as I could. Someone cracked me again on my temple and I went limp, dazed and nauseated with pain. My limbs were heavy and refused to do what I ordered. I was powerless to stop them, and one of them quickly carved a *C* into my cheek with her knife. My skin opened under the blade, a sharp, bright pain tracing the edge of my jaw. Warm, sticky blood flowed out over my cheek to run down and drip off my neck.

"Now what, my lady?" asked one of the goons.

"She doesn't want to talk," Ki-Iseul said. "So cut out her vocal cords. She doesn't need them."

It hit me that I really was going to die. I was already losing a ton of blood from the deep cut on my cheek—I'd never survive losing my vocal cords. I let myself go completely limp while my brain went into hyperdrive. *I really might die here.* The lab rats wouldn't know what had happened to me. If my stupid parents ever, ever came back, they wouldn't find me. They'd never find me. It would serve them right.

My cheek stung horribly and felt sticky. I smelled the sharp, coppery scent of my blood, heard it dripping to the street. *Get yourself out of this, goddamnit,* my brain commanded. Feeling me go limp, their hands loosened ever so slightly on my arms and legs. The cold, sharp tip of a knife pressed against my throat—they really were going to cut out my vocal cords. Time for some desperation.

With one last-ditch effort, I gave an almighty heave, snapping my feet downward and my arms in. They were taken by surprise and I got myself mostly loose. In the next second, I unfolded my wings from beneath my poncho—not all the way—I was hemmed in, couldn't extend them fully.

There were gasps. Tentative hands reached out to touch my feathers.

"You're a freak!" one of the henchmen exclaimed.

"You're the one with the forehead horns," I pointed out, then crouched down and jumped. Hands grabbed my feet again, but I was able to whip my wings open, gaining altitude. I soared upward, kicking my feet free. The street went silent. Every head turned. I'd kept my wings a secret from the outside world for ten years, and it felt like a failure to blow their cover now. But it had been life or death.

I glanced down again at the Chung gang, just below me, out of reach, and the guy pointed to his horns. "These are *fake!*" he protested.

Shaking my head, I stroked down hard again with my wings, blood from my cheek spraying in the wind as I deliberately whacked Ki-Iseul and another soldier together. Their heads banged hard and they dropped, stunned. And then I was soaring upward, free, untouchable, leaving a trail of blood behind me. By the time they realized their guns would still work on me, I was much too high.

CHAPTER 14

For the first time ever, I didn't give my mythical parents a full half hour on my corner. I was practically guaranteeing that this would be the day they showed up.

I flew high enough to be out of sight, but I knew I had totally rocked the world below—news of the freak bird-girl would no doubt travel everywhere in the City of the Dead. I really hadn't had a choice. I wasn't going to die to keep my secret. It just meant that I had to—

My head swam for a second. I took my hand away from my cheek and saw that it was coated thickly with blood. Looking down, I saw that my whole right side was red with blood, soaked down to my boots. And I was dizzy.

Flying took real strength, and I was weak, was losing too much blood, and was still several kilometers from home. Where was I? I flew downward till I recognized the buildings below—this was one of the few nice areas of the city, where trees still grew and houses and cars and people were clean. This was where Pietro lived.

I straightened out my arms and legs, heading downward

fast. If I lost more blood I would just drop out of the sky, breaking all my bones and probably my wings, too. Anyway, it was Pietro's fault that this had happened to me. Time to ante up.

The Pater homestead—palace—was on the outskirts of the neighborhood, not far from the high stone walls of the city. It was huge, covering an entire city block, with an enormous protected courtyard in the middle. Its smooth plaster walls were painted a warm terra-cotta, and most windows above the second floor had balconies. The palace had its own ten-foot walls, and they'd had the brilliant idea of gluing broken glass bottles on top, to keep Paters in and Opes out. I counted three armed guards wearing the Pater colors, and I knew I'd no doubt missed some.

All the same, it wasn't hard landing in a tall oak tree to wait for an opening. From where I clung I could see directly into Pietro's room—its balcony's glass doors were open. As I watched, the hallway door swung open and Pietro entered his room by himself, closing the door behind him. Time to take a chance.

When the guards were out of sight, I left the tree, flew to the balcony, and landed without a sound. Quickly I folded my wings but not before Pietro had turned to see me, alerted by my shadow.

He gaped at me. I tucked my wings beneath my poncho. His mouth opened but no sound came out. I didn't know what to say, either—like, surprise?—but then realized if I didn't sit down, I would *fall* down.

"Here," he said, pushing his desk chair at me.

I collapsed onto it, trying to stay conscious.

"What the hell happened to you?" he asked. He tore a shirt from his closet, balling it together and pressing it against my bloody cheek. It was some kind of soft fabric, nicer than anything I've ever owned or felt.

"The Chungs were looking for witnesses to yesterday's duel," I said, unable to keep bitterness from my voice. "I didn't tell them anything, so they marked me with a C, for Chung." I gestured to my face, which was now numb with pain. "They were about to cut my vocal cords out, 'cause I wouldn't talk."

"But you escaped, thank the gods," he said...letting his voice trail off. "I'm...guessing you flew away?"

I shrugged, and Pietro rolled his eyes. "Wings? Seriously, you've got wings and you never told me."

He was half impressed, half pissed, but I didn't have the energy to fight. I only shrugged again, and Pietro pulled the blood-soaked shirt away from my face, then went into his bathroom, returning with a warm wet towel. Gently he started cleaning the cut, and I felt fresh blood seeping out.

"You need stitches," he decided. "And new clothes. And a bath. Don't go anywhere."

Before I could protest, he had left the room. Had this been a terrible mistake? Had he gone to call the police, or worse, *his father*, who hated my guts?

CHAPTER 15

I tried standing up but sank back down again, my head swimming. I pressed the towel against my cheek firmly, trying to stop the bleeding. In general I tended to heal really fast, but this was pretty much the worst injury I'd ever had that wasn't a broken bone.

The door opened and I looked up in alarm. Pietro stood there, leading an older woman into his room. Then he closed and locked the door.

"This is my friend," Pietro told the woman, whose jaw dropped at the sight of my wings sagging tiredly out of my poncho. "I need you to stitch up her face, and anything else she needs."

The woman closed her mouth. She wore the standard Pater uniform, but hers had "Dr. Morelli" embroidered on it. "Yes, my lord," she said faintly, which tickled me. Pietro was barely sixteen, only a little older than me. But he was a prince. A *my lord*! I tucked that little nugget into my brain, determined to bring it out sometime to give Pietro a little razzing. I wondered if I could get the lab rats to start calling me "my lady." It was worth a try.

"You've lost a lot of blood," the doctor murmured as she

worked. She'd given me numbing shots, and I couldn't feel the needle and thread moving through my cheek, thank the gods.

"Yep," I agreed, feeling really tired. The numbness felt like it was spreading past my cheek, down into my throat, like even talking was just too hard.

"I'm going to give you a couple shots to kill germs," she said, tying off the thread and biting it loose. Then she swabbed the whole area with something that smelled like the cheap booze a lot of Opes resorted to when they couldn't get dope.

"Okay," I said.

"And I'll give you some tablets for pain," Dr. Morelli said, straightening up and putting her tools in a black biohazard bag. "When the numbness wears off, it'll hurt like hell."

"Yeah," I said glumly. "I figured." I mean, that's pretty much my theory of life, anyway.

Pietro thanked the doctor, got her promise of secrecy, and let her out. Then he stood looking at me, tapping one finger against his face.

"Should we talk about the wings now?" he asked.

I shrugged. "I guess I was experimented on, like a lot of kids," I said.

"Can I look?" he asked.

Frowning, I nodded, and Pietro slowly removed my poncho, seeing the big slits I had cut into my T-shirt. I felt him carefully move the fabric aside and gently touch my covert feathers with his fingers. I almost jumped when I felt his warm hand between my shoulder blades, stroking my smooth skin.

He leaned back and looked at me. "How come I never saw these when we were kids?"

"'Cause I keep 'em *hidden*," I said with exaggerated patience.

"I don't think you were experimented on," he said, and I opened my mouth to argue, but Pietro held his hand up, stopping me. "Or at least, not for these wings. There's no scars, no grafted seams, nothing. They look like they grew out of your back naturally. Totally a part of you."

I'd always wondered but had never wanted to ask any of the lab rats to look. We'd all seen our share of pain; asking someone to look at more was just cruel. *But if I wasn't experimented on...what did that mean?* I shuddered a little at the thought, but Pietro seemed intrigued rather than grossed out.

"I assume they work?" he asked, rocking back on his heels.

"Well, *yeah,*" I said.

"I'd give anything to have wings like that." Pietro looked wistful. "They're beautiful. *You're* beautiful."

Slowly he rose, leaning over me, one hand on the back of the chair. My eyes flared as his handsome face came closer and for the first time I saw him not as my childhood pal Pietro but someone new and different. Someone who had just saved my life.

Holding my breath, I watched as his lips came closer to mine...and suddenly the emotions of the day, the adrenaline, the loss of blood, and the fear all caught up with me. I put my hand against his chest, stopping him.

"Gonna barf," I said, and lurched to the bathroom.

CHAPTER 16

The McCallum Children's Home had wretched, green-tiled showers with bad lighting that gave off the feeling that unspeakable monsters in the water pipes could come up through the drains and grab our feet. Besides that, I didn't trust the cleanliness of the water from the showerheads. Once Calypso got a rash that only showed up after we cleaned her, so we didn't shower too often. By the time Clete and Moke were twelve, they *stank*. We all figured we'd rather be dirty than get sick.

Pietro Pater had, in his own private bathroom, a deep porcelain tub that could have held at least three lab rats. There was soap that smelled like flowers. The water was steaming hot.

"Come here," Pietro said, and before I realized what he meant to do he had pulled my cut-up, blood-soaked T-shirt off and thrown it in the trash. My eyes were wide as I stood there in pants and a sport bra. He reached for my pants button and I grabbed his hand.

"I can do it," I said, a blush rising.

"Okay, but they go in the trash, too," he said. "I'll find something for you to wear." He put his hands on my hips as if gauging my size, then looked me up and down until my face heated. "Geez, you're tall," he said, and straightened up to look me in the eye. He was maybe two centimeters taller than me. *Maybe.*

I was starting to think that I had died on the street below, and this was some dead-dream, not reality. My world was harsh, dirty, and dangerous, and that's what I was used to. Pietro's world was rich, clean, and full of anything he wanted or needed. I had no idea what that felt like.

"What are you thinking?" he asked. "You have a funny look on your face."

"Is this real?" I blurted.

In answer he stepped closer. I smelled his clean scent, the laundry detergent of his clothes. I was about to step backward because he was too close, but he put his arms around me, tilted his head, and held me in place with one hand gently cradling my chin.

"This is real," he said softly, and kissed me.

I'd never been kissed on purpose before; had never kissed anyone else except Calypso. And that wasn't like this. There wasn't anything like this.

Pietro pulled his head back a fraction. "Quit thinking," he said, and kissed me again. This time his mouth was firmer on mine, and just when I got panicky about running out of air, I remembered to breathe through my nose.

I wound my arms around his neck and pressed closer, tilting my head opposite to his so we could kiss harder. I don't know how long it went on, but finally he pulled away and smiled. His face was as flushed as mine, and he had blood smeared on his cheek and shirt.

"That's all I've been able to think about since I saw you that day," he said. "You have to believe that I gave my second no orders to kill the Chung prince. I was as shocked as you were. Please believe me." I looked into his dark brown eyes, saw the earnestness on his face. Maybe he was telling the truth. Maybe his dad had given the order without telling Pietro.

I stepped backward and nodded awkwardly. "I'm going to get in the bath," I said.

"Let me know if you need help washing your hair."

"Uh-huh," I said. But no way would I take him up on it. We couldn't pretend to just be friends or even just a couple of kids anymore. Not after a kiss like that.

That bath, no lie, was the highlight of my entire existence. I sank into the hot water, submerging myself to get my mohawk wet, just for the delicious feeling of being surrounded by pure, clean water. It was heavenly, lending serious weight to my already-dead theory. When I surfaced, I stretched my wings out to dry, letting them hang over the back of the tub. Rinsed of dust, they were prettier than I remembered.

The bathroom door cracked open. I was about to yell when a hand quickly put a stack of clothes on the stool by the door. "Here!" Pietro said. "Hope they fit."

Turns out, when my hair isn't full of City of the Dead grease and dirt, it's fluffy like a donkey's mane. It was still black and shiny, but so soft and silky. My skin was a whole shade lighter than what I thought it was. And the bathwater was so gross and dirty that I quickly drained it and rinsed the tub out before anyone could see it.

The clothes, including bra and underwear, fit. It was a pair of soft, worn jeans and then a gray, long-sleeved T-shirt. He'd already cut slits in the back for my wings. Right now I had so many emotions flooding my mind that I didn't know what to do, what to think. I was still a bit light-headed, super tired, and super hungry. Why had I come here?

"Come out, you big chicken," Pietro taunted me from outside the door. Then he seemed to realize what he'd said and laughed. "Chicken!"

I opened the door. "Very funny. Like I haven't heard that before...my lord," I added, giving him a snide smile.

Just then there was a quick rap on Pietro's door. It opened slightly before he had given permission, and frowning, Pietro walked quickly over.

A servant poked her head in and whispered, "My lord, your father's coming!"

"He's out of town!" Pietro said.

"He's back and headed this way!" She looked terrified.

"Thank you." Pietro closed the door and locked it.

"I'll go," I said, picking up my ratty backpack. I hated for it to touch my nice new clothes.

"I wanted you to spend the night," Pietro said in a low voice, holding me by the elbows. "I want us to be close, like we were when we were kids."

A booming voice in the hallway shouted, "Pietro? Where is my son?"

"I need to go," I said again. "He hates me."

Pietro didn't deny it. "When will you come back?" he asked urgently, as his father tried the doorknob.

"Pietro! Why is this door locked?" his father bellowed.

"I don't know," I said. "Sometime." I gave him a tiny smile and then took a running jump off the balcony. I snapped my wings out, feeling them catch the air, and I rose swiftly into the night, headed home.

CHAPTER 17

My head was full of Pietro, Pietro, Pietro the whole way home. His kiss. The way he smelled. How he had helped me, protected me from his father. The other half of my mind was totally focused on that bath. *Oh, god.* It felt like only seconds until I realized I was over the McCallum Complex. I did a slow left, checked the yard out, then came down quickly behind the big garbage dumpster, like usual.

Pietro's life was full of light. Full of rich fabrics and polished wood and warm-colored lamps creating pools of comfort. As I walked toward the doors to the common room, I tried not to feel achingly bitter about my life. And my parents. And my life. And the lab rats. And my life.

Clete was waiting for me and pushed through the doors eagerly to meet me. He opened his mouth to speak but then noticed I looked different. His up-and-down examination of me felt quite different from Pietro's. That memory brought a flush to my cheeks.

"Where have you been?" Clete asked. "What's all this?" His hands gestured to my clothes, my clean hair, the huge, throbbing stitched-up wound on my face.

I searched, wondering how to explain what had felt like a dead-dream. Pietro's house, his hands, the Chungs' cutting a C into my cheek, and the only hot bath I could ever remember taking. But Clete cut me off.

I was just about to say that I would tell him later when he waved his hands again and blurted, "It doesn't matter. Listen, Hawk—everyone's gone!"

I looked through the big glass windows. The common room seemed completely empty. Smiling tiredly, I said, "Did you guys come up with a new exit? Are they hiding?" I was in no mood for this, but they didn't understand that. They wanted to play hide-and-seek for real, have me try to find them and test out their new spots. I'd either have to play along or disappoint them by being too wiped for one of the few games they could play.

"No!" Clete said as I opened the glass door. "I mean they're gone! The soldiers took them!"

I stopped and looked up into his face. Usually he spoke slowly and dully, like the way he moved. When someone said something funny, it took him minutes to smile. Now there was fear and outrage in his voice.

"This better not be a joke," I warned him. "I will NOT think this is funny."

"It's not a joke!" he said. "You know how we all bugged out this morning?"

Had that been only this morning? It felt like five years had passed since then. I took a pain pill out of the bottle in my pocket and popped it open, dry-swallowing it.

"Yeah?"

"The others must have waited a couple hours, then surfaced,"

Clete said. "But I—I fell asleep there, under the floor. I only woke up when I heard Calypso screaming. Then I heard heavy footsteps and Moke fighting back and Rain trying to get away."

He looked anxiously into my face as if I would already have a plan in place, because that was my job—knowing what to do. But I had nothing. I sat down heavily in one of the school chairs at a table and put my aching head in my hands. The numbing shot had worn off, and my cheek strained against the stitches every time I swallowed, or spoke.

"What should we do, Hawk?" Clete asked, all of his tension in his voice.

"Let me think for a minute, Clete," I said. "What time did you hear them?"

Clete looked at his watch. "I guess…around two? I had missed lunch."

"Okay. Let me think." The soldiers probably hadn't taken the lab rats off campus. At the other end of this huge complex were the Labs, where the doctors and scientists conducted their experiments on Opes, kids, and prisoners on death row. The lab rats were probably there. The question was—how could we get them back? And if we got them back, how could we keep them? They would never let us keep them. Which meant we all had to leave. Leave this place forever.

So I needed to come up with a plan to rescue the kids and escape to some new place far away in the city, where we wouldn't be found. We couldn't *leave* the city. Not unless we wanted to die in the desert.

And this plan had only one chance of working. If it failed, we were all dead.

CHAPTER 18

"This better work," Clete muttered anxiously.

We were dressed in our usual coveralls, heading down the long corridor to the laundry rooms. As if nothing was wrong. As if I hadn't lost most of my family in one day. As if rescuing them—if possible—would make me lose the only home I could remember. As if rescuing them meant I'd never see Pietro again.

Overhead, the dim lights flickered. My mind raced with adrenaline-fueled ideas—how to break the kids out, how to escape. If only they had wings! It would make all this so easy. And where could we live? Maybe way in the northeast corner of the City of the Dead? People didn't ask a lot of questions there.

"Hawk?" Clete's voice brought me back to the now. He was pointing at a sign that said, HALLWAY CLOSED DUE TO REPAIR. TAKE MAIN CORRIDOR INSTEAD.

An armed guard stood there, gesturing to an open door. "Stay in the exact middle of the prison corridor," he warned us. "Go single file. And don't let the shit they say bother you. There's another guard at the end who will get you to the laundry."

"Uh, okay," I said, and motioned to Clete to go first. Just a little hiccup, I told myself. We weren't going to come back through this hall anyway. From the laundry room, the Labs were across another big courtyard and down another long hall. Since I could fly, I could go anywhere. But I had to think of Clete. Maybe I could get him out, stash him somewhere, then get the others and go meet him? My head pounded with all the possibilities, and my cheek throbbed with pain, despite the pills. Despite my brain running on automatic, the rest of me was weak from loss of blood, the pain in my cheek hot and burning.

"Heyyyyy, baaaay-beeee!" Startled, I realized that we were walking through the main jail of the complex. We walked single file in the exact middle of the concrete floor—if we veered right or left, reaching hands could grab us.

"Hawk?" Clete muttered again.

"I know, Clete," I murmured. "It's okay. It's almost over. You're doing great." For all his weird habits and hyper-brain abilities with computers, in some ways he was like a little kid.

We were almost through. Some prisoners were throwing things at us—chalk, toothbrushes (the rubber kind you put on one finger, because you can't stab anybody with those). Basically anything they could part with, which meant anything they couldn't turn into a weapon. They shouted things that made the back of Clete's neck go bright red, but I didn't have time to listen to them. I had to plan.

Okay, Hawk, I thought, *let's start thinking about the Labs.*

The Labs were very bad. Being taken to the Labs meant your time was up. That keeping you alive wasn't as important as

McCallum finding out if you could live through a new biological weapon, or a new vaccine, or a new treatment for getting all the heavy metals out of your blood. I'll save some time here and tell you the answer is no, to all. You do not live through it. If by some reason you sort of do and they bring you back to the Children's Home, you won't last long. You'll be like a corn husk, like a walnut shell, with nothing inside. Then you'll die, and whoever's left calls the soldiers and they take you away again, this time to dump you over the city wall with the rest of the trash.

"Phoenix!"

Automatically I looked up, looked around. And realized with horror that it was the new prisoner talking. He was looking at me through the bars in his cell. I gave a fierce frown and prodded Clete between his shoulder blades so he would hurry up.

"Phoenix!" the prisoner said again. He pushed his face between the bars, staring at me. I ignored him.

"I knew it was too much to hope that you would still be waiting for us after all this time," the prisoner said, speaking loudly to make sure I heard. "But I still hoped. And then I saw you from the courtyard!"

My jaw was tight as I marched forward. A few more steps and I'd be past his cell.

"I'd recognize you anywhere," the creep went on. "Because you *look* like *me*. Phoenix, I'm your *father*. Don't you remember *Dad-man*? And *Mom*?"

My eyes flared and I turned slowly to look at him. "My name is Hawk, asshole! I don't need your crap and your lie…"

My voice trailed off as I realized that, actually, he *did* kind of look like me. Without the mohawk, the tattoos, and the piercings. And a man. But we had the same black hair, black eyes, thin nose, narrow mouth.

Suddenly my exhaustion and loss of blood made me sway, made the jail go fuzzy and gray for a moment. I grabbed Clete's shirt and managed to keep my balance. He'd turned at the criminal's words and now was looking back and forth between us.

"I don't *have* parents," I bit out. "You think I would be *here* if I had *parents?*"

The killer winced as if I had slapped him. "You *do* have parents!" he said, his voice hoarse. "Your mom and I named you *Phoenix*. We've been trying to get back to you for *ten years*. Your mom is…an amazing revolutionary. Her name is *Max. Maximum Ride*."

I held on to Clete as the floor went out from under me, and then I fell, down, down into darkness.

PART TWO

CHAPTER 19

Max

I ran out of wall space to mark the days going by maybe a year ago? Three years? No idea. I'm not super tied into reality these days.

These days. The Powers That Be had been especially cruel, putting me on the top floor of Devil's Hill. Its real name is McCallum Island Penitentiary. No one calls it that, and Devil's Hill is a much more fitting name, anyway. But here on the top floor, my window—maybe twenty centimeters by forty, forty-five centimeters?—I've never gotten used to this metric crap. Anyway, the "window" that's too small for any humanoid of any age to fit through, and yet has thick bars every four inches—damnit—*ten centimeters*—anyway, that window actually looks out on *sky*. I can see blue sky. I can see scary dark thunderclouds roiling toward me. I can see lightning flash, making my cell glow for a metric fraction of a second. I can hear birds, seabirds, calling hoarsely to each other, but I usually can't see the suckers.

And I sure can't join them, fly freely among them, swerving and dipping and wafting along on a warm updraft, like I used to.

Sometimes I think that's exactly why they put me here, in a cell with a window. Other prisoners would think this was the high life, would do just about anything to get a glimpse of the view I've got. Not me. For me, that window and slice of sky is pure torture. And torture is what McCallum's good at, making me think about being free. Being able to fly. Like I used to.

Like I used to. That's the phrase of the moment. Of the Year. Of the Years. Everything I'd once had, had once been, was *like I used to*. Thoughts started to creep coldly into my mind, the savage fingers gripping my memory and forcing me to see— Iggy. The Gasman. Angel. Nudge. And...Fang. And my baby. My baby Phoenix. Because Max + Fang = Phoenix.

I'd been there when she'd first walked, first spoken (her first word was *Why?*), and first flown. I couldn't call it flying, actually. Just the memory of it made me laugh. Have you ever laughed at the thing that caused you the most pain of your life? That was me, remembering five-year-old Phoenix, running and jumping, letting her wings out. She'd been practicing constantly, working on her down-push so she'd have enough power to catch air in her feathers.

This time she was astonished as she rose three feet into the air, five feet, seven feet, still working her wings, already sharp and beautiful even at five years, their colors a glorious mix of Fang's and mine.

"Get ready," I murmured to Fang.

"On it," he said out of the corner of his mouth.

And at ten feet in the air, she crashed into the apple tree she was under. How could she have not noticed that she was standing in its shadow? She rose right up into it, breaking some small branches, getting scratched...and totally losing her focus and momentum. She made an anguished, silent face, then fell, a disappointed, feathery mass, into her father's arms—where she promptly had a temper tantrum at not being allowed to immediately go back up.

"That was so goddamn cute," Nudge had said.

That was as far as I got down memory lane before it turned into Memory Road to Hell, and the pain of losing them, losing *all of them,* just gutted me, left me kneeling on the ground, pounding the concrete until my fists bled. "No, no, no, no, no, no, no!"

And that's why I try not to remember. Anything. My "childhood." My awkward teenage years, which were spent on the run from Erasers, crazed robots, mad teachers, anarchists—

Then the explosions. The chaos. The destruction that had forced us underground for years. Phoenix had been born underground, had spent her first few years living in tunnels, like a rabbit or a mole. When we surfaced, when she felt actual sunshine on her toddler face, reacting with pure shock to the outside world, my heart had burst. She had pointed at the sun and said, "What's that?"

No kid should live in a world where they don't know what the sun is, I'd told myself. And I'd promised I was going to make up for the hell of her first years with nothing but paradise to follow.

But paradise couldn't last forever. Here my memories began to shred and fragment, overlaid with the constant, head-splitting noise of McCallum, day and night. He promised, cajoled, reprimanded, raged. None of it meant anything. I saw others shrink beneath his weapon of the Voxvoce, which made grown men and women cry and fall to the ground. Sometimes they just screamed, hands over their ears, trying to escape the lances and blades of vicious noise, their own sanity winking in and out, like my memories.

My mind grew cloudy and my memories faded like woodsmoke as soon as I tried to capture them. I didn't know what had happened or why me and my flock were suddenly on the run again after years of peace. I'd tried to remember so many times, until tears ran down my face, and headaches raged along with my temper.

I'd been interrogated. That was just a Sunday walk in the park for me—I could be interrogated all day long, and in the end, the questioners would be ready to tear their hair out, more frustrated than I was by a long shot. I'd be fine. Bloodied, sore, but fine. That is, as long as I knew that Phoenix was safe with her dad or one of my flock. No one else. Ever.

Then...I don't know what happened. I really don't. I can't even imagine what kind of scenario would have made me leave my baby, my firstborn. The world must have been about to end.

I'd been wounded—a wing, my arm, my ribs broken on my left side. I couldn't fly. Could barely run. A rib had punctured my side and it was running blood till I was dizzy. I'd been holding Phoenix...her small feet getting soaked with my blood.

Fang had found an ally—someone we knew and trusted. She would take care of Phoenix and hide her till we could come get her. And so, with Rose less than a hundred feet away, with me screaming and sobbing and bleeding, Fang had put me on his back and flown away from our child. I'd watched her grow smaller, her tiny, confused face following our ascension, drops of her mother's blood falling down like rain.

Then...what? We'd been shot out of the sky? We'd lost the rest of the Flock? We'd been separated?

All I know was that I had woken up in this cell on Devil's Hill. McCallum ranted at me day and night from a vidscreen right outside my cell. The days had passed. And passed. And passed. Till I had run out of room on my walls to mark them. That had been a year ago? Three years? Once I tried counting my marks, to try to get a grasp on how long I've been here, but the number got pretty high, pretty fast, and I'm not ashamed to admit that maybe I lost count on purpose.

I'm not super tied into reality these days.

Call it a coping mechanism.

CHAPTER 20

"Wake up!"

The bucketful of cold disinfectant splashed over me. At the last second I remembered not to open my eyes because I surely didn't want that stinging crap rolling into them...if that was all they were throwing at me.

"Get up!" The wooden handle of a mop cracked across my back even as I rolled out of bed, pinching my wings and making me spout things I might regret.

"I'm *up,* you *dick!*" I shouted, swiping my wet hair out of my face. The disinfectant was yellow-green and smelled exactly how you'd think prison disinfectant smelled: nasty, with a side of nauseating. The only plus side of it was that I didn't have lice...usually.

Why was this inmate/janitor in my cell? Because these cells *don't have doors.* Long ago, McCallum decided that the fewer prisoners he had to feed, clothe, and house—however horribly, for any of those things—the better. Fewer inmates means—and stay with me here—*lower costs,* which means *higher profits.*

His answer was not to educate the inmates or give them

therapy so they'd get out sooner and be less likely to come back. *Noooooo*. That would be too kind. McCallum is not kind. He is a shithead of the highest order. Which I guess is a contradiction in terms, but I'm gonna go with it.

Anyway, his answer was to *take all the doors off the cells*. We were free to wander anytime, anywhere we wanted. Escaping was impossible—it was pretty rare that anyone even tried. The last person who'd tried actually made it into the sea. Obviously trying to swim the twenty miles to the mainland. Finally he turned back, made it onto the mossy, seaweed-covered rocks of Devil's Hill. The warden wouldn't let him back in. He clung to the wet, slimy rocks, begging to come back to the prison he'd hated. Soon he was shaking and red-eyed from the cold, constant saltwater washing over him, drying on his skin, dehydrating him with every wave. They gave him no food, no fresh water, no mercy. His begging turned to shouting turned to shrieking turned to screaming and sobbing. His fingertips got worn away by clinging to the wet rocks. Salt crusted around his eyes, his mouth. I'd wished I could help him, but there was just no way. At last one of the big waves washed over the rocks, and when we looked again, he was gone.

So people don't try much.

And yes, they'd jailed even the sky. Above us was a thick iron cage, designed to be unclimbable, unbreakable. It went over the whole jail. They knew I had wings, of course. They'd seen them during the first delousing spray. Knowing they had a cage over the whole island, they didn't have to worry about my wings. But they had. I was a high escape risk.

My wings were handcuffed behind me. Or, wing-cuffed.

Once a month they made a big deal of taking off the cuffs and letting me stretch out to my full—let me do some quick math—five and a half meters. They jeered and gave me shit and called me a freak as I rolled my shoulders and ruffled my feathers in ecstasy. But, you know, you have to get up *pretty early* in the morning to come up with an insult I hadn't heard before. So I tuned them out.

They were supposed to give me a solid three minutes. I never got more than one. Then they pulled my wings tight behind me, barely letting me fold them into their natural shape, and cuffed them together again. It was painful. I couldn't sleep on my back. I couldn't use my wings to fly or defend myself or to scare people who still believed in demons. Frankly, that would have been the extent of my entertainment here on Devil's Hill.

"Up and at 'em, freak!" the inmate shouted.

"I swear, Marty, when *I'm* the janitor you're gonna wish you weren't a germ!" I snapped back. "'Cause I'm gonna disinfect your ass!" I narrowed my eyes and tried to look as mean as possible, which used to be enough. I'm guessing my physical appearance has gone *downhill* these past few...maybe a half-decade?

Marty giggled and kicked his rolling bucket with his foot, moving out of my cell. I wrung out my long hair and tried to get a grip.

"Today is your day to die, abomination!" a new voice screamed.

I got ready to look bored—a death threat was just your average Tuesday here—but backed up quickly when I saw who was jeering at me. It was Kenton, and Kenton was effing nuts. Also, he had a shiv, maybe made out of a broom handle. He could do a lot of damage, and he had me backed into my cell, which was not on my list of advantages.

I put my hands up. "Kenton! I don't know what you're thinki—"

"Thinking 'bout the coins I'll get if you die!" he howled, circling around me, so excited at the idea of the payout that he'd forgotten to trap and kill me first.

"Someone paid you to kill me?" I asked quickly, moving to the right, toward the hall where other inmates were already gathering, already taking bets on the outcome of this match. If I could keep him talking, keep him distracted, I might still come out of this walking, not rolled out on a gurney.

"Paid to kill the freak!" he nodded, grinning wildly, looking like, well, like a Devil's Hill inmate who was effing nuts.

"Who?" I shouted, but he was done talking.

Kenton roared and leaped at me, slashing down with his shiv, and carved a neat gully out of the concrete wall. He should be using that thing to dig an escape tun—

He made another lunge and I jumped aside again, but he'd been paying more attention than I'd given him credit for. He was edging me back into the cell, back to the corner with the window. At least I might die with a view.

My heart pumped harder, adrenaline waking up my brain, my nerve endings. My eyes moved fast, calculating his moves. Except he was crazy, unpredictable. I kept ducking, taking big sweeps from side to side as he stabbed the air again and again with his shiv. He was getting closer to trapping me. None of my fellow inmates would help me—they were already arguing over who would get my cell.

Shit, Max, think! I ordered myself—and came up with an idea. If this didn't work, I was dead.

CHAPTER 21

Kenton screamed and swiped at me again. I leaped back, hitting the wall, and his shiv cut me over one eye. Warm blood ran into my eye and down my face, blocking out half my vision. When Kenton pulled his arm back again, I pushed off from the wall and dove toward the floor, landing outside my cell on top of other prisoners' feet. They parted around me, making space. Nobody wanted to be too close to me when Kenton was taking such sloppy swipes with his shiv.

Keeping low, I shot my way through the crowd and raced down the hallway to the stairs. Kenton shrieked as he followed me. So, someone had paid him to kill me, huh? I'd have to find out *who*.

My wings were cuffed behind me, and I've been in jail way too long, but that didn't stop me from being tall, thin, and real light-boned. So as Kenton barreled down the hallway, shiv flailing, I looked around, then nodded to myself. Out here, I had a lot more options, more environmental factors in my favor than in that cramped cell.

Shiv raised, Kenton screamed and charged at me. Behind

me were the stairs leading downward. In front of me was a throng of eager prisoners, parting to let my wild-eyed attacker through. I wiped the blood out of my eye and got ready. When he was about five feet away, Kenton tucked his shiv arm in close and hunkered down, then gave a bloodcurdling scream of delight and sprang at me. I jumped straight up in the air and watched him pass under me like a wretched, rabid freight train.

In midair he realized his mistake and craned his head upward to stare at me. Time stood still while our eyes met; I saw the fear in his. I'm not sure he saw the pity in mine. His arm arced up even as he began the long, painful tumble down the stairs and he gave one last, desperate stab with his shiv... just barely piercing my side. If I'd been hovering with wings, it would have stopped there, a mere scratch. Since I wasn't, Gravity did her best to kill me by bringing me back down to earth— right on top of the shiv. I sank onto it as I landed, crying out as five or six inches of rough, filthy wood penetrated my side.

Then Kenton was an awkward, bony lump at the bottom of the stairs, and I was crouched on my bare feet at the top, blood still running from above my eye and now a fresh trail from my side.

Kenton's raspy voice muttered weakly: "I killed her, I killed her, I killed her! Now I get coins, coins, coins!" He was jubilant, totally thrilled at the idea of getting paid in coins that—by the look of him—he wasn't going to live long enough to spend.

Suddenly I felt like I was drowning. I stood up with difficulty as the crowd of prisoners came to gawk at Kenton. "Finish him off!" more than one voice cried. "Finish him!" "Kill him!" "Kill him!"

"No," I said as I shook my head, pushing my way through the crowd. I wasn't in a hurry to finish off that guy, even if he was responsible for the shiv sticking out of my side. I got out, feeling like I was about to faint. These poor inmates, prisoners at the end of the world, didn't know who I was. They didn't know how many people I had killed in my life. Actually, neither did I. Let's say *a lot*. I was tired of killing. Also, I felt like I was about to die myself.

I made my way to a landing, a trail of blood behind me. Nobody followed me, since I'd made it clear I wasn't going to be delivering any more violence. It was more entertaining to watch Kenton die in a heap.

I looked down at the broom handle sticking out of my side. It may have pierced my lung. I was guessing it had missed my heart, since I was still, you know, *alive*. But I had to make my way to the Infirmary, fast. "Okay, on three," I muttered. "One...two—" and then I yanked the broom handle out, gasping with an almost blinding pain. The wood brushed against ribs as I pulled, tugging at my bones as if it wanted to pull them out with it. "Three. Oh...oh, *holy shit*," I said weakly. "Oh, that sucked *so bad*."

Amazingly, I had the presence of mind to keep the freaking shiv as I tiptoed down the stairs, past Kenton, down more stairs and more stairs, and now I was hugging the wall and stepping in my own blood. The chants of the inmates above me were fading, replaced by the rushing sound of my blood in my ears, the thumping of my heart. Was it getting slower?

I knew where the Infirmary was—we all did. Everyone here had survived beatings, attacks, near-starvation. They'd patch you up just enough to dump you back in your cell so you could live to fight another day.

I didn't think I would make it. I was sure I was going to collapse here in the hallway and just...bleed out. Kenton would get his coins after all—or whoever ransacked his cell after he died would. But I kept telling myself, One more step, one more step, one more step...

Until I found myself in front of the swinging doors to the Infirmary. I pushed through, more like *fell* through, and then sank to my knees on the floor. Then I let go and spiraled down, down, down into a cold nothing-world where there was no pain.

CHAPTER 22

When I came to, a thin, gray-faced little man was hovering over me, watery brown eyes peering at me from behind silver-rimmed glasses. One lens was cracked.

I tried to bolt upright in case this was a dire situation, as it so often was when I woke up. He put a gentle hand on my shoulder.

"Lie still." Then he whispered, "We're giving you blood."

Now I was really awake and aware of a pinching feeling in the crook of my elbow. "No—I can't have regular human blood! It'll make me sick!"

"I know," he said quietly, patting my shoulder. "Because of the two percent avian DNA."

"Uh, yeah?" I mean, it was obvious that I wasn't entirely human because of the glaring pair of wings on my back, but how did he know the actual percentage?

"It's okay," he said, still speaking softly. "This is modified plasma and fluid. It won't cause a negative immune reaction. But you had just about bled out."

I pulled my prison jumpsuit open, seeing my underwear

drenched in blood. A rectangle in my side had been cleaned and painted with disinfectant. A messy, uneven row of staples held my shiv wound shut.

"I used to be better," the doctor said sadly. "I used to be a great surgeon. Now I'm on Devil's Hill, barely able to do my job. They only give me the most basic material, because I'm just an old Ope."

Now I could see the dilated pupils, the shaking hands of a doper. Most of the inmates here were dopers. I'd come within a hairsbreadth of succumbing myself. It was another feature of a McCallum penitentiary: easy access to dope. There had been so many times when I'd just wanted this reality to go away. I knew dope would make me feel like I'd been wrapped in cotton, moving through life in a cozy sleeping bag. It had definitely seemed like the way to go, but not often. Maybe only about fifty million times. Not more than that. I don't know what kept me tied to this reality, this life.

Did I think I would ever see Fang and Phoenix again? No. Not really. But every time a shadow fell across my slit of a window, my heart skipped a beat. Every time I heard a female inmate fighting back against a guard, my heart skipped a beat and I thought—could that possibly be Phoenix? How old would she be now? If she was alive. I knew this was stupid, pathetic, a waste of time. Most likely I would never see them again, my love and my child.

But there was always the tiniest chance, let's say maybe even 2 percent, like my DNA. And it was really clear to anybody that saw me that even 2 percent can make a huge difference. So that's why I never went the Ope route or just let some shiv find its target because I'd gotten so tired of avoiding them.

I looked up into the eyes of the little doped-up doctor who had done such a sloppy job patching me up. He was embarrassed.

My head fell back against the unwashed pillow. "What do they want from us?" I asked, my voice as low as his.

The doctor shook his head. "I don't know. Repentance? Their entertainment?"

"I don't even know how I got here, what I did," I said.

"You've been here longer than I have," the doctor said. "If I knew your crime, I would tell you."

"My crime has always been that I exist," I said tiredly. "Me. I'm the crime." I shot him a look. "Maybe you could uncuff my wings? Say it was impossible to treat me with them cuffed?"

"Yeah, and have them cut off my dope supply?" The doctor looked horrified. "No way!" He busied himself with removing my IV and covering my wound with laughably inadequate Band-Aids, a bunch of them. "Okay, you're done," he said. "Time to get out of here."

It wasn't even close to time for me to get out. In a regular hospital they probably would have me in recovery for twenty-four hours, at least. But I wasn't in a regular hospital, I was on Devil's Hill. And this wasn't a regular doctor; he was an Ope, waiting for me to leave so he could take another hit of his dope stash. I nodded, sitting up slowly. I was still a bit light-headed, but felt a lot better. "Thanks, doc," I said, holding out my hand.

He refused to shake hands, instead backing away, like maybe freak DNA was catching. "All I've done is patch you up so you can fight another day—to the death," he said. "Go. Go!"

"Okay. But thanks," I said. "I won't forget it."

"You will." The doctor sounded resigned, not angry. "They always do."

There was nothing to say to that. When I left the Infirmary, I saw that my section was outside for our hour of sunlight and exercise. I needed some sun.

CHAPTER 23

I went outside, trying not to limp but of course limping. Every step felt like it was tearing the staples out of my side, and the wound had started leaking blood again. The doc had given me a paper packet of something to rub into it if it got infected, which I was positive it would. The packet said "Sulfa Powder, Veterinary Use Only." But it was what I had, and given my wings, laughably appropriate.

Everyone turned to look when I came through the metal door. Our outdoor exercise space was about as big as our cafeteria—concrete paved and walled, with the iron-bar cage overhead. We couldn't see shit, except whatever the sky was doing overhead. Not a place where you could appreciate the varied, wondrous beauty of the outdoors. I'd flown over forests, lakes, clear mountain streams...

"Good job on Kenton, hey," a prisoner said to me. She was tall and had very white skin and a shaved head.

"What do you mean?"

"He died, didn't he?" the woman said indifferently.

"I didn't mean to kill him," I said. Now I would never know

who had hired him to kill *me*. This was all so stupid. Maybe it was the new plasma talking, but I was just so sick of this whole asinine kill-or-be-killed policy.

"Well, he's dead." The prisoner spit a gob of something onto the cracked pavement. "You'll get an extra ration tonight."

Yes, of course. One of the unspoken features of Devil's Hill was that murder wasn't necessarily treated like a crime... it was more like something you were rewarded for. Fewer prisoners meant more profits, right?

And extra rations? Was that something to get excited about? Oh, boy, more swill, I thought. I stepped away from the inmate in case she suddenly, you know, *tried to kill me* for extra *food rations,* and looked at my fellow prisoners.

"Listen, guys," I said, raising my voice. "We have to stop this!" Cameras were no doubt recording us, and no doubt I'd be flogged or something, but I couldn't stay silent. Not anymore. Someone had been hired to kill me, and had been only too happy to do it, knowing that he'd get his payout, plus a little extra from the prison system itself.

"Stop what?" One guy, whose skin used to be brown but had dope-faded to a kind of gray-beige, looked at me, puzzled. He rocked back and forth from one foot to another, his hand jittery. He'd need another hit soon and would do anything to get it—kill his cellmate? The person next to him in the pen? Me?

"Stop killing each other!" I shouted so everyone could hear me. "We're not animals! We've got nothing against each other! Why do we have to keep fighting, killing each other for no reason? Just because they want us to?"

Another guy, short and dark, rubbed his chin thoughtfully. " 'Cause they give us extra rations if we kill somebody."

Okay, his logic was sound, I'd give him that, but holy mother!

"Extra rations of the crap they call food?" I yelled. The prisoners were now gathered around me, many looking scared, glancing at the cameras. Some of them might agree with me, but that didn't mean they were going to go against McCallum, not with all those eyes on them.

"We could take turns each giving *one spoon* of food to someone else. *That* person would have a huge meal, and we'd only be down *one spoonful*! Think about it! We don't have to kill each other! We don't have to be trained...*dogs,* doing stuff to make them happy! They get off on this shit, you know? What if we just said, *No more?*"

Some inmates were looking intrigued by this novel idea of no more killing, but others were shaking their heads, looking either scared or angry.

"I *like* killing people!" someone in the back shouted. "And they give me dope when I do!" There were many nods at this.

There was no chance of talking my way around that. Dope was a powerful motivator. Much stronger than me.

"Look," I said, trying again. "Dope or not...We. Don't. Have. To. Kill. Each. Other. Don't you get it? Why don't you get it?" Why was I even bothering? They wouldn't ever get it. They were prison-sick like I was, dope-sick like so many, but they weren't champing at the bit to get out—not when you could get free dope.

I was trying to think of what else I could say, what could possibly reach the people they had once been, the people who might still be inside.

"In fact, I think I'm hungry!" A thick, heavyset woman lunged forward and knocked down a man. She jumped on him, grabbing his hair in her meaty hands, and banged his head against the concrete.

"Stop!" I pleaded. "This is what they want us to do! Stop!"

"Maybe I *want* to do what they want me to do!" The woman laughed, showing several dope-rotted teeth. The man beneath her had quit fighting, almost like he agreed with dying. Blood ran from his head. Finally, the woman stopped as did the horrible, mushy sound of the pounding, and she leaned over the guy's face, checking for life. "Extra rations for me!"

The crowd had been whipped up into excitement by this gross spectacle, and now several other fights broke out that would of course be to the death.

I guess more people were extra hungry tonight.

CHAPTER 24

Overhead there was a metallic whirring sound. As I watched, a metal crane that I hadn't seen before stretched out over the exercise area. A mass fight had broken out and no one seemed to notice the crane but me. Prisoners were shouting, crying, shrieking, cursing as they bashed one another for extra rations.

"What in the world?" I muttered, looking up. Maybe they're building more cells. Maybe that would be the next reward—kill your bunkmate, level up to a suite.

The vidscreens in the exercise area had been playing staticky, cacophonous noise designed to get on whatever nerves we had left. Now they changed to McCallum's blistering red face. Next to him, a list of crimes was scrolling down.

"Pay attention, you worthless vermin!" he shouted. It took a minute for the inmates to quit fighting and look at the screens. Some of them dropped what they were doing instantly; others kept going, too lost in the process of killing to break away.

"There is a traitor among you!" McCallum shouted, finally gaining everyone's attention. "Someone even lower than the rest of you! A dirty scumbag who didn't follow the rules! All

I ever ask is that you follow the rules! Is that so much? Everyone has rules. I have rules. I follow them. Why is it so hard for you?"

The prisoners looked at one another, then slowly started edging away from me, already following the path McCallum had laid out for them. Overhead, a big metal clawlike thing scuttled out on the crane.

Why does everyone always assume that it's *me*? These people barely *knew* me. Is it something I was born with? Suddenly, I thought of Phoenix, always asking why. Questioning the rules Fang and I had laid out for her. Okay, maybe it was something I was born with, and I'd probably passed it on, too.

I'm hardly the only rule breaker here, though...I mean, it's a prison! It's true I was just shouting about rebellion, but—

The metal claw zipped down a cable on its line...until it was right over my head. I don't know why, but I didn't run when the metal claw opened slowly. It hovered above me, mesmerizing and enchanting me. It was so perfect, so beautifully made, and operating with precision. There was something almost calming about that when everything else was hopeless. My pleas for everyone to stop fighting meant that three more people had died. What was the use of even trying anymore? The claw dropped down and closed roughly and surely around my waist. It awoke a whole new level of pain from my stapled wound. I didn't really care. I needed to stop caring—about everything—before I lost my mind. Everybody I knew who didn't give a shit was happy.

"What should we do when a person can't follow the rules?"

McCallum demanded. "You tell me. I'm asking you. What should we do when a person just can't follow the rules? I'll tell you. I'm McCallum, and I get to decide. I have to decide everything. So I'll tell you. This person is hereby sentenced to death!"

That person was me.

CHAPTER 25

What was *wrong* with me? How many times had I told my flock to *never* give up, to fight back *always,* that there was *always* hope? Like a *million*? And here I was, so apathetic that I'd just let an evil claw grab me, as if I were a cheap stuffed animal in a carnival game! One second of apathy, one second of giving in to the sweet nothingness of not caring anymore, had landed me here. Now I attacked it with my hands, scrabbling to pull its metal arms apart. Was this going to...*pinch me in half*? That thought made my throat constrict with terror.

"Take that traitor to the Judgment Room!" McCallum shouted from all the vidscreens. "Anyone can tell you—she's an infection! Everyone knows that! Her crimes are many! I don't even have time to go into all her crimes! But they are many, I promise you!"

So much for the Judgment Room, I thought, still trying to pry the claw apart. "Sounds like I've already been judged," I shouted.

I heard the whirring before I felt it, then it was *oh, my god, are you kidding me?* This weird device wasn't a *killing* machine—it was designed to *move* prisoners, painfully, awkwardly. It rose several inches in the air till my feet dangled uselessly above the ground. Then it changed tracks with a screeching jerk that made me scream. My body swung uselessly in its grip and I tried to hold on so my injury wouldn't have to bear all the weight. I tried to reach down with my feet to kick out at anything close by. But I was completely helpless, feeling the metal pinching into my skin, feeling the slow, warm trickle of blood I couldn't afford to lose.

I swear, they made this thing just for me. A last, final insult before I died. They were going to make it seem like I was flying one last time, teasing me with the idea of it. The claw moved forward. The voices of the inmates had gone silent when the claw came out, but once I was captured their murmuring and questions swelled again. A minute later I couldn't hear them.

I punched the claw, which just caused more sickening pain from my injury. I was sure the clumsy staples were popping out from the pressure.

"Stop this!" I shouted. "I'll *walk* to the Judgment Room! Enough theatrics! Let me out! Goddamnit! You goddamn— ow! Goddamnit, that *hurt,* you assholes!" The claw had swung me against the rough stucco of a wall, and now my knee was bruised and a lot of skin was scraped and stinging.

My fingers were gripping the metal arms, trying to hold on and support my entire body the best they could. Still the pod moved, switching from track to track. I went through entire buildings—some I'd never seen before, never been in. I went through other exercise yards, where prisoners' voices went silent as this horrific contraption whirred past. That was part of the idea, I'm sure—they were making an example of me. An example of the traitor.

The pain in my side was blinding. My eyes were watering. My throat was so tight I couldn't even swallow, could barely get breath down. My fingers, holding on to the claw's arms, were cramping and turning numb. I couldn't hold on much longer.

Having Phoenix had been painful. In a different way than this, of course. But it had been painful. I'd never had a mom to help me, we were underground, there weren't tons of midwives or doctors, and there sure wasn't anesthetic. When Phoenix finally was born, and I quit swearing, I knew that I would do anything, anything at all, to make sure I'd always be there to help her. Always, always.

And then I had left her when she was only five. In my mind I could see Rose hurrying toward us from half a block away. I saw Phoenix, tall and thin for her age, standing at the corner. Fang held her shoulders and spoke into her ear, again and again. She nodded and looked at him, her black eyes confused and worried. I was trying not to show how bloody I was, how my wing was broken, how near I was to death.

And Fang. Fang who I had loved my whole life. First as a sort-of brother, then as a friend, and then...as the person who made my heart jolt, who showed me how deep and strong and overwhelming love could be. I remembered his kisses, the strength of his arms, how it felt to lie with him, feeling him all against me.

Hot tears leaked from my eyes and ran down my face.

Fang. I had missed him, ached for him, for so long. Years and years. Phoenix. My mother's heart had felt ripped apart, empty, unnatural without my baby by my side. To be alone here for so long had been the worst punishment I could imagine. Not knowing what had happened to either one of them—surely I would be able to feel it if either one had died? Wouldn't the fabric of the universe be ripped in some way that I could feel? If I'd ever gotten out of here and found that Fang or Phoenix had died—I knew I wouldn't be able to go on. For me, a world without them was a world I didn't need to be in. Real apathy would have taken over then. They could've pinched me in half. Sent a dozen guys at me with shivs. Set me on the rocks when the waves came in. I wouldn't have cared.

Except, even thinking about those scenarios automatically made my mind whirl with how I would escape them. The rocks were the easiest; obviously if I were anywhere outside, one of the Flock could...

Oh, god. Angel. Nudge. The Gasman. Iggy. Any one of them would have been able to spring me out of here. The fact that they hadn't meant one of two things: They had no idea where I was, or they were dead. I couldn't remember what had happened to injure me so badly—so badly that leaving Phoenix in a safe place seemed like a reasonable thing to do.

Suddenly the claw came to a jolting stop and my body swayed in agony. Slowly, slowly, the arms loosened while I clawed at them. Then they were open and I dropped to the ground.

Here was the Judgment Room.

CHAPTER 26

Hawk

I woke up on one of the folding tables in the laundry room—
Clete had carried me, despite not really liking touching people.

"I fainted?" I asked unnecessarily.

"Yep," he said, reaching past me to throw some soiled towels into one of the big machines. The crisis was over and he was
sticking to his schedule.

I sat up, and everything went filmy, black spots in my vision.

"Some of the prisoners tried to grab you," he said. "I
stomped on a couple arms."

That made me grin, though I still felt light-headed.

"That guy said he was your dad! How stupid does he think
you are?" Clete said.

"The weirdo? The worst of the worst? The kid killer? I guess
he thinks I'm pretty damn stupid," I said and slid off the table.
I must have been hallucinating when I thought I saw the resem-
blance to myself. I didn't have parents. They would have come
and gotten me. They wouldn't have let me live like th—

Clete was still automatically putting laundry in the machines and starting them.

"He said we looked alike," I went on, hearing snideness in my tone, some anger. "Which part? My tattooed eyeliner or my boobs?"

Clete looked at me, met my eyes—something he almost never did. "He's not your dad. You should just forget about it, refocus. We still got to rescue the other lab rats." He eyed me worriedly. "You still up for it?"

"Damn straight," I said and got busy, loading as many machines as I could—until Clete and I took our "break." We left the laundry room casually, looking bored, but as soon as we were out in the hall, we flattened ourselves against the wall and waited. After the guard's footsteps faded, we hurried down the hall, trying to be as silent as possible.

The Labs were in another building, across a courtyard. We opened the door to the courtyard slowly, catching it as it closed to prevent it from making the slightest sound.

"Stick to the shadows," I murmured to Clete, and he nodded. I wished Clete hadn't heard that weirdo say he was my father. I didn't ever want to talk to Clete about it again. I silently took in a deep breath, trying to put all that out of my mind.

It took us two long minutes to cross the courtyard, precious minutes of our so-called break. We didn't have much time.

In the Labs building all the doors were alarmed, opened only by keyed ID tags worn by the guards. We waited, standing behind a tree, until two guards marched out. Before the door could close behind them we had slipped through, as silent as air.

CHAPTER 27

Unlike our complex, the Labs were lit bright, the hallways clean and fixed up. Like the scientists were so much more important than us and the prisoners and the Opes trying to get clean one last time in the hospital.

"Any idea where they are?" I whispered to Clete. His day job was to work on their tech, and usually that meant the Labs.

He nodded. "Lab K. But hang on."

Clete took something out of his pocket, pushing back wires and SIM cards and who knows what else. Then, looking to make sure we were alone, he quickly popped the cover off the door alarm, undid some chips, put in another chip of his own, tightened something using his fingernail, and put the cover back on. It had taken literally less than one minute.

"What was that?" I whispered as we continued warily down one hall.

"I just unlocked the doors everywhere in this building," he whispered back, and my eyes opened wide.

"Awesome!" I murmured, impressed.

"Except for people who hold key cards. Their cards will

relock the doors, so they'll still have to use their card, or a code or whatever. But they'll be unlocked for everyone else."

"That is…so amazing," I said very softly. For years I'd been hearing Clete talk about his coding, his secret projects, and how they were going to change the world. I'd never actually believed him. But this—this was sophisticated, useful stuff. It made me see Clete differently. Like, if he can do something like that, maybe the app he was talking about when we folded laundry isn't so insane, after all.

As we padded softly down the hall, I tried hard not to think about what might be happening in Labs A through J, or L to Z. Awful stuff that should be criminal, maybe even was criminal. Not that it mattered. These were McCallum's Labs. His City. He made the laws and decided which ones to enforce. McCallum decided who the criminals were, and he certainly wasn't going to name himself. If I ever met him in real life, I would kneecap him. Promise.

In this hallway, Clete and I stuck out. We didn't have white coats, we were obviously kids, and together we were three point eight meters of freak. We couldn't blend, so we had to not be seen at all.

Which is why when we heard murmured voices, we grabbed the first doorknob we saw and yanked. To my relief, the door opened silently—no lock. We found ourselves in a dimly lit room…of horror. It was quiet, almost peaceful, with nothing but the barely noticeable hum of machines and the constant soft bubbling of water or something. Ten tables were laid out in neat rows, with a person—or what used to be a person—on each. Machines made their chests go up and down, like they were in a coma or something. The burbling sound was all the tubes going in and out of them. Some tubes had clear liquid, some had red, like blood, and some had a weird, milky blue solution.

Here was Science and Progress in McCallum's world. The same science that had made my friends: had made Clete into an Ope, made Moke blue, made Rain's skin look like a rain-splashed window, and made Calypso...into Calypso. Superchild.

Clete and I were both so grossed out that we couldn't look away, couldn't pay attention to the outside voices. Finally, it occurred to me to open the door a sliver and listen. It was all clear, and I motioned to Clete. He nodded, looking haunted, like he'd had a really bad dream.

I opened the door and we went out, leaving those things behind.

CHAPTER 28

We had to quickly hide one more time before we got to Lab K. Every door opened to us, which in some ways I was sorry for—the more doors we walked through, the more nightmares I was going to have. I'd seen stuff in these labs I'd never forget. It was making me hate all humans. All regular people. The only ones I'd met or seen had been complete assholes.

Other than doors that were usually locked, I didn't see any alarms or cameras. Like they were certain no intruder would make it this far. This was their clean, white kingdom of experiments. Where they could get away with anything and no one would ever interfere, or try to stop them.

A slow rage was building in me—I tried to shove it down so it didn't mess with our mission, but now it felt like it would shoot out the top of my head at any second. If I ran into a scientist, I would shove his nose up into his or her skull.

Clete elbowed me, pointing to a door sign. Lab K. This was it. If they were alive, our friends would be here. I clamped my fury down, but it still smoldered, like coals in my belly rather than an outright fire.

Meeting Clete's eyes, I nodded, and he slowly pushed the door open. Like the other labs, this one was dimly lit. There was a wall with a big glass window in it, like for people to spy on this room. Behind the glass, I could see a table with computers on it.

This room was so dim that it took my eyes a minute to adjust. Soon I saw that there were no tables in here, no cages or anything. But two walls had big thick iron rings stuck into them, and my family was chained to three of them. Rain and Moke, sitting on the floor with their hands chained above their heads, looked forward dully, as if they hadn't noticed us yet. A third person hung by one arm, skinny legs folded underneath the unmoving body. Calypso.

I clapped my hand over my mouth hard, the anger rising back up in a hot wave that wanted to come out in a scream. Calypso's eyes were closed, the thin white arm she hung from stretched taut. Her head was low, lifeless. I understood Rain and Moke's dull looks, why it seemed like nothing mattered to them anymore.

Calypso was dead.

CHAPTER 29

I knew the second Clete saw her because I heard his quick intake of breath. I whirled, slapping my hand over his mouth so hard that I'd probably leave a mark. I waited until his eyes showed that he was under control. We stared at each other for a long time, and had a whole, silent, freaking convo about finding Calypso like this, being too late to save her life.

We'd have to figure out a way to break or unlock their metal wristbands, but first, I needed to comfort my friends. I knelt next to Rain, touching her shoulder, and she turned her head slowly. Her eyes saw mine, but they were fixed on something far in the distance. I checked over my shoulder—there was nothing. When I turned back, Rain was smiling, her streaked face looking happy for maybe the first time in her life.

"Butterflies," she said dreamily. "They're real. They exist."

I wasn't going to take the time to argue that they'd gone extinct long ago. "Listen, Rain, we've got to get you guys out of here! Have you tried to get your hands out of the rings?"

Rain didn't move, didn't react to my words. It was like she was looking through me to another world. "I'm in a car," she said, sitting up a bit straighter, turning her head back and forth as if looking through car windows. It was the creepiest thing ever. She made the quiet humming of a car as if I didn't exist.

"Rain! Focus!" I said sternly, shaking her shoulder a tiny bit. Her fluffy, cloudlike hair waved back and forth, and that was when I saw it: a tiny, green blinking light behind her ear. I moved her hair aside and looked at it closer. I had just reached out a fingernail to see if I could scrape it off when Clete stopped me.

"Don't!" he whispered, pushing my hand away. "I think it's a parietal stimulator."

"Uh-huh and what now?" I asked.

"I think these probes go deep into their brains. Moke is in another world—not even here, just like Rain. I don't think they know that Calypso is—gone. And they definitely don't know that we're here."

"Well, *shit*!" I said.

"We can't rescue them like this," Clete went on quietly. "They wouldn't be able to come with us—they're tripping, basically. Maybe on Rainbow."

Rainbow was a street drug. Not every Ope liked it, but the ones who did were nuts. "Goddamnit," I said, my mind racing ahead for possible options.

"Should we...try to get Calypso?" I asked. "Get her body out of here?" I took a deep breath and tried to swallow the thought. Until this moment I hadn't let myself even stand next to the idea. Now, with Rain and Moke tripping happily, I had to face the worst thing I could think of: losing Calypso...and maybe having to leave her dead body behind for the lab to get rid of, thrown out with the rest of the trash.

Moving soundlessly, Clete and I scooched across the chilly floor to where Calypso hung by her left hand, the rest of her crumpled on the ground. Seeing her bare feet shot a dart into my heart. I'd washed these little feet, warmed them, found shoes for them, and pushed them out of my face while sleeping. Now all that was over. My eyes felt hot, my tongue was thick, and my brain was shrieking. I reached out and touched her wristband. Holy mud, it looked like it had been soldered onto her. Who would do that to a...freak?

The four little antennas growing on her back made her a lab rat. Literally something—not someone—to be experimented on. This was so ugly. I sat back on my heels for a second, trying not to let my thoughts and feelings run away with me. Trying to think of a way to get her out of here. Wondering if Rain and Moke had a chance, with their pari—whatevers glowing green behind their ears. I frowned. I pushed aside the wild red tangle of Calypso's hair. She had one, too.

"Can we take her?" I mouthed to Clete. He shook his head slowly.

"Almost certainly has a tracker," he whispered.

Then Calypso opened her eyes, and I almost screamed.

CHAPTER 30

Clete had me in a death grip, his fingers digging into my shoulder more deeply than Ridley's talons ever had. I didn't know if he was doing it to stop me from screaming, or himself, but either way, it worked. I took a deep breath, forced myself to look back into Calypso's gaze, into her new eyes.

"Calypso?" I whispered, wondering if she was still in there. I tried to lift her, get her into a more comfortable position, but she only collapsed against me.

Her mosaic eyes focused on something in another world, and my heart sank. She wasn't reacting to her name, or my voice, at all.

"I had an orange once," she murmured, smiling at nothing. Then she turned her head, as if in response to someone else talking. "No. I don't know. That's a pretty shirt. Hmmm." Her voice was quiet and calm and she tapped her index finger against her thumb. No idea why.

I tried to at least stand her up, so she wouldn't be hanging, but she sagged again immediately and said, "A pond!"

Clete put his hand out and tugged my shirt, telling me that

we needed to go. I looked at him helplessly. How could we leave without them? How could we save our family?

He tilted his head slightly and whispered into my ear. "We'll go back home. Come up with another plan. I need to research their probes."

I nodded, though I hated it. I tucked Calypso's hair behind her ear, and eased her body back so that she was leaning against the wall. It was the least I could do ... the only thing I could do.

We had no trouble retracing our steps—we both could map places in our minds and remember them. I could also always tell if I was facing north, south, or whatever, but Clete couldn't. He just committed every turn to memory, then did it in reverse.

When we were back in the laundry room, it all started to feel like a dream. Nightmare, I mean. Had we really gotten into the Labs? Had we seen those awful things, seen the zombies of our family? Here, with the heat and steam and familiar smells, the same Opes shuffling in, getting their mops and brooms—it was so ordinary and everyday that, if I tried, I could probably talk myself into believing I'd hallucinated it all. Maybe something I ate had been laced with Rainbow. I could almost believe it.

Wanted so bad to believe it.

CHAPTER 31

Clete and I finished at the laundry and started to head back to the Children's Home. We were still staying there, still calling it home. Nobody had come for us, which must mean that three kids had been enough for—whatever they were doing, with the blinking green lights and the Rainbow effect. Holy mother.

"We'd need a way to carry them," Clete said. "Like on a gurney. We'd have to...maybe blowtorch their bracelets off. But the entire band will get really hot and it'll hurt them. How do we use a blowtorch and not burn them to a crisp?"

I didn't have a response, but I knew Clete didn't really need one, either. He was thinking out loud, coming up with plans and tweaking them as he went. A shouting voice interrupted his thoughts, and mine.

"Phoenix!"

I looked at Clete with an oh, god, not this again look. Clete gave a tired, sad bit of a smile, and I waved at him to go on without me. He was exhausted, and my day couldn't get any worse. A street gang had carved up my face, marking me. My family was in chains and possibly altered for life. There was nothing a child killer who claimed to be my father could say that could shock me more than what I'd seen in the Labs.

"Go on, get some sleep," I said to Clete and he continued on the path toward the Children's Home.

The tiny window opening into the hall was enough for the criminal to see us—if he was standing on his chair, on his bed.

"Phoenix!" he whispered. I could see only his eyes and eyebrows and the top of his head.

"My name is Hawk!" I whispered harshly back.

"Okay, Hawk," the prisoner said patiently. "Listen. I'm your Dad-man. Don't you remember me? You and me and your mom—we were always together."

I crossed my arms over my chest. "Sure we were, creep. Leave me alone!"

"Hawk! Wait. I've been looking for you for years!"

"Okay," I said. "Prove it. Tell me something about myself. Anything."

"You have wings," he said, and I froze in place. "They're dark brown with tan undersides—more like your mom's than mine. But you have a spray of black feathers around your shoulders— so black that when they're in the sun, they look iridescent."

I bet my own gang couldn't have described my wings so well.

"I know because I'm Dad-man," he said, apparently reading my mind. "I was there when you were born."

"Were you there when I was left by myself on the street?" I asked, practically spitting.

"Yeah, I was," he said, sounding surprised. "But you *weren't* left on your own—a good family friend, Rose, was ten meters away from coming to get you. We didn't leave till we knew she was super close."

"*No one* came and got me," I said, putting all the meanness I could into my voice. "I was *left* by *myself* on a *street corner*. I was a *little kid*."

"Rose was almost there," the murderer said more strongly. "We saw her! She was ten meters away!"

I sighed. "You know what? I'm tired and depressed and not going to argue with a child killer." Once again I turned to go, but he said, "Why are you depressed?" Almost like he gave a shit. That's not something you heard on the streets. Nobody cared about a stranger. But this guy...either he meant it, or I was so run-down and hard up that I'd talk to anybody right now. Even him.

"The rest of my friends—kids I live with—have been taken to the Labs, where they're being experimented on. Clete and I tried to rescue them, but we couldn't."

He said, "I can help."

Without turning around, I waited. If he really was a child killer then he was certainly crafty, probably had a whole book of lies and tricks in his head to get people to do what he wanted...But he knew that stuff about my wings, and I was flat out of options.

He said, "I have friends, too—people your mom and I grew up with. Some of them are waiting for me in the city. I wasn't supposed to get caught, get put in here. You can go find them— tell them what happened. They can probably help."

"Probably isn't good enough," I said, feeling exhausted. The glazed look in Calypso's eyes had seared a hole in my heart. "I need promises."

"They'll *help* you," he said more strongly. "They know more about rescuing freaks than anyone in the world." He put his mouth closer to the tiny window and whispered directions to where his friends were. Flying directions. "And hurry—if these labs are like labs I've known, time's already run out. Tell 'em Fang sent you."

I gave him one last look: should I trust him? No. I shouldn't trust him. He was a child killer. The worst of the worst. But he had known my wings. *My wings.*

"Wait—you say you're my dad. So you have wings, too?" I almost smiled at how easy it was to catch him in his own trap. Let's see how he lied his way out of this.

"Of course," he said, sounding surprised again.

My eyes and my mouth were all as round as O's as I heard a fluttering sound, and then saw big black wings raised behind him. He moved them up and down while my heart skidded to a stop inside my chest. Wha—

"*Who are you?*" I whispered in shock. Before he could answer, I turned and ran.

CHAPTER 32

I'd flown above the City of the Dead a million times. It was always the same: choking smog, factory chimneys billowing clouds of steam. All the coal dust hovered in the air till nighttime, when it sank to the ground for Opes to sweep it up and try to burn it again in their cheap little stoves.

Tonight the air felt colder, denser. Like smog soup. I looked over at Ridley, flying so beautifully even in this industrial goop, and she looked back at me calmly.

"Am I stupid for trusting him?" I yelled over at her.

Her yellow eyes blinked at me. I kept flying.

The Guy with Wings had given me directions to Sault Tower, way south and west, right on the edge of the green and greasy river. It had been supposed to be a luxury high-rise at some point—some point before McCallum. Which I couldn't remember. Anyway, it'd been left unfinished. No one lived on the top three floors, the only ones of a hundred that had been completed.

I landed on the roof; Ridley flitted down to sit on my shoulder. Silently I opened the rooftop door and headed down the dark, plywood stairway. Had this been a trap? Was I being set up?

The sound of a shotgun's ammo clinking into place made me certain. There's a life lesson for ya: Never trust a child killer.

"Since you're about to die," said a cool voice, "got any last words?"

My mouth was dry from flying, my eyes watering from pollution. All of a sudden this seemed like the worst idea ever. I'd been so stupid. *Deadly stupid.* I took a chance on trusting a stranger in order to save my family, and now I was going to die in a dark hallway because of it. I swallowed a couple times and then in the darkness someone said, "Is that...Ridley?"

Ridley snapped her head toward the voice and peered into the black. She gave a sudden squawk and left my shoulder, her long, deadly talons leaving indents in my skin.

"How—" I started, then coughed, some of the smog from outside leaving my lungs. "How do you know Ridley?"

"Fang gave her to..." a woman said, then stepped into the light. She was really pretty, in the same way Rain was, but she didn't have rain marks all over her. Her skin was smooth and brown, and her hair was pulled tightly back into a ringlet-y ponytail. Ridley sat on her shoulder and was trying to preen her, touching her powerful beak gently against the woman's skin. When the woman looked at me, she frowned, tilting her head.

"Do we know you?" said a man's voice. One by one they stepped closer, where the dirty moonlight glowed through an empty, unbuilt wall. There was a tall guy, taller than me, with super-white skin, pale white hair, and pale blue eyes. Another guy, not quite as tall and not quite as thin, came into the light. He was the one holding the shotgun. His dark blond hair stuck up on his head, and he had blue eyes, too, but darker than those of the Ghost Guy.

"No," I said shortly. "But your friend said you might help me."

"Fang gave this hawk to Phoenix," the woman said, coming closer. There was that name again.

I'm used to getting stared at, be it for my height, my pierced everything, and ever so rarely, my wings. This felt different. They were all squinting at me, like they were trying to remember if I'd robbed them once or something.

"You don't know me," I said again. "And I don't know you, but your friend said you could help me and time is running out. So will you, or what?"

"Hm," said the blond guy, but he didn't lower the shotgun. "Iggy—"

"On it," said the tall blond guy, and he walked toward me. I stood still like a trapped rat while he reached out long, gentle fingers and carefully touched my face—after he'd started somewhere around my stomach. I realized he was blind and took his hands, moving them up, up, up to my face.

"Careful," I said, touching his palm first to the still-stinging cheek where the Chungs had cut a C into me. He nodded, acknowledging my injury, and Ridley flew to *his* shoulder, preening her feathers and shaking them, the way she did when she was super happy.

"Jeez, you're tall," the blind guy said. His fingers traced my nose, my eyebrows, and the curve of my ears, skimming over the various studs, rings, points, and hoops along the way.

He drew in a shuddering breath, one hand on my shoulder. "Guys—this…is Phoenix! Taller and older."

"My name is *Hawk*," I said, but they were coming at me now, no shotgun, just a trio of grown-ups staring at me. Except the blind guy, who kept touching my face, my eyebrows, my earlobes.

"Hawk!" I tried again, but it sounded like "Baw!" I'm one point eight meters tall, but they were all as tall as I was, or taller. Only the woman was maybe an inch shorter than me. Slowly they surrounded me—one of my favorite positions— and then they were all hugging me. *Hugging* me. Like, with *hugs*. I stiffened, not knowing what to do with all the affection from people I didn't know, and trying to keep everybody from bumping the wound on my face. My shoulder felt wet—I peered down and saw it was because the woman was crying.

It was so awkward and uncomfortable I almost threw up. Also, I couldn't breathe.

"Phoenix, Phoenix, Phoenix!" the woman murmured. She drew back, her face wet with tears, large brown eyes shining. She took my appalled face gently in her hands. "Is it you? After all this time?"

"No," I said tensely. "It's *Hawk*, after like a *minute*."

"Gosh, whose daughter does she sound like?" the blond— not blind—guy said.

I thought about the inmate saying I was his daughter, but didn't say anything. Better to keep some tricks up my sleeve.

"I'm Nudge," the woman said, hugging me tightly. It took all my self-control to stand there and take it. "Don't you remember?"

"Iggy," said the blind guy, reaching out and wiping away

the woman's tears. How he knew she was crying or where her cheeks were, I don't know.

"Gazzy," said the other guy, holding the shotgun behind him. "The Gasman."

"We're the Flock," the woman said, like that should mean something.

"Flock of what?" I asked, totally confused. Then I stepped back, mouth open, as pair after pair after pair of enormous, powerful wings unfolded in the moonlight.

CHAPTER 33

My whole life, I'd been the only person I knew with wings. Calypso had antennas, Moke was blue, Rain had rain skin, and I'd seen a thousand poor freaks with everything from horns to see-through ears (I know—*why???*) to multiple sets of fingers, toes, and boobs. But I'd never, ever seen another pair of wings, till the prison guy had raised his.

Just then the blare of the Voxvoce sounded loudly in the city a hundred stories below. Like me, it didn't seem to bother these people.

"Who *are* you?" I demanded. "*What* are you?"

"Have you looked in a mirror, kid?" said the Ghost Guy. Iggy. "We're like you. Or, you're like us. We're the *Flock*."

"We're *your* Flock," the woman—Nudge? What kind of a name is *that*?—said.

"I have no idea what you're talking about," I said flatly. "But my friends are being hurt, and I was told you could help me. Now, are you in or out?"

"Ooh, voice from the past," the blond guy—Gazzy?— murmured.

"Who told you we could help you?" Nudge asked gently.

"This horrible prisoner, at the place I live at," I said. "He's the worst of the worst, they said. A child killer."

"You live in a prison?" Iggy asked.

"I live at a Children's Home in the same complex as the prison," I explained, thinking of all the seconds ticking by, seconds of Calypso hanging by one hand while Rainbow rotted her brain.

"Did he tell you his name?" Nudge persisted, like she just wasn't going to stop. Oh! That's why her name was Nudge! Got it.

"He said to tell you Fang sent me," I said.

"Yes!" Gazzy punched the air. "She knows where Fang is!"

"Okay, now, Fang is at this children's home?" Iggy said, suddenly all business.

"No!" I said impatiently. "Fang is in *prison,* which is part of a much bigger complex, with things like this children's home, but also a lab."

"That's weird," Gazzy said. He looked at the others. "Isn't that weird?"

"We specialize in weird," Nudge said dryly, then motioned to me. "Come on, sit down, eat something while we come up with a plan."

"My friends are in danger *now,*" I said.

Nudge sat down on an upturned wooden box and started rustling in a big leather backpack. "I know, honey. Would it be better for you to rescue 'em while you're hungry, or rescue 'em when you're not hungry?"

I stood there, thinking. It's like she nudges you toward doing that, too.

"Better sit down. She doesn't give up," Iggy said, moving past me to another crate. His skinny knees stuck up like two triangles when he sat.

"We have doughnuts," Gazzy said, folding his wings in. Their wings were like mine, folding not once like Ridley's, but twice, to rest neatly on either side of their spines. It was a comforting sight to see; someone like me, for the first time, ever.

I sat.

"Okay," said Nudge, handing me a doughnut. "Tell us about this complex."

For the next twenty minutes I stuffed my face with doughnuts, then a bunch of dried fruit—like dried on purpose, not just old and yucky—then a little mesh bag of all kinds of nuts. Then a couple more doughnuts, not even all that stale.

In between mouthfuls, I drew them a map of the complex in the thick dust on the floor. I showed them how it looked when I flew over it, where the gates were, the few windows, doors, and how they were guarded. I drew the long walkway to the Labs and showed how the prison was kind of off by itself but not far away. In a tiny box in one corner of one building, I scratched out the main room and the little sleeping closet of the Children's Home.

"That's where you grew up," Iggy said, rather than asked.

"Uh-huh," I said. "There used to be a lot more of us, but now there's only five. The last one we lost was Veil. You could sort of see through her, but she couldn't pass through walls or anything. They took her like six months ago. She hasn't come back. They never come back."

"And now they've taken everyone else," Gazzy clarified.

"Yeah," I said. "Everyone but me and Clete. Me because I was…somewhere else, and Clete because he hid." My face heated and turned pink as I thought about where I'd been, and with who. Kissing Pietro felt like a thousand years ago.

"And you got injured how?" Nudge asked.

My hand went to the C on my cheek, the flaming, red skin puffy under my touch. I told them about the Chungs and the Paters, Ones and Sixes, the street fights and the constant battle for pride and protection—one that the street rats like me ended up in the middle of, all too often. What I didn't tell them was that I'd been sitting in a high-end tub, then been kissed by the Pater prince not too long ago. They didn't need to know that. My blush got deeper. Nobody needed to know that.

"Okay," said Iggy, standing up. "Let's go."

CHAPTER 34

I jumped to my feet. "Wait a second!" I said. "We don't have a plan!"

"We're going to go rescue Fang," Nudge said, sounding surprised. "Then your friends."

"My friends first," I said, realizing that all my drawings and explanations had given them the only bargaining chip I had. They'd fed me doughnuts, and I'd downed them without question, happily giving away all my info while my brain drowned in sugar. I was a moron.

"Fang first," Iggy said mildly. "Then he can help save your friends."

I remembered the first look I'd had of the prisoner: strong and solid. If he was a decent guy, having him on our side to bust my friends out would be a good bet. But if he wasn't...I shook my head. I was so down and out, this is where I'd landed. Trusting strangers.

"That prison is pretty solid," I reminded them. "Fang is on death row. I mentioned the thick walls, the guards, the guns, right?"

"Yeah," the Gasman said, sounding surprised. "Figure it's pretty standard prison stuff."

"And we're just...going to go break Fang out?"

"Yeah," said Nudge, smiling at me. "It's okay, sweetie. We do this kind of thing all the time." She pulled on the leather backpack. I noticed Gazzy had a larger, black backpack, and so did Iggy.

My stomach was grinding, all the doughnuts taking a turn for the worse as I realized these people were actually going to do this. Part of me hadn't thought this was real. I'd totally expected to come here, meet a bunch of creeps who would blow me off—or worse—and then have to figure this out on my own. The idea that three strangers, grown-ups, would *join me* and help make this happen—it was a lot to take in. Of course, they hadn't saved anyone yet, and, I reminded myself, promises were easy to make. And even easier to break.

"You okay?" Iggy frowned at me. But he was *blind*.

"How do I know that you'll help me get my friends out?" My voice sounded like a lost little kid's, and I made it stronger. "Maybe you'll rescue Fang and then ditch me." I stuck my chin up in the air, my lips tight, to show this would be no more than a small glitch. Like, if they're going to screw me, let's take the surprise element out of it and just screw me now.

All three of them turned to really look at me, their faces shocked.

"How could—we would *never* ditch you!" the Gasman said.

"You're one of us, Phoenix," Iggy said. "I mean Hawk."

Despite obviously itching to hit the sky, Nudge came and sat next to me, putting her hand on my knee. A cold wind whistled through the skeletal building, whipping plastic sheeting around. I wanted to shiver but forced myself not to.

"Sweetie, I don't think you understand," she said. "You're part of the *Flock*. You're not being invited in—you *are* in. You were a missing piece, and now you're back, and we'll never let you go again." She raised her head, and a thin shaft of moonlight highlighted her tan skin and one brown eye. "Okay, that sounded more stalkery than I meant. But to us you aren't a stranger, though we haven't seen you in ten years and you definitely look different." She smiled. "To us you're a member of our family."

"You don't even know me!" I said loudly, getting to my feet. This was all getting super sticky, and I felt furious but didn't know why.

"That's the thing about families," Iggy said. "We don't have to know you. Hell, we don't even have to like you. But you're in the Flock anyway."

"Just like that," I sneered.

"Just like that," Gazzy agreed.

I sat down abruptly again and reached for a bottle of juice. It was slick and sugary in my throat, chasing down the last of the doughnuts. My body was burning through all the sugar, eager and ready to fly, but I was still thinking. What Iggy said about families was right; I knew what it was like to make one rather than be born into one. And I knew—really well—that you didn't have to always like each other. But that word— *family*—hung in the air, and I had one more question.

"Did the pris—did Fang really kill some kids?" Was I the possible daughter of a murderer?

"He may have," said Nudge calmly. "If he thought it was necessary, he would."

"Why would it *ever* be necessary to kill a bunch of *kids*?" I cried.

Nudge's voice was quiet when she answered. "Because sometimes, death is, in fact, better than life. Only in the most extreme situations. Only when death is...a mercy." She stood up and shook out her wings, ready to fly. "And you should know that, better than anyone."

One last smile and she ran and jumped off the building, a hundred stories up. Energized by possibilities, sugar, and curiosity, I ran and jumped after her.

CHAPTER 35

Max

The concrete I'd fallen onto was wet and slimy with mold. All I felt was my familiar enemy, pain. Pain in my head, pain from my scraped knees, and big pain in my side where the arms of the claw had definitely popped some staples. What kind of sick asshole would make a big claw to move people? Give me ten minutes alone in a room with them. But first maybe give me ten days of recovery.

Slowly I stood, refusing to show how much I hurt. One by one, pink, purple, and green floodlights snapped on, making my skin look revolting, like I'd already died and started to rot. Looking up, I saw they made *everything* look revolting—then I almost gasped in disbelief.

"Oh, come *on!*" I shouted, blinking against the pink flood-lights shining in my eyes. "*This* is the Judgment Room? It's more of a judgment *courtyard,* isn't it? You used the stupid claw to bring me *here?*" I was about *thirty meters* away from where I'd started, in this separate little block in the prison yard!

So the whole claw-grabbing thing had been *pointless*! Except it had been scary, I'd thought I was going to die, and it'd hurt like almighty hell. Other than that, pointless.

But, I guess that *was* the point, wasn't it? Hurting me and scaring me. These sick, sick assholes. When would I ever stop being surprised by them?

This courtyard was open to the prison inmates, who were held back by the twelve-foot-tall chain-link fence topped with razor wire. Hundreds of prisoners crowded against the fence, watching eagerly. This was something kind of new, after all. They could see normal, everyday violence in the courtyard. The people mover had promised something different, and man, did it look like McCallum was going to deliver.

There was an operating table in the courtyard. It wasn't padded or lined with sterile sheets. It was plain metal, beat-up, with fringes of rust around its edges like it'd decided to grow a beard. It was chained to the ground. It had iron loops welded on it.

This was looking...not good.

I did a fast 360, in seconds memorizing the courtyard layout, the one entrance/exit, the high walls, the slimy wet concrete floor. The ceiling was open, which wasn't saying much, because this whole place still had the thick iron-mesh cover over it. So there'd be no sudden up-and-aways. It felt like a hundred years since the Flock had named that particular maneuver. Since then I'd used it probably a million and a half times. Could not use it now. My wings were still banded, but even if I could use them, I'd never be able to claw my way through that cover. *Shit.*

A door I hadn't noticed before opened in the concrete-block wall. The sad-sack doctor who had helped me earlier entered, carrying a black bag. The green floodlight highlighting him did not improve his looks, turning his gray Ope skin into something even more sinister. When the door closed, it was almost impossible to see where it had been. I glanced into his eyes to see any intent to help me. Instead of sympathy, I saw ... anticipation. He set his black bag down on the metal table.

The constant blare of the vidscreens around the prison yard changed to a horrible, ear-piercing crackling, and then of course McCallum came on, his wide, tan face filling the screen. Because we needed him to make this scene complete.

"Traitor!" he said with a sneer. For some reason his voice always made me think of oil. Any kind of oil. He just seemed—oily.

I was still in all kinds of pain, and all I wanted to do was kill some nameless prisoner and lie down on their cot because my cot was too far away. I didn't even care who it was, at this point, just as long as it emptied up a bed nearby. *Nice,* I thought to myself, *and you were just arguing for us to stop killing one another—what, half an hour ago?*

When I didn't respond to his accusations of being a traitor, McCallum yelled, "You're unredeemable! Another piece of human trash!"

Well, 98 percent human, I thought. I brought one hand up and looked at my fingernails. They were broken and bloody from clawing at the metal arms.

"For far too long you've been flouting the rules here," McCallum went on. The fat rolls around his eyes showed whiter than his tan cheeks. I noticed his lips were wet. *Ew.*

"We've given you shelter and food, and how have you repaid us? We've tried to rehabilitate you..."

Oh, they so had *not*. *No* one had *once* tried to rehabilitate me. All they did was let you loose in here with the other criminals, and probably took bets on who would last.

"For ten years!" McCallum finished.

My head whipped around, first to look at a single McCallum screen, then at the doctor.

"Wait—*what*?" I cried.

CHAPTER 36

"The time has come to show you you're not special! You are not above the law! You're just a prisoner like anyone else!" McCallum yelled.

"Okay, right, right," I said, "but what did you just say? About time?"

McCallum started to say something else, but then someone off camera seemed to want his attention. He stopped and looked away, then looked straight into the camera, as if he were looking right at me. It was really disturbing, and my mind was reeling.

"I said we had been trying to rehabilitate you for *ten years*," he said, all pompous wind and certainty.

"No," I said, my eyes narrowing, filled with purple light. Out of nowhere, a tiny microphone hovered over me on a thin wire. "It has *not* been ten years!"

Apparently, I was now being transmitted to him directly, because he leaned closer to the camera and said, "Ten. Years. It's a long time. A long time to be in prison. A long time to

learn the rules. And a *very* long time to put up with your inso-
lence and bad behavior."

No...this was impossible. The green floodlight swirled in
circles against the concrete walls, creating a sickening effect.
I thought I'd been here...a long four years, maybe? I tried to
think back to when I'd first come here...all my memories of
this place were kind of hazy, not set sharply in my mind. I put
my mouth to my hand, trying not to scream. If I had been here
ten years...did Fang have Phoenix? Were they safe?

"For all of your crimes, you deserve death!" McCallum went
on. "For your insurrection, your hundreds of betrayals. You've
tried to undermine the state, to create *more* infidels. For these
and your many other crimes, you deserve to *die*. But it would
be too easy to simply kill you." McCallum didn't seem to notice
that I was one second away from turning into a screaming banshee, and it wasn't because of his words, or the things I was
being accused of. I was still stuck on something else.

Ten years! He must be lying. I swayed on my feet, then
quickly righted myself and stood tall, ignoring the floodlights.
He was lying about *everything*—I'd never tried to insurrect
here or create infidels. I had no idea what he was talking about.
Unexpected tears filled my eyes as I drew sharp, quick breaths
in through my fingers. It couldn't be *ten years*. Phoenix had
been five when we'd been forced to leave her with Rose Simmons, a friend we'd made in what was left of England. To find
Rose in that miserable hellhole, the City of the Dead, had been
amazing. I hadn't wanted to leave Phoenix! But Fang could
carry me or her. Not both. Not even he could do that, and he
was the strongest person I knew.

I'd been dying. I could barely remember it. I remembered crying, trying not to let Phoenix see my broken wing, the blood...

"So instead, we're going to do what we should have done a long time ago," McCallum said in a silky whisper, as if to get my attention. "We're going to cut off your wings."

CHAPTER 37

The invisible door opened again and ten armed guards marched in, their boots squelching in the slime.

"Turn off those lights," McCallum said. "This is something I want to savor."

Something about that flicked some recognition in me, but my mind was still whirling from his ten-years lie (which *might* be true!) to them wanting to *cut off my wings*. And then he gives me the gift of ten guards. It was something to focus on. It was something to do.

I felt like beating the hell out of someone, so this should work out.

I let my shoulders drop, keeping my hand over my eyes as if I was about to cry. The guards, unsurprisingly, split in two and moved to surround me. I was as tall as most of them but because of my bird DNA I was incredibly lightweight. *These guards could have almost a hundred kilos on me.*

I inhaled. McCallum, for once, was quiet.

From behind my fingers, I glanced out, quickly assessing their weak spots. Holy moly, they weren't even wearing helmets or shin guards. Years of working in a prison full of Opes that were easily manageable had made these guys soft. Sure, they had stun guns—far more powerful than tasers, one hit from a stun gun and I'd drop like a brick. But they had to get close enough to reach me...

"Okay, lady, get over to the table," one gruff voice said.

I shook my head and sniffled.

Someone moved closer behind me. With no warning, I suddenly dropped and shot my leg out, sweeping it under his legs. He fell with a satisfying *oof,* and I stomped on his knee, feeling the break. The joint cracked under my heel, the sound just as loud as McCallum's stupid voice. He coiled up, screaming in pain.

Nine stun guns were pulled. I did a handstand, kicking away two guns. They flew through the air and fell with a clatter five meters away.

Rough hands tried to grab me, but these prison clothes were super loose, making it easy to wiggle away. Two more guards came at me. Springing up, I chopped my hand down in a ridge strike, aiming for one's gun arm. I heard delicate human arm bones break—so satisfying after thinking about my broken wing, all those years ago (but not ten! Surely not ten!)—and a guard sank to the ground, screaming and holding his arm.

I hit another guard with a hard palm strike to his nose, breaking it and shoving bone shards toward his brain. He, too, went down, but that one wasn't moving. That made three in the last eight seconds.

"Maximum!" McCallum said, sounding like a father. "We all know you can fight! Stop this pointless display—you're only making it worse for yourself."

"Worse than having my wings cut off?" I snarled, spinning backward to punch a guard in the kidney. When he staggered a bit, I jumped up and snap-kicked his head sideways. He dropped. They just weren't making guards like they used to.

Another snap kick to a guard's left ear, and he fell to his knees, his stun gun skittering across the ground. I punched someone else right below his ribs, then clapped both of my hands over his ears as hard as I could, rupturing at least one eardrum. He yelled and dropped his stun gun, then fell against a concrete wall. I'd lost count, but there were only a few left.

"What—who are you?" one guard shouted, trying not to look afraid.

"I'm Maximum Ride, you son of a bitch!"

And a roundhouse kick to the side of his neck, disrupting nerves and blood flow to his carotid. He looked confused, then melted to the ground.

I felt the brush of a stun gun against my arm, so I whirled and slammed it out of the guard's hand. "I think you use the pointy end," I said, then punched him hard in the gut. When he folded, I grabbed his head and smashed it down on my raised right knee.

Then it was me and the remaining two guards. I saw one swallow nervously, obviously wishing he was armed with a regular gun or even a taser. The ground was littered with broken, bloody, or unconscious guards—the ones who had tried to get close enough to me to use their stuns.

"My legs are longer than your arms," I pointed out, and he lunged toward me, gun out. I ducked and snap-kicked his knee, making it bend forcefully in the wrong direction. Moaning, he fell hard but still tried to swipe at me with his gun. I stomped on his wrist, breaking it, then kicked the gun away.

When I looked up, the last guard was disappearing through the hidden door.

That was when I felt the hard stick of a needle in my neck. I slammed it away, spinning to see the washed-out doctor, who had snuck up behind me.

The hypo flew against the wall, but the doctor didn't look worried. His eyes gleamed with excitement. What had happened to the man who did his best to patch me up when I got hurt? The guy who had moaned over his lack of decent supplies? I looked hard into his eyes and found my answer. He was tripped out, for sure, fresh dope running through him like water. No wonder he was happy. No wonder he'd do anything they asked him to. I lunged for him, hands out to grab his skinny neck ... but my arms were limp noodles, not obeying my command.

"Oh, fu—" I mumbled, and fell to the ground.

CHAPTER 38

For what felt like hours, my only objective was to open my eyes. But it was an impossible task, they were so heavy. And every time I got close, something told me it might be easier to just go back to sleep. That it might be easier to just give up. No, I argued with myself. No. Because of Fang. No. Because of Phoenix.

Trying with all my might, I resisted my own instinct to remain unaware. I was still locked in darkness. For who knows how long. Finally, I was able to swim upward toward consciousness, and I blearily opened my eyes just a slit.

I was in an...operating room. Super-bright lights shone down and I hazily saw people in doctors' robes hurrying in and out of my line of vision. The walls had chipped paint peeling off their cinder blocks. So I was in a *bad* operating room. Probably the prison's. Awesome. At least they'd taken me out of the courtyard. Apparently letting the prisoners watch me be operated on might make an example, but letting them see me take out ten guards all by myself might give them ideas.

Plus, I had the *worst* headache. Very carefully, I twitched one finger a tiny bit to see just how drugged I was. Bird-people have superfast metabolisms, so we process things like food, drugs, and water much quicker than regular humans.

In fact, I was hungry now. Maybe I should kill the doc for extra rations. I bit the side of my cheek, trying not to laugh at my own joke.

"She'll be out cold for another couple hours," I heard someone say.

"I don't want her to feel any pain." That sounded like the sad-sack doctor who had dosed me. Maybe there was a little bit of decency left in him, after all.

"Has anyone ever done this before?" the other person asked.

"Not as far as I know," said the doctor. "I'm so excited to get my hands on her—usually I just do autopsies. This is a whole new world."

What was a whole new world? I wondered. My body? Just working on the living? Or was there something more sinister implied in his words? Metal instruments clinked on a metal table, and I quickly revised my opinion—there was definitely not anything good left in this man.

"What are you going to do with the wings?" the voice asked.

Oh, my god. *My freaking wings.* That's right! They were going to cut them off!

"He's going to examine them," said the all-too-familiar voice of McCallum. As usual, he spoke too loudly, and I struggled to keep from wincing. "And try to graft them onto someone else! I would love to have a platoon—no, a *flock*—of winged soldiers!"

I felt my eyes grow hot with possible tears and tried to blink them away without looking like it. Various megalomaniacs had been trying to make winged armies my whole life. Could I just tell them that it never, ever turns out well? God, *I* wished a flock of winged soldiers would come get *me*, right now! I hadn't seen my family in ten goddamn years! But it would take a miracle for them to burst in now and rescue me from this maniac!

"You have extra paralytic medicine, if necessary?" the doctor asked.

The other someone, who I'd realized was a woman, answered softly, "Yes. But she's out deeply—her heart rate is dangerously slow. And we'll be using the restraints, of course."

My heart rate is almost always very slow. It speeds way up if I'm fighting.

"This is a first step toward real equality," McCallum said. "Keep up the good work, doctor. And turn her to face away from me—I want to see the whole operation."

"She'll be facedown," the doctor told him. "To give me more access."

"Of course," said McCallum. "Carry on!"

"We're going to need more people to turn her, if you want her facedown," said the woman.

The doctor was silent, but maybe others were watching, too, because a few seconds later I heard the clomping of heavy boots, a door opening, more clomping.

"Help us turn her," said the doctor.

"Is she asleep, like *super* asleep?" one of the soldiers asked warily.

"Yes," the doctor said.

Do I try to jump up now, fight everyone? Wait till I feel

the first scalpel? My hand hurt and when I looked downward through my slitted eyes, I saw an IV going in. The time to get up was now!

I mentally pictured myself leaping off the table, kicking the doctor in the throat, then chopping his neck until he lost consciousness. Maybe I would put him on this table, see how he liked it.

The problem was, when I told my body to spring off the table, it telegraphed back, Nobody home. Then I realized I couldn't see. Couldn't open my eyes again. Was heading to painless, floaty dreamland. Shit.

CHAPTER 39

Hawk

I'd never, *ever* flown with anyone else, *ever*. Now I was flying with three people who were *like me*. Actually *like me*. They weren't gaping and gawking like the Chungs had when I had to use my wings to escape. They weren't calling me a freak. They thought I was *normal*.

They were all older than me and their wings were a bit bigger. I bet they were stronger. I couldn't *believe* they were up in the sky with me. The sky had always been...all mine. Mine and Ridley's. I kept looking around, surprised again to see them there. I had to work hard to stay in front, but I did. After all, I was the one who knew where the complex was. I was the one who had told them where that prisoner was. They needed me.

But not as much as I needed them.

Okay, all right. First we would rescue—Fang. (What kind of a name was *that*?)

Anyway, first we would rescue Fang, and then I would hold

them to their promise to free my gang. Then Clete and I would detox my people—however long that would take. Rainbow might have a pretty name, but a person could turn ugly once you took it from them. I hoped Clete had been hanging tough all this time, trusted me to come back.

Iggy, the blind guy, stayed in formation, to my left, behind the blond guy. Gazzy.

As if he could feel me looking at him, Gazzy spoke. "You ready for some action?"

I didn't know what that meant. "Well, I guess we'll sneak in, the way I usually do? Like go through the laundry and down the long hall—"

"Hm," said Gazzy. "I was thinking a little plastic explosive on the roof, go in through there?"

"Explo—you mean like a bomb?" I said. "Where are we gonna get that?"

Gazzy grinned at me.

"He likes blowing things up," Iggy said.

"But—the prison is built pretty solid," I said.

"Listen," said Nudge (I liked her best so far, even though she was kind of soppy). "If you ever hear one of us say *Duck!* or *Drop!* or anything like that, *do it.* Immediately and without question. Okay?"

I wasn't used to taking orders; usually I was the one giving them. But Nudge wasn't smiling, and I sure as hell didn't think she was joking. "Uh...okay?" I said.

"She is dead serious," said Iggy.

"Okay?" I said. Like, who *were* these people? Just gonna go break their friend out of *prison*? With a *bomb*? "Do you guys do this often?" I asked, not trying to be a smart-ass. Just then a bug flew into my mouth. Gross. It happens pretty frequently—bugs of all kinds smashing into my face like it's a windshield.

"We've broken a lot of people out of a lot of jails," Gazzy admitted. "It's an occupational hazard."

"What occupation?" I asked.

Gazzy grinned at me. "Being the Flock."

Nudge moved so she was right over Gazzy, their wings moving in sync on each downstroke and upswing. It was amazing. They'd flown together so many times that this was easy for them. My mouth dropped open when the *blind* one moved beneath Gazzy. Now all three of them were flying in synchronization. How did they know one another? Were there any more of us? I had a million questions.

"Okay," said Nudge. "Fang is on what floor of the prison?"

"The first," I said.

"So the roof is out," Nudge said.

"The side, then," said Gazzy. "Not as good—it's harder for people to follow us through the roof."

"If you went through the roof right in the middle," I said, "we could drop down to the first floor, get Fang, and then—"

"All fly out through the roof," said Gazzy. "Excellent. Good thinking, Phoe—Hawk."

I didn't say anything. I was used to being the roughest, toughest person around, the one other people came to for help. Now these three strangers were, like, so much more experienced. They weren't *blinking* at the idea of blowing up a roof to break a prisoner out of jail. They had done it before. A lot. Maybe *they* were criminals. I snuck a side glance at them, flying in sync. I didn't care if they were criminals. They were flying like me, leading a life of crime like me. And I needed their help.

CHAPTER 40

One good thing about the coal smoke and general smog—it made landing on rooftops super easy, even when armed guards were supposed to be watching said rooftops. Like all the buildings in the complex, Incarceration had a flat concrete roof, dirty and covered with tar-paper patches.

After I'd landed, all hot from flying, I noticed the Flock staring at my wings.

"What," I said.

"They're Fang's wings," Nudge said very softly.

"And Max's. Underneath." Gazzy's voice was sober.

A thousand painful emotions hit my heart at the same time. They were saying that Fang really was my dad. So I had a dad, a real dad! Which would be *great* if he weren't a *jailed murderer*. Also, he had abandoned me when I was really little, so eff him! Him and my mom both! I never wanted to talk to them again!

I knew my emotions were flying across my face as quickly as we'd flown across the sky. Nudge was watching me and I'm sure she could see me move from elated to angry in point two seconds. I folded up my wings and stuck my chin in the air. "They're *my* wings. Now where's this explosive?"

We had to duck periodically as the Incarceration floodlights swept over the roof, but it was no problem. I watched as Gazzy took a lump of modeling clay out of his backpack and handed it to me.

"We want long, thin flat sheets," he said, showing me how to smack it and stretch it.

"Where's the *explosive*?" I asked again. Why was he having me play with clay? Had they been lying to me? Was this all a joke?

Gazzy looked at me in surprise and held up his own modeling clay. "This is it."

"C-10 then, Gaz?" Iggy asked.

"Easier to get than Semtex6," Gazzy told him. He'd already molded two flat sheets and had laid them in a row across the roof. I handed him mine, still confused. He saw my face and explained, "C-10 is a moldable explosive. But it doesn't explode by itself, so it's great to carry around, have handy. Not even a bullet could make it explode." He leaned toward me eagerly, warming up to this topic.

"Here we go," Nudge murmured as we all automatically ducked from the floodlights.

"What does C-10 stand for?" I asked.

"Composition number ten," Gazzy said happily, laying down two more sheets. "It's made up of a bunch of different things. They keep making it better, refining it. This number ten stuff is amazing—easy to control its explosion, much lighter in weight, and you use much less than C-5 or even C-8."

Nudge met my eyes and gave me a pointed look, like, *Do not ask him about explosives again.*

The Gasman gazed off in the distance, I guess thinking about how awesome C-8 had been or something. We all ducked under the sweep of the floodlights, and Iggy said, "Ready, Gazzy?"

"Oh, one more thing," Gazzy said, getting back to work. He fiddled with some gadgets, pressed a wire down all the thin sheets of the C-10, then stood up and nodded. "Let's go over here." We all flattened ourselves toward the edge of the building, and Gazzy punched some numbers into his phone.

"Duck!" Nudge said, and I dropped my head to the roof and covered it with my hands. Instantly, no questions—just like she'd told me to.

There was an amazingly huge explosion. The roof shook below me as the whole building swayed. Glass sprayed from the windows in the Labs, and there was immediate chaos. Lights swung wildly, alarms shrieked, and from below I heard hundreds of people yelling.

We crawled forward through the debris of concrete chunks, heavy metal wire, and bits of light fixtures. There was a big, rough hole in the middle of the ceiling, about two and a half meters wide and a bit more than three meters long.

Nudge, Iggy, and Gazzy looked at one another and smiled, then turned to me.

"Let's go get Fang," Iggy said.

CHAPTER 41

Max

The metal table was cool beneath my cheek. I had drooled, and I felt sticky from it. Hey, this is the unvarnished account of my life, okay? You don't want gross stuff, don't read it!

I felt a cold draft on the skin of my back. It all came back to me in one horrific thought: they had *cut off my wings*. Oh, my god. A bird-person without wings is just a...*person*. A tall, weirdly skinny person. I mean—Fang had a metal wing. It worked. But two metal wings? Two wings that weren't part of me, my body, my brain? I couldn't see how they could work. They might as well go ahead and kill me.

"What are we waiting for, goddamnit!" McCallum wasn't worried about waking me up. It sounded like he was right there, but he was on a vidscreen.

"I had to rethink my strategy!" the doctor said testily. "The micro scan showed some nerves and arteries looped across an unexpected bone between the wings!"

"An unexpected bone? Surely you can do better than that, doctor. Pretend she's a holiday turkey. And I. Want. A. Wing."

I hated McCallum so much. But…thoughts started lining up in my numb, drugged brain. They…they hadn't operated yet! And yes! I sent a signal to my primary feathers, and they responded, *Right here!* I still had my wings, I still had my wings!

That meant—I had to ditch this place. I was on my own. I couldn't hope for anybody to break me out, couldn't hope for the doctor to have a change of heart and be a decent man. This was on me. I was cold, and on an operating table surrounded by insane people, but surely I had a few things going for me?

Okay—one thing: I wasn't nearly as sedated as they thought. Two: I recognized this place—after all that circus entertainment outside, I was just here in the goddamn Infirmary! Knowing where I was helped because I knew where I had to get to, and how to get there, but the location was still a bummer.

I couldn't fly out—I'd have to run.

Below my hand with the IV drip, I felt the thin, soft tubing that was delivering the sedative. With two fingers, I very slowly pinched the tube shut.

"Why can't you just cut the nerves and whatever?" McCallum asked.

"Because." The doctor now sounded irritated. "We don't know what will happen if I cut the nerves and the arteries. It could kill her. Plus, you want the wings grafted onto someone else? We'll need those nerve endings!"

Well, that was a relief. If I died I wouldn't have to live without my wings. Maybe I was imagining it, but did I already feel a little more conscious?

"So what?" McCallum said. Without his usual continuous shouting of threats and verbal abuse, he sounded so different. Like a real person. That was a disturbing thought, that a real person could think and behave like McCallum.

"So then you would have wings that we'd try to keep viable with ice and saline, and a dead person. Voilà. How impressive is that? But if I can get these wings off without killing her, then you have wings, plus a penitent person. That would be much more compelling, much more of a lesson."

McCallum was quiet. The only sounds were the tiny pump not pumping drugs into my IV and the clatter of more metal surgical tools on a metal tray.

"How long will this take?" McCallum asked.

"I have an image of her back right here," the doctor said. "I'm going to study it for a few minutes and come up with a plan."

"I'll check back in five minutes, then," said McCallum. "And I have an idea—we can broadcast the whole operation. Everyone from the Council to the lowest Ope will see it!"

"Why?" That was the nurse, and everyone seemed surprised that she spoke. "I'm sorry," she said immediately.

"Why?" McCallum's voice was soft, like the subtle hiss of a snake. Then he roared. "Because she's a Freak, and we can make an example of her! Because I'm McCallum! And I say so! Five minutes!"

The screen went blank, then was quickly replaced by a vid of three kittens singing a song about loyalty and honor. It was such a catchy tune I almost started tapping my foot along.

"Goddamnit." The doctor's voice was so low that his nurse

probably hadn't heard it. But I have birdlike ears, and I heard it. I managed not to gasp or twitch when his hands smoothed the skin between my wings at the top of my shoulders. I hadn't been touched in prison—my reputation made sure of that—so it was hard to lie still and feel someone else's hands on me. He pulled my wings open a little bit so they were out of the way and rubbed their upper joints, feeling where the bones separated. He was really gearing up to do this.

How awake was I? Was I strapped down? I didn't feel it.

Get up, Max, I told myself sternly. *You are Maximum Ride and you will get off this goddamn table and run, you hear me?*

Do. You. Hear. Me?

CHAPTER 42

Hawk

I'd never done anything like this, but it was awesome. We just tucked our wings along our sides and dive-bombed down to the cold concrete of the first floor of the prison. The explosion had also ripped open a bunch of the cells on the third floor, and prisoners were running out, free. They gawked at our wings, but were too thrilled at their newfound freedom to ask questions.

On the first floor. I raced toward Fang's cell, with Gazzy and Iggy right behind me. Nudge was shooting guards left and right with a dart gun. "We try to keep the body count low," she had explained to me. "Part of our personal growth."

"This is it!" I said breathlessly as we reached the intersection of cells. I grabbed the bars of the cell as if I could just yank them out. Then the three of us stood there silently while chaos erupted all around us.

The cell was empty.

I felt Gazzy looking at me, and Iggy turned his head in my direction.

"This is where he was," I said lamely. "This is where I saw him."

"Damnit!" said Gazzy, wiping sweat off his brow. "What now?"

"You lookin' for that murderer?" The skinny, dirty prisoner in the next cell had pushed his face between his bars.

"Yes," Gazzy answered quickly before I could say anything.

"They took 'im this mornin'," the prisoner said. "Open these bars and I'll tell you where."

"You don't know where!" I yelled, furious and embarrassed.

"Do, too," the inmate insisted. "Open these bars!"

"Iggy?" Gazzy said, and Iggy went to the next cell, feeling his way along the bars till he came to the big lock on the cell door.

He pulled some metal picks out of a pocket and put them in the lock. His face was calm concentration, despite the roar all around us. Loose prisoners were everywhere, others shouted to be freed. They pelted us with "gifts" offering the best of what they had in their cells if we'd only let them out—extra toilet paper rolls, dirty pictures, and some (I'll admit) pretty decent personal artwork. The floor was littered with stunned guards, their hands still on their guns.

"Okay," Iggy said, and the lock clicked. The prisoner stared and pushed the door open. I grabbed him by his inmate jacket and shoved my face into his.

"Where's the prisoner from this cell?" I snarled, using my meanest face and voice, the ones that usually made people cry.

"She's so cute," I thought I heard Nudge whisper.

"They took him to execution this morning," the inmate said, cowering a bit.

I stared. *"What?"*

"They took him to execution," the inmate said again, starting to look surly. "Over by the mess hall."

I let go of his collar. "So you're saying he's dead? They executed him?"

"I only *said* that they *took* him to *execution*," the inmate said pointedly. "Don't know if he's dead, do I?"

"Phoe—Hawk," Gazzy said. "Where's the mess hall?"

It took me a second to organize my brain cells and my internal map of Incarceration. Then I pointed to the hole in the ceiling, and we flew up, toward the gray-green night, leaving the riotous wreck of the prison behind us.

CHAPTER 43

The Flock and I landed silently on the mess hall roof, ignoring the blazing searchlights, all of which were below us, the dogs barking hysterically, the shouting, the gunfire. The loose prisoners were making their way to the fences, attacking guards in the yard, and trying to force open more cells to free their friends. Everything below was in chaos; nobody was paying attention to what was going on up on the roof.

"Let me do a quick three-sixty," Gazzy said, and Nudge nodded.

As silently as we had landed, the Gasman took off, not making a sound with his wings. Nudge, Iggy, and I lay on our stomachs on the roof as I tried not to let stupid thoughts and emotions run though my head. I couldn't stop thinking about Calypso, and her kaleidoscope eyes, the blank stares of Moke and Rain. They were lost in a dreamworld, waiting on me to save them. And I was stuck on the roof of the wrong building still trying to help free this Fang guy. *Their friend*, I reminded myself. *Not mine*. Time was running out for my gang, and we still hadn't achieved anything. Another couple hours and there wouldn't be enough left of their brains to rescue. I exhaled sharply, my breath spinning up a cloud of dirt in front of my face. *Keep focused, Hawk.*

When Gazzy landed, his sneaker dislodged two small pebbles. That was it. I could land without stumbling, but there were usually drag marks. I was going to have to practice take-offs and landings. If I lived through tonight.

"Found him," Gazzy said tersely.

"Alive?" Nudge asked.

"I can't tell," Gazzy said. "He's tied to a post in the execution square."

Ohhhh. It came back to me—the time I'd been flying overhead in the daytime, which was unusual. I'd glanced down at Incarceration in time to see a prisoner get shot, slump down. That was where Fang was.

"He's not...standing up," Gazzy said in a low voice.

"Let's go," Iggy said.

Nudge let out a breath but said nothing, just got into a crouching position, below the searchlights. One by one they jumped off the roof, swooping low toward the ground and then rising sharply. I tried it, almost face-planted into the ground, then rose shakily after them. There was so much I didn't know about flying. Because until now, there hadn't been anyone to teach me.

CHAPTER 44

The execution square was on the edge of the compound, away from everything else. Everything else except McCallum, of course, and his occasional Voxvoce, which went everywhere in this damn city.

For a few moments, the Flock hovered above the execution square. I don't know how to hover, so I would downstroke and rise up about ten feet, then let myself fall. I felt stupid, like I should have figured all this out on my own.

"Okay, swoop down, cut him free, swoop back up with him," Nudge said, and the other two nodded, hovering in the air like… like mosquitos or something. "Who's going to carry him?"

"Me," Iggy and Gazzy said at the same time. There was a pause, then they both said "Me" again.

"Me," Gazzy said again. "Iggy drops down and sets him loose."

"But—" Nudge began.

"You're not as good at lock picking as he is," Gazzy said. I saw from Nudge's face that she couldn't deny it.

I hadn't wanted to actually look at Fang, in case he was dead. He might be my dad. He might be dead. Finally I forced myself. In the dark courtyard, there was one prisoner hand-cuffed to a post. He was slumped forward, not moving. The wall all around him was stained with blood, some of it super recent, alarmingly bright.

I swallowed hard, scanning him for signs of life. I couldn't see any. There was a vidscreen in front of Fang's limp body, of course. I remembered what McCallum had said when they brought Fang to the prison—we do prison right! Yep, prison and murder, and making sure everyone knew who was in charge. Right now families all over the city in their homes were beaming at a glowing McCallum on their TVs. But they were able to look away, if they wanted to. Part of the punishment for a prisoner would be having to stare, all day, into that confident jerk's mug, huge and oily and just out of reach.

Maybe some of them did walk away "rehabilitated," truly believing that McCallum wanted the best for them, was here to protect them, and the city. But I bet most of them just died wishing they could crush his face.

"Okay, let's go," said Iggy, and he and Gazzy dropped down to the ground.

I couldn't swallow.

Iggy immediately set to work on a handcuff, while Gazzy took out his canteen and splashed some on Fang's head. Did he twitch? Then Gazzy pulled Fang's head back by his long, black hair and tipped water into his mouth just as Iggy got one hand free.

Fang slumped down, held up by one hand. Just like Calypso. Gazzy propped him up so Iggy could work on the other metal cuff. Nudge was hovering, and I was trying to hover and not succeeding.

The vidscreen in front of Fang changed to McCallum's broad, tan face and small blue eyes. "This is for you third-shift workers who are making the City of the Dead productive, even while others sleep!" he boomed. "I know it's the middle of the night! But I have a show for you that you won't believe! We have found a freak to end all freaks—someone who drank the water before it hit the water-cleaning facility!" He paused to let everyone laugh, then said, "We have a true subversive, loyal citizens. Someone who would destroy what you own, what you believe, what you want. But we're going to show her that in our city, we don't want subversives! Traitors! People who don't trust their McCallum!" He gave a big smile. "Citizens, we've captured a bird-person, and we just can't rehabilitate her!"

Nudge's head whipped downward and she stared at the screen. My breath caught in my throat. Iggy and Gazzy both froze and looked at the screen.

"We've tried and tried, but she's bad to the bone," McCallum said ruefully. "So in a little while here, we're going to cut off her wings! See how subversive she feels then!"

On the vidscreen, a fast montage of images scrolled by— images of a young woman with brown hair and brown eyes. Usually she was spitting at the screen or shown beating up other prisoners or guards. Once she flew upward and clung from thick metal bars, screaming into the wind, her wings out-stretched behind her.

They were my wings. The underside...was identical to mine.

Below us, Fang blinked blearily, his face a mass of swollen bruises.

"Max?" he said hoarsely.

CHAPTER 45

In moments Iggy had freed Fang's other hand. That cuff was apparently attached to an alarm system, because as soon as it popped open, klaxons sounded, floodlights lit the gruesome, garish courtyard, and we heard tramping booted feet.

"Let's go!" Gazzy said, taking Fang on his back. He jumped into the air, pushed downward hard with his broad wings, and rose into the air. Iggy rose more quickly beside him, and Nudge and I surrounded them as we all shot through the grim clouds that almost always covered the City of the Dead.

Below us, people shouted and fired into the air but couldn't hit what they couldn't see. In seconds we were well out of any bullet range.

"Max," Fang said again, one arm looped around Gazzy's neck, with Gazzy holding it tightly.

"Yes, Max!" Nudge said. "Max is alive!"

"Or will be for another half hour," Iggy said darkly.

"Max," Fang mumbled, then seemed to fall asleep.

Ten minutes of fast flying high above the city brought us back to the Flock's base at the top of the tall, skeletal building.

We circled it a couple times to make sure it wasn't surrounded, there weren't snipers anywhere, nothing unexpected.

We landed on the same floor I'd found them on, what felt like several months ago. Gazzy set Fang down gently onto one of the pallets they'd been sleeping on, and Nudge quickly went to him. "Iggy?" she said.

Iggy began to feel Fang's face, tracing over the lumps of swollen purple flesh, his hairline, his ears and chin.

"Fang! I just can't believe it!" Nudge said, starting to cry. "And now Max!" She turned to me with a tear-stained smile. "And Phoen—Hawk. Oh, my god, we're going to be all together again!"

She hunched over Fang as sobs shook her slender body.

"No bones broken, amazingly," Iggy said, after feeling Fang's feet. "Just really banged up, dehydrated, starving, et cetera. The usual."

"It's not usual to find Fang," Gazzy said hoarsely. "And Max! Guys, we have to get our shit together and go get Max!"

"Not so fast," I said, and clicked a bullet into the chamber of my gun. Three heads turned in shock.

"Hawk, what's going on?" Nudge asked.

"Your next step will be going with me to save my friends, down in the labs at the McCallum complex," I said slowly and deliberately. "You promised. And I will hold you to that promise, or this night will get very ugly, very fast."

I was smart. I didn't point the gun at any of them. I pointed it at the person they all cared about the most, the person we'd just risked everything to rescue. I pointed it at Fang.

"Where did you get the gun?" Gazzy asked.

"From a prison guard, earlier," I said, and he nodded.

Nudge was looking at me, smiling through her tears. "God, you're just so adorable!"

Gazzy and Iggy smiled, too.

"You're a lot like your mom was, when she was your age," Iggy said.

"People keep telling me that," I said snidely. "But you're not going to get to know me better if you don't come through on your promise." I spread my feet apart for better balance and kept the pistol trained on Fang.

Gazzy shook his head in admiration. "I really like this girl."

Were they trying to fake me out? Lull me into a false sense of security and then turn on me?

"Food?" Fang croaked, propping himself on one elbow.

Nudge rummaged in her leather backpack, pulling out small, high-calorie stuff you could eat on the run. She held out an energy bar to me, and I shook my head, eyes flicking from it, back to Fang, still on the business end of my gun.

"We've been looking for Max for almost ten years," Fang said, meeting my eyes.

"You're going to help save my friends," I said.

"Drink some water," Nudge said briskly, rolling a bottle to me. I ignored it, let it bounce off my foot.

"You know she won't give up," Fang said, speaking to the others.

"Yeah," Nudge agreed.

"Yup, got that," Gazzy said.

"So...we go save her friends, yada-yada-yada, then find Max," Iggy said conversationally, then took a swig of juice.

176

"Okay," Nudge said. "You're right. We promised. We'll save your friends first. Then go find Max, and hope we get there in time. Put this in your pockets so you can eat on the way."

She threw a granola bar at me. I caught it in midair with one hand and stuffed it in my pocket, keeping the gun leveled on them.

Fang sighed heavily, then got creakily to his feet. "Max," he said wistfully to the others.

"Yes, Max," Nudge said, getting ready to jump off the side of a hundred-story building. "We'll get there in time. We will, Fang."

Fang said nothing more, just jumped out into the night, his wings so dark they were almost invisible.

I waited till they were all out, then I jumped, too, keeping my gun trained on Fang.

Moke, Rain, Calypso—I'm coming for you.

CHAPTER 46

"Fill me in!" Nudge shouted at me as we flew.

I'd told them to fly back toward Incarceration. Fang's bruised face had flinched at my words, but he hadn't changed course.

"They're being held at the Labs," I said, then gritted my teeth. The Flock knew that. Blinking against the greasy clouds, I wondered which facts were important.

"How many of them?" Gazzy asked.

"Three," I said.

"Good fliers?" Iggy asked.

"Uh...not fliers at all?" I said, and four pairs of eyes focused on me. "They're just...well, freaks," I said. "But they don't have wings. I'm the only person I've ever seen who has wings. I mean, till now."

I focused on flying while everyone looked at me. I was used to being stared at, but not by bird-people. *They'll get over it,* I thought grimly, trying to move my wings more smoothly yet forcefully, the way the others seemed to.

"Okay," Nudge said, raising her voice to be heard. "You'd called them freaks, and I just assumed—"

"Moke is taller than me," I said. "He's...his skin is blue. Rain is really pretty, younger than me, but her skin looks like it's melting? Like from acid rain? Calypso is almost eight. Sometimes she knows things before they happen. She's started growing antennas out of her back."

I tried to breathe *in* on my upswings and *out* on my hard, downward pushes. I'd never tried to improve my flying before— it'd been enough to fly at all. But looking at the Flock, it was like I'd been on level two, maybe, of the Flying Skill Scale and they were all like on level ten.

"But they can walk?" Iggy kept up with us easily, never running into anyone, knowing when to land and all.

"I'm not sure," I admitted. "They're all doped up. Plus, there's Clete. He's okay, in hiding, not locked up or doped or anything." I hoped this was still true. He'd been clean for a long time, but we'd been through some shit lately.

"So we each take one," Nudge said, speaking to the Flock. She counted off on her fingers: "Moke, Clete, Rain, and Calypso. Fly them to safety."

That was another thing I had to figure out—where was "safety"? Then I thought of something else. "Clete weighs about...maybe a hundred and ten kilos? And Moke is probably eighty, eighty-one kilos."

For reference, I'm one point eight meters tall, and weigh less than fifty kilos. Iggy was the tallest of the Flock, almost a head taller than me, and weighed, I guessed, less than sixty-five kilos.

"A hundred and ten kilos?" Fang repeated, his voice still raspy.

"Shit," I said miserably. "I didn't think about any of this. I just want to get them out of the Labs."

"And then?" Iggy asked, sounding a bit ticked off.

"And then I'll figure it out!" I said loudly, working my wings extra hard to shoot ahead of them. We were close enough to the Labs that I had to trust them enough to take the gun off them. I'd need my hands free when we got there. "I always do!"

There it was, right ahead of me: the Complex. Which we'd just left an hour before. Inside, I was furious and embarrassed about my lack of planning. Had I thought we'd just go back to the Children's Home to wait for the next time they needed lab rats? The truth was, the only places that were at all safe were the tops of tall, empty buildings. And what would my gang do up there? Plus, more and more I'd heard about the families of the Six starting to move into the empty buildings, make new headquarters there.

"The Children's Home is down there," I said, pointing. "I'm gonna go down, see if my friend Clete is there."

"Okay," Fang said.

"Okay," I said awkwardly, then angled my wings back and flat to dive. What did Fang think of me? Was he disappointed in me? Had he hoped for someone else for a daughter? Did it upset him that the first thing I did when we broke him out of jail was point a gun at him?

If *so*, he should have goddamn *been* here for my childhood, goddamnit! Because the truth was I might have pointed a gun at him anyway!

I landed quietly behind the trash dumpster in the courtyard. I'd scanned the area for guards but couldn't see any. Over at

Incarceration, the place was lit up like Crismins, floodlights everywhere, choppers circling overhead.

Well, a lot of prisoners had escaped. And there was a huge hole in their roof.

The double glass doors to our main room were unlocked and I went inside. It was dark. No sign of Clete anywhere. I tiptoed over to our sleeping closet and opened the door. It was empty, too.

Please, just be here and be okay, I thought.

CHAPTER 47

Kneeling down, I pounded my fist on the floor three times, then three times again, then once.

"What is that, some kind of code?" Fang asked quietly from behind me, and I almost jumped a foot in the air.

A trapdoor opened in the floor right next to Fang's foot, and Clete's relieved face popped out. "I'm glad you're here," he said. Then he saw Fang's foot, followed it up to Fang's swollen, black-and-blue face. "Oh, you got out."

"Yes," Fang said, holding out his hand for Clete. After looking at it for a moment, Clete took it and came out of our go-to hiding place, then closed the trapdoor and kicked the blankets over it.

"You must be Clete," Nudge said, coming through the door. Iggy and Gazzy were behind her.

"I thought you were gonna wait till I came back or called you," I said irritably.

"We're not big on waiting," Iggy said. "Is this Clete?" He homed in on Clete and immediately began touching him lightly all over. I knew it was to get an idea of Clete's height and weight, but Clete took a big step back. "Hi, I'm Iggy," Iggy said much too late.

"Gazzy," said Gazzy.

"I'm Nudge," Nudge said, smiling. Clete seemed to relax a bit.

"Are we gonna go rescue everyone now?" he asked.

"Yes," I said. "Put your shoes on. Any guard action while I was gone?"

"Yeah," Clete said, putting on his sneakers. "Lots of searching and yelling—but it's all over at the actual prison, probably because you got Fang out. Been quiet over here since then. We gonna do tunnels, this time?"

"Yep," I said, feeling grim. "We're gonna do tunnels."

"Are these kids locked up?" Gazzy asked.

I nodded. "They were yesterday. Locked with a chain and a metal cuff around one wrist."

"I can do those," Iggy said.

"Right," said Fang. "Then we'll walk out of there?"

"Back into the tunnels," I said, pulling the door open and making sure the courtyard was clear.

We all crept out and I led them behind the dumpster. Very quietly I braced my back against the concrete-block wall and put my feet against the dumpster. I moved it slowly and almost silently, an inch at a time. The Flock immediately put their hands on it, moving it much more easily than I had always done by myself.

"Here," I said, pointing at the ground. "Sewer. I usually don't use this one 'cause it's under the dumpster, but it's the closest one."

Nudge knelt and carefully moved the round cover, revealing the black tunnel below. She looked up and smiled. "This is just like old times."

I had no idea what she meant by that, but lowered myself down, knowing that rusty metal rungs were set into the tunnel wall, starting about two feet down. In a minute all six of us were down the ladder and standing on either side of the filthy sewage flowing down the middle. Fang was last, and he had somehow managed to pull the dumpster most of the way over the manhole cover before replacing it. They were all so much better at this than I was.

"We're not far from the Labs. This way," I said. Three small lights clicked on and I stared at Nudge, Gazzy, and Iggy—all of whom had tiny flashlights shining from their wrists.

"Oh, not those fancy watches again," Fang groaned.

"You just wish," Nudge said, waving her hand around.

"Um, I was going to lead the way by memory," I said, "but light is always good."

I still led, but the way was lit dimly by their little watch lights. Was it better to *not* see what was around you, down here? Maybe. I hadn't known there were *quite* so many rats and bugs and slimy things—and those were the things that were alive. The rest of it...better not to think about. We were on our way to rescue my family, at last. It felt like a year since Clete and I had seen them, doped up and hallucinating.

"Oh," I said, trying to sound casual or professional or something. "Um, one last thing. *Two* last things. One, I'm not totally, *totally* certain that the kids will be able to walk; and two, they might, just *maybe,* you know, try to *resist* being rescued."

Behind me, footsteps slowed.

"What?" Gazzy said.

Clete said, "They're tripping; they're on Rainbow. They probably won't know who we are or what we want. So they might fight us."

Footsteps stopped. I swallowed hard. This might be the last straw for the Flock. They might leave me.

CHAPTER 48

"We needed to know this earlier," Fang said.

I turned quickly. "Why?" I said, chin in the air and hands in fists at my sides. "Would it have made a difference? Would you not have come? Yeah, when we saw them, they were hallucinating. It doesn't matter! We came and got you even though you might have been dead, you know that, right? Whatever state they're in, we have to get to them! Before the experiments start!"

"Before there's nothing left to rescue," Clete agreed, not picking up on the tension in the air.

There were several moments of silence, and some looks passed between the four members of the Flock. Then Fang started walking again and the others followed.

I turned around, my back stiff, and almost stomped along until I realized my stomps were probably spattering gunk over Clete's legs. After a silent minute, I stopped beneath the tunnel that led up to the manhole cover closest to the Labs.

"This is it," I said.

"Okay," Nudge said, then came closer, edging around Clete until she stood next to me. "A team has to share every bit of information they have, so that they can work together," she said.

"If one or two know something the others don't, it makes it more dangerous for everyone. See?" Her voice was kind, and she put her arm around my rigid shoulders.

I nodded, feeling my cheeks heat. The staples holding my cheek closed had been pulled and stretched so often in the last couple hours that I'd gotten used to the constant stinging, burning, aching pain.

"So!" Nudge said. "Is there *anything else* we should know before we go *blow* this joint?" She made it sound almost funny, almost fun, and I thought for a minute.

"This cover opens up right next to the main ventilation intake for the Labs," I said. "It'll be hard for all of us to sneak in—so some stay in the ducts and help the gang get up there?"

Nudge nodded. "Then what?"

"Then we get back out the ventilation tunnel, probably back into these underground tunnels, until we're far enough away?"

"The Six," Clete said, reminding me, as he rocked back and forth on his feet anxiously.

"Oh, yeah, the Six," I agreed miserably, glancing right and left down the dark tunnel.

"We know about the Six," Gazzy said quickly. "What about them?"

"A lot of their, like, money laundering and illegal dope making happens in these tunnels. Not necessarily this particular tunnel," I added. "But if we run into them, it'll be...messy."

"We're running out of time," Fang said tensely.

"Yeah," I agreed. "Let's just do this." I started up the rickety rungs leading up to the Labs courtyard. "You guys sure do talk a lot," I muttered.

CHAPTER 49

Holding my breath, I went up the rusty ladder rungs first. One of them came off in my hand, and I shouted down to the others that there would be a gap, and where to expect it. At the top I listened through the cover's holes and heard nothing except far away klaxons. Everybody was at the prison. Probably. I hoped.

This cover was between the back wall and the Labs building so we were pretty well concealed. I was proud of myself for bringing my knife with its screwdrivers so I could take off the ventilation cover.

"One at a time, shimmy upward," Nudge said. "Heating and cooling ducts aren't super strong."

"I know that," I muttered. I hadn't known that. Carefully, trying to make no noise, I shimmied up the duct as directed, and soon the six of us were spread out across where three ducts intersected.

"Do you know where your friends are?" Nudge whispered almost soundlessly.

I nodded. "Me and Clete will go get them."

"Gazzy and I will follow you," Nudge told me. "To help get them up into the ducts."

Clete and I set off toward the inner labs. Almost as soon as I turned my back, I heard Fang say, "Max is out of time, Ig!"

"I know," Iggy said quietly. "But we promised. This should go quick."

I wondered where Max was and what they were saving her from. They'd said Max was my mom, but I wasn't even on board with Fang being my dad, and I *knew* him. So Max wasn't in my picture, except as a person on a billboard sometimes.

Glancing back, I saw that Clete was so big that he almost took up the whole duct. "Do you know where you're going?" he asked softly.

"Yeah," I whispered back. "How you doin'?"

"I need to get out of this duct," he answered. I could hear the tension in his voice. He'd always been a little hair-trigger with his emotions—most of the time he was fine, but when things got to be too much, he melted down. And his emotions were big. We had to get to the kids before that happened.

Because I needed more pressure on myself. Holy mother.

I'd always been able to know where I was, known how to get back to a place, known if I was pointed toward the sun or whatever. Maybe that made up for my not being so good at this rescuing stuff.

Anyway, I crawled along, turning here, hanging a left there, trying to move fast in case Clete's steam was building up. From the vibrations of the duct I knew that Nudge and Gazzy were following us. Too bad Nudge wasn't my mom. She seemed kind of momlike, as far as I could tell. I didn't have much to compare her to.

Behind me, Clete gave my pants' leg a tug. I'd almost passed the vent that led to the small room where the kids were shackled.

"I know!" I hissed. "I was just checking things out!" Except that was completely untrue, and I'm guessing Clete knew it.

"K," Clete said, and I felt bad for snapping at him. He was stuck here right along with me, and probably freaking out more than I was. I needed to remember that.

I moved so I could look through the vent. I was dreading what I might see—three bodies shackled to a wall? My family, starved or doped to death? I braced myself: this could be truly grim and heartbreaking. Leaning close to the vent, careful not to breathe any dust out into the room, I peered through the narrow metal slats.

Frowning, I leaned closer, until the slats made impressions on my forehead. I scanned the room from one corner to the next, seeing the shackles, seeing where the dusty floor had been disturbed.

What I didn't see? Moke, Rain, or Calypso. They were *gone*.

CHAPTER 50

Max

I was tensed to leap off the operating table when the universe actually cut me a freaking break: a young guard came running in, telling the doctor to come quick because there was a huge fight happening outside and one of the other guards had been cut badly, was bleeding all over the place.

"I can't come, I'm busy right now!" the doctor snapped at him, still holding up the picture of my back, trying to decide where to cut first.

"You're...the only doctor," the guard said hesitantly. "And it's a guard, not another prisoner."

The doctor put down the x-ray, and his hands hovered over my wings, his fingers absently stroking the skin between them. My flesh crawled, and it was a test of my superhuman self-control that I didn't just throw up all over the table right then.

"Sir?" the guard said. "Please...she's bleeding out pretty bad."

There were a few long moments where the only sound was the beeping of the machine monitoring my heart rate. I tried to make sure every muscle was totally relaxed, and even let some drool come out of my mouth. As a survival tactic.

"She's out?" the doctor barked at the nurse.

"Yes, doctor," said the nurse. "She's still on a drip. I'm about to add the paralyzing agent. Then I can put the breathing tube down her throat."

"You have ten minutes!" the doctor told the guard. "And *you* make sure she's still out and prepped for surgery by the time I get back!"

"Yes, doctor!" the nurse said.

Gosh, it was *awfully quiet* after they left. But clearly, I was going to have to say *No Thank You* to the *paralyzing agent*. I had just opened my eyes a slit to make sure I knew where the door was when the vidscreen jumped from some kids getting praised for ratting on their uncle to the man himself: McCallum.

"*Where's my wing?*" he roared.

Behind me, metal instruments clattered on a metal table—the nurse was rattled.

"I—I'm sorry, sir!" the nurse said. "The doctor was called away for just a moment! As soon as he gets back he'll begin the procedure—everything is prepped and ready!"

"He what?" This was said in an almost normal tone, if by "almost normal" you mean only slightly menacing.

"He—he was urgently called away..." the nurse said, faltering. "A guard was injured and he's the only doctor..."

The nurse was clearly hating her life just then. And that gave me an idea. Was it a *good* idea? Time would tell. Was it a *smart* idea? God, no. But if my ideas had to be *smart* for me to do them, I'd never get anything done.

Suddenly I sat up, hearing the nurse's shocked indrawn breath. Grabbing the IV that I'd been pinching shut, I pulled it out of the back of my hand.

"Wait, no!" the nurse cried.

"Better call the doctor back. You're going to need him!" I snarled, then grabbed the small rolling table where the scalpels and forceps were laid out.

"Guards!" McCallum bellowed, right before I smashed the table into the vidscreen. I had the pleasure of seeing his look of surprise right before it went to static.

"You want a wing!" I muttered as I picked up the biggest scalpel from the floor. "Find yourself a goddamn brain first!"

"No, please," the nurse begged, and I just shook my head at her pathetic plea. I had no intention of hurting her, but she didn't need to know that. There was one set of doors out to the inescapable courtyard and another set before that heading into this building. I rammed through the inside doors, knocking down four guards who were on their way in.

"Out, out..." I said, looking wildly for an exit sign or a window with sky—anything. There! A door to the outside, with only two guards. I ran up as they gaped at me and gave them a double flying kick, one to each head, before they had even aimed their rifles. Then I landed on one knee, with one palm down, like I'd seen a superhero do in one of Gazzy's comic books.

I burst through that door, then stopped dead, my heart seizing inside my chest. I was back out in the goddamn freaking *prison courtyard* with a fenced-in cover. My daring escape had gotten me *nowhere*.

CHAPTER 51

Hawk

"They're deeper in," Clete whispered. Sweat had broken out on his forehead, and I could smell the fear radiating off him. Behind him in this air duct, Nudge and Gazzy must have been thinking I was crazy. Or stupid.

I could barely see around Clete's bulk, but I caught Nudge's eye and made motions to say I was going farther in. Her eyebrow raised, and I quickly turned and started crawling as fast as I could down the duct. Each room in this place had at least one air vent, and I looked through every single one as I went past. I heard Clete crawling after me—what choice did he have?

Finally I stopped for a second. "There are no people anywhere," I said softly. "Where are the doctors or the guards?"

Clete said, "They must be at the prison. Helping or something."

"Then where are the rest of the gang?" It was the middle of the freaking night and I was almost weeping with exhaustion and frustration. Then I remembered that I was Hawk, *goddamnit*! I straightened my back and swallowed my tears. Setting my chin, I made a decision. "Let's go to the end of this duct. If we don't see them by then, we'll turn around."

"Without them?"

I didn't meet his eyes. "Yes."

CHAPTER 52

Max

I'd let myself believe that I'd find a way out of the prison, maybe through a break in the metal bars or something. I'd pictured myself running, taking off, finally free after—who knew how many years?

You've gotten stupid, Max, I told myself. *You let yourself have hope*. Hope...sometimes it was just as dangerous as dope.

Already guards were running at me, tasers ready, guns raised.

With nothing to lose I jumped high in the air, whipped my wings out, and pushed down hard. Beneath me, the rabble seemed suddenly quieter. The metal cage over the prison wasn't too far up, maybe forty feet, and I reached it in about a second. I landed, grabbing the grid of thick metal bars, bracing my feet against them.

I was trapped, stuck, going nowhere. And still, even knowing all that, it felt damn good to fly. I stretched my wings out, enjoying the freedom.

McCallum appeared on the vidscreens in the courtyard. "Shoot her!" he screamed. "Don't hit her wings!"

Bullets began whizzing past me and I pulled my wings in. With a grim smile, I wrapped the end sections around me, a cool, feathery shield they didn't dare damage. McCallum himself gave me the best safety net I could ask for—he wanted my wings unharmed? Great! That made these things better than a bulletproof vest.

No more bullets came at me, though below I heard shouting and feet running. It sounded like the big prison riot was pretty much over; watching me get shot off the cage was better entertainment.

One thing about feathers—you can't see through 'em. Very slowly I edged them away from my face and immediately a bullet came so close to me that it singed some of my hair. Shit.

"You're trapped!" McCallum yelled from his vidscreen. "You might as well come down! We'd rather take your wings off you alive than dead—but either is fine with me!"

That asshole.

What to do...what to do...Peeping out again, I saw the skinny sad-sack doctor shouting orders to the guards, staring up at me with fury. I bet he wished he hadn't helped me, before. He probably wished he'd just let me bleed out from the shiv in my side. He'd said he was just an old Ope, but I bet his version of flying wasn't half as good as mine.

Hey, here's a thought...

With no warning, I dropped off the ceiling cage, plummeting toward the ground. Prisoners started applauding—they probably thought I was going to kill myself. You are shit out of luck, guys, I thought, letting my wings stream out behind me. *Right* as I was about to splat against the stained concrete, I grabbed the doctor and *whooshed* upward! People gasped as I reached the ceiling bars almost instantly, holding the doctor with one arm around his skinny middle.

"What are you doing?" His voice sounded tense and squeaky—guess he wasn't used to looking down from forty feet up.

"Max." McCallum's voice now sounded calm and patient. "Max, come back down with the good doctor. Even with him, you're still trapped. Really, what can you do?" He was all reason and logic.

Blinding strobe lights spattered against me, holding me in sharp focus against the bars. Guards were raising long ladders against the walls. What was their plan? Were they going to climb the cage to get me? Or maybe they were angling for a better shot?

"You can't win this, you know," the doctor said. He was trembling and his voice was weak. His hands gripped the arm holding him, as if afraid I'd let him go. To be honest, I had totally considered it. I mean, I could hold him for hours. But not forever.

"I don't need to *win*, hack," I said. "I only need to come out *even*."

With that I let go of the bars and swept downward, zigzagging to avoid the bullets ripping through the air around me. The doctor squealed and then suddenly screamed. I reached the bars way on the other end of the courtyard and held on.

"I'm hit!" the doctor yelled, trying to hold his leg where he could see it, assess his own damage. "I got shot!"

"Gosh, I bet that hurts, huh?" I asked. "Whoa, you're dripping blood on everyone below you!"

"Eff you, you goddamn freak!" the doctor shouted, squirming in my hold.

"Hold still!" I said. "Unless you want me to drop you right now!"

The doctor stopped, his body rigid with pain.

"I've been shot before. It hurts like a mother," I said sympathetically. "Almost as bad as getting a shiv in the side and having some hack staple it shut."

More bullets hissed through the air around us. The doctor looked down and screamed, "Quit shooting, you idiots! I've already caught one bullet!"

A slight sound made me look to my right. *Hm.* I squinted against the bright lights to see that guards were climbing up the outside of the cage. It would be super hard for a person to climb up the *inside* of the cage, but much easier to climb up the outside. In a few minutes I'd have bullets coming at me from front and back.

Looks like it was a bad plan, after all.

CHAPTER 53

Hawk

Clete was horrified by me saying I'd leave without the gang. But—
I knew the Flock was anxious to leave, to go get this Max. And I
could hardly ask them to crawl around in air ducts when the kids
could be anywhere. They wanted to save my mother...my supposed mother. What a laugh. Well, I didn't need them anyway.

I kept crawling down the duct, which was mostly pitch-
black except for the air vents from each room, shining a bit of
light. There weren't too many left before I'd have to stop, tell
Clete I was abandoning most of our family.

"I need to get out of here," Clete whispered from in back of
me. "I can't breathe."

There were three more striped rectangles of light ahead of
me. We'd be turning around soon. Suddenly I felt a whoosh,
and air started flowing strongly past us. The next few feet
showed me why—there was a giant fan on my right, so powerful that I couldn't help leaning toward it as I crawled past.

"Careful," I told Clete, who was gulping mouthfuls of fresh air.

I crawled past a vent, scouring the room for any sign of the kids. Nothing. The closer I got to the end of this duct, the more a sense of dread wrapped its clammy cloak around me. We might not ever find them. I'd blown off any feelings I had about losing them, but now those feelings seemed bigger than me, bigger than Clete, bigger than this whole building.

We might not ever find them. They might be gone forever.

"No, *no, no, no!*" I froze as the piercing scream echoed through the duct, filling my ears.

"That's Calypso!" I told Clete and scrambled toward the sound.

They were in the second-to-last room. I'd been moments away from leaving them behind.

Peering through the vent, I saw that Calypso was strapped down to a hospital bed, like a troublesome prisoner. Which I guess she was.

"Argh!" The animal-like roar came from Moke. Looking through the vent at an angle, I saw that Moke had grabbed the thick bars on the one window and was shaking them, trying to break them or pull them out. When he couldn't, he just kept yanking on them and shouting.

And Rain? I had to lie flat on my stomach to see her. She was curled up in a ball beneath Calypso's hospital bed, so still I couldn't tell if she was alive. Calypso screamed again, Moke roared again, and I waited wide-eyed for guards or doctors to come running. But they didn't.

"They've gone crazy," Clete said, not bothering to lower his voice. "And I think Rain's dead."

Those were the exact same thoughts I was having, but I didn't want to admit it, not even to Clete.

"We have to try," I said, and started kicking at the air vent. It was screwed in from the room side and there was no way for me to get it out neatly.

"I'll do that," Clete said, and I gave way. It would take his mind off his fear.

At the sound of the first kick, Calypso turned to look, her face red and wet with tears. The only thing she could move was her head, and no doubt she was seeing dust falling and plaster chipping.

"Rats!" she said. "There's rats in here!"

"Rats?" said Moke and let go of the window bars. Coming closer to the wall, he peered upward.

"Moke!" I called over the sound of Clete kicking. "It's us, we're here!"

There was a noise of breaking plaster and creaking metal, and the vent fell out into the room, leaving a space about two-thirds of a meter wide and a third of a meter tall.

I put my head out, checking what I was about to jump into. "Moke! We've been looking all over for you guys!"

I couldn't wait for them to meet the Flock, see the expressions on the gang's faces when they saw adults like me, with wings.

"Can you get Calypso free?" I asked, pulling my head in and sticking my feet out.

I lowered myself carefully, glad the ceilings weren't higher.

With one last little jump, I was in the room and trying to hug Moke.

He pulled back and looked at me blankly. "Who are you?" he said. "What's wrong with your face?"

I couldn't believe he was joking around. I rushed to Calypso's bed and started undoing the straps around her arms. "Hey, sweetie," I said gently. The pupils in her blue eyes were so wide I could hardly see the color of her irises. I checked her neck, beneath her wild red hair. It was there, the tiny, blinking green sensor.

Like Moke, she looked at me with zero recognition. "There, one hand free," I said, and no sooner was it free than it shot out and grabbed my shirt.

"Got any dope?" Calypso asked, her voice ragged and raw.

CHAPTER 54

I unhooked Calypso's fingers from my shirt.

"Yeah, sure," I said miserably. "Up in that duct. You just need to climb up there to get it." I managed to free her other hand and she clapped them together to get feeling back, then rubbed her wrists where the skin was broken.

Clete was staring at her, and now we met eyes. I shrugged a tiny bit, like, what am I gonna do?

He gave a small nod, then explained to Calypso that he would help lift her into the vent, where friends of ours were waiting.

"Friends with dope," Calypso said, smacking her lips hungrily.

"Yeah, okay," Clete said, sounding as miserable as I felt.

Up in the duct, Nudge was looking down, her face both worried and I guess understanding? She knew my back was against the wall here, and she also knew that having our rescuees out of their minds was a ... complication. So I didn't even want to mention that they were all chipped. That would come later.

"Moke?" I said, standing in front of him. "Time to go, bud." I pointed to the vent that Calypso was being lifted into.

Moke swallowed and looked around as if I hadn't spoken. His large fists were clenching. "I need..." he began.

He needed to get his ass up in that vent *now,* I thought.

Again he looked right through me. "I need—"

Clete touched his shoulder. "Come on, man. We gotta go. Soldiers comin'."

Moke said nothing, so Clete and I pushed and pulled him over to the wall, on totally high alert because a punch from Moke would really hurt.

I left Clete to deal with Moke and went back to Calypso's bed, where Rain was curled up. I watched for a second—she wasn't breathing. Goddamnit. We were too late. I was torn. No way did I want to leave her body behind to be experimented on, but could we carry her as well as wrangle Moke and Calypso?

Gently I touched her back. It stiffened. *It stiffened?* She was alive!

"Rain?" I whispered. "Rain, sweetie? Time to go."

Slowly, stiffly Rain turned her face in my direction. "Need dope," she mumbled.

I started to offer her the imaginary dope in the air vent, but my breath was snatched from my lungs. *Rain...*I stared at her, wanting to throw up. They'd already started their experiments on her: her eyes were gone. *They'd taken her beautiful hazel eyes.* Her eyelids were shut, the lids collapsed into empty sockets. Holy mother.

"Need dope," Rain said again, reaching a hand out to me. I took it.

"Okay," I said, hearing my voice quaver. "I need you to come with me, okay?"

Docilely Rain uncurled, her lithe body now weak from lack of food. She tried to stand up, banged her head on Calypso's bed. She hadn't known she was under it.

"Come on," I said again, guiding her out from beneath the bed. Suddenly my ears pricked—was I hearing boot steps? Feeling their vibrations? "Come on!"

She let me take her hand, though she obviously had no idea who I was. I led her over to the wall and helped her climb up on the table. Nudge looked out and reached down, pausing when she saw Rain's empty eye sockets. Between the two of us we got her up into the duct, then I jumped up.

The boot steps were definitely louder now, and too late I realized that we had left a huge, broken hole where the vent had been—it would take even the dumbest guard about a second to see how their prisoners had escaped.

"Go, go!" Nudge whispered, pushing me after Rain.

I told Rain to crawl and she did, sometimes tentatively feeling the duct with her hands. Behind me I heard the door open, heard guards shout, then there was a small *pop!* and a fizzing sound.

Nudge began crawling rapidly after me, saying, "Go! Hurry!"

I barely heard the two guards drop to the floor as I raced with Rain and Nudge down the maze of air vents that would take us back to safety.

Safety. My ass.

CHAPTER 55

Max

Pretending to drop the doctor and hearing him squeal like a scared little pig had been fun, the first half dozen times. Now I was bored. What we had here was a classic standoff: They yelled, Come down and don't drop the doctor! And I yelled, Screw you! We'd gone back and forth like this for a good half hour. Every once in a while they tried to shoot me, and I let the doctor scream at them for that; each bullet that came near me barely missed him as well.

As to the busy beavers who'd climbed up the outside of the cage, well. I'm just faster than them. *AND I CAN GOD-DAMN FLY, YOU MORONS!!!!!* When one got too close, I let go of the bars (making the doctor scream) and shot over to one and kicked their ladder out. One by one they'd swung backward at the top of a very tall ladder, their faces outraged, surprised, and terrified, right before they hit the ground.

Now, all was quiet. The prisoners below weren't even interested anymore, since the violence was only sporadic and nobody had actually died yet. The doctor was starting to feel a bit heavy. He was a decent human shield as long as he didn't wiggle, but something had to change, and it didn't exactly help that I didn't care a whole lot if he *did* get shot. There was a time in my life when I could have kept this up forever, but I'd been in prison a long time, and I couldn't stay up here all night. God, it felt like this had been going on *forever*. When had it all started? Had it been only...it must be way after midnight. So it was just *yesterday* that they had grabbed me, held that mock trial, tried to operate on me.

What's your next step, Max? I asked myself. *Your next big plan?*

CHAPTER 56

Hawk

Okay, Hawk, what are you gonna do? I asked myself. We'd gotten the three lab rats out of the ducts and were now moving through the underground tunnels again.

We had a few issues:

1. All three lab rats were raving, out of their minds, and desperate for dope.
2. Sure, we were in the tunnels, but where were we going? Not back to the Children's Home, that was for sure, but where?
3. Fang was desperate to leave us. Well, he was good at that, wasn't he?
4. I needed a place that would be safe for the kids, where they couldn't get into trouble, where Moke, Rain, and Calypso could make noise while they were coming down off their dope. I didn't know any place like that. The top of the unfinished building was safe in a way,

but I knew one of my gang would end up walking off
the roof by accident. And they couldn't fly.

5. The longer we stayed in these tunnels, the more
likely it was we'd run into trouble.

I counted these off on my fingers, my spirits sinking with
every step. Finally, I edged past Iggy to talk to Nudge. Very quietly, I admitted that this was as far as my plan had gotten me. I
didn't know what to do now.

I felt like a total failure, and I *hated* having to admit a weakness to anyone. I mean, *really* hated it.

Nudge put her arm around my shoulder. I immediately
hunched so it would fall off but caught myself and let it happen.
I had to make some sacrifices here.

"It's okay, sweetie," she whispered. "You've done great so
far. I've been thinking about your friends—they're not great
travelers right now, you know?"

I nodded and then I stepped right on top of something dis-
gustingly squishy, because things had to be worse right now.
Swallowing my swear, I said, "I can't think of anywhere to put
them where they'll be safe."

"I know a place," she said, and left me to work her way back
to Fang.

She knew a place? We had a place to go? I was furious at
myself for not having thought through the plan this far, but
also felt huge relief. For so long, I'd been the only person I could
really rely on, *really* trust. I mean, I love my lab rats—they're
my family—but in a pinch? I was my own go-to person.

Even though I hardly knew her, my gut told me I could lean

on Nudge. And Gazzy. And Iggy. I could. Fang, I wasn't so sure about.

Suddenly Iggy pushed past me, holding Rain by the hand. "There's a fire down the last tunnel, on the left," he said. "I think the Sixes are here, and they're sending scouts ahead. We gotta get out of here!"

"There's an exit twenty meters up and on the right," I said quickly. I knew this city's tunnels like I knew the cracks in the ceiling of our sleeping closet at the Children's Home. We might be moving through almost total darkness, but I knew exactly where we were.

"Let's go!" Iggy said, and took over my place as leader.

Without stumbling, walking into the sewage, or turning face-first into a cement wall, Iggy led Rain and the rest of us to the exit.

"Where does this come out?" he asked me.

"One street off the main street," I said. "It's a bad area, but close to a good area."

"Okay," Iggy said, and started to climb the rusted, filthy metal rungs.

"Why?" Rain protested, not sounding like herself at all.

"Please, Rain, just do it," I said firmly.

"To get some dope," she said, and started to climb.

Whatever. Nudge went through next, then a dark, furious-looking Fang, who was guiding Moke by a firm hand at the base of his neck. Behind us, I saw the very dim lights of a pair of scouts, checking to make sure the tunnels were clear.

"You go," Gazzy said, digging around in the pockets of his big leather belt.

"Clete?" I said and motioned him upward. I hadn't heard any shouts or gunfire, so I was assuming it was okay up there.

Now I heard the scouts shouting, the faint sounds of their booted feet running toward us.

"Come on, honey," I said to Calypso and picked her up so she could grab the first rung. She started to climb. "I can smell dope!" she said excitedly.

"You," Gazzy said, motioning toward the rung.

"I'll go last," I said. "Hold those hoods off for a while."

"Hawk, I'll take care of these guys. You go, see what's happening up there."

There was nothing I could do. I started to climb.

I was almost to the top when Gazzy's blond head appeared at the bottom of the ladder and he started scrambling up. "Go, go, go!" he said, pushing at me. I practically jumped up the next meter and then leaped to my feet.

There was a boom! Followed by the sounds of tiles and plaster falling from the tunnel ceiling. Gazzy shot out of the manhole, slammed the cover back in place, then sat on it.

A second later the cover hovered several inches above the manhole. Gazzy hung on tightly. It dropped back into place with a clang, and Gazzy got up and dusted off his pants.

"Now where to?" he asked.

CHAPTER 57

An excellent question. I looked for Nudge and saw her standing shoulder to shoulder with Fang, who was gesturing angrily, sometimes pulling at his long black hair. Nudge's cheeks turned pink as she, too, began to argue.

It was so late—probably hours after midnight. I bet Ridley had her head tucked under her wing somewhere high and dry. I was glad she was safe and not caught up in this mess.

I was tired down to my bones, almost faint with hunger, and so thirsty that I was ready to drink the gross water from the pothole in the street. Clete looked super unhappy, too. His kind of normal routine had been shot to shit tonight.

I went over to him. "Hey, honey. How you doin'?"

There was misery in his eyes.

"I know you're tired," I said. "And hungry and thirsty?"

He nodded, shifting his weight from one foot to another.

"Well, I couldn't have done this without you," I said. "You're my hero."

He looked at me, a little smile on his lips.

Fang threw up his hands and stalked off. Nudge called after

him and he stopped but didn't come back or even turn around. He was ready for flight.

Looking back at our weird group, I saw that Iggy had taken charge of Rain, was talking to her, making sure she didn't wander off. *Oh, my god, Rain's eyes,* I thought again. Gazzy was on Moke duty—he still didn't know who any of us were and kept asking for more dope, only coming along with us strangers because we promised him more. I was hanging on to Calypso. She was pretty small for her age, barely to my waist. Of course, I'm weirdly tall. We were all hunkering down in the deep entrance of a building, on a lonely, abandoned street with no lights. I'd eaten here a bunch of times, had made deals here...back when I flew alone.

"Okay, here's what we're gonna do," Nudge said, gathering us in closer. "We, meaning all of us, are going to take your friends to a safe house. There's room for Clete and these three can dry out there, with good folks. So, Hawk is going to carry Calypso."

What was this place she was talking about? I pretty much knew every inch of the City of the Dead, and I hadn't seen anywhere like that. A safe house, with good folks? Ha!

"Iggy is going to carry Clete," Nudge went on, and Clete's face went white. "Fang is going to carry Moke, and I'll have Rain. Gazzy's going to take rear point with all weapons ready. Got it?"

"Yeah," I said. "But where are we going?"

"We're leaving the City of the Dead," Nudge said simply. "To a canyon city, outside of these tall walls."

"There's nothing out there!" I said sharply. "Only desert! I know! I've flown out there and seen it!"

"Maybe you didn't go far enough," Nudge said calmly. "It's pretty well hidden."

My back pressed against the dirty building wall, my hands clenching and unclenching.

"What's the matter, sweetie?" Nudge asked me in surprise. "It's a good place—we know the people who run it."

"There's nothing out there," I insisted. This was just like when I was five. I thought I'd had a family and they were going to leave me again. Last time they'd left and not come back; this time they were lying to me, telling me they were going someplace that definitely doesn't exist.

"No, it's there," Gazzy said firmly. "So everybody, get on your horses!"

"What's a horses?" Calypso asked, her fevered brain latching on to that one word.

"They're made-up animals," I said shortly. "They're not real; just in books."

Calypso nodded.

Gazzy wrinkled his brow as if he wanted to say something but changed his mind and looked away.

"Fang!" Nudge called. "Let's go!"

My breath was coming fast, as if I'd just run up ten flights of stairs. They'd gotten us this far. They'd said I was one of them. They'd helped all of us. But I knew this city, knew it inside out and knew the places beyond it. Knew there was nothing.

"Hawk?" Gazzy said.

My forehead was damp with sweat, and I bet I looked as white as Clete did.

Shaking my head, I said, "I can't do it. I can't leave the City of the Dead."

CHAPTER 58

Max

My life totally sucks, I mused as the prisoners below chanted my name. Some of them were rooting for me, some of them against. All they knew was that I was providing some entertainment. McCallum was on every vidscreen, sometimes talking to me, sometimes shouting, sometimes coaxing. I still had a death grip on the doctor and had tuned out his pleas, threats, and wiggling.

Then the glitch happened, the glitch that would change the course of my life.

My left-hand fingers were turning white from holding on to the bars of the ceiling cage, so I quickly shifted the doctor (he shrieked) and clamped my right hand around a bar.

McCallum's broad, fleshy face blurred and pixelated for a second, and then *yours truly* was on all the screens in the prison. Someone was talking: "For those of you just joining us, we're watching as longtime freedom fighter Maximum Ride leads her captors on a less-than-merry chase. It's been some hours now."

My mouth dropped open and I almost lost hold of the doctor. Down below, everyone was silent, in shock. I mean, *my face* was on the screens! I tore my eyes away to look for the camera. The screens showed me doing that! Quickly I judged the angle of the camera—it was practically eye level with me! *But where was it?* I have good eyesight, an eagle's eyesight, so let's say *good,* and I didn't see *any* camera or lens or anything up there.

I looked back at the screen, which was a close-up of me and the doctor. Was this being broadcast to the world? To one country? To one city? Was someone somewhere learning about what had happened to me for the first time in years? And wow, I...I...really looked like *shit. Yeah, world, finally see my face right now when I look the absolute worst!* This was *great* timing!

"How will this end?" the female voice went on. "No one knows! But we'll bring updates as we get them!" The screen crackled and McCallum was back. I mean his *back* was to his constant camera and he was waving his arms and screaming as several people ran around like kids playing freeze tag.

It wasn't what we were used to seeing. McCallum was always calm, always in control...always facing *you,* always watching. But not right then—he didn't seem like he was calm, or controlled, and for once I had been the one watching him.

The screen went black again just as an extra-long, extra-bad Voxvoce dropped everyone to their knees. The doctor tried to curl up, moaning, his hands over his ears. I decided it was a good time to let go and was down before anyone realized it, dropping the doctor on the ground and immediately flying back up to perch on one of the courtyard's tall walls.

Then McCallum said, "Okay, people!" He was smiling wide on every vidscreen, but his smile looked kind of strained. "Today must be Crazy Day, right? I don't know what that fantasy newscast was about, but you know that McCallum News is the only trustworthy news! There was no truth to that so-called newscast, and whoever put that up on your vidscreens is going to pay for it, I promise you."

Slowly the people below me, prisoners and guards, began to recover. Some had tears streaming down their faces, some looked like all the blood had drained out of their heads, and two or three had barfed. I was still immune to the Voxvoce poison, so at least *something* was going my way.

"Yes, that glitch was most disturbing," McCallum said smoothly. "No doubt the work of deviant troublemakers. We have to stamp their kind out, don't we? We don't need to be upset about their lies, do we?" He smiled, his dark eyes twinkling like sunshine on a beetle's back. "Don't worry, my dears! You can bet I'll find out who did this disturbing thing. In the meantime, let's join Lacey Lamb as she learns an important lesson about telling the truth!"

A cartoon started and I looked away, still wondering where that camera had been. There were no choppers overhead, no drones. I'd be able to see them even in the night's darkness. The only things besides me (and the doctor, we can rule him out) who'd been up on the ceiling cage were the usual rats, mice, roaches…

I looked up again. Could one of them have been fake? Or carrying a camera? Who had arranged it? Who still cared about me, even if it was only to see me fail?

Of course, it was while I was musing, pondering my life choices, that a tightly woven net dropped over me and yanked me up into the air.

McCallum interrupted a couple screens of Lacey to gloat. "Got you now, little birdie! I'm patient, probably the most patient man in the world, but you've certainly been getting on my last nerve!" He chuckled and seemed to nod at someone. Then the screens went back to Lacey Lamb while I hung there like an onion in a grocery bag. And that's what I got for letting my guard down for *one second*. That's what I got for being merciful and putting the doctor down before I became too weak, and dropped him.

My life sucks.

CHAPTER 59

Hawk

"Sweetie, you've got to trust us on this," Nudge said.

I shook my head. "I've followed you guys long enough. Thanks for helping me get my kids out, but this is where we get off."

"There are cities besides this one," Nudge said. "There are different *countries,* different lands...*you* were born inside an underground haven during a nuclear winter. It wasn't this place. You *came* here. You can *leave* here. At least once, and to save your..." Nudge seemed to be searching for words.

"Family," I said tautly. "They're my family."

Fang stalked over to me, tension rolling off him in waves. "Look, Hawk. You're a smart kid, you can think this through. One, I have to leave to go save your mother. Two, you've got four kids who can't fly, three of them about to go through dope withdrawal, unless you're planning on keeping them hopped up. Three, you can't go back to that...place. Four..." his voice softened a tiny bit. "You're going to be wanted, your face flashed on vidscreens everywhere. The jail breakout, the rescue of these kids. You've got nowhere to go. You have to come with us. I will give you one minute to think about it."

Gosh, he'd suddenly put his dad-wings on. This was super annoying because he was...right. I couldn't do this alone. I needed the Flock, and the kids needed me.

"Fine," I said, trying to hold on to some dignity. Looking at Nudge, I said, "I'll check out this tent city. But if it's messed up, we're turning around."

"Got it," Nudge said, and went to Rain. Iggy helped Rain put her arms around Nudge's neck, told her how to lie still in the middle of Nudge's back so Nudge's wings could still move.

"This is the best trip I've had yet," Rain said, smiling.

It took me a second to realize she meant Rainbow trip, a trip inside her mind. And as Rainbow made fun trips for Rain to take, it was also poisoning her brain. Another month and she'd be shuffling around, begging for a few coins so she could buy more. Regular dope was horrible—Rainbow was a thousand times worse.

"Oh, uh, good," said Nudge, not understanding.

"Come on, Calypso," I said. "I'm going to give you a piggyback ride, k? And you're going to hold on super tight, got it?"

"Sure," Calypso said, and obediently climbed on my back. "You're taking us to get more dope."

I let out a deep sigh and didn't say anything.

There was no trouble getting Moke onto Fang's back—all we had to do was tell him we were taking him somewhere with dope—and then all that was left was Clete on Iggy.

"No, I don't think so," Clete said faintly.

Fang came over, Moke's weight not slowing him down.

"Get. On." Fang's voice was like black ice.

"Heights," Clete mumbled, rocking on his feet. His hands began flapping—he was really, really super upset.

I hoped Nudge would come over and talk to him—I didn't know what to say: I didn't want to do this, either.

Surprisingly, Iggy began speaking in a low, calm voice. "So, Clete, you don't like heights, huh?"

"No." The hand-flapping continued.

Iggy put his hand on Clete's shoulder. "I understand. Most people don't like heights. And most people wouldn't have been able to do everything you did tonight to help rescue your friends."

"Hawk said I was a hero," Clete remembered. I smiled at him.

"We're all heroes," Iggy said. "And Hawk, and all of us, need you to be a hero for another ten minutes. Think you can do that? I think you can."

"Ten minutes?" Clete asked.

"Ten minutes," Iggy said. "You can do it."

"Okay," said Clete, and climbed onto Iggy's back. He must have outweighed Iggy by half, but Iggy barely seemed to feel it. I guess all of us bird-people are superstrong, not just me. I was learning so much.

"You know, I have a plan that's going to take the whole city down," Clete said as we moved to an open area to take off. Iggy vaguely said, "Oh, good," and the rest of their words were lost to the night as Iggy ran, snapped out his big white wings, and took off.

I was next, Calypso's slight weight making no difference in my takeoff.

One by one, bird-people just like me took to the sky...and headed out of the city to some Other Place.

CHAPTER 60

I hadn't been lying when I said I'd flown out, away from the city. Of course I had. I could fly; the first thing I'd wanted to do was fly away from the City of the Dead. The only thing out there was desert. Naked hills, bare, sandy stretches that couldn't support an ant, much less people. I'd gone out there and had never seen a single living thing. No place to escape to. Nowhere to go. Nothing to see.

The Flock headed northwest, where the land was somehow even more desolate. I saw no lights, no structures, no sign anywhere of a safe place. I mean, I trusted Nudge so much. She wouldn't lie to me. But I knew there was nothing out here, knew it deep in my bones.

We flew over a bunch of canyons, some of them with rivers. I'd never been out this far. We were eight minutes out; Fang had two more minutes to make me trust him more.

A minute and a half later, the Flock started backstroking their wings so they could drop down. There was a narrow crevice here, maybe two meters wide? It was black, barely visible.

One by one they dropped through, wings out, managing their descent.

I'd never dropped down into a crack in the earth. I had no idea what was down there. I'd taken such a huge, stupid chance, and had to keep on taking it because Fang had been right: I truly had no other place to go.

Carefully I aligned myself sideways over the crack, as the others had done. Then I dropped down, too, trying not to scrape Calypso off my back. Where was the floor? How far down did I have to go? Shit, the crevice grew narrower as I went down and I glanced to both sides to see if the Flock had gotten stuck. I felt my pin feathers rub harshly against the rock and angled them so I could still move but not get stuck.

"Ouch," Calypso said, her voice still dreamy. "I'm dreaming that a rock monster swallowed us whole." She laughed and tightened her arms around me, apparently okay with this fate. I definitely wasn't.

"Sorry," I breathed, peering anxiously below us. Then we were out! The rock opened like a huge bell below us. I saw the rest of the Flock watching me, smiles on their faces. Clete, Moke, and Rain had gotten off, and Clete was looking at me anxiously. I smiled reassuringly at him and landed with as much grace as I could possibly manage, given what I'd been through during this long night.

Calypso slid off my back and sat down on the ground, talking quietly to herself, her eyes closed. Clete came over and I did our weird hug where I put my arms out, pretended to hug him, then pulled them back. He wasn't crazy about being touched.

Moke was running his hands through his hair, making it

stand up wildly. He looked upset and angry—the Rainbow was having a Mokelike effect on him, just like it was having a Calypsolike effect on Calypso and a Rainlike effect on eyeless Rain. It was like it was taking all the parts of their personalities and making them stronger, larger, too big for the bodies that were supposed to hold them. Rain had sunk down, curled up, and was moving her hands gently in front of her face, as if writing something that she could still see.

Now I could look around. I had to press my teeth together so my mouth wouldn't drop open like a gaping fish. The Flock hadn't been lying to me. There *was* a village here, spread out beneath the enormous, endless overhanging canyons. Multiple "streets" branched off from this entrance, winding away as far as I could see. Dim, predawn lights were coming on as the inhabitants woke and started their day.

Buildings were carved into the stone sides of the canyon. Some of them were obviously businesses, their windows stocked with wares. But sometimes I could see curtains hanging at a window, or even plant boxes that made me think it was a house.

Not just a house. Someone's home.

There were rows and rows of them leading up and back to the very last wall of this overhang, and the village continued on the other side, leading through connected canyons. In the middle of this main canyon, water flowed quickly, strongly, through a narrow channel. Most of it was covered with walkways to the other side, but I could still see and smell it as it rushed by.

I inhaled deeply. Yes. I could smell the water, and right away

I knew that it was a water smell, like, of the water itself, not the chemicals or sewage or whatever always pollutes water. I thought maybe if I took a bath in this water, I might actually come out clean.

"Where does the water come from?" I asked.

A man I hadn't noticed before stepped forward. "We're lucky—we have two separate natural springs in Tetra. We still filter the water, but mainly for sediment. This water is continuing to create our home, digging it a tiny bit deeper all the time."

The man's skin was very dark—he was much shorter than me and had a nice smile and straight red hair. I could hardly see his eyes because his smile had almost squeezed them shut. He came toward me and I automatically tensed, moving one foot backward to be in a strong fighting stance.

Still smiling, he came toward me very slowly. "My name is Durrel."

I shook his hand, still tense and awkward. All this civilization was going to wear me out. "Hawk."

CHAPTER 61

"Okay, we have to go," Fang said abruptly. He still seemed wired with tension and looked like shit. It felt like a month since we'd broken him out of prison—had it really just been yesterday? His face was bruised, he had big dark circles under his black eyes, and his cheeks were hollowed out like he had something in him, sucking him dry.

He didn't look like someone who'd be all geared up to go somewhere. Gazzy went to him, put his hand on Fang's shoulder, and said, "We gotta eat, man. Birds need *fuel,* ya know what I'm sayin'?"

Fang gave Gazzy a look that, if he looked at me that way, I'd either run or pull out my knife. Probably run. Fang was pretty much the only person in the world I'd run from. He was that scary. Sometimes.

Clete edged over to me and whispered, "I'm hungry, too."

As soon as he said that, my innards suddenly felt like they'd been empty for days or maybe weeks, like I was just waiting for someone else to admit to the weakness of being hungry. I looked at Calypso, talking to herself, Rain, writing her invisible words, and Moke, who looked ready to kill something. When was the last time their captors had given them anything but dope or Rainbow?

There was a carved-stone bench nearby and I sat down on it, my legs shaky. I pretended to be interested in its carved decorations, stuff out of kids' books, like that kind of rat with the super fluffy tail. I ran my fingers over it, trying to remember the word for this made-up animal. Fox? That sounded right. Like I'd told Calypso about horses, they weren't real. Unless... I let my hand fall away. I didn't think this canyon was real. I didn't think my mom and dad were real. I'd never really liked being wrong, but I guess sometimes it's not a bad thing.

"Hello! Hello! Welcome!" A woman came up, this one with light tan skin, short, shiny black hair, and black eyes like Fang, only like a thousand degrees friendlier.

I guessed she was some kind of ware seller, trying to get the newcomers to fork over some coin. But I was surprised when Nudge hugged her. They talked quietly for a few minutes. The woman looked over Nudge's shoulder at me, the lab rats, Fang. She smiled and nodded several times, taking Nudge's elbow. Then she went to hug Gazzy and Iggy. She seemed to know not to hug Fang, who was pacing nearby, or me, who was giving her the uninterested-in-your-wares look.

"Hello, Phoenix," she said warmly, and my eyes narrowed. "My name is Ying. I run the care center here. Nudge says some of your friends are addicted to Ope, and are also on Rainbow right now," she said, shocking me. Her voice was kind, but she was kind of throwing it right out there, you know?

Fang clapped his hands. "We. Have. To. Go. Now," he said loudly.

"Hang on, Fang," Iggy said. "We're making arrangements."

"Uh-huh," I said to Ying, pointing subtly to Moke, Rain, and Calypso.

"At the care center we can wean them off the drugs," Ying said. "We've had tremendous success with many nomads who have found us. Would you like us to take care of your friends?"

Oh, god, yes, I thought, then felt so guilty. *I should be the one taking care of them.*

Someone put their arm around my shoulder and I whirled.

"Hi," Nudge said. "I just wanted to pop over and remind you that you yourself are still technically a child, so let someone else take care of them for a while, huh?"

Outraged, I opened my mouth, and Nudge shoved a burrito into it. It was hot, smelled fantastic, and tasted like it might even have real cheese.

"Umph," I said, taking hold of it, biting off a mouthful. I swallowed almost without chewing, feeling the beans and cheese and tortilla starting a party in my stomach. "Oh, god," I murmured as I wolfed down a second bite.

Ying smiled. "I'd like you to let us take care of your friends."

I chewed and thought. I didn't know where I was going, what I'd be doing. It sounded like the Flock was going to go rescue their friend Max, the rebel. The freedom fighter. Possibly my mother. I didn't know.

This place was paradise, unless it was all a cruel sham. But I knew tricksters and shams, and Ying didn't feel like one. You can't fake that sort of kindness. Sadly, I finished the burrito and admitted that actually I probably couldn't take care of the lab rats the way they needed. I was so used to being the one in charge, the one who took care of—everything. To hear that, to the Flock, I was still (technically) *a child* was their mistake, one I'd have to correct soon. I'd stopped being a child the day I was left behind on the corner.

"There's also Clete," I whispered, wiping my mouth with the back of my hand. Some cheese stuck to me and I ate it, licking my hand clean.

"The tall boy, there?" Ying asked, pointing to Clete. Clete also had a burrito and a drink, too. He looked happy.

"Yes. He doesn't like change," I said. "Or new people. And Rain"—I pointed—"they took her eyes. Just a few days ago she had eyes."

"You guys have been through a lot," Ying said, her hand on my arm. "The wound on your face—it looks fairly new. I could help fix it up a bit."

"We go through a lot every day. It's kind of what we're used to. But usually, we're doing it together. So I should stay and help."

"No," Gazzy said, walking up to us. He handed me a small, heavy, vestlike backpack. "Put this on. You're coming with us."

CHAPTER 62

Five minutes later I was flying over the desert. The sun, just coming up, was radiating out amazing colors of red-peach-gold light. At home, dawn was gray—you just noticed that suddenly you could see more stuff, most of it pretty ugly.

This—this was so different I wanted to cry, but I'd take that secret to the grave. The greasy gray-green haze over the City of the Dead was completely gone. We were in a sky of blue, blue, blue—the bluest blue. It was so easy to breathe—I could gulp deep breaths of air and not cough, not have to swallow a bad taste.

Speaking of taste, the vest Gazzy had given me was full of pockets, all stuffed with *food*. There had been two more burritos, some filled with scrambled egg (maybe real?) and sausage that didn't taste like cardboard. Every pocket had cool new food, all of it 1,000 percent better than anything I'd ever had.

It helped to know that the lab rats were getting the same food. Saying good-bye had been hard, especially since the more I wanted to leave, the guiltier I felt. In the end I had fled, jumping straight up and flying out of the cavern like the Flock.

"Don't think about it," I muttered, and unclipped the

clear tube leading over my shoulder. Why was my vest heavy? Because I was carrying thirty liters of water on my back! Anytime I wanted I could just unclip the tube and drink! And it was all water from Tetra, which was amazing. Anything I'd drunk before now had been like—old laundry water or something. This was a totally new thing. It tasted like blue sky.

And the desert. I'd never seen it during the day. In the sunlight and clear air, the desert was beautiful, shades of colors I didn't even know the name of, shadows playing in all the ridges of sand, almost making pictures below us.

Gazzy had told me this would be a long flight. He'd asked what was the longest I'd ever been up in the air, and I'd told him maybe an hour? I mean, I always took little breaks on top of buildings whenever I wanted, you know? Why worry about building up your stamina when you've got no place to go?

Now I noticed that my wings were getting tired. The Flock was getting ahead of me, little by little. I wondered when or if the Flock was going to take a rest stop, but there was no way I'd ask for one.

About two and a half hours out, I was definitely flagging. The desert was slowly giving way to swaths of trees, most of them I didn't know the names of. The only time I'd seen any trees in one place was inside Pietro Pater's walled garden. It had been green there, full of trees and vines and grass and the heavy scent of some tiny orange flowers growing on a trellis.

I took a sip of water to clear my head. Pietro was another thing I wasn't going to think about.

Soon the ground below us was completely covered with trees no one was growing on purpose, like in a garden. They were just *there*: wild trees.

"Time for a break!" Gazzy yelled, and I thought, *Thank god*. Then I thought that this new sun was the most beautiful, most powerful thing I'd ever seen. So I thought, *Thank the sun*. The sun would be my goddess, like some people at home worshipped little statues.

It was such a relief to be able to slowly circle a small clearing and finally come to a still-graceless landing, this one caused by my total exhaustion. I flopped onto the grass, hearing the buzzing of insects and the calls of birds I'd never seen. I left my wings outstretched so they could cool and drank water for a long time.

When I finally sat up, the Flock was sitting on the grass, eating.

"Come on," Iggy said to me. "Eat fast so we can get back up."

"How much further is it?" I asked, then could have slapped myself.

Fang looked at me. "Are you wiped?"

Yes. "No, of course not," I said stiffly. "I'm just curious, is all."

"Better eat something," Nudge said, her mouth full. "We have a way to go."

"I...I'm out of food," I said, and four pairs of eyes widened and looked at me.

"Did some, like, drop?" Gazzy asked. "Or did you actually eat everything in your vest?" I thought I saw a smile trying to escape his mouth, but everyone else looked serious.

I looked off to the side, trying to act cool. "I was hungry."

Gazzy broke out laughing, and after a moment Nudge joined him, then Iggy. I even saw Fang smile slightly.

233

"I guess this is the best food you've had in a while, huh?" Iggy said, giving me one of his hand pies. I wished I could be proud and say no, but let's just say he drew his hand back with no fingers missing.

"It's the best and most food I've had ever," I said, cramming the pie into my mouth.

"Are you going to be okay to fly over water?" Fang asked.

"Sure, why not?" I asked, spitting crumbs.

"We're going to be over water for a long time," Fang said. "We won't be able to take rest stops. It's an *ocean*."

I frowned. "What's an ocean?"

CHAPTER 63

"I mean, I know it's a lot of something, like an *ocean* of potato flour or something. But what's this an ocean of?" As usual, I felt like an Ope-addled idiot. There was so much I didn't know.

Nudge was the first to speak. "This is an ocean of water, and it's literally called 'the ocean.' There are a couple different oceans, but we're just flying partway over one."

"I don't get it," I said stubbornly.

"So...your schooling has been lax," Iggy murmured, which totally pissed me off.

"My schooling has been *nonexistent*!" I snapped, jumping to my feet. "I was stealing food from *dogs* and begging for coins when I was six! Then I was scooped up and brought to the Children's Home, and you all saw what that was like! At no point during my life has there been 'schooling'! And you all know whose fault that is, right?"

I turned and stalked away, but not before I saw a look of shock and horror on Fang's face. *Because he had left me.* Because he and Max had given me that fate. That look...was what finally convinced me that he was my father. Now I knew for sure.

"Hey, it's okay!" Gazzy called after me. "Our schooling was totally lax, too! I taught myself to make bombs from online videos!"

"I read some old encyclopedias," said Nudge. "Then I would pelt everyone with facts."

I turned around and leaned against a tree, a little calmer.

"But who taught you guys to read?" I asked.

They all looked at one another and then answered at the same time, "Max."

Nudge stood up and brushed off her hands. "Do you need anything else to eat?" she asked me. "We've all got extra." Gazzy started to say something, but she shot him down with a look. "How much water do you have left?"

I hadn't known we were supposed to be rationing it. "A bunch."

Fang had been very quiet since I'd snapped. Now he came over but didn't look me in the eye. "We'll be flying over nothing but water for several hours," he said calmly. "Longer than our flight here. There's no land, no place to stop. Can you make it?"

Oh, my sun, no. "Yeah. *Of course.*"

I felt Nudge and Gazzy exchanging looks. A tiny, weaselly part of me was maybe hoping that one of them would insist I stay here. I would protest, they would be firm, and I would finally give in. Then I'd take a long, long nap beneath these weird trees.

Fang looked like he really wanted to do that, but in the end no one insisted.

Shit. I mean, it sounded like, like, a lot of water? With no banks or *edges*? I couldn't picture what they were describing.

I took a couple of deep breaths, adjusted my vest, and tried to look ready to go.

"Okay. Let's do this!"

One by one the Flock ran and leaped into the air, snapping their wings out. It was still amazing to see other people's wings. Nudge's were beautiful, a soft brown, with shades of white beneath and black speckles on top. Fang's were solid black, so shiny that they looked almost purple with the sun on them.

I didn't have time to linger over Gazzy's and Iggy's—it was time to fly.

Just like them, I ran and threw myself into the sky.

CHAPTER 64

Okay. An ocean. "The" ocean. It was goddamn big. Obviously, I'd never seen that much water, or even flown over any natural water except the rivers and smaller lakes we'd passed this morning. And—when I saw it ahead, my brain could barely process it. It was trees, trees, trees, then sand like in the desert but only a thin strip. Then, just water.

When we left land behind and were suddenly over the ocean, it was like—like I didn't know how to fly over water. Without land underneath I felt like I would just drop out of the sky.

We were up higher than I'd ever been. There was way more wind, sometimes with us, sometimes against us. There were still goddamn bugs. But below us, only water. Above us, only sky. I was in a dream, only no dream I'd ever had.

"Why is it colder now?" I called to Gazzy, who was the closest to me.

"The higher you go, the colder it is," he called back. "We've been so high that the air is actually thinner, with less oxygen. That's a trip."

I was gonna take his word on that. Breathing in deeply, I

felt cool air filling my lungs, filling everything inside me with, like, life or something. I felt clean and fresh, I wasn't hungry, I had water anytime I wanted it. This was the most wonderful, fantastic, unbelievable feel—

"Can I make a suggestion?" Gazzy said. He'd pulled closer to me while I'd been glorying in how fabulous it all was.

"Yeah?" I said without enthusiasm.

"Okay, you see how you're flying, and like everything except your wings is kind of hanging down? Like your body?"

"Yeah?"

"Okay, see how we're flying, how we push our heads forward and arch our backs and hold our legs parallel with our wings?"

I looked. Yes, indeed, so they were.

"So?" I said, ready to defend my personal flying choices.

"So our way is more streamlined," Gazzy said. "We're blocking less air, making less resistance."

"Okay," I said.

He sighed. "It's easier," he said gently. "It takes less energy. You don't get as tired as fast."

Ohhhhh. Hesitantly I tried it, arching my back, using my leg muscles to hold them parallel to my wings.

Oh, my sun, it made *so much difference*! I was practically *gliding* along, not having to move my wings nearly as hard or as fast!

"I'm like a bullet!" I said happily.

"Yep," Gazzy agreed. "Once you get in the habit, you won't have to think about it. You wanna see something else?"

"Yeah!" I said. I'd been flying my whole life, and now someone was teaching me how.

"Angle yourself to the left of me, about two meters past my feet," he said.

"Okay," I said, doing as he instructed.

"Now you're in my slipstream," he said. "Do you feel the air coming off me? It's like a little air current. If you put yourself into it, basically I'm doing some of the work of you flying. Feel it?"

"I think so," I said, trying to angle myself better. I could feel the airstream, but it was hard to stay in it.

"If you'll notice," he went on, "the rest of us do that naturally. We all take turns being the one in front, because that's harder. The rest of us angle ourselves out in a vee-shape, to take advantage of the slipstream."

"Oh, my sun, I think I'm in it!" I said excitedly. I hardly had to use my wings at all, when I was in it. I kept falling out or going above it, but now I actually knew it existed.

Oh, this was amazing! I breathed in, working on being a bullet in Gazzy's slipstream. This was *awesome*.

Which is why I was so not ready five minutes later when I felt myself completely. Run. Out. Of. Steam.

With no warning my wings lost every ounce of energy. They seemed to weigh fifty kilos apiece. It was harder to breathe. My throat was closing. I had tunnel vision, then couldn't see anything. I tried to yell for Gazzy, for anybody, but all I could get out was one last gasp.

And then the sky went black, and I was dropping like a rock toward the endless ocean.

CHAPTER 65

I blinked and drew in breath. I was still falling. I tried to stop myself with my wings, but at this speed they almost snapped off. I cried out in pain and folded them in. Now I was falling faster.

I yelled but my voice was snatched away by the wind and I couldn't even hear it myself. I'd never flown so high. Now I was gonna hit the ocean and it'd be like a plum hitting concrete. Still—I was glad I got to do all this before I died.

An entire minute had passed. The longest minute of my life, and I'm including listening to Clete's endless plans to bring the city down. The rushing air made it hard to look up, and when I tried I couldn't see the Flock. We all have amazing eyesight, but I doubted they could pick me out against the ocean from nine kilometers up.

Almost a whole other minute passed. I managed to turn so I was falling face first. Below me I saw waves, blue-green ripples. Something jumped out of the water! Several somethings! Really big, smooth, shiny, jumping in arcs. Some kind of fish. I bet Nudge knew what they were.

In the City of the Dead they farmed fish in huge tanks. These were wild fish. I hoped I didn't kill too many when I disintegrated against the water.

The ocean smelled salty. If I reached out, I could almost touch it. I guessed I had about three seconds left. I closed my eyes.

Something like a freight train hit me sideways. It took several seconds to realize I wasn't wet. I wasn't wet? I wasn't dead?? Opening my eyes, I looked up to see that Fang was carrying me in his arms. He'd come down and snatched me up at the last second before death. He'd seen me, caught me, and now was surging upward with powerful wing strokes. Before, because I was the only flier I knew, I'd prided myself on flying almost as good as Ridley. Now I knew that Fang and the Flock *did* fly as good as Ridley.

I hoped Ridley was okay and knew to wait for me. Or maybe she knew to get the hell out of there, which would be good, too.

"I need you to climb on my back," Fang said, looking down at me. "I can carry you much longer on my back."

It was hard to look tough when he'd just saved my life, but I tried anyway. "I don't need you to carry me."

"Yeah?"

Before I could answer with a hard *Yeah,* Fang dropped me. Just let go of me and let me fall.

Because I wasn't ready, I was in the same position as before, where I couldn't whip my wings out because the high speed of falling would probably snap the bones. I watched him become smaller very rapidly above me. He was grinning.

I gave him the finger and crossed my arms over my chest. When I dared to look up again, he was laughing.

Then he dive-bombed, the way I'd seen Ridley go after a rat. He came down amazingly fast and scooped me up.

"I need you to get on my back," he began again.

So I did, because this flight was too far for me and he couldn't carry me forever in his arms. But I didn't have to be pleasant about it.

CHAPTER 66

Max

One has so much time to reflect, doesn't one, when one is hanging upside down in a net? Especially when one has a puffed-up blowhard *yapping* at one *incessantly*. Every so often, McCallum would demand some answer to some stupid question. I was usually off in a daydr—*daymare*—and he had to repeat it several times.

After the second time, he had a guard use a taser on me (tied to a long pole—it was ridiculous). I had to point out that being tasered made *speaking* physically impossible for a while, and also tended to build up ill will. Was that what he wanted?

Then it was back to the yapping. Two and a half meters below me, the doctor looked sulky, the prison warden seemed about to have a heart attack, and the prisoners, who had stayed up the whole freaking night to watch this circus, had mostly fallen asleep in place.

I kept thinking about that amazing glitch in the news feed, and where the camera had been. Who had made that happen?

Why? Had it helped anything, anywhere? Had it hurt? McCallum had definitely seemed upset by it, that was for sure. If they could get a camera that close to me, could they get like, a grilled cheese sandwich within reach?

All valid questions. If I ever met these people, I was definitely bringing up the question of the grilled cheese sandwich.

"Maximum…" The voice was silky, cajoling, and it slithered into my ear. "It's pointless to keep fighting. You're the last of your kind, and you should want us to pursue any means to make more of you."

I kept my face blank, but inside it was like a cold hand had seized my heart and squeezed. What did he mean, last of my kind? The rest of the Flock was out there somewhere, fighting for freedom! *Weren't they?* Did McCallum know something? Or was he just saying it to upset me?

All these years, the only thing that had kept me going was the sure knowledge that Fang had gone back to get Phoenix, and that they and the Flock were living somewhere, probably looking for me and plotting to liberate the planet, one stupid regime at a time.

I wriggled to get more comfortable, making the net sway. As soon as they got tired of this, I was going to chew my way out and go back up to the welded bars of the prison's all-encompassing cage. I'd already managed to quietly fray some of the rope. McCallum couldn't be right. I knew my family was still out there, maybe still looking for me.

"You'd hate to die, knowing that you could have created more of your kind but chose not to? Are you ready to let humanity down like that?" McCallum sounded totally reasonable.

"Humanity," I said, "of which you are a part, can kiss my ass!"

"Maximum," McCallum said, "don't make this decision in such a heated moment. We'll let you hang there for a while, give you time to think. When you get tired of hanging upside down in a net, just yell. We'll be ready to talk."

The screen went blank, then a cartoon came on about some kids exploring in the woods. They find something important and didn't tell the nearest adult. No! They schlepped all the way to a government office and told *that* person. I don't even know what they found because my net had been swinging the wrong way round at the time.

McCallum was wrong—I did want to create more of my kind...but not by giving them my wings. I had, in fact, already created one. Where was Phoenix now? My heart ached from the lack of holding her. She'd been so amazing, even at five. Determined, headstrong. I hoped she hadn't given Rose Simmons any problems. You just had to know how to deal with her. She could be stubborn, grumpy. But not for long. I remembered cuddling her after a bath when she was all clean and sweet-smelling. I missed her so much I thought I would go crazy sometimes. And where was Fang, my love? Oh, god, did any of this have any point at all? Was I just delaying the inevitable?

My net swung around again.

Maybe I was. Maybe I was being stubborn and stupid and making the wrong decisions. It wouldn't be the first time, and god knows it surely wouldn't be the last.

Because I was going to bust out of this joint if it was the last thing I did.

One simply had to figure out how.

CHAPTER 67

Hawk

Turns out, riding over an ocean with someone else doing all the work wasn't so bad. Except for the part where they played "Drop the Phoenix." Other than that, it was great.

"Uh-oh..." Iggy said.

I clung tighter to his neck. "No! Nooooo! No more Drop the Phoenix!"

"I think I might have to..." Iggy said.

"Noooo!" I shouted. "Goddamnit! This isn't fun!"

"Might have to... *drop the Phoenix*!" Iggy yelled, and did a fast spin so he was flying upside down and I was trying not to plunge to my death.

Nudge and Gazzy laughed gaily because apparently it didn't *bug* them to see a teenager hanging on to save a life she'd already almost lost.

"Goddamnit!" I shouted again, trying to kick Iggy. "My name is Hawk!" I managed to land a good one right on his butt.

"Yow!" he said, and quickly pried my fingers loose.

My howls of outrage were lost to the wind as I fell. I didn't even try anymore. Just kept my wings tucked in, my arms crossed angrily over my chest, and a sour expression on my face. Then I waited.

Sooner or later, maybe in about three kilometers, someone would come fetch me.

This time it was Fang. He came down like an arrow, swooped me up, then almost flung me onto his back. I quickly grabbed on.

"Do not," I said icily, "play that game again, you sick bastard."

I felt Fang chuckle beneath me, though I couldn't hear it.

"It's weird," he said with fake innocence as we soared upward. "How you manage to fall every time, and your name isn't even Phoenix! That's bizarre, don't you think?"

He asked me that every time. My first three responses, none of them polite, had earned me a quick return to "Drop the Phoenix."

I tried for something neutral. "Maybe...maybe you guys have me confused with someone?"

He turned his head so I'd be sure to hear him the first time. "I think we're all pretty sure that you're both fantastic and obnoxious, an almost guaranteed outcome of Max plus Fang."

I started to say something about where the obnoxiousness had come from but pressed my lips together. *No more Drop the Phoenix.*

"Do you know for sure where we're going?" I asked instead.

"Yes."

"Do you know for sure Max is there?"

"Eighty percent sure," Fang said.

"What happens if this is the twenty percent?"

"Then we keep looking. It took almost nine years to find you. I came to get you while the others kept looking for Max. I figured out the best way to you was through the prison. And right when I got myself arrested in that hellhole of a city, Gazzy found Max."

The air rushed through my mohawk and made my longer hair stream out behind me. My eyes watered from the chilly wind but I didn't dare let go to wipe them, or my nose, for fear of triggering a Drop the Phoenix. A thousand other questions filled my head, but I didn't know where to start. He said—they all said—that he was my dad. And I knew I looked like him. Somewhat. Okay, a lot. Did that mean I got to ask him anything? He was still scary sometimes. I'd seen him get angry, and I didn't want to get him angry at me. At least, any more than I had to.

Gazzy, Nudge, and Iggy had been helping to fill in the blanks. But just a little. As if there was some stuff they didn't want to tell me. Some things it hurt too much to remember or talk about. I was like, you're talking to someone who grew up on the streets of the City of the Dead. I bet you can't shock me.

Except they could shock me, and they did. They shocked me every time they were kind or acted like they cared about me. Or when they wanted me to be with them on purpose. Sometimes just by looking at me. Nudge could make me practically cry by the way she looked at me.

I mean, was this going to be my life from now—

"Uh-oh," Fang muttered and nodded at Gazzy.

"No! No more freaking goddamn Drop the Phoenix!" I

bellowed. "If you drop me, I'll take a bunch of your hair out with me, I swear by the sun!"

"No," Fang murmured, reaching way back to pat my shoulder. "Look. Up ahead."

There it was, shining in the middle of this freaking huge ocean. It looked like an enormous rock, but there was a metal cagelike thing covering the whole place. Right now, three helicopters were hovering over it. Soon we were close enough to hear megaphones.

I glanced at the others. They looked grim.

"Looks like we found Max," Nudge said with a tight smile.

CHAPTER 68

"What is that place?" I asked Fang.

The Flock had quickly risen upward and was now circling about four kilometers above the rock, the helicopters, the noise.

"Here, switch to Nudge for a minute," Fang said, angling over her. Something in his voice made me do it without question, jumping off of him and landing on Nudge's back, perfectly between her wings, aligning my body with hers. Weird that I already trusted these people enough to try something like that.

"But what is that place?" I asked again.

"It's one of the highest-security prisons in the world," Gazzy said, his voice unusually solemn.

"Why...is Max in prison?" I remembered why Fang had been imprisoned—for killing a bunch of kids. I almost didn't want to know about Max.

"A job went wrong," Nudge said simply. "Max was caught. This was only a few months after she and Fang left you with our friend. She's been missing for ten years." Her voice sounded thick with tears, and I saw her quickly swipe one hand over her eyes.

"What makes you so sure she's down there?"

Gazzy answered, finding a current and gliding in a big circle. "One, this is the last Class D prison left for us to check. If this doesn't pan out, we'll move on to all the Class C prisons—like any of those could hold her. Two, the metal cage on top. Putting a cover on high walls, on a rock two hundred kilometers from anything in the middle of cold, shark-infested water, seems a bit like overkill. Makes you wonder what they've got in there."

"Just a bit," Fang said, peering downward.

"Three," Iggy said, now continuing, "experience has shown us that if we suddenly find a bunch of police, or military, or mercenaries all having a hysterical meltdown over something, then that something is Max."

"Uh...how many times has this happened?" I asked.

Gazzy tossed me a small, heavy brown paper bag. "Here, hold this."

I caught it one-handed.

"Okay, can you fly now?" Nudge asked.

I moved my shoulders, flexing my wings to test for strength.

"Yeah, pretty sure I can pull my own weight," I said. Holding Gazzy's paper bag close to me, I let go of Nudge and shot my wings out fast. Instantly the wind caught them, shooting me backward about thirty meters before I found my rhythm and flew to catch up. The hours of rest, and some food, had been as good as eight hours of sleep. I felt recharged and ready for anything.

Gazzy tossed more bags to the others. I was working to stay in Iggy's slipstream, paying attention to how my body was positioned, like I'd been taught. "What are these?" I asked, shaking my paper bag. *Please be more food,* I begged silently.

"Bombs," Gazzy replied, not looking over. "Don't shake it, don't squeeze it."

Iggy giggled beside me. "If Gazzy hands you something, it's pretty much always a bomb. What, were you hoping for lunch or something?" He chuckled again.

"No," I said, putting as much snideness in my voice as I could. "I meant, what *kind* of bomb. Obviously. Jeez." I held it somewhat away from myself—the "Don't shake it, don't squeeze it" directive kind of freaking me out.

"Here we go," Fang muttered. "You made the mistake of asking Gazzy a bomb question."

Gazzy turned to me, his face lighting up. His long, dark blond hair whipped around his face and he tucked it behind his ears, only to have it slip free again seconds later. "In some ways, it's a basic IED—improvised explosive device," he said. "They can be anything from little smoke bombs—I love those, been experimenting with colors—to, like, honking big things that can blow a hole in a city, or reach down to a subway, or take out a tall building."

"Uh-huh," I said, deciding I hadn't really wanted to know that information. I should've been more specific—Do we have a plan??? What are we doing??? We couldn't keep circling forever—for one thing, big dark gray clouds were sliding in below us. Nudge pointed downward and we slowly sank through them so we could still see the prison. The clouds were heavy and full of water—they left me damp, my feathers beaded with droplets.

A rumble of thunder sent vibrations through my body like I

was sitting on trolley tracks, and I wondered if this was dangerous. Sometimes the clouds over the City of the Dead kind of leaked, but there usually wasn't thunder. Should I be worried? I was holding a bomb beneath a gathering storm. Glancing at the others, I saw that they were intent on what was happening below.

Three helicopters hovered above the metal cage. From this far up, the flickering lights of the vidscreens looked like lightning bouncing around a big courtyard. Rain began to fall, quickly turning into fat, hard drops pelting painfully against my face.

"Gather in!" Nudge shouted, just as another rolling drum of thunder echoed through my chest and stomach. Beneath the clouds, the wind whipped against us, pushing us in all directions. I tried hard to stay close to the others. My bomb was getting wet. Was that bad?

Iggy flew near me. "That's the Flock for ya," he said, making himself heard above the storm. "We do great, necessary, exciting things. But you know..." he shrugged. "We sorta play with death a lot."

Oh, awesome.

CHAPTER 69

"Drop lower," Gazzy directed, his hair plastered against his face. He brushed it away with one impatient hand.

"Try to stay above and behind the choppers," Nudge added.

"Do we have a plan?" I couldn't help asking, then wanted to smack myself.

"Yeah," Iggy said, sounding surprised. "We're here to rescue Max!"

I pressed my lips together, but the words escaped anyway. "Like... *more* of a plan?"

Fang answered tightly: "We don't have numbered diagrams. We have to take in all the factors involved in the moment, including stuff like storms, which we couldn't predict."

I turned a bit so he wouldn't see the hurt on my face. He was short-tempered, irritated with me. No more questions, I told myself. Just relax and go with the flow.

Gazzy and Nudge were talking, nodding, moving their hands in the air.

We were all sopping wet. I was chilly, shivering, the heat of flying washed away by this goddamn rain that kept getting in my eyes. I suddenly remembered celebrating Clete's made-up birthday last year. It'd been almost cozy, and I'd stolen a whole cake from a bakery way down the Main Line, where they didn't know me, wouldn't watch me the second I walked in.

Everything had been so much simpler, then. I remember how I thought if I ever found my parents that everything would be okay. Not that I'd have one fly me directly into a lightning storm and yell at me while we attempted to jailbreak the other one.

Another bout of muscle-clenching shivering swept over me, and I thought, *You know what? To hell with this!* I'd never been quiet or obedient in my whole life! The Flock might do great, exciting things and play with death a lot, but that wasn't exactly big news in my world. I'd been playing with death since I was left behind as a child, and the reason I survived wasn't because someone was looking out for me. It was because I was calling the shots myself. It was time for Hawk to be Hawk.

"Look!" I said loudly, and four heads turned. "Either we're going down or we're not! We don't have one stinking idea of the sitch down there or 'all the factors involved in the moment, including stuff like storms'!" I used my nastiest voice when I quoted Fang, and instantly saw his face go flat with anger. Well, tough shit. I've been mad a few times in my life, too, and it hadn't killed me yet.

"We're in the middle of the *freaking* goddamn *ocean*, there's a crazy freak show happening in the prison below us," I shouted, "and I'm holding a goddamn *bomb* in a goddamn *paper bag*, and that *paper bag* is *wet*!"

To emphasize this, I jerked it out in front of me. The wet

bag ripped, the bomb dropped out, and it fell like, well, like a bomb.

"Frick!" I hissed and started to dive after it, but Nudge grabbed my backpack.

"Stay up here!" she ordered.

"It might not explode," Gazzy said, lying through his teeth. "I mean, it would need a detona—"

CRACK!

Lightning and thunder happened at the same instant, almost blowing my eardrums out, making every hair I had stand up straight.

Directly below us, one of the choppers exploded into a fireball, its pieces scattering like confetti. At the exact same instant, lightning hit the prison, blasting a hole in the heavy metal cage. There was another huge explosion, this one catching a second chopper in its wake, snapping off its rotors, making it spin downward in crazy circles. It hit the rocks of the prison island, its larger pieces sliding into the water, fuel bubbling up to burn on the surface.

The explosions barely reached us, though we felt the shockwave five kilometers up. It was the nearby lightning strike that had cooked our brains.

"Tha wa inshting," Gazzy said, his words slurred. I could barely hear him, could barely remember to move my wings to stay in the air.

Dazed, I looked around at the others. Everyone's hair was standing up, including Nudge's tight curls. I felt like I might barf—my ears were ringing and my vision had a blue flash burn from the lightning. The rain pouring down on us felt really good right now but it also made our entire bodies into living conductors.

"What happened?" I said when I could speak.

"We almost got hit by lightning," Fang said, looking pale and disheveled. "And your bomb hit a chopper right when the lightning did, so—"

"Everything go boom," Iggy said. "But guys—*Max is down there.*"

"Well," Fang said, eyeing me. "We didn't have a plan, but you just created one hell of a distraction. Let's hope it didn't kill your mother."

CHAPTER 70

"Max!" Fang cried, and tucked his wings back, face pointing downward. He went through the air like an arrow, dropping incredibly fast, like I'd seen Ridley do.

"I'm sorry," I whispered, trying to see through the billows of smoke being shot through by rain as he disappeared into them. I had just blown up like half the prison, two choppers, and who knew how many people—including Max. *I might have just exploded Max. Who might be my mother.* Who the Flock had looked for for ten years.

"Good one with the paper bags, Gaz," Iggy said angrily, and shot downward after Fang.

"Oh, like I knew it was going to rain!" Gazzy yelled after him. He looked at me. "It wasn't your fault. I put them in the goddamn paper bags. Trying to go plastic-free, the environment, you know." Then he was gone, too, and Nudge and I hovered beneath the roiling, blackening clouds. She said nothing, didn't even look at me before going after her friends, her family, the Flock—leaving me up here alone.

Shit. I had nowhere to run, had no idea where we were

except, you know, *ocean*. The only land was beneath me, and I'd set most of it on fire. With no options, I tucked my wings back, angled my head down, and got ready to plummet fast, from this high up, for the first time in my life.

BOOM!

Light flashed so bright it hurt, and I couldn't tell if my eyes were open or shut anymore. I was plummeting, but not like I'd planned. I was in a free fall, my legs, arms, and wings spinning out of control. There should have been wind rushing in my ears, but I heard nothing. My vision was gone. My hearing was gone. My body wasn't responding to what I told it to do. I was a rock, falling, falling, falling.

Hitting the water felt like I'd been slammed down onto a brick. It knocked the wind out of me, and panicking, I gulped in a big mouthful of salty water. I'd landed in the ocean, but I was still falling, still going downward when life was the other direction.

Kid, you're gonna die.

I put my hand over my mouth. I tried to see something, anything. Zigzagging sparkles of light danced through my vision, but everything was going darker and darker green. I couldn't breathe, and I'd never learned how to swim. The City of the Dead didn't exactly have any bodies of water clean enough to put your own into.

Crap, crap, crap, Hawk, get it together. Get it together or die. NOW, RIGHT NOW!

Carefully I spit out the water in my mouth. I knew I was going to puke but tried to hold it down. Pulling my wings in tight, I turned and spun until I saw water that was lighter. Lighter water meant sky. I'd seen turtles swim in the meat market, and I imitated them, moving my arms and legs. I needed air.

Was the water lighter? How long was this gonna take? I didn't have that much time! My lungs were about to explode. Blue light shimmered inside my head. Another few seconds and I would just...let water in...

When my head popped out the water, I couldn't believe it. It was still raining, the sky still the color of the worst bruise I'd ever had. I sucked in air, threw up, sucked in more air. When my head cleared, I remembered the endless flight here, the bomb, the prison, the Flock diving down to see if Max was still alive.

They'd left me. I guessed I'd been hit by lightning? My whole right side burned. I'd thought being numb and unable to control my body sucked, but feeling the pain wasn't much better. Now I was bobbing in the wide expanse of the ocean, alone. The Flock had no idea where I was. *Which meant I had to find them.*

Turns out, once something has been set on fire, it's pretty easy to spot again. Spirals of white and gray smoke twisted upward from the prison, and screams reached me across the water.

Once I'd seen an angry Ope push a mangy dog into an open canal. The dog had swum to the other side, climbed out, then given the Ope a look that promised an infectious chomp the next time they met.

I remembered how the dog had swum, head above water, four paws paddling.

I couldn't survive here on my own—and I didn't want to.

I wanted to be one of the Flock.

I hoped I hadn't killed Max.

I started paddling toward the prison.

CHAPTER 71

Max

Rain did not help my hanging-in-a-net situation. I could barely move, and now I was soaking wet. These had been the longest, weirdest couple of days I'd had in a while, and I'm including that time when ill-placed food dye had made us all crap purple for a week.

Rain, of course, did not slow down McCallum. "This person"—he flashed a picture of me on the screen, and I still looked like shit—"has broken every rule our city has! She has assaulted helpless Opes! She has written anti-government graffiti all over our beautiful community! She has assaulted government officials! She has said that all government officials should be put to death!"

Okay, *that* one I could get behind. The others had been shown with doctored footage of me supposedly doing all those crappy things. I mean, I would *never* assault helpless Opes! Those people had enough problems!

A certain, all-too-familiar *chop chop chop* sound made me

look up. Several helicopters had joined our party, which meant that McCallum had his icy heart set on getting me out of here. No doubt he would move me to a different hidden hell-hole where he could cut off my wings without anyone watching. Like, who has *more than one* hidden hell-hole? How many does he need, for god's sake?

I was...just so tired. How long had I been fighting? How much longer was I supposed to fight? What did it say about my life that my happiest years had been spent in an underground bunker during a nuclear winter?

I missed the Flock with a fierce, sudden urgency. I missed Fang so much. And if my arms couldn't hold Phoenix again before I died, then even dying would be pointless. I know I'm strong, and I'd proved it countless times, but sometimes even I get tired and beat down.

Suddenly all the vidscreens crackled behind me. There was a blur of numbers and then that same reporter from before was on the screen. To my horror, she showed a close-up of me swinging slowly in the hanging net! I saw my face, battered and bruised, my eyes widening, appalled. I had been a people's hero, once upon a time! Now I looked like—a pathetic loser. Not strong. Not a fighter. And again, where the hell was this goddamn camera???

Holding on to the net with wet, clawlike hands, I pulled myself painfully to a stand. The me on the vidscreen did the same thing, looking less like a loser, more like a fighter—one that still had some fight left in her.

"This is the nightmare that McCallum is so afraid of!" the reporter said. "Maximum Ride has never assaulted a helpless

Ope! She has only ever tried to help people find freedom! Freedom from tyrants like McCall—"

Then McCallum was back, a bit tilted at first, then quickly straightened. His face was almost purple with rage. "Do not listen to anything that traitor says!" he bellowed. "She will be dealt with! And so will Maximum Ride!"

The view of the vidscreen turned away from McCallum, up into the pouring rain to focus on the armed helicopters. One of them had just dropped a rope that reached the top of the wire cage. A man in an orange flak suit started descending. Then a bulky package dropped right past him from higher in the sky. I turned from the screen back to real life as the package fell through the bars and rolled a good twenty meters away.

Huh, I thought dazedly. That looks just like one of Gazzy's— muscle memory instantly curled me into a tight ball, face and head down, back to the bomb, and then there was a huge crack of thunder and a blinding flash. A second later, an explosion blew my net sideways, slamming me against the wall. Still I kept curled tightly, hands over my ears, eyes shut. I'd lived with the Gasman too many years to get exploded like an amateur.

Familiar smells of ozone from lightning, that weird, plasticky smell of C-something, and hot metal almost cheered me up. Recognizing the scent of fire as I hit the wall a second time, I stuck my hand through the net, scrabbling for anything to cling to. There was a rough plaster window ledge and I grabbed it, holding myself still so I could see what the hell was going on.

There was a smallish crater in the ground of the courtyard, maybe a bit less than six meters across? Every window on this wall of the prison was broken, every vidscreen shattered. Most of the inmates were flattened, some holding their ears and moaning, blood coming from in between their fingers. I looked up: the lightning had ripped a big hole in the cage bars, and I could see rainclouds.

That had been a Gazzy bomb for sure, I thought, scanning the skies. *He must be alive!* Then the clouds parted and I...I saw...four...four bird-people. Coming down from the heavens for me.

CHAPTER 72

I was hallucinating. The bomb, the lightning—they'd knocked my brain sideways. Now I was hallucinating, seeing the only things I would ever want to see again.

"Max!"

That was Fang's voice. Those were Fang's wings. Even without the sun to make them shine, I'd recognize those black wings anywhere. This was Fang's face, visibly older, inches from mine, outside the net. Iggy, then Nudge flew down. The three of them supported the net while Gazzy tried to unhook it. I didn't know how much time we had—not everything had been destroyed. The warden and the doctor had been in the courtyard, but I couldn't see their bodies now.

"Hurry, hurry, hurry," I breathed, and then Fang gently put two fingers through the net and stroked my cheek.

I almost fell apart. This was a dream. A dream, and I would wake up soon, be in my rotten cell, and I just couldn't stand it—

"I love you," Fang whispered. Hot tears welled in my

eyes. "I never stopped looking for you. I'm so glad we found you."

Putting my mouth over my hand, I almost doubled over with happiness, with joy, and with fear that this somehow wasn't real. I realized I was gasping with sobs, my chest aching. "Please be real," I choked out.

CHAPTER 73

Hawk

Swimming is so forking hard, so much harder than flying. I saw the prison rock and paddled as hard as I could, but it was taking forever to draw close to the prison. Waves kept breaking over me, the waves that had looked so pretty from above. Now I hated them. In fact, I hated water. I never wanted to see another ocean.

"Ouch!" My paddling foot had hit something hard. A rock! The water was getting shallower. Then my other foot felt one, and soon there were enough rocks to walk over, all the way. They were slippery and I almost got my foot caught between two of them, but at least waves were only coming up to my waist instead of over my head. At last I was at the prison, standing on the tiny bit of earth that surrounded it. This must be the huge, boring backside of the main building. I stood for a minute, getting my balance, shaking water off my feathers and out of my ears—for whatever good that did, it was still pouring. But I needed to buy myself some time, time to think of what to do.

Had the Flock left without me? Was I abandoned—again? Should I jump into the action in the prison? Had they already rescued Max? Or...had they found Max's body? The one I'd dropped a bomb on. Maybe Fang and the others had found her that way, and decided they were all better off without me blowing up people by accident.

If they'd left me, I was dead: there was no way to fly home by myself. Not home, I corrected—but to Tetra. I could maybe—just maybe—return the way we had come. Or—I could totally miscalculate and end up running out of energy with nothing but ocean and sky all around me. I shivered. One near-drowning was all I needed for a lifetime, thanks.

I shook my feathers again, moved my wings up and down. Despite their recent soaking, they felt fly-worthy. I took a running jump off the spit of land, hoping I didn't crash facedown on the rocks. I didn't! I went upward, feeling new strength flowing through my veins as my wings carried me easily above the smoke and the chaos.

I looked down through the torn-open metal cage—there was a crater below with lots of bodies around it. Some of them were starting to move. And then I saw the Flock! They were gathered around someone in a hanging net. *Oh, my god, that must be Max!* I hadn't killed Max! But why weren't they setting her free? There was still one live attack chopper circling overhead!

CHAPTER 74

Max

"Are you real?" I gazed at Fang, reaching my own fingers through the mesh to touch his face, the unusual growth of stubbly black beard. The last time I'd seen him, he'd been barely twenty-one.

"Yep, and I'd love to prove it later, but right now..." he said, his voice grim. He looked up at Gazzy. "Speed it up! We've gotta split!"

I turned my head and saw the woman that Nudge had become without my witnessing it. She was beautiful, though tired, gaunt, her face smeared with ash. "Oh, Nudge!"

Tears ran down her face, streaking the ash.

"Gazzy, and Iggy—you guys—" I said, my voice choking up.

Then a new face joined the circle, the harsh face of a teenager who'd seen too much. My eyebrows came together as I took in the black hair shaved into a long mohawk, the tattoos, the piercings, the black eyes...

"Don't you guys carry knives?" she snarled, pulling a long

blade out of a sodden boot. In a second she had sliced the net open from my head to my feet—I almost fell out of it. "Better split," she advised, and spit, picking some ash off her tongue. "They've still got some hell up their sleeves." Then she pushed down with powerful wings, wings that were black on top and brown on the bottom, with white primaries at the tips.

I got tunnel vision and felt cold all over. "Is that..." I managed, and then I fainted, for only like the thousandth time of my life.

PART THREE

CHAPTER 75

Hawk

"No," I said, not bothering to smile. The woman named Danae gave me a pleasant, confused look. This deep in the canyons of Tetra, people mostly used candles instead of electric light, so there was a warm, cozy feeling in this room. I could feel the steam wafting off the deep bath—but I had no intentions of going anywhere near it.

"I've put healing herbs in it," she offered, like that would make me change my mind. "You've got some burns on the side of your body that could really use the aloe in that water."

"No." I crossed my arms over my chest.

Danae looked like she'd never had an unwilling bath-taker, and maybe she hadn't. Until now. But I had taken a long, horrible bath in a cold, horrible ocean only like ten hours ago, and there was no way I was gonna dunk again.

"It's nice and warm?" she tried. "And I have some nice clean clothes for you?"

I didn't bother to respond.

A loud rap on the wooden door made both of us jump.

"For god's sake, Hawk, take the goddamn bath!" Gazzy shouted. "You smell like a goddamn ox!"

There was silence for a few moments.

I jerked my head at the hooks on the wall. "You can leave the clothes."

The last luxurious bath I'd taken had been in Pietro's house. Both times I'd been injured; both times had been/were embarrassing and fabulous. Maybe that's why I hadn't wanted to get into this water; thinking about Pietro and our one kiss was just too hard. Still, I almost fell asleep in this bath. Danae was right. The hot water was nothing like the ocean, and the herbs were doing their work, soothing the burns from almost getting struck by lightning. But finally I got out, dried off, and put on the first clothes I hadn't stolen.

"Where is she?" The voice was startlingly familiar, but I couldn't place where I knew it from. Then my breath caught in my throat. Max.

Maximum Ride, my possible mother, the one I hadn't accidentally blown up.

There was a knock on the door, but I was already opening it. She, too, had been cleaned up and bandaged, her matted, rats' nest of brown hair now untangled. We stared at each other.

"Phoenix," she said softly.

"My name is Hawk."

She nodded and swallowed. "The last time I saw you, you were five years old."

"You missed all the exciting stuff," I said with a sneer.

"Fang has…explained to me," she said, her voice breaking.

She put one hand over her mouth and shook her head, then tried again. "I didn't know about anything that had happened until ten minutes ago. Fang told me."

I didn't say anything.

"Has he told you?" she asked.

I shrugged.

"I was dying," she said simply. "I was bleeding out. Fang couldn't carry both of us. We had a good, loyal friend, Rose Simmons. Fang saw her running toward you, there was no reason to think she wouldn't get to you. She waved us away. Fang picked me up, we took one last look at you, and then we left."

Her face was very pale and she was so skinny that her cheekbones jutted out and her shoulders were like right angles. For a moment she put a hand over her mouth again, then went on. "We thought it would be for two or three days. Long enough for Fang to drop me off somewhere safe where I could get patched up and then he'd be back for you. Two nights at the most, we said."

"Someone told me to stand on that corner every day, for a half hour," I said harshly. "You know when I quit? Like *four days ago*! When I met *them*!" I moved my head to mean the rest of the Flock.

Max's clear brown eyes bored into mine. I saw depths of pain and hurt—the same things I saw in the rest of the Flock. "Do you remember a car accident?"

I frowned. Car accident? The sound of brakes shrieking, the heavy thump, the screams of passersby, a car horn blaring and blaring and blaring...

"Neither of us knew that Rose was hit and killed by a car,

two seconds after we left," Max said. "While I was healing up, I was abducted by McCallum. Fang went back to get you and found that Rose was dead. No one knew where you were. He searched the City of the Dead, and he waited by the corner for two days, but you didn't come, no one who had seen you came—Fang lost both of us in two days."

Well, okay, that sounded bad.

"Then he was framed for acts of terrorism in a different territory and was taken away. Put in prison until recently. The first thing he did after getting out was head for the City of the Dead, to find you."

I actually didn't remember the first few days after they left me on the corner. Their faces, voices, still didn't seem familiar to me. But just a few days later I was sitting on a street curb, eating an apple core, and it suddenly occurred to me that I was supposed to wait on the corner. That was the first day I waited. So it could be true, that Fang came to look for me and I wasn't there, couldn't be found. It could all be true.

"Listen, Phoenix—you're part of the Flock, whether you want to be or not," Max said, her voice firmer. "So I want you with us, by our sides, no matter what."

I tried to look bored but failed. "My name is Hawk. By your side, doing what, exactly?"

"Taking down one evil regime after another." Max grinned, looking years younger. "It's what we do."

CHAPTER 76

"Will she get better?" The doctor, Mikaela, and I looked through an opening into a healing room. The hospital section of Tetra was weirdly big and super protected. As soon as Max had left, I'd gone to check on my friends—because I might have found my mom and dad, but my friends were still my family. Ying, the doctor I'd met before, had pounced on me and insisted on cleaning up my cheek. I'd been braced, but she'd numbed everything, given me two shots, and then took out the thick black stitches. Instead, she'd glued the edges shut, and the whole thing was much smoother and less noticeable.

But now I was looking at Calypso as she moaned quietly, tossing and turning on a bed. Every so often she barfed. A helper caught it in a basin, then wiped Calypso's face.

"Oh, yes," Mikaela said firmly. "She, Rain, and Moke are all detoxing. I'm afraid it's an unpleasant process, but completely doable. We've detoxed hundreds, if not thousands, of citizens."

"She's just a kid," I said, my chest aching.

"Yes," Mikaela said. "And like most kids from the city, she's malnourished, needs other meds to keep her from getting sick, and is really small for her age."

My face went cold. "I did the best I could. It's not like I was stealing from a health-food store!"

Mikaela remained calm. "Hawk, *you're* a kid from the city. You, too, are malnourished and need other meds to keep from getting sick."

"I'm not small for my age," I pointed out.

Mikaela's laugh sounded so...I don't know—open? Like she knew she could just laugh and it would be okay? "No," she agreed. "You don't have antennas, either."

"So is she a bug-kid, like I'm a bird-kid?" I asked. I'd always wondered.

"We don't know," Mikaela said, not sounding bothered by that. "I guess we'll find out." She laughed again. "Do you know why Moke is blue?"

"Something about silver?" I said.

"Oh, that would do it," Mikaela said thoughtfully. "Talk to you later, sweetie." She headed off down one of the tunnels that looked like striped, twisted clay. She was humming.

This place was weird. It's like people were happy for no obvious reason.

"Hawk!"

I turned at Clete's voice, amazingly glad to see someone familiar, someone I totally knew.

I almost ran to him, and he looked shocked when I hugged him.

"Boy, Clete, am I glad to see you!" I said, and his uncomfortable look made me remember why I never did this, never hugged him. I took a step back, but let the smile stay on my face. "It feels like I was gone for a week! What have you been doing?"

He said, "You seen Calypso, an' Rain, an' Moke?"

"Yeah. The doctor says they'll detox okay. But it'll take a while."

"Yeah." His face brightened. "They got real food here! An' computers! An' the people are nice, too. I like it here, Hawk."

"What's not to like?" I asked.

"I don't wanna go back to the city," he said, getting what I thought of as his "brick wall" expression.

"I don't think you have to, bud," I said. "I think we're welcome to stay. Or at least, you and the other kids are."

"And you?" he said, concerned.

"To be honest, I'm not sure what my plans are right now," I said. Like, if the Flock actually really wanted me, if I wanted to go with them...

"Oh, really?"

I tensed, already knowing that voice too well.

Fang came up behind me, put one arm around my shoulder, and gave me a sideways hug. "God, your killer scar is much less intimidating," he said. "And you're so clean—I hardly recognized you," he said.

"Look who's talking," I sneered.

He did look super different from the scraggly, dirty prisoner he'd once been. He'd shaved. His hair was dark and shiny. He smelled a hell of a lot better. I guessed I did, too.

"Speaking of plans," he said, "I need you to come with me."

"Why?"

"There's someone you need to meet."

CHAPTER 77

"Hang on—this place is a maze," Fang said, frowning.

I couldn't give him any shit, because he was right. Tetra was one cavern or tunnel after another. Sometimes we crossed through a thin strip of sunlight from an open canyon above, and twice we'd gone over a small wooden bridge that crossed a narrow stream.

"Where are we going?" I asked for like the fifth time. "Just stop and ask someone!"

He gave me his narrow-eyed glare, and I mimicked him. But the next person who walked by was in fact grumpily asked for directions. She also pointed out the small signs everywhere, saying where stuff was. But god forbid we should rely on those!

"Maybe some punk moved 'em all around—you don't know," Fang muttered as we charged down yet another tunnel.

"Yeah, can't trust all us young punks," I said, sarcastically.

Finally he stopped in front of a door, checked its number against the one *written on his hand,* and opened it. "Okay, we're back," he said, walking in.

I looked past him to see a large living room–type situation, kind of dark, as so many rooms here were. Max stood up, smiling at me, and I prayed this wasn't some kind of family thing I was nowhere near ready for. Then I saw Gazzy sitting on a sofa, eating something. He waved at me.

"Come get some eggs and stuff!" he said.

Okay, then. I walked in and headed for a small alcove with a kitchen in it. Iggy—*Iggy*—was cooking? My head swiveled right and left as I looked to see if anyone else thought this was, you know, *dangerous*? But it was all business as usual with the circus bird-family!

I grabbed a plate and stood still as Iggy—*Iggy*—dolloped scrambled eggs (I really think they were real) onto my plate, and toast and the best bacon-flavored krill I'd ever had.

I'd ignored Max since I'd come in, ignored when she and Fang hugged each other for an uncomfortably long time, ignored when they both glanced my way, murmuring softly. Instead I sat down at a convincing wood-grain table and started shoveling chow in.

"Ooh! Hawk!"

I smiled up at Nudge as she hurried over and gave me a quick hug.

"Are you sure he should be cooking?" I whispered, motioning my head toward Iggy.

Nudge chuckled and whispered back, "Trust me—he's a thousand times better than the rest of us."

"Are you done?" Fang asked impatiently. "There's someone we want you to meet."

I took a last slug of coffee, looking at him. Something in me told me this was important; it was why he'd brought me here.

But everyone in the Flock was already here—Max, Fang, Iggy, Gazzy, and Nudge.

I wiped my mouth with the back of one hand and stood up. They all looked expectant. I hadn't noticed the slightly open door at the far end of the room, but now a small wolflike creature bounded out of it, mouth open to show its long, sharp canines.

I felt a quick flood of adrenaline, the way my hands tensed for action, the way my feet tightened for kicks.

It was coming straight at me, and no one was stopping it, no one moving to help me. Was this some kind of test? I'd never seen a wolf this small before, or this dark, nearly black.

"Stand down, Phoenix!" Max said sharply.

Shocked, I straightened to look at her, and the small wolf seized that moment to leap at me, landing so it could brace its fat, fuzzy paws against my knees.

"Hi! I'm Io!" it said. "An' you're Phoenix, but I'm s'posed to call you Hawk an' I never met you before but you used to know my dad an' he isn't here right now he had to stay home and help Mama but he said I could come an' this is my *first mission* only I'm s'posed to stay back and be careful."

I stared down into blue eyes, seeing the pert, triangular ears, the ruff of fur framing a face. A dog's face? A *little* dog's face? Then it hit me: it wasn't the dog talking. Oh, my god, I was so stupid. One of the Flock threw their voice to mess with me. Those asswipes.

A light, silvery laugh made me look up to see a teenager, maybe almost twenty, coming toward me. She was a good head shorter than me, with fluffy, light-blond hair that curled around her face. She wasn't vidscreen pretty, but there was something about her that kept my gaze locked on her face.

"It was really Io talking," she said with a smile. "And that was real bacon, not bacon-flavored krill, and this table is actually wood, not just wood-grain."

My mouth opened to ask where the mics were, but then I realized that those had been *thoughts*—I hadn't said any of that out loud.

The blond woman laughed again. "And yes, certain members of the Flock are often total asswipes."

"Hawk, this is Angel," Max said, coming over to us. "The last member of the Flock. More important, she's the leader of our worldwide group—a group called Freedom."

CHAPTER 78

"No, no—I want to hear," Gazzy said. "Which ones of us are asswipes?"

I shook my head, embarrassed. "I didn't mean asswipes," I muttered. "More, like, you know, *jokesters*."

"She meant asswipes," Angel said, almost doubling over with laughter. "Oh, my god, you guys—if I wasn't sure she was your kid, I'd be totally sure now after hearing her thoughts for two seconds!"

My face was red and burning and I didn't know what to do. I felt a soft pat right below my knee.

"You know, if you sit on the sofa, then I could sit next to you." Io started trotting to the long sectional sofa against the wall. Numbly I followed her and sat down. She was a little too short and chunky to make it up, so Nudge gave her a boost. She snuggled next to me and put one paw on my leg. "There," she said. "Isn't this nice?"

"Uh-huh," I mumbled, looking at the floor.

"You don't remember Total?" Max asked, coming to sit on my other side.

"Total of what?" I asked.

Io laughed a kind of doggy laugh. "Total's my dad, silly! He told me all about you. He says you used to pull his ears when you were a baby."

I had zero idea of what she was talking about. "So, Total's a dog?" I asked Nudge, because she seemed the least nuts of all of them. "And he talks?"

Max reached across me to rub Io's ears. Io preened and closed her eyes. "Total is one of the Flock, and so is his...wife. Yes, he talks. He's a small, black, Scottie-like dog. You don't remember him? He used to crawl into your crib all the time so you could nap together."

I practically gave myself a hernia from trying to remember this, and I couldn't. Not even a little bit. Now I had Io to deal with. I didn't like animals. I had never cuddled with a dog— the only ones I'd seen, besides pompom dogs in fancy cars, had been street curs with fleas, ticks, diseases.

"You can pet me if you like," Io said in her little-kid voice. "Everyone says I'm totally silky."

"Oh." I made my hand into a flat shape, experimentally, then lowered it to Io's head. I gave a couple of hesitant pats, and then Max took my hand in hers and drew it down Io's head to her side.

"Whoa, you're all fur!" I said. I'd thought she was chunky because she was basically melon-shaped, but beneath the fluff I felt little ribs, her small shoulder joints. And...something else. Some kind of weird growth on her back. I drew my hand away, not sure what was wrong with her.

"That's my wing!" Io said proudly and stood on all fours.

287

She screwed up her muzzle and shut her eyes, and I almost jumped when two small wings popped out of her fur. They were each about thirty centimeters long and folded only once, not twice like ours.

A talking dog with wings, I thought in a daze.

"My dad has wings, but my mama doesn't," Io said, turning her head to look at hers. "So not all of us have 'em. But I do! Watch!" She fluttered her little wings, then took a jump off the sofa. She stuck the four-paw landing. "See?"

"Oh, that's...cool," I said. Had someone put Rainbow in the food? What the hell was going on?

"Okay, Io, my turn to talk," Angel said, pulling up a chair to face me and Max. "You guys, come over here so I don't have to shout." Iggy, Nudge, and Gazzy got chairs, and Fang sat next to Max, their hands immediately intertwining. Io scrambled back up on the sofa and curled up next to me, resting her head on my leg.

"Isn't this nice?" she whispered up at me again, and I nodded.

"Let's talk about liberating the city, okay?" Angel asked, and everyone nodded.

I frowned, now positive that they had put Rainbow in the food. Max had mentioned Freedom, their "worldwide group." But Angel was barely older than I was, and let's face it, this was a pretty scruffy group of weirdos we were working with, myself included. *I mean, they don't make plans or carry knives so I'm unsure how a worldwide group sprung from all of this.*

Angel smiled at me then, and too late I remembered that she seemed able to read minds. Goddamnit.

Still smiling, Angel went on, ticking things off on her fingers.

"Now, one, McCallum keeps control of the people by being everywhere, all the time. Two, he uses the Voxvoce as a punishment and warning. Three, he runs the factories that make the dope that keeps a large percentage of the people addicted and docile. Basically, he controls, directly or indirectly, everything. Especially the mass communications equipment."

Everyone was quiet, digesting this.

I didn't know how this worked, so I cleared my throat and held up a finger.

"You can just speak, sweetie," Angel said.

"I know something McCallum doesn't control," I said.

CHAPTER 79

"Go on," Angel said.

"The Six," I said. "They don't seem to answer to McCallum. They run a lot of things in the city, but just for themselves."

"The Six," Angel said thoughtfully. "Nudge?"

"They're the six most important families in the City of the Dead, like Hawk said," Nudge clarified. "There's the Harrises, the Chungs, the Stolks, the McLeods, the Diazes, and the Paters. Between them they've carved up all the import-export businesses, banking, loan-sharking, and drug supply for more than just dope. Like some of the uglier street drugs."

Had I just betrayed Pietro? I felt a pang in my heart—I'd been purposely trying not to think about him. Was he thinking about me? Had he even realized I was gone?

"They're run like the old mafia families, from Before," Nudge went on. "They have the family heads, then captains, soldiers, freelancers. I think the Pater family is the biggest, or at least most powerful."

I kept my mouth shut, concentrating on Io's fur so Angel couldn't read my mind.

"How do they fit in with McCallum?" Fang asked.

"We're not positive," Nudge said, "but we assume they pay him a percentage of their profits or help him in law enforcement. We don't know for sure how it works—it's just what we suspect."

"So what are we going to do?" Iggy asked.

"Well, we want to bring McCallum down," Angel said, as if this was actually doable in some way on some fantasy planet. "And we want to balance out the Six. If they can run the city without doping people or extorting them, we could work with that."

" 'Extorting' means making them give you stuff," Io whispered, squirming closer so she was almost in my lap.

"Okay," I whispered back.

"So what are our plans?" Gazzy asked.

"It would be great if we could just blink McCallum out," Angel said, rubbing her forehead. "If I could get close to him, I could take him down. But no one seems to have ever met him in real life."

"My friend Clete might be able to help you with that," I said hesitantly. Clete always talked about his big plans—now he had to put up or shut up. I hoped I wasn't going to embarrass him by putting him on the spot. "He's a whiz with computers, and he said that he'd tapped into the city's mainframe." He *had* said that, hadn't he? I realized that I usually tuned him out when he spoke.

"Go get Clete," Angel said to Fang, and Fang nodded and left. "Any more ideas, Hawk?" She smiled and said, "It's weird for me to call you Hawk—I knew you as little Phoenix. And now here you are, tall and badass. I'm so happy Fang found you."

So, Angel was a person who spoke her mind and didn't screw around—just like me. Now I saw why sometimes people were uncomfortable around me; I didn't know what to say.

"Ideas?" she prompted me.

I thought for a moment. "Getting the Six to agree on something—anything—is going to be hard. They hate each other."

"And yet I think I can get them to agree to be in a room together," Angel said, grinning. "Somehow."

"Is that...I mean, is that a good idea?" I asked doubtfully. "Like, wear a bulletproof vest."

"We'll be okay," Angel said firmly. "And you're coming, too."

CHAPTER 80

After seeing the ocean and Tetra and the grassy plains and a forest, to go back to the City of the Dead felt like a huuuuge step backward, let me tell ya. As soon as we got near, the pollution hovering over everything and the permanent smog that blocked out the clear sun made my chest hurt on the inside. I hated leaving the white, fluffy clouds that until last week I hadn't known existed.

Angel flew point and I was proud of myself for automatically taking my place in the vee, staying in her slipstream as best I could. It was getting easier. Angel's wings, of course, were pure white, top and bottom. Last night, she had explained more of what needed to happen in the city, but most of it had to be done by the citizens themselves, once they were free of dope and McCallum and any controls the Six had over them.

I'd thought Angel was dreaming, like *way* too optimistic about being able to help the city, but I didn't say anything. Mostly I just nodded at Io, who whispered explanations—some I needed, and some I didn't.

When Fang had come back with Clete, Angel took Clete

into a far corner to talk privately. Clete got really excited, rocking back and forth and flapping his hands. They talked for almost half an hour, and when they finished I realized that Io had completely climbed onto my lap and fallen asleep and I was forced to hold her like she was a basket of eggs—a hot, fuzzy basket of eggs—until she woke up.

Now here we were, flying back to the place I'd never wanted to see again, the place I thought of as filthy, rotten, evil, unsavable. How could Angel see anything different? Why were they bothering? I remembered Max saying, "It's what we do."

My gut clenched as we flew over buildings I knew as well as Calypso's freckles. They had seemed normal, before—but after the clean, natural, beautiful caves and caverns and rooms of Tetra, I saw these buildings as they were: filthy, gross. The unfinished skyscrapers looked like the skeletons of huge animals that had died in place and hardened.

"There," I said, pointing. "That's the factory that makes the dope. You see the people lining up?"

Angel nodded. "McCallum—the government—supplies dope to anyone. If you're on dope, you can't think. If you can't think, you can't get angry about what the government's doing."

I'd never looked at it that way. I'd never looked at it in *any* way. It was just how things were. I'd never thought of McCallum as the *government*. He was just McCallum. I'd been blind my whole life. Blind or *stupid*. I hadn't *thought* about *anything* except getting food for the kids, how to keep the cops off my trail. I should have known something was wrong here. I should have been smarter.

My face heated and I was so mad at myself. Why did the

Flock even want me around? What had Gazzy said? *We don't have to know you...We don't even have to like you.* So... maybe they *didn't* like me. Maybe they thought I was stupid, just a street punk.

Angel turned to look at me again. "Staaaaahhhhp! Oh, my god, you're giving me a headache!"

Startled, I stared at her, then glanced at the others to see if they'd heard.

"They didn't hear. I'm only talking to you."

Oh...*sun,* her mouth wasn't moving.

"Listen," Angel's voice said inside my head. "We think you're amazing. You survived in one of the worst cities on this continent, all by yourself. For ten years. That's incredible. Not only that, but you are, without a doubt, the kid of two of my favorite people. You've inherited the best, and maybe the worst, parts of both Max and Fang. I would want you around *forever* just to watch *that* play out."

I looked down, embarrassed.

"We can talk more about this later," Angel's voice said. "Right now, we've got work to do. We're here. Got your bulletproof vest on?"

"No! I don't even have one!" I burst out, and five heads turned to look at me in surprise.

Angel's eyes laughed at me. "Lol," she said.

CHAPTER 81

The meeting was in a building I'd never landed on. It was a super-fancy restaurant that I'd only walked by like twice. Up in this part of the city they didn't like strangers, and I would have stuck out like a...dirty street punk.

We landed in the alley behind the restaurant. This felt more homey—it was all concrete and bricks, dirty, smelly, with three trash dumpsters lined up. I knew that at the end of the alley, I could turn right, then left, and about twenty meters down was a manhole that would drop me into a tunnel that would connect up with other tunnels that would eventually lead to the Children's Home. It took a lot of willpower to not paw through the dumpsters, see if there was any good food in there. You wouldn't believe what some places threw out.

"Okay," Nudge said briskly, "I've had confirmation that at least two representatives from each of the six families will be here. So everyone keep alert, and if this goes south, get out and meet up outside the city."

"Oh, this is definitely going to go south!" Gazzy said cheerfully, patting his pockets.

Angel stopped him with a hand to his chest. "Brother, we spoke about this. We're here to reach a peace agreement."

"Sister," Gazzy said in a singsong voice, "I know that. But I'm always prepared. Just in case."

Angel gave him a narrow-eyed look, then turned and opened the back door, which led to the restaurant's kitchen. Several cooks and waiters nodded at Angel as if they knew her. Maybe they did. If Angel told me she knew everyone in the entire city, I'd believe her.

A guy in a waiter suit said, "They're in the private room upstairs."

Angel nodded and led us to the most amazing staircase I'd ever seen—fancier even than the one I'd caught a glimpse of at Pietro's house. *Pietro.* Would he be here tonight? I hadn't seen him since he'd patched me up...oh, sun, that had been only four days ago? Five days? Impossible.

Restaurant sounds of plates clinking and polite people talking followed us up the carved wooden stairs covered with blood-red carpet so thick, even Clete could sneak down them.

The meeting was in a big room that had glass all around it. Anyone could see what was happening in it. That was smart. Angel pulled open the door and we all filed in. Everyone here was well dressed, and clean. They looked smart. They looked capable. They looked...nothing like me.

Oh, man, I was in way over my head. I stared at my feet. Why had Angel wanted me to come? I didn't know anything about this kind of situation.

"Staaaaaahhhhp," Angel's voice said. I didn't even look up— she was talking only to me, inside my head. "You're here to *learn.*"

Oh. That made sense.

"My name is Angel," she said out loud. "Thank you for coming. Can everyone introduce themselves?"

"Kieran McLeod," a big man with red hair said. "This is my brother, Mike."

Angel nodded.

"My name is Mark Chung." He was older, with straight gray hair and four earrings in his right ear. In the Chung territory, you pierced your ear for every person you killed yourself. They must have thought I was a goddamn maniac because my ears were all pierced, my nose was pierced, my eyebrow...

"I'm Koi Chung," said the woman next to him. She was pretty, but one cheek had a slight dent in it as if it'd been knocked in and not set right.

Next were the Harrises, Shiv and Chris. Shiv looked just like her name, like she'd been made out of something else, in prison. Chris looked nervous, twisting the tablecloth in one hand.

"I'm Kim Stolk," said the next woman, who looked as if her face would crack if she smiled. "This is my son, Trevor." Trevor was maybe twenty, brown eyes, tightly curled blue hair, and had a "Gonna kill Mom soon" air about him.

"Santino Diaz," said a dark-haired man. He seemed impatient, his gaze on the others dismissive.

"Dom Diaz," said a guy who looked like he might be Santino's twin. But his smile was easy, he was chewing a toothpick, and he clearly thought this whole thing was a joke.

"Pietro Pater," a strong, clear voice said, and my head jerked up. It was him. My heart lurched and I took in a shallow breath. He was one of the Six. I shouldn't even like him.

I'd seen him involved in a killing that happened just to keep the family's pride intact.

"Pietro's uncle, Felipe," said a dry voice.

"Good, everyone's here," Angel said, pulling out a chair. "Now, we all have the same objectives," she began.

And then the door blew open, Pietro's father filling the doorway. And he was not happy.

CHAPTER 82

"What the hell is this?" Giacomo Pater roared, and spit on the floor. He gestured to Angel, then looked around the room. "This stranger crooks her finger and you weaklings come running? And for what? For peace? Is that what you're telling me? Peace? We got peace here! All of you dumb shits stay out of my territory, we got peace, eh? I don't care what you do on your own turf, you don't poke your noses into my business on mine. *Bam!* We got peace! See? We don't need a little girl to come here and call us to a fricking meeting! What's *wrong* with you guys?"

Every one of the Flock was tensed and ready for action, including Angel and me. We felt the heavy, thudding footsteps in the hallway before we saw them, two of Giacomo's soldiers. They slammed through the doors, their long rifles out in the open.

"Mr. Pater," Angel said firmly, "your population is aging and dying, and dying too young. How many children do you see around? How many people that you send to the Infirmary come back? They die there, even with minor wounds! Your air is dirty, your water polluted, and almost half the population is addicted to something! You call that peace?"

Giacomo waved a meaty hand at Angel. His wavy dark hair was streaked with white, but he still looked youngish somehow. "You're seeing things! Come to my house, at the top of the Pater territory—my air is clean, my water sweet. You're making too much of minor problems!"

Angel stood up, bracing her hands on the table. Giacomo's bodyguards dropped their weapons into a shooting stance.

"These problems aren't minor," she said mildly. "And just because they don't affect *you* doesn't mean that they don't affect tens of thousands of other people. The City of the Dead is a good name for this place."

"Look, you," Giacomo said, pointing his finger at Angel. "You keep your nose out of our business, eh? You're a stranger, maybe you're not seeing things properly."

"I'm seeing them fine," Angel said, her voice flat.

"What my father is trying to say," Pietro began earnestly. I automatically winced, wondering why he was so stupid—this was not the time to speak up.

"*Your father says what he means to say!*" Giacomo Pater shouted at Pietro so loudly that the windowpanes shook. "You don't ever explain for me, boy! Why are you here in the first place? I just found out about this meeting! Ready to knock your old man out of the nest?"

"No!" Pietro shouted. "Not at all! But when you're out of town, I represent the family!"

"You represent the soft, spoiled, weakling that your mother made you!" Giacomo screamed back. "Not my family! Not me and surely not the family business! Not the one I built from the ground up!"

"Talk about that later!" Angel said, clapping her hands. "We need to—"

But it was too late. Giacomo pulled a pistol and took a shot at his own son, his bodyguards spraying the ceiling with bullets as a warning. Gazzy lit two smoke bombs, one red, one blue, and rolled them under the table.

"Duck!" Nudge yelled. I'd learned to do that without thinking when she said it, so I dropped to the floor. She was there, too, leading me to one of the wooden panels of the windowed wall. When she pushed it, it swung open, and we scrambled through as fast as we could.

Then we belly crawled down the carpeted hall to the fire exit, glass spraying all around us as the windows were shot out. Screams of pain and anger were everywhere, but I couldn't tell if Pietro's voice was among them. I didn't know if his father had gotten off a successful shot or not. We reached the fire exit and took off, shooting up into the sky like rockets. We hovered over the greenish-gray clouds for a couple minutes and were quickly joined by Angel, Iggy, Gazzy, Max, and Fang.

Angel looked breathless. They all had smears of red or blue powder on their faces.

"Okay," she told me. "You know how I said you were there to learn?"

I nodded.

She pointed down, where we could barely see faint wisps of colored smoke coming out of the building. "Yeah. Don't do it like that."

CHAPTER 83

Max

Yeah, that had gone well, if you call a total failure "well." I was surprised—the Angel I knew could pretty much make anyone do anything. Ten years later, I'd figured her personal power had only increased, but it definitely hadn't worked this time. God, it was so weird to see everyone ten years older. And the first time I'd seen my unhealthy, bony, but clean face in a mirror—well, let's just say it had been a shock. Fortunately, ten-years-older Fang still loved me. And ten-years-older Fang was hot, hot, hot.

Oops, I realized the Flock had left me behind while I spent too much time thinking about how hot Fang still was—we were circling and changing altitudes a bunch of times to make sure we weren't being followed by drones. *Okay, come on, Max. Use your remaining brain cells.* I'd been briefed on the City of the Dead and the people involved. And I was glad that Hawk had brought useful intel.

I glanced over at her, flying in Gazzy's slipstream. She didn't fly well. I mean, she was fine, she wasn't a rock dropping out of the sky, but she wasn't that smooth or graceful, and it kind of hurt to see my kid struggling instead of just being a natural at flying. Just then Gazzy told her to roll her shoulders back and use those muscles. I saw her try it, then cursed myself for not giving her the tip on my own.

We were here, the three of us: me, Phoenix, and Fang. We were flying together, like I'd dreamed we'd do ever since she was born. I should be bursting with happiness, but instead I was almost rigid with tension. I'd been apart from the Flock for ten years. Once we had been a finely tuned guerrilla unit. I felt we could slip into those roles again, given time. But Phoenix? The last time I'd seen her, she was five years old. If she'd lived with Fang or the Flock this whole time, she might be ready to take her place in our unit. But not like this. She was street-smart and knew the City of the Dead really well, but she didn't know our ways, and the street was clearly where she belonged; not the sky. At this point, she was basically tagging along.

When Phoenix was about two, and the memories of how totally heinous childbirth was had sort of faded a little, Fang and I talked about having more kids. But we were still living underground, the world was still deep in a nuclear winter, and it didn't seem like a good idea. I wondered now if we should have. If having a sibling like her might have helped make Phoenix more...well, more like one of us.

"You know—"

Phoenix's voice startled me out of my memories.

"You know," she said, "I've been thinking about Giacomo's paranoia—that he thought Pietro would try to take over the family business. I mean, Pietro is my age. And I know him. We were pretty good friends. I don't think he'd overthrow his own father, and I don't think he'd be supported within the family, either."

Phoenix wasn't Phoenix anymore—she was Hawk now, only a few years younger than I'd been when I had her. And she was talking to me like a grown-up. And she was taller than me.

"Max?"

She was looking at me, frowning slightly.

"Sorry," I told her. "Lost in thought. But I'm listening. What about Uncle Felipe?"

"I don't think the rest of the family would want someone so young in charge," Phoenix said. "And then there's all of the Six. Are they McCallum's bitches, or what?"

My daughter talked super rough. The same way I did when I was her age. Of course, she'd had to grow up rough, on the streets. Alone. Somehow she had survived. Probably by developing the same kind of skills I'd developed as a little kid. No line too far to cross. I shuddered a little bit, thinking of the things I'd had to do, wishing my kid hadn't. The guilt swelled up from inside, heavy like a rock. I was surprised I could keep myself aloft.

And now I was doubting her, after everything she'd been through. I tuned in again to listen to her voice—a little husky, sharp as a knife when she wanted it to be.

"Nah," she was saying, thinking out the answer to her own question. "McCallum would never share power with anyone else. So how did the Six manage to carve the city up? Why does McCallum let them have any power at all?"

I looked at her. "Point your toes," I said. "Keep your body up and high, parallel to the ground, and point your toes."

One black-eyed look at me. One blink. Then she pointed her toes, or as much as she could in her heavy black army boots.

"It's about being as streamlined as possible," I said. "Like a missile."

"Uh-huh."

Maybe I had been a bit abrupt. "Tell me more." I went on. "You know this city so well. You know all the players."

That earned me a "God you are so stupid" look. So my mom skills were right on track...and so were her teenager skills. Looks like I'd better stick to what I know best. Flying.

"Okay, this sounds like it's not true, but it is," I said. "But you go faster by taking long, deep strokes with your wings, instead of shorter, faster ones."

Her face closed, anger erupting at yet another tip from me. "Gosh, too bad I didn't have any goddamn parents to teach me all this crap when I was little!! Then maybe I'd know how to do it right!"

And with short, fast strokes, she zoomed away from me, from the Flock, headed for Tetra.

"Sweetie, I love you," came Angel's voice inside my head. "But my god are you a freaking idiot. Leave her alone, for god's sake!"

"How can I leave her alone?" I screamed. "She's a total rookie! She's gonna get us killed!"

Angel was silent.

CHAPTER 84

When I finally dropped through the narrow gap that led down into the entrance of Tetra, I was in a totally pissy mood and felt ready to let that kid have it. Like, *my* childhood hadn't been a *picnic*, you know? I didn't exactly have anybody holding my hand, either. Basically it had sucked, then been awful, then terrifying and heinous, enlivened by little bursts of horrible! None of the Flock ever had parents, so where did Hawk get off acting like she was the only traumatized person in the whole world? Boo-hoo for the poor orphan!

I was stomping toward the quarters we'd been given when I ran into Angel.

"Please," she said seriously, standing in my way. "Have some chocolate. I'm begging you."

I opened my mouth to bite her head off, but she popped a piece of chocolate into it instead.

I hadn't had chocolate in fifteen years, since the world had exploded. My taste buds blew up, that unmistakable scent of cocoa and fudge and chocolaty goodness flooding my mouth.

"Oah mah dod," I said, chewing with my eyes closed.

"Listen," Angel said, now that my jaws were practically glued shut with chocolate. "I hear you, about Hawk. No, she's not a perfect puzzle piece in our little family. She's not a trained sniper, she can't swim, she's not a great flier. But you said it yourself. She knows this city, knows the players. She's tough, can fight, has a knife in her boot. You need to cut her some slack."

I swallowed, then said, "Ange—what if cutting her slack gets us all killed? Believe me—she's my baby. When we left her it tore my heart out, and I made myself sick, thinking about her, wanting her back, hoping she was okay and with Fang. But this is *now,* and *now* we have an important mission to do, a dangerous mission. You know that a weak link *means people die.*"

Angel took the other half of the chocolate bar and bit off a small piece. Her face wasn't melting with pleasure the way mine had. I knew my words weren't landing well with her, chocolate or not.

"I'm not saying she can't be valuable," I said more calmly. "She knows everything about this city. She can provide useful intel. She can stay hidden and help coordinate communication. Or something."

Angel gave me the sideways glance that still made me nervous.

"She and Clete have important roles in the rally tomorrow."

"Huh?"

"The rally," Angel said. "Remember? That we're planning? It's tomorrow and I've gotten confirmations from a lot of people that some of the main players will be there. I want Hawk to help identify them. And she has to be with Clete when he brings the city down."

"Why does she have to be with Clete?" I asked, my eyes narrowing.

"Clete functions better when Hawk is around," Angel said. "And I need him to be in the middle of the rally. So that's where Hawk will be, too. It'll be taking place in the city's largest open space—Industry Park. We've worked hard to get the word out."

I snatched the rest of the chocolate bar. Angel didn't deserve it. "I don't want her there," I said. "And you shouldn't, either, if you cared at all about the safety of the Flock." With that, I stomped off, the chocolate suddenly bitter in my mouth.

CHAPTER 85

Hawk

Did Angel have a dark side? I really wanted to ask one of the Flock but didn't want to piss anyone off...especially Angel if she *did* have one, because something tells me it would be super bleak. If she was really like she seemed, then she might be my favorite person ever, which of course, just makes me more suspicious of her. Nobody can be that good. Not in my experience.

I mean, she can't be my favorite person ever, anyway, because I still have my lab rats. And Nudge. Nudge was definitely in the top two grown-ups who were my favorite—neither of which were my parents.

Max—well, Max just got on my nerves.

I was headed to the Care Center when Fang appeared out of the shadows so suddenly I took a swipe at his face. He dodged it easily, which only made me more irritated.

"Yeah?" he said cautiously.

"Creeper!" I said. "Don't just lurch out of the shadows at people!"

One side of his mouth rose slightly. He smiled even less than I did, which was saying something. "I've always lurched out of the shadows at people. It's what I do. There's someone above that wants to talk to you," he said, pointing up to the narrow opening that led to the outside world.

I crossed my arms and tried to stare him down, but it didn't work. "Who could possibly be above that wants to talk to me? Everyone I know is down here."

"It's that kid from the meeting of the Six," Fang said. "The one whose dad took a shot at him. He came here in an ultra-light about an hour ago."

Pietro? He had made it out of there alive, after all! How had he found out about Tetra? I looked at Fang's dark eyes, wondering if Pietro's coming here meant Tetra was in danger. Having any one of the Six here could be bad news. Fang must have seen the worry in my eyes.

"Is he your friend?" Fang asked.

I frowned. "He was when we were kids." The truth is, I didn't know what we were now. There was a weird kissing moment, but I also couldn't say for sure that he wasn't a cold-blooded murderer. Both things made the question of whether or not Pietro was my friend pretty complicated.

"Go talk to him." Fang said.

So far, nothing the Flock had told me to do had been bad. Crazy and dangerous, sure. But not *bad.* They hadn't steered me wrong. They seemed to mean everything they said. Even Max.

"Fine," I said, and took a couple steps before I jumped up in the air and snapped my wings out with a satisfying whoosh. When I glanced down at him, he had a weird look on his face. What was it? I soared through the opening into the night air and then I realized what I'd seen on his face.

Pride.

I landed—I'd been working on landing silently and gracefully, like the Flock.

"Hawk," came a voice out of the darkness. "Thanks for coming."

I didn't answer him right away, instead just looked at Pietro, trying to get a read on him. Had he really been trying to overthrow his dad? If he had, then this was a dangerous meeting—not only for me but for Tetra. As far as I knew, no one in the City of the Dead knew about Tetra. I certainly hadn't. How had Pietro found it?

"What do you want?" I asked.

"I wanted to tell you...something."

I turned and walked out into the desert. Unlike the City of the Dead, where it was never really night, out here nighttime was a deep, velvety blackness, with no streetlights or stoplights or store signs or anything. I walked out into the dark, leading Pietro away from the entrance to Tetra. He didn't need to know any more than he already did—which was already too much.

The dirt beneath my boots was hard-packed, dotted with dead brush. Pietro followed behind my long strides, trying to keep up. Was Pietro my friend, like Fang had asked? Could I trust the boy following me out into the darkness, or was he a danger to both me and this city—the one place I felt safe? My thoughts made me tense, my shoulders hard as iron as I walked.

But Fang knew where I was, and with who. He wouldn't have sent me up here if he thought Pietro was a threat. And he'd be on guard to keep Tetra safe, just in case.

"Hawk!" Pietro called from behind me. "Wait! I need to tell you something important!"

CHAPTER 86

"Yeah? Like what?" I called over my shoulder. "Like how that supposed peace meeting with the Six turned into a bloodbath?"

Even in the dim starlight I saw the anger on Pietro's face. "That was my father, not me!"

"Why were you even there?" I demanded, still walking, my eyes sweeping the area around us. It seemed like I was alone, at least.

"I was there because my father was out of town," Pietro said. "Damnit, stand still for a second!"

I stopped. He came to stand in front of me, put his hands on my shoulders.

"My father was out of town," Pietro said more calmly. "I thought he was staying out on purpose in order to miss the peace meeting, so that nothing could be accomplished. I went, so at least someone in the Pater family would be there. Then *he* showed up."

He dropped his hands and walked away from me, his back rigid. I waited.

"Now I wonder if the other five knew that my father

wouldn't show—or maybe just some of them did," he said, turning back to me. "Some of them might actually want peace. But the Chungs, the McLeods, and the Paters," he said bitterly. "We don't. My father didn't want me ruining everything by brokering peace with his enemies."

"Because...it would interfere with business?" I probed, hoping to gain some useful information out of this to take back to the Flock.

"What's the worst thing that could happen to him?" I asked. "Or his business?"

"Those are one and the same," Pietro said, looking unhappy. "You can't separate my father from the business. They feed off each other."

I tried not to let the look on Pietro's face get to me, tried to keep this meeting strictly a fact-finding mission, nothing personal. But what had never occurred to me was that you could have a dad and still be unhappy. Pietro clearly was.

"Okay," I said. "So what's the worst thing that could happen?"

Pietro looked up. "Peace."

My mind raced ahead, wondering what that meant, following a logical path to get to the answer. I was so lost in my own thoughts that Pietro's next words took me by surprise.

"If only I could trust you," he said.

"Trust *me*?" I exclaimed, my eyes wide. "You don't trust *me*? How can I trust you? I saw that Chung kid dead in the street, remember."

Now Pietro looked surprised. "I told you that wasn't my fault! And you must have believed me. Who did you come to when you were hurt?"

I clenched my hands in my pockets so my fingers wouldn't automatically go to the C-shaped scar on my cheek. *C* for Chung.

"I came to you because the Chungs thought I was your girlfriend! I figured it was partly your fault it happened at all. You might as well be part of the cleanup!" Also because I hadn't thought I could fly twenty more meters without dropping from the sky. That, too.

"Oh." Pietro frowned and looked back toward where the City of the Dead made a fungus-like orange blob on the near horizon. "I had hoped it meant that you trusted me."

"Trusted you?" I shook my head. "We haven't really been friends since we were kids," I said, and he winced, causing a twinge of guilt in my gut. Time to change the subject. "What did you want to tell me? You said it was important."

He looked at me again, his face sad and older than it should have been. He shrugged.

"It doesn't matter. It isn't important after all. And you're right—we don't really trust each other."

I gaped after him as he took off toward his ultralight, first walking fast and finally running, as if he couldn't breathe the same air as me for one more minute.

CHAPTER 87

"I can't," Clete said. "It's bedtime." He looked at his watch anxiously.

I'd found him in one of the meeting rooms when I returned from seeing Pietro. A couple of Tetra's leaders were with him: Bimi, a small woman who always looked like she could use a trip to the toilet, and Terson, a guy who was built like one of the prison guards from back home. I guess if you can't fly, climbing in and out of this place must really build up the pecs.

"Hawk!" Clete looked happy and relieved to see me. "Tell them it's bedtime."

Clete liked order and for things to happen the way they were supposed to. At the Children's Home, it had been hard to be predictable. When you don't even know if you'll eat every night, it's kind of tough to keep regular meal times. Still, I'd tried my best. Any bump in schedule could make Clete melt down.

"Yep, it's bedtime," I agreed, and saw Tetra's leaders get tense. "What's going on?"

"Clete was showing Terson and me his plans to help tomorrow," Bimi explained.

"What plans?" I asked, some of the tenseness leftover from talking to Pietro seeping into my tone.

Clete stood up, all two meters tall and hundred ten kilos. He swallowed anxiously and looked at his watch, painfully aware that it was now *past* bedtime.

"I can disable the Voxvoce," he said. "And like their guns and all."

"We just need to understand how," Bimi said.

I looked at Clete, remembering the promises he had made while he folded laundry back at the Children's Home. "You've been working on this for years," I said. "Do you have it now? Can you disable guns and the Voxvoce, really, truly?"

"Uh-huh. Really, truly," he said, nodding his head. "I promise, Hawk."

I patted him on the shoulder. "Good enough for me! Go to bed."

Smiling, Clete grabbed his beat-up computer and hurried out of the room.

"He likes to keep a schedule," I explained to Bimi and Terson. "If you made him stay here one minute longer, you would've seen a meltdown big enough to pollute Tetra's air as badly as the City of the Dead."

They looked unhappy, glancing at each other as the door closed behind Clete. "We really need to understand how he plans to do this," Terson said.

"Why?"

"Because we're counting on disabled weapons at tomorrow's rally," Bimi said. "If Clete's plan doesn't work, people could die."

"That's like, a *Tuesday* for me," I said, shrugging.

The door opened and the whole Flock came in, pushing Terson and Bimi closer together, almost shoulder to shoulder. They frowned, having clearly lost control of the whole meeting.

"Hey," Nudge said. "I hope everyone is ready for tomorrow. We've invited the Six families, but also everyone in the City of the Dead. We flew over and dropped leaflets a few minutes ago."

"It was like tee-peeing a whole city," Gazzy said cheerfully.

"You invited everyone in the city?" I said in disbelief. "And the Six?"

"Yes," Bimi said. "So you see why we're anxious that Clete's plans work."

"He said they would," I said defensively. Inside, I really, really hoped that Clete knew what he was doing. Because if he didn't...I mean, I had a few things on my conscience already. I didn't need the bloodbath of an entire city added to it.

"Okay," Gazzy said, clapping his hands. "So the plan is to meet at Industry Park in the City of the Dead at ten tomorrow. "Max is gonna speak, and maybe Angel. Iggy, Nudge, and I are going to be on the perimeter."

"What about me?" I asked. "I can do overheads, or undergrounds. I know that city like Calypso's freckles."

"We were hoping you would be with Clete," Bimi said. "To help him or protect him."

I nodded, liking the sound of that. If anybody would be able to keep Clete together during the rally, it'd be me. My eyes bounced off of Max's. She hadn't spoken to me at all; hadn't even acknowledged that I was in the room. Why was she watching me? I flipped her off. Gazzy laughed, quickly covering it with a cough.

Terson cleared his throat. "I hope you understand that very few Tetrans will be at the rally. We've escaped the City of the Dead, and most of us never want to go back for any reason. But there are about six of us who will go with you. Your mission is worth it."

"Toppling totalitarian governments is always worth it," Max said.

"It's what we do," Angel said. "But…" She gave everyone a hard stare. "In order to topple governments, you need to get a good night's sleep."

I awoke too early on the day of the rally because I'd dreamed I had an anvil on my chest, making it hard to breathe. I opened my eyes to find that I really did have a weight on my chest. The dim blue nightlight outlined a pair of pointy, fuzzy ears.

Io leaned down and whispered, "I can't sleep."

I patted the space next to me and she hopped off, turned in a circle three times, then curled up and closed her eyes. One paw reached out and rested on my arm. Soon gentle snores filled the air. Ridley, on her perch in the alcove, blinked once at me. I made a face back, then tried to sleep. I knew the rally was going to be hard.

I just didn't know how hard. Or how high the price would be.

CHAPTER 88

I'd never seen so many people from the City of the Dead in one place, ever. Industry Park was a huge rectangle of dirt, with some depressed bushes and a couple of broken benches—not the kind of place you wanted to hang out. Opes didn't even crash here unless they didn't have a choice. But it was the biggest open area in the city, and since everyone was coming, that was what we needed.

There were many, many Opes, no doubt hoping for food or begging opportunities. There were tons of regular people, too—clean people wearing nice clothes, talking on phones, looking insecure about having wandered into the wrong side of town. On the sidelines, raggedy street performers juggled, spit fire, walked on stilts, hoping to pick up a few spare coins for their talents. I was pretty sure no one here had any idea what was coming. It wasn't going to be a picnic, and sure as hell was no circus.

So far I hadn't seen anyone from any of the Six, and I hoped they wouldn't come. Nothing was improved by adding the Six. The Flock thought they could win against them somehow, but that sounded like a Rainbow fantasy.

Now the crowd started murmuring, looking at the large stage that had been set up with towers of speakers on each side. Where had all this stuff come from? I saw some words stenciled in white on a speaker and squinted, using my hawk-vision to see.

It said: "Property of the Pater Family. Use only with permission."

Had Pietro helped them? Was that what he had wanted to tell me at Tetra? I prayed the Flock hadn't gotten those speakers from Giacomo, because if so, they were full of dynamite or something.

As for me, I was with Clete toward the back of the crowd, on top of an enormous statue of McCallum. I'd flown here before dawn, and Fang had brought Clete. I felt better knowing that Clete was secure up here. He hated crowds, and this one was turning into a doozy.

"There's so many people," Clete said, sounding nervous. He shifted anxiously on McCallum's wide stone shoulders. Below us, even more people streamed in through the park gates.

"When are you supposed to do it?" I asked.

"When Angel gives me a signal," Clete said. "She said to be sure to wait for her signal."

"Okay. And ... you're positive it'll work?"

"Yeah, I'm positive." Clete opened his computer and looked at the cracked screen. "I have two different programs. Well, three, but two we'll use today." His fingers clicked on the keys.

On the buildings around Industry Park, huge vidscreens were showing their usual fare: stories about people being loyal, cartoons about animals following the rules, and harangues by McCallum.

Attention shifted from the screens to the stage when Angel appeared, motioning for people to quiet down. She tapped the microphone to make sure it was on.

"Many of you may have heard about the revolutionary Maximum Ride," she began loudly, and a chill went down my back right between my wings. That was my mom. The revolutionary Maximum Ride. Someone I'd idolized and looked up to...until I found out she was my mom. Then I treated her like crap. Huh. Weird.

"But you may not have seen her," Angel continued. "She's been in one of the deadliest high-security prisons that any government has. She has defied death, not just once, but many times. And she defied death to be here with you today."

People started clapping. Clete followed along, and I elbowed him to be quiet, not wanting to give away our position.

Max strode onto the stage, her usual poncho hiding her wings. Her long brown hair hung down her back, and her eyes were overly large in her too-thin face. Somehow she still got everyone's attention: the crowd got quiet. Max stepped up to the mic and held the stand tightly.

"Thank you for coming!" she shouted, and the crowd whistled and clapped. Even some of the Opes stood still and looked toward the stage—her voice was that commanding.

"Sorry if this speech is kind of rough," Max said, trying to be heard over the vidscreens, which were still spewing their dreck. "I haven't given a speech in ten years."

More clapping. Max seemed to be thinking of what to say, as if she were shuffling invisible pages. Then she looked up and said, "Why are you all here today? This City of the Dead has been marching along for decades, just as it is. So why are you here to listen to a revolutionary?"

Below us, I saw people in the crowd turn to look at one another. Just then the vidscreens changed from McCallum ranting to a typical cartoon meant to suck little kids into the McCallum way.

Max looked over at a screen and watched it for several long seconds as the crowd moved restlessly. People outside of the park were listening now, craning their necks to see Max on the stage. The streets were filling with rally goers, blocking traffic. Horns were honking angrily. What was Max doing? Trying to start a riot?

Some weird sense prickled the hairs on the back of my neck. I looked at Angel, who seemed calm. She hadn't given Clete any kind of signal. He sat next to me, tight as a piano string. I patted his knee reassuringly, but I didn't know if I was doing it to calm Clete, or myself. Something was off. Something was about to happen.

CHAPTER 89

"Look," Max finally said, pointing to a vidscreen, where a McCallum newscast showed sniffer dogs at work. "You see those sweet dogs sniffing out a traitor?" The crowd nodded and murmured yes. "Those dogs...those dogs are sniffing clean air. Clean, clear air. Look at that blue sky. That's awesome, isn't it?"

"I don't understand this," Clete whispered.

I shook my head. "I don't, either."

"And they're walking on green grass!" Max continued. "Clear blue skies, healthy green grass! *Those dogs* have a better life than you do! Where's *your* blue sky, and puffy white clouds? Do you even remember them? When's the last time you walked barefoot over fresh green grass?"

Thousands of heads swiveled to look at the vidscreen closest to them. It was true that the dogs looked like they were living in paradise. They sure weren't living in the City of the Dead. The crowd's murmurs grew louder.

"How long has it been since you saw blue sky?" Max shouted. "How long has it been since this city was clean and up-to-date? Since your water was safe to drink?"

Heads with every color and texture of hair tilted up to look at the ever-present depressing gray-blue bank of clouds, heavy with smokestack fumes. Clete and I carefully moved behind McCallum's head, out of sight.

"What I don't get," Max said, taking the mic off its stand and walking across the stage. "What I don't get is—*why is this okay with you*? Who among you is upset that the city you live in, that you're raising your kids in, is ugly and poor and dirty?"

Hands raised hesitantly, people glancing around to see if anyone was watching them, if punishment would be immediately doled out.

"There's no money!" someone yelled.

"Okay, there's no money," Max agreed, walking to the other side of the stage. "What else?"

"There's no jobs!" someone else shouted.

"Right," said Max, nodding. "What else?"

"There's no one to talk to! At the city offices, they're all empty, or filled with people who don't care and aren't going to help you!" That was a third person. Up on stage, I was still watching Angel, my eyes flicking between her and Max. No signal so far.

"Right," said Max. "The city officials don't care. What else?"

Everyone started yelling then. I heard "There's not enough food!" and "The police are corrupt!" and "There's too much organized crime!"

Max was quiet, listening. "Okay," she said during a lull. "You guys have a lot of real complaints. Now I'm going to ask you again: *Why is this okay with you?*"

The crowd was stunned into silence.

"*Because apparently* it is," Max went on mildly, walking around the stage. "If it *wasn't okay,* you would have done something about it. Right?"

"You don't understand!" someone shouted, and a few voices agreed.

"I *do* understand," Max said with solemn authority. The crowd went quiet again. "But I'm here not to be your fairy god-mother and wave my wand and make everything okay. I'm here to teach *you* how to *make* it okay."

Concerned silence. I watched Angel intently, but Max was grabbing my attention, I had to admit. My eyes kept pivoting back to her, riveted. She was magnetic. She was my mom.

"Each of you has the *power* to change things in this city," Max said, coming back to the middle of the stage and putting the mic into its stand. "But just a little bit, right? Because each one of you is only one person. But take *all* of you—"

Suddenly there was a reverb on Max's words. All the vid-screens changed to show Max's face, then pulled out to encompass her with her arms outstretched on the stage. The huge vidscreen Max looked this way and that, searching for the camera. I looked, too, and didn't see anything.

Frowning, half watching the vidscreen, Max went on. "*All* of you together—look at how many of you *want* change! All of you together are as big as an *army*! And you have the *power*! The power to take ba—"

Just then a screaming sound made me clap my hands over my ears. Something hot whizzed past us, maybe three meters away? In the next second the upper part of the stage's ceiling exploded and burst into flame!

"We're under attack!" Max spoke from where she crouched on the stage. She gave a cough from the smoke and said again: "We're under attack!"

CHAPTER 90

A harsh cry from above rang out, recognizable even in all the chaos. Above me, Ridley tilted her wings back and forth: danger coming. Then a clanking, rolling roar filled my ears even as the huge statue shook.

I leaned past Clete to look down the street, nearly losing my balance when I saw what Ridley was trying to warn me about. There was a *tank* rolling down Fourth Street. An actual *tank*, marked with the lotus flower symbol of the Chung army! Chung soldiers marched alongside it, roughly pushing people out of the way.

"Hawk?" Clete said, sounding worried.

"It's okay," I said softly and patted his hand, but I could tell that it was not okay at all. Sure, this was an anti-government, anti-McCallum, anti-Six rally, but a *peaceful* rally. At least...it was until someone blew up the stage. But, the armies of the Six never get involved—they let the police force handle everything. Yet here they were, in uniforms and helmets and guns, like a private army. An army of Chung fighters.

Because I was so high up, I could see far across the park.

JAMES PATTERSON

Diaz tanks and soldiers, marked with their gold crosses, were entering the park from all sides. The marching soldiers shoved people out of the way, and the long guns on top of the tanks circled threateningly.

"What's happening, Hawk?" Clete sounded scared, so I'd have to make this lie good.

"Um, the army is here to go to the rally," I said as I made sweeps of the park, rating the likelihood of danger. About an eight on a one-to-ten scale: it was all going to shit. How could I get Clete out of here? Fang had been able to carry him, but I couldn't, and I'm the strongest fifteen-year-old ever. But we were way high up. Maybe we could just stay here, ride out the clash? Mostly I had to keep Clete calm through it all, which... he was already rocking back and forth, as much a danger to himself as the gathering armies below. If he slipped off this statue...

Suddenly I heard a horribly familiar sound: machine-gun fire. It was unmistakable, even after only hearing it once in my life, on a bad, bad night. Now I saw it in daylight: the flaring sparks from the barrel of the guns; bright red splotches exploding on people's backs, sides, faces, heads; how those people crumpled; how other people screamed and ran, some trying to carry the injured, others trampling them in their rush to save their own necks.

The line of soldiers at the edge of the park was just firing into the crowd. Not even aiming. On the huge vidscreens, Max's face looked outraged, even amid the smoke and falling embers.

"Gaz!" she shouted.

Angel dodged the blazing bits of canvas as it fell. She came to crouch next to Max, raised her left hand, and made a chopping motion with it.

Next to me, Clete nodded. He hit four keys.

The shooting stopped abruptly, sparks no longer flying, no more red splotches spattering across the crowd.

Clete wiggled a bit, smiling.

All around the square, soldiers were looking at their guns, some shaking them, unloading and reloading them. No matter what they did, they couldn't get them to function.

"That was you?" I asked Clete.

"Yep," he said. "The government put a chip in all of their weapons, so if someone grabbed a gun away from a soldier, they couldn't shoot it. I deactivated their chips!" He was almost chuckling.

"Clete," I said, "you are a stone-cold genius."

And he was, but that didn't mean we were out of danger. The guns might not shoot bullets anymore, but they were still weapons. Army soldiers were using their rifles like baseball bats, slamming them into people's heads, their shoulders, their sides. Again, people began crumpling, or screaming and running away.

There was no place to run. Everyone was pushing against everyone else. I saw an Ope fall, holding up her arms. Panicking people, afraid for their lives, ran over her. One single person stopped and tried to rescue her, some guy in a hoodie. He grabbed her arms, hauled her up over his shoulders. She was unconscious, maybe dead. But he fought the crowd to get out of the square. I gasped when his hoodie got pushed back—it was

Pietro! What was he doing here? Why was he trying not to be recognized?

Then I realized—the tanks and soldiers on the far side of the park were Paters.

Max grabbed the mic again. "Who's responsible for this *slaughter*? The Six! The Six have too much power! The Six must be stopped!"

Angel tugged on Max's shirt, and the two of them ran off the back of the stage. A moment later, I saw them shoot into the sky like rockets.

"Stop the Six!" someone shouted below, and others took up the chant. "Stop the Six! Stop the Six!"

Next to me, Clete happily joined in. "Stop the Six!" he yelled.

"Shh!" I snapped and elbowed him.

Too late. Someone below looked up. Ridley screamed. A soldier took a long knife from her boot, her eyes intent on us.

"No!" I shouted, snapping a wing out to shield Clete.

Thunk! The blade went through my wing cleanly, pinning me to Clete's back.

"Oh!" he said, looking at me in surprise. Then his eyelids fluttered and he fell backward off the statue, taking me with him.

CHAPTER 91

We landed hard, my wing ripping with the impact. Clete was on the ground, but I'd landed facedown on a small stone edge around the statue. A fast, freaked-out self-check told me I'd broken at least two ribs—a feeling I knew well enough. Quickly I spit dirt out of my mouth and sat up, feeling the grinding pain in my chest, the searing pain in my wing.

The soldier who'd thrown the knife was staring at me, looking from my face to my wing and back again. Moving fast, I grabbed the knife, swallowing a scream as it left my wing, and hummed it at the soldier, burying it deep in her chest above her ribs. She blinked a couple times, then sat down as if wondering why she suddenly couldn't breathe and felt like shit.

"Clete!" I leaned over him, pulled him to face me. "Clete!"

His innocent face was calm, his eyes unseeing. I shook him. "Clete! Goddamnit! Clete! Come on!" I knew why he wasn't answering, knew the only reason why Clete could be this calm, even amid a panicked crowd. But I just couldn't let the truth into my brain. "Clete! Come *on*, let's go!"

The riot continued around me—people tripping over us. I

heard the whining rumble of the tanks, the shouts and screams of pain and fear, and still I sat there next to my friend. My brother. Looking up dully, I saw that I was right in the path of a tank's tracks. I had to move, fast.

Stifling a sob, I pushed Clete next to the statue so he wouldn't get run over. Then I saw it: a manhole cover, right beneath the Chung tank. I dove for it just as the tank's caterpillar tracks began moving. My heart pounded like never before as I pried the cover up with my fingernails. The treads were almost on me, but I threw myself into the hole feet-first, hitting some rungs before landing some twelve feet below. My ribs took another blow and I cried out, the pain squeezing around my chest like an iron band. I looked up as the tank's treads crushed half the manhole cover into place, flattening it like tin foil.

Weeping, I crawled deeper into the darkness, the truth surrounding me like a cold wind.

Clete was dead.

CHAPTER 92

I gave myself three minutes to get my shit together, broken ribs, dead friend and all. If I gave myself more than that, I'd panic. And I couldn't afford to do that, down here in the dark. I was shaking, panting, felt dizzy and sick. In the darkness I could hardly see my wing, but I knew it had a big rip in it, my feathers were stained dark with blood. My heart was practically banging against my ribs; whenever I moved, my broken ribs ground together and it was impossible to not gasp with pain.

I had only one thought: Clete was dead! I'd known him practically my whole life, had slept near him every night I could remember.

Shit! Wiping snot from my nose, I whispered every swear word I knew. Then I stood shakily. I had to find the Flock. Taking off my loose jacket, I folded my wing in tight, then tied the jacket around it and my broken ribs. Could I even fly? I wasn't sure.

Above me I still heard screams, pounding boots, metal hitting metal, metal hitting bone. I heard the shouts, even louder than the screams: "Stop the Six! Stop the Six!"

Okay. I was beneath Industry Park. I needed to get somewhere clear where I could try to take off. Clete's body was still up there. I couldn't do anything about that. Keeping close to one curved wall, I headed north.

As I moved through the city's tunnels, I tried to think my way through this. Where had Max and Angel gone? Where was the rest of the Flock? They were probably all carrying bombs, right? I wasn't sure—they hadn't included me in a lot of the rally planning. Did they not trust me? I remembered Max's words about how I was a rookie who would get them all killed, and I winced. She hadn't been wrong. I hadn't known what to do or how to protect Clete, and now he was dead, gone forever.

Was I supposed to meet everyone back at Tetra?

"Stop the Six! Stop the Six!" the crowd was still chanting, despite the soldiers coming at them. There had been tens of thousands of people there. None of the Six's armies could beat that many people, especially if they didn't have guns. So the mob might actually be able to do something. But what? The soldiers above were only lackeys. The real power behind the Six was safely ensconced somewhere, no doubt.

The only way to stop the Six was to—storm their palaces? Actually, only three of the Six—Chungs, Diazes, and Paters—had shown up with muscle today. They were the ones to focus on. I thought of Pietro, disguised, hanging out in the crowd, helping that Ope, even though he could've been killed trying. I thought of Giacomo, telling Pietro not to have anything to do with me.

Well. I knew whose palace I wanted to see stormed.

CHAPTER 93

Max

"Did you see her?" I asked Iggy. We were flying south, away from the rally. Rally! Try riot! Those armies had been told to go in and slaughter hundreds, if not thousands, of innocent people. People whose only crime was wanting clean air, clean water.

"You're asking the wrong freak, obviously," Iggy said dryly, and I rolled my eyes because duh, I knew that. Of course Iggy didn't *see* anything.

"Yeah, sorry." I dropped back to Angel and Nudge. "Did you guys see her?"

"No," Nudge said, looking concerned. "One minute she was on the statue, the next, she was gone. They both were."

"So maybe she took off, flew off somewhere," I said. I scanned the skies around us, but tamped down on the rising panic, refusing to let myself worry. Phoenix had made it clear that she didn't need any advice from me, so, *whatevs*. It hadn't been *my* idea to have her up on that statue of the huge nimrod.

"Hm," said Angel, obviously listening in on my thoughts.

"You guys ready?" Gazzy came closer and opened his vest to reveal more small bombs than I'd known about.

"Did you see where Phoenix went?" I asked him.

"No," he said. "But she's tough, I'm telling you. Wherever she is, she's kicking ass and taking names."

"Yeah," I said, my panic only subsiding a little. "What's first on our shit list?"

Nudge pulled a literal list out of her pocket and tried to read it. Since we were at twelve thousand feet, going fast, it was like trying to read toilet paper. She squinted, held the paper tight. "The dope factory," she announced at last.

"Let's hit it," I said, and pushed down hard with my wings.

Three minutes later we were over a god-awful ugly building, our eyes burning from coming down through the green-gray sludge they called "clouds." I felt like I was wearing a scuba suit filled with sand, and it wasn't only the air quality making me feel that way. The unbearably itchy and irritated feeling went below my skin, and since I knew myself horribly well, I knew it was because I was upset that I didn't know where Phoenix was.

We were expecting bullets to come at us, but it would be okayish; at this altitude, there was too much wind for regular machine-gun bullets to be super accurate. Still, they could now see us, so we could kiss our stealth plan good-bye.

"Okay," said Gazzy. "Remember to pull their strings at the last minute!"

I had already dropped mine. "Strings? What strings?"

"It's a new design," Gazzy called over to me. "An added safety feature! Ya gotta pull their strings or they don't go off. Cool, huh?"

"Oh, damnit, Gaz!" I said, already dropping out of formation.

"Max, don't!" Angel's voice was already fading high above me.

I could see my bomb—just a second ago it had landed on the roof of one of the dope factory's buildings. I could see it because it was neon pink. Gaz was trying to make them more festive.

Of course, this close, the guards' aim would be much better—but they weren't shooting. I landed for a split second, grabbed my bomb, and bounced back up to take flight. I saw the guards' furious faces, saw them yelling and throwing their guns down on the ground. *Of course!* I laughed—Phoenix's friend was supposedly able to dismantle guns. I hadn't believed it, but it looked like he'd come through.

Now I could see the simple cotton string Gazzy had rigged up. I pulled it, the bomb vibrated slightly in my hands, and I dropped that sucker.

Whoosh! Something fast and hot hit one of my wings, spinning me sideways. Had the bomb gone off too early? I was falling fast, losing altitude and gasping for air. Keeping my head together, I forced myself to straighten in midair and beat my wings—which hurt like hell—something was really wrong with my right wing. I looked sideways—it wasn't broken—I could move it. But it was burned, and where it was burned, a line of feathers fifteen centimeters wide had been scraped away.

"They're shooting flares!" Iggy yelled.

"Are you okay?" Angel asked, coming closer to me.

"No," I said, gritting my teeth and motioning to my wing, now spinning a rivulet of blood into the air.

"Oh, shit," she said, and deftly pulled a bomb string with her teeth while she did another one in her hands. She hummed them both downward, one, two, and we watched as large chunks of the factory exploded and went up in flames, the hot gust of air buoying us higher. Trying to ignore the burning, searing pain of my wing, I looked behind us and saw a dark figure shooting toward us.

Oh, thank god—Fang.

Then I saw the look on his face.

CHAPTER 94

"What *happened,* baby?" Fang asked, flying directly over me, matching wing stroke for wing stroke.

"They're shooting flares. And rockets," I said tightly. My wing hurt so freaking bad. Using it was definitely making it worse. "Where's Phoenix?" I craned my neck to look at him, and the dark expression on his face made my stomach knot.

"Next is the so-called Hospice House!" Nudge shouted and motioned where we needed to go. She took point and the rest of us vee'd out in back of her. Gaz was throwing bombs to us— Fang deftly caught his and dropped one into my hands.

"Do. You. Know. Where—" I started.

"I found Clete, the kid she was with, who stopped the guns," Fang said.

"What did he say? Was Phoenix still with him?"

Fang was silent for several seconds, and I wanted to swing my left wing up and *fwap* him in the face. "He's dead."

I just blinked.

"He was lying at the base of that stupid statue, dead," Fang went on. "His computer was smashed into atoms."

"And . . . Phoe—" I began.

"She wasn't there," Fang interrupted me. "But there were feathers covered in blood, and more blood in a trail to the street."

"Then what?" I asked faintly as my own blood seemed to leave my head in a rush. I shook my head and tried to clear away the fog taking me over.

"Then nothing," Fang said. "I didn't see her body—we don't know she's dead. But she's injured, for damn sure. I don't know if she was taken captive . . . or what."

Every single stroke of my wing felt like it was being hit with a blowtorch, over and over. Plus, it was now weaker than my other wing. Which meant I had to force it even *harder* to go up, go down.

We were flying right below the noxious city clouds and could easily see hordes of people swarming up the main avenues, looking like honeybees. They split off into different directions and I assumed they were heading for the Sixes' home bases. We had whipped them up into a frenzy, and now they were going to try to overthrow their corrupt overlords.

Even though guns weren't working, the soldiers had shown that rifles could still maim and kill, and now they were shooting flares and rockets. Lines of broken and bloodied bodies showed where the crowds had been. Even with my raptor vision, I couldn't pick out a body with a black mohawk, piercings, tattoos, and army boots.

That was good, right?

Fang's strong hands reached down to rub my shoulders, pushing aside my hair. "She's okay," he said. "I know that it'd take more than an army with tanks to stop her. She's strong."

"She's untrained," I said. "She's naive. She doesn't have the exper—"

"She's kept herself and her friends alive for ten years," Fang said.

I didn't say anything but yanked the string out of my lime-green bomb and hurled it down onto the hospice with every bit of anger and fear I had. It took out a quarter of the top two floors, shattering windows, flinging bricks and mortar into a sunless courtyard.

"That's my girl," Fang said, dropping his own bomb.

"What do we blow up next?" I asked.

CHAPTER 95

Hawk

I'd been walking for almost an hour, just to get way north, to where the Paters had their estate. I'd tried jogging and running, but it'd made my wing start bleeding again. My jacket was soaked, and I was definitely leaving an easy trail behind me. I'd also had to wade in icy water up to my chest, then stoop and walk almost bent double for almost a kilometer, my ribs pressing against my lungs and nearly stopping my air flow.

So now I was walking as quietly as I could. The worn leather soles of my boots were surprisingly silent, even over trash, tile, and wet cement. Every so often when I crossed beneath a manhole close to the surface I would stand and listen, careful not to let the dots of sunlight fall on me. I still heard angry hordes. I still heard the rumble of tanks and thousands upon thousands of feet as they tromped north. There was a huge contingent headed for the Paters'. I'd never seen anything like this, where all kinds of people from the City of the Dead joined together

Ernie leaned over me, grinning. "My lord Pater said double wages and extra beer for whoever caught the freak, an' I'm gonna enjoy it, I'll tell ya!"

I will never live down the shame of how little effort it took them to knock me down and chink my wrists together behind me. It was probably the easiest thing they'd done all week. I was injured, exhausted, had seen Clete die...all of a sudden I felt like I had no idea who I was or what I was doing. All of my confidence and swagger was gone, knocked out of me, just like my wind.

The two servants pulled me behind them with a rope around my neck—the understanding being that if I caused trouble, it'd be easy enough for them to drag me—and other servants cheered when they saw us. I was guessing their lives were super bleak, since catching a teenager was cause for cheering. Or maybe they would be punished for *not* cheering.

The men took me down a flight of stone steps, past the big wine cellar and cold pantries that Pietro and I had played hide-and-seek in so many years ago. Every so often it gave Ernie a giggle to suddenly tug on my neck rope to make me stumble. So far I hadn't actually fallen, *so screw you, Ernie*. Each time he tugged and I managed to keep my feet, I felt a little better. They might be tiny victories, but I was still winning them.

Since our childhood, vidscreens had been added in the hallway every ten feet or so, and of course the McCallum channel was playing nonstop.

"Remember," McCallum said, wagging a finger at the screen as we trudged by. "If you steal from your employer, you're really stealing from yourself! And if you see someone stealing from your employer and say nothing, it's the same as if you yourself stole!"

God, I hated him. I grabbed onto that hate, let it burn like a small fire in my belly, the only thing keeping me warm. At Tetra I'd heard someone call him a megalomaniac, and I hadn't known what that meant. They had explained it. Now I could confidently think, "What a complete asswipe megalomaniac" as we took another turn and went through a door into an empty room. I'd been expecting a jail cell, so this seemed better. At first.

Maybe this had once been a break room, or the servants' living room. It was a bleak, run-down shell now, with the plaster ceiling falling in, mold growing in the corners, the floor covered with a thick layer of dust.

Ernie turned me roughly and unchinked my hands, then yanked the rope from around my neck so hard it left burning scrapes in my skin. But I didn't cry out. It was one more thing I could add to my pride column.

"Be good, girlie," the other guard said as they left. "Someone'll be back to get you in a while." The heavy wooden door closed behind them, and I heard keys turning in the two locks.

"Goddamnit!" I swore, standing still as I adjusted to the dim light. This was not a good situation, and by "not good" I meant it was pretty freaking bad. The only window was a thin slit way up on one wall. I could get to it, of course, what with the wings and all, but there was no way I'd fit through it.

I realized just how much my ribs hurt with each and every breath, and how my poor wing was still dripping some cloggy blood every so often. Large, dark drops fell from my feather tips onto the dirty floor. I followed them down, sneezing as clouds of dust reached my nose.

Okay, think! This is a mess. No one is coming for you. Only you can save your own ass. Get on it!! It's like my own private McCallum Channel in my head. The Hawk Channel.

Could I fly up to the window, break it, and yell for help? Maybe, but what good would it do if I can't fit through the window, anyway? I could lie in wait for whoever came to get me, but with a bleeding wing and my breath only coming in short gasps, I don't know if I could take them—and I doubt there'd only be one. I started to feel deflated again, spinning my finger around one of the drops of my own blood. Some slid under the nail, sticking there. I'd been in tight spots before, and more often than not with other people counting on me, too. Where was my confidence? Where was my absolute conviction that I am Hawk, and I will survive? Where was the brilliant, unexpected show of power and brains that would get my sorry butt out of here?

Stuck somewhere in my mind, that's where.

I just had to get it out.

CHAPTER 97

Max

"They're just...so pretty!" Gazzy said, lobbing one bomb after another, making sounds to match. *"Pyoon, pyoon, pyoon!"* He gave me a cheerful smile, his long blond hair streaming away from his face. "It's like old times." Fondly, he looked down at the fires, the multiple explosions that his bombs had made. He sighed, his happiness almost overflowing.

Flying by his side, my own arms full of IEDs, I saw the destruction, the few dead people who hadn't gone to the rally, the shattered glass, crumbled bricks, gnarled and twisted metal studs, the plumes of smoke rippling upward. I couldn't feel the same way, not when I didn't know where Phoenix was. Or if she was even alive.

"Outgoing!" Iggy said, hurling a bomb down on a parking lot filled with army vehicles—cars, motor scooters, armored vans. One after another they exploded as their gas tanks heated up. "Better than any video game! Gaz, remember that time at the cabin?"

"That was like three lifetimes ago, but yeah, I remember," Gazzy said. "These schmucks deserve it, too!" Squinting a bit, he took aim, tilted a wing, and hummed a bomb down onto the biggest McCallum screen. It burst into a thousand pieces of glass, shooting sparks into the air and raining shards onto the people below, who screamed and ran for cover.

Gazzy looked first at me, then at Fang and Nudge. "Did you see that? Gotta say, today's models are a huge improvement over paper cups taped together, with a push-nail igniter!"

"Yep," Iggy agreed. "These are way more explosive, much easier to aim. And the feathers are a nice touch."

Gazzy's newest inventions were shaped like toilet-paper tubes and had three feathers notched into the end, like arrows. They landed where we aimed them, which was something new and different, and also meant less chance of collateral damage.

"Circle back," I called, angling my wings to turn in a big circle. I tried to ignore the throbbing pain the flare had made on my wing. I could still use it, which was the only thing that counted. Gritting my teeth, I kept moving on. The five of us flew right below the smoggy clouds of the city, searching for new targets. "God, there are already so many fires," I said, looking down. Smoke was flowing up from just about every city block.

"You can't make an omelet without breaking a few eggs," Iggy said wryly.

We flew in a big vee, with Fang taking lead. "This isn't a game though, guys," he said, speaking mostly to Gazzy and Iggy. "This is *war*. We might be up here dropping bombs like B-17s, but down there, they're going to figure out how to shoot us and how to kill us. So keep your guard up. They might be sitting ducks, but don't forget that the only difference between them and us is that we're flying ducks."

"Okay, that's it for the shit list," Nudge said, raising her voice so we could all hear. "We hit the dope factory, the death hospice, that horrible empty Children's Home, a lot of the prison, a whole bunch of the government buildings...what next?"

"I say we join the people below," Gazzy said. "For one thing, as much as we've done, we seem to have missed McCallum's headquarters. He's still yapping."

It was true. Far below us, huge vidscreens showed McCallum's purple, furious face, as he railed against the protesters and shook his meaty fists at nobody. "I am just like your father!" he was shouting now. "Like your father, you can trust that I know best! And like your father, I'll be punishing the wrongdoers!"

"Pretty sure he's talking to us," I said.

"Can't believe we missed him," Fang said, flying over me, touching my back with his cool hands. "We hit just about every place we thought he could be."

"We gotta find Phoenix," I said flatly. "Either her or her body. I need to know what happened to her. And, dead or alive, I want her back."

Of course everyone nodded, happy to follow my lead. Hell, most of them liked her more than I did. But she was still my kid, and there was zero chance that I was going to lose her again. So all we had to do was comb an entire freaking city, thousands of bodies, tons of wreckage...

"Okay," Angel said. "You want to do that now, or—"

I looked at her, her unfamiliar grown-up face, her sharp, wise eyes. Long, long ago, she'd been like my baby, my child. Like Phoenix, she'd grown up without me. I hadn't been there for either of them.

"Maybe we should storm the castle first?" said Gazzy, gliding closer. "If we help the Paters fall, that'll spell the end for the rest of the Six."

"I vote Paters, too," Angel said.

"There's a huge crowd heading up the avenue toward their estate," Fang said.

I was a mom *and* a member of the Flock. I wanted my child back, but I also wanted to finish what the Flock had begun. The two sides were having their own battle, one in my mind to match the streets below. I shook my head, told myself I needed to concentrate.

"Let's go blow up the Paters," I said slowly, and angled my wings to turn east-northeast. "Let's reduce their castle to rubble!"

And that decision, right there, was the turning point for *everything*.

CHAPTER 98

Hawk

I was in the bowels of the Pater homestead, locked in a room. For all of the thousands of fights I'd been in, I'd never, not *ever*, been *trapped*. Never been without an escape route. I knew this whole city from the air and underground, and I'd memorized escape routes from every possible place I could be cornered.

I'd just never counted on being cornered under the Pater mansion. The City of the Dead was a wrecked place where you could count on rot and rust to help you out of a tight spot, punching your boot through a weak spot.

But this was different. This place was built to hold people. There was the one heavily planked door, double locked, and one weensy window way up high that was too narrow even for a tall superthin bird-kid to slip through. That was it.

I'd paced patterns into the dusty floor—circles, like a chained dog, my blood mixing with the dirt to create filthy footprints. There were two places where the plaster was broken away down to the skinny wooden laths, and I'd tried punching through them. My knuckles were scraped and raw. It would have taken about a thousand more punches to get into the next room, which for all I knew looked just like this one, with another locked door. Besides, I didn't have the strength to break through a wall. My sides ached, my breaths coming in gasps.

The only other thing in here was a fireplace—not a huge, ornate one big enough to roast an ox, but a small one, big enough to *almost* warm mistreated servants. I imagined them crowding it during the long winters, the fire producing more smoke than heat.

Hm. I kneeled to look at it better. Yeah. It was tiny. Squinting, I lay on my back, slid into the hearth and looked up. And saw—*maybe saw*—a tiny bit of light, very, very far away. *Could that could be sky?* Maybe. Maybe not. I was underground, and the mansion went on for another three stories above me. That would be a long freaking chimney. And one hell of a tight climb.

But I was desperate. The jerks who'd locked me in had promised that someone would be back to get me soon. I assumed it wouldn't be to give me tea and cookies.

Oh, my god, tea and cookies would be so, so good right now. So would a little bit of medical attention, I thought grimly.

Getting stuck in a too-narrow chimney would be bad—they'd only have to shoot up or shoot down and I'd be a goner. Or worse, I could get stuck and die slow.

I measured the opening with my hands. There wasn't a lot of space, but whoever was coming back for me might have something worse in mind. And it wouldn't take them long to figure out where I had gone, either. I needed to move, now. Taking a breath, I scooched into the hearth and tried to stand.

"Achoo, achoo, achoo!" Just standing up I had knocked so much soot off the chimney walls that I was black from my head down to my hips, which was where I was stuck. I mean, I could still probably get back out, if I wanted to. My shoulders were scraping each side of the chimney, knocking loose more grimy soot. I wasn't sure if I could climb higher, or not. I was starting to feel...*terrified*.

I had to try. And I had to do it now. I sank down to gather my muscles and gave a big jump upward! Automatically my wings tried to snap out...and became feathery chimney brushes, sending a storm of soot into my eyes as I ascended. But not far.

Now I was about three meters up, braced in a small chimney with my hands on one side and my feet on the other, my wings pressed tight against my sides. My injured wing was bleeding again, the dark drops falling down below letting anyone who showed up know exactly where I'd gone. My ribs hurt so much that I would have cried, if I was the crying type. But crying wasn't going to get me out of this. Only upward motion would.

I reached forward, feeling for a fingerhold. Right above me, the chimney narrowed, probably to make a hearth for a fireplace on the first floor. I bet it was a much bigger fireplace, one for the family, not the servants. If I could climb out, I might be able to find a window. And if I found one of those, I could fly to freedom. But if there was a hearth, why didn't I see any light?

Carefully, dislodging approximately fifty kilos of soot with every movement, I crept upward. Soon my eyes were level with the hearth, but...this one had been bricked in. *Of freaking course.*

That's why there wasn't any light. The Pater family had probably updated the whole damn mansion. For all I knew the fireplaces were just for show, and not actually connected to the chimney.

Soon I worked out a system of moving hand-hand, then foot-foot, and made it up to the hearth on the second floor, which had been partially closed in and replaced with a gas heater. I heard people talking and eagerly listened, but it was a couple of servants, anxious about the crowds they could see off in the distance. I wanted to scream, *Clean the goddamn chimneys once in a while, will ya, goddamnit?* But I didn't. If I got caught again, locked up again, I didn't know what I'd do.

I kept climbing. Ideally, I would have been able to jump four stories high, popping out of the top as fresh as a just-picked apple, but I couldn't. My legs had nothing to push off of, and were exhausted anyway. *Flying* upward also would have been *great,* but my wings were almost four meters across. I couldn't spread them, and I didn't know if my injured wing would support me, either.

Third-floor hearth, also bricked in. Freaking awesome.

But now there was definitely light above me. My muscles were shaking and I'd slipped a bunch of times. Soot was in my eyes, ears, nose, and mouth and had trickled down my neck beneath my shirt. I could feel it in a fine layer across my entire scalp. I would probably never be clean again. I didn't care. It wasn't like I'd been all that clean for the past ten years, anyway.

"Keep. Going. Hawk!" I hissed, and made myself move hand-hand, then foot-foot.

I heard pigeons. They made little cooing noises, calm and soft.

Suddenly the light above was mostly blocked! Had they found me? Was this where I would die? All someone had to do was lean over the chimney stack and fire!

Feeling like my blood had left my brain, I looked up. And saw...pigeon butts and little pigeon feet. Several fluffy gray pigeon butts, partially blocking the flue. How did they keep from getting sooty?

"Sorry, guys, coming through," I whispered, and poked one with my finger. The bird jumped up with a squawk, which alarmed the other birds.

When I hooked my fingers on the flue's edge and pulled myself up, several indignant pigeons were giving me the stink eye, hopping around and making it clear that I was in their territory, and they weren't happy about it. Too bad. I was out in the air again. And that, my little pigeons, belongs to everyone.

I hauled myself the rest of the way out the chimney stack, to fall to the red tile roof. I just lay there, facedown, feeling my sweat rolling, cutting dirty paths through the soot all over my body. Carefully I spread my wings out—they been squished against me for a while and were numb. I wished I could just go to sleep here. I wished there wasn't a revolution. I wished I knew where the Flock was.

I wished Clete was alive.

But, thank sun, I was out.

CHAPTER 99

It took a minute, but other noises started to get past the soot in my ears, other noises that were louder than the pigeons, who had finally settled. I shook my head to dislodge the soot, making the sounds clearer. Oh, good: What I was listening to was McCallum. Because he never shut the eff up.

"This misguided betrayal will only backfire onto you all!" he was ranting. "Where would you be without me?"

"Definitely someplace else," I whispered, my eyes still closed.

"What would you be doing? Who would be taking care of you?" he demanded.

"Definitely something else," I decided. "And, myself."

"You citizens need to stop this pointless foolishness and go home!" McCallum said. "If you do, I may possibly forgive you in time. Who knows? *Possibly.* So drop your weapons and go home! What you're doing is treasonous!"

I raised myself up a little and peered over the roof to the big vidscreen mounted on the building across the street. McCallum, red-haired and red-faced, was pointing at the camera. He leaned back, took a breath, and went on, "Are you serving your city, your *home,* right now? Or are you attacking it? If you're trying to attack your city, then you're attacking *me* and you're committing treason! Who am I going to take care of? Treasonous people or patriots? People who love their leader, or not? Huh? Who? *You tell me.*"

Oh, sun, I hated him so much. What a bastard! What an *unholy creep*!

Peering over more, I saw soldiers, some of them wearing Pater colors, wandering around in the streets. They were prepared for a fight—but their guns looked weird. I squinted, peering down to get a better look. Their guns were *old*—not the new ones with the chips that Clete had disabled! Old guns *didn't have chips*—so they weren't disabled. They could *shoot*! I edged backward on the roof before someone spotted me. Crap! I needed to warn the Flock, wherever they were! And I needed to not get shot myself—I already had a gash in my wing. I was just hoping I could still fly.

Suddenly, stopping McCallum just seemed so...*impossible.* I was only a kid. An awesome, kickass kid, but still. What could *I* possibly do? Right now, I couldn't think of a damn thing. I didn't even have one of Gazzy's bombs to drop down the chimney I'd just climbed up.

I sighed, feeling very tired and sad. Time to leave, before the guards came back and found that room full of soot and empty of myself.

CHAPTER 100

I stretched my wings out experimentally, knowing that flying was going to suck.

"Just do it," I whispered, and launched myself off the roof, beating my wings hard because I was only three stories off the ground. Catching the wind made the cut in my wing feel like it was ripping, and I shrieked inside my head.

"Hawk!" someone shouted. Pietro.

I glanced back and saw him standing on the balcony outside his room on the second floor. He was waving at me almost frantically, but I shook my head and started to bank to head south.

"I know where McCallum is!" he shouted.

Whaaat? I turned in as tight a circle as I could manage, looking everywhere for hidden snipers or soldiers. I didn't *think* Pietro would betray me...but I also didn't know what I could believe anymore, or who I should trust.

I got close enough to yell, "What do you mean?"

Quickly Pietro put his finger to his mouth, telling me to be quiet, and again motioned me closer.

Not sure if this was a huge mistake, I headed for his balcony, soot sliding off my wings in sheets when I landed. "What do you mean, you know where McCallum is?"

He looked me up and down. "What the hell happened to you? You a chimney sweep now?"

"Later," I said, and got ready to jump off the balcony.

"No!" he said, grabbing my arm.

I turned to stare at him, and he let go, his face flushing.

"Look, I know where McCallum is," he repeated. "Where he's *got* to be. I can take you there, if you want."

"Yeah?" I said, sneering. "And why would I want to?"

His brown eyes met my darker ones, his face more serious than I'd ever seen it, even than the night he'd come to talk to me at Tetra. I didn't know if I trusted him then; I didn't know if I trusted him now.

"We *have to kill McCallum,*" he told me, in a voice barely above a whisper. "It's up to you and me. We've *got* to take him out!"

CHAPTER 101

"Kill McCallum?" I exclaimed. "Trust me, I'd love to! But he's everywhere...yet somehow nowhere. He's on every vidscreen in the city, but no one's ever seen him in the flesh!"

"I think I know where he is," Pietro said.

"Okay, where?" I asked. "Tell me, and I'll go take care of it."

"We go together," Pietro said. "You'll take me to him."

I gawked at him. "Like on *my back*? Are you *serious*?"

"Not strong enough?" Pietro smiled, his mouth slightly cock-eyed, like he was teasing me.

"I'm strong enough!" I said, offended. "But I swear, if this is a trick, if you're leading me into a trap—"

Suddenly Pietro took my face in his hands and kissed me. It might have been nice, it might have lasted longer—but he pulled away in an instant, a black halo of soot around his lips. "Hmmm," he said.

I rolled my eyes to hide the fluttering in my chest. "You're gonna get a lot dirtier, if we're flying together. But if you're serious, then wrap your arms around me. One over, one under," I said, showing him. "Keep your body in the exact same line as mine. If you're off to the side and I'm trying to turn—"

"Yeah, okay, like a motorcycle," he said, his arms tightening around me. My ribs hurt, but I'd positioned his arms so that he wasn't putting too much pressure where I was injured. As for the weird fluttering in my chest...I'd worry about that another time.

This was just one more thing in a long list of incredibly stupid things I'd done recently. I didn't know if I could trust him, and I definitely didn't know if I should have let him kiss me. Plus, there was a big chance we'd jump off the balcony and go splat on the courtyard below, if he was too heavy. I'd never tried anything like this.

"Go!" Pietro said. I took a deep breath to fill my lungs and extra air sacs, moved my wings up and down to test their strength, and then one, two, three...

"Jump!" I said, and we both pushed off from the balcony. Sure enough, we sank very, very low before I got into a rhythm and beat my wings with everything I had. We rose, gaining altitude just as soldiers came tearing around the house. They took aim, then lowered their guns: if they shot me, Pietro would fall hundreds of feet and die. If they missed me but hit their master's son, they'd be in for a world of hurt at Giacomo's hands.

Concentrating on a strong upward move and an even stronger downward one, I managed to get us a couple thousand feet in the air. Let me tell you, it wasn't easy. Pietro was only a few centimeters taller than me but at least twenty-five kilos heavier? It was only my bird-kid super strength that kept us from plummeting to the ground like sooty rocks.

"We've never been this close before," Pietro murmured into my ear.

"Nope," I agreed, deciding not to remind him about the time I took a bath at his house. We might not have been as close then, but I was certainly wearing less. I turned my head so my words wouldn't be torn away by the wind. "Where are we going?"

"Downtown, close to Industry Park. Where the tall buildings are."

I nodded and adjusted course slightly, uncomfortably aware of the heat of his body. His fingers moved over my rib cage slightly, which hurt, then one hand moved to hold me around my hips. I'd never felt anything like this and wondered what he was doing. Was he adjusting his grip so that he wouldn't fall? Or was he flirting?

"You know," he said, leaning close to my ear, "you're amazingly skinny. I can feel all your bones. Even through the soot."

"That's it," I said, leaning into a steep bank. "You're going down."

"No, no!" Pietro said, clinging tighter and wrapping his legs around me.

"Don't do that! I can't balance. Or steer!" He unwrapped them.

Our motions had dislodged more soot, and he sneezed onto my neck. "Oh! Sorry!"

"Just tell me. Where. Exactly. Are. We. Going."

"The Marble Tower."

The Marble Tower. I knew it—everyone did. Once it had been really beautiful—the tallest building in the city—where every vidshow or talkie program was made. Sometime in the last decade, a lot of its middle had fallen out, leaving just the skeleton of its metal structure. Its once gleaming marble siding was as gray and graffitied and filthy as the rest of the city. I thought it'd been abandoned years ago.

"Huh," I said.

"Yeah. It used to be this...shining masterpiece," Pietro said. "I've seen pictures of it from when it was first built. It was supposed to be a beacon for the City of the Dead. Now it's just covered with *grime* and is halfway destroyed."

I circled as we approached what was left of the building. It was a colossal wreck, steel beams visible in places where time—and probably the crap air quality up here—had eaten away at it.

I kept dropping, circling the building, checking it for signs it was being used. I saw nothing—no soldiers at the bottom or middle, no lights on, no movement at the windows.

"If you're lying," I said slowly.

"If I'm lying, you can drop me, right now."

"Do *not* tempt me," I said—and then I saw it.

CHAPTER 102

Max

A thousand feet below us, the Pater estate was mostly in ruins. We'd seen at least thirty servants fleeing the destruction.

"We gotta do a couple more passes," Fang said as we circled high overhead. "I can see some structures underground, and he might have an escape tunnel."

"Okay," I agreed. "Two more sorties and then we'll regroup, make plans. Gaz?"

Gazzy flew over me and I held my hands up. He quickly dropped three IEDs and I caught them, stashing two in my pockets.

"Be fast," Fang reminded me. "They got their hands on some old guns."

"Got it," I said, starting to drop. "See you in a few." I flew strongly in a wide circle, well out of range of any soldiers, then started dropping altitude quickly, aligning myself with my target. I worked up speed, dropping and flying as rapidly as I could. I held one bomb and at the last second pulled the string and hurled it down into what I could see of a basement. Instantly I rose in a steep climb, hearing rifles being shot, and then feeling the hissing heat of bullets as they got *way* too close to me.

When I was a kid, this kind of stuff hadn't fazed me at all—it was only now, when I realized what I could lose—that I was squeamish.

Not that I would ever admit it to anyone.

I had two more explosives and decided to concentrate on the western end of the estate that was still relatively intact, so I circled once more and got ready to dive. Even from this height, I could see all the guards and soldiers, their weapons trained on me. Not everyone had been able to find an old rifle, but I still needed to make this snappy.

Folding my wings in back of me, I took out both bombs and held them close to my chest, then let myself point downward. *Let's see how they handle six hundred kilometers per hour,* I thought, seeing the world streak by below me.

They pointed, they shot. I ripped the strings out with my teeth and aimed the bombs, dropping them when I was barely twenty meters off the ground.

And, up! I raced toward the sky, hardly able to see because of my speed. Then I heard a whistle and something hit my head. It knocked me sideways, dazing me. There was tremendous pain, and suddenly I was falling, my wings out, making me spiral like a pinwheel as I plummeted downward.

CHAPTER 103

Hawk

Pietro had felt me stiffen. "What? Did you see something?"

"I think so." I tilted my head, automatically rising, wrinkling my nose at the smog I was sucking in. A thousand meters later I said, "I'm pretty sure I saw some soldiers in the deep shadows of the bombed-out middle. And the upper floors—when we went past a corner, we couldn't see through the windows to the other side. They've got the windows covered or blocked. They'd only do that if they were trying to hide something."

"Whoa," Pietro said. "Good eyesight! From the ground those black windows don't stand out at all."

"People expect 'em to be dirty, like everything else in this city."

"Okay," Pietro said, letting that opening for a crack pass. "Drop me off at the middle? I'm going to try to get to the top floors."

I caught an updraft and floated on it for a minute, resting my wings, thinking things through. The long tail of my mohawk streamed out in back of me. Flying is…beautiful, and part of me was dying to bank and head west, back to Tetra. Leave the City of the Dead behind me. Take Pietro away from Giacomo. Both of us starting fresh—not to mention clean—someplace new. That would be so—wonderful. Great. Awesome. Every other good word.

Instead.

"I'm going to rush into the middle superfast and then put on hard brakes," I told Pietro. "Get ready to jump or fall off as soon as we're over something solid. Then we'll take out the soldiers and head upstairs."

"Okay," Pietro said.

I banked, turning in a big circle that would give me enough time to build up some speed, even with this *tremendous weight* on my back. "Hang on!" I aligned my body with the building, pointed my toes the way Max had told me, and gave my wings everything I had. A fresh shot of adrenaline coursed through me, and my fatigue and pain faded away. Only one thing mattered now: to stop McCallum. Any way I could.

Pietro may have made some little sounds, but they were lost to my speed, my power. There was a big empty circle in the middle of the Marble Tower, as if it had been shot by the biggest bullet in the world. That's where I was heading. I felt Pietro's grip increase, felt his face burrowing into the crook of my neck.

In maybe three seconds we were there. I shot into the empty space at probably two hundred kilometers per hour, then backbeat my wings, dropping low enough so my boots could skid along the floor. Pietro rolled off as I continued to slow—and just as my toes reached the edge of the other side of the building, I stopped.

Turning, I folded my heated wings quickly, then rushed back to where Pietro was jumping to his feet. Almost instantly, two guards ran at us, their long rifles held like clubs.

I jumped sideways, hitting one in the chest with both feet. He staggered backward and I whirled with a roundhouse kick at his rifle, which clattered to the floor. A snap kick at his helmet made him reel backward, followed by a powerful uppercut punch under his chin that made his eyes roll up into his skull. He fell like a sack of rocks.

I looked up to see Pietro standing over his guard, holding something small and black. "Taser," he said, wiggling it at me.

"Nice. Take the easy way out," I said.

Pietro only shrugged. "It was a Christmas present."

I spotted a metal staircase and nodded toward it. Pietro went in front of me, stopping at the first stair to turn and face me. "This is gonna be my fight," he said. "You should clear out while you can. Thanks for getting me here. I won't forget it."

"You can either start climbing or get out of my way."

"Look, Hawk—"

"Move it!" I said. "My last Christmas present was a shank, and I'll use it if you don't zip your lip and start climbing."

CHAPTER 104

Max

Old habits forced me to straighten up and fly, damnit! I broke the free fall, but with both hands holding my head. A thick trail of blood spun away from me, and it felt like if I moved my hands, I'd be holding pieces of my skull.

"You got it?" Fang asked, appearing right under me. "Want a ride?"

"Man! Yeah," I said. "But let me puke first." I turned my head and did exactly that.

"Hate to be down there right now," Gazzy murmured.

Gratefully I landed on Fang's back, hardly making him sink, as if I were no more than a wish flower. I closed my eyes, held on to him with one hand, and kept the other one on my head. Blood streamed down his neck, falling to the ground like rain. It would leave a trail that anyone with half a brain would be able to follow.

"Relax," Fang said. "They can't reach us, even with old guns."

The Flock landed on the top of a tall building right at the edge of the city. Iggy grabbed me as soon as Fang's feet touched the ground and lowered me to the red tiled roof.

"Okay, move your hand," Nudge said, taking my wrist.

"My brain will fall out."

"If it does, I'll push it back in," Nudge promised, and pulled my hand away.

"We don't have time for this," I said, somewhat weakly. "We're at war, and we need to find Phoenix!"

"You're totally right," Nudge said. "Try to bleed slower."

I scowled, but that was hard to do because I was also half smiling.

"Got the first-aid kit," said Iggy, kneeling by me.

"You got hit by a bullet," Nudge said, her careful fingers parting my bloodied hair. "It looks like it impacted pretty hard, but it just grazed you. You got a hell of a hematoma, though. Wouldn't be surprised if it cracked your skull a little, underneath."

"So...she's *literally* so hardheaded that a *literal* bullet *literally* bounced off her skull," Fang said.

"*So* funny," I muttered.

Nudge smiled a bit as she clapped a wad of cotton onto my wound. "Hold this," she told Iggy.

Quickly, deftly, she wound a surgical dressing around my head.

I sat up, waves of nausea making my head spin. I concentrated on not puking again. Iggy gave me some tepid water to drink. I did, then wiped my mouth on my sleeve.

"We still haven't hit McCallum, apparently. He's still broad-casting," Angel said, putting one hand gently on my head. "Close your eyes for a second."

I closed them. She kept her hand on me and gradually my breath and heartbeat slowed. My thoughts changed from stat-icky, smeared pixels to cohesive sentences and pictures.

"Okay, you're fine," she said, and I opened my eyes, feeling 1,000 percent better.

"Let's go find Phoenix," I said, and one by one, we ran down the slippery tile roof and leaped into the air.

CHAPTER 105

Hawk

From the middle of the Marble Tower to the top was about thirty floors. I took the steps three at a time, passing Pietro at one point and leaving him way behind. My bird-kid systems of strength and oxygen delivery just worked better.

Soon I stood at the bottom of the stairs to the sixtieth floor and looked up. Like twins, two hefty guards armed with new guns stepped into view. I'm sure they were *very impressive* to the uninitiated, but I'm about as initiated as one gets.

"Hi, boys," I said. I dug a scrap of paper out of my pocket and scrutinized it. "This says the geocache is up here some-where. Did you guys beat me to it?"

"Private property!" one of them snarled. "Get lost!"

I climbed a couple steps. "This isn't private property—it's an abandoned building! And it's got my geocache in it! Now get out of my way!"

Very quietly, Pietro's tired footsteps reached my ears. He'd finally made it.

One of the guards aimed his gun at me and sighted down the barrel.

"I'm two meters away," I pointed out. "It's not like you gotta have crackerjack aim."

At last, Pietro rounded the staircase behind me. "What's going on?"

"They won't let me get my geocache!" I said, turning and winking at him so he'd play along.

"Got no idea what that is," Pietro said, like a moron. "But I'm Pietro Pater, this is my dad's building, and you need to let us up."

Well, okay, that was another approach. Maybe better than bluffing.

"We got orders to let *no one* in," one guard said.

"We're going in," I said firmly. "We can do this the humiliating way, or the *super* humiliating way. Up to you."

Once again the guard put the gun to his eye and sighted down the barrel.

I went up a step.

He aimed right at my heart and pulled the trigger from half a meter away. *Click!* Nothing happened.

I let out a breath. No matter how much confidence I had in Clete, having a gun fired at you point-blank is still pretty scary. "Sorry," I said, smiling at the guard. "The chips inside your guns are having a day off."

With a roar of rage, the guard lunged at me, swinging his gun like a club.

I grabbed the gun and used the weight of his own swing to yank him off the stairs, flinging him down to the stairs below me. Right as he jumped to his feet, I stomped on his instep, then whirled and kicked him behind his knee. He sagged but recovered quickly. I spun and knocked the gun out of his hands with an axe kick. It clattered to the ground and I grabbed it, swinging it at his head. *Wham!* I clocked him right on the temple and he staggered, his eyes crossed.

I glanced back at Pietro, who was just barely holding his own against the other guard.

My guy had recovered and surprised me with a fierce uppercut that made my teeth smash together. I saw stars but stayed on my feet, ducking down and aiming a completely enraged kick at his kneecap. There was a satisfying snap, immediately followed by a scream of pain, and my guy was curled in a fetal position, holding his leg.

I smashed him in the head with the butt of the rifle—a pity move to knock him out. There's nothing quite like a shattered kneecap to make you wish for unconsciousness.

The other guard was still swinging his gun at Pietro. I took a little hop, unfolded my wings, and flew over them to the top of the steps. The guard's mouth dropped open and he stared, which gave Pietro time to hook his foot behind the guy's ankle. They tumbled together down the last few stairs and ended with Pietro leaning way over the guy, still holding on to the gun. But something was wrong—Pietro was way too still.

Then I saw the blood running down the rifle, saw the smile on the guard's face. He lifted one booted foot and gave a mighty shove, and Pietro simply fell to the side, his eyes closed. At the end of the rifle was a bloody bayonet.

I only had time to scream, "Pietro!" before the grinning

guard had jumped to his feet and was lunging up at me with the bayonet still dripping my friend's blood.

"Oh, you son of a bitch, you're gonna pay for that!" I swore.

He only grinned wider, unaware he was looking at death's face.

I jumped up as he swiped at me, then whipped my wings out, startling him when the last bit of soot left in my feathers flew into his eyes. For just a second I hovered above him, inches out of his reach—then I whammed him with the hard, bony tip of my right wing, knocking the rifle away. In the next second, both my feet smashed into his chest with everything I had. It drove him backward in one brutal move against the stair railing. His arms windmilled, his smug face now alarmed.

I landed, grabbed his feet, and yanked them upward, flipping him the rest of the way over the railing.

He yelled for a surprisingly long time as he went down, his screams rising above the smog as he fell.

"Pietro!" I said, falling to my knees next to him. I opened his shirt, afraid of what I'd see. It was bad—close to his heart and pumping out sluggish blood. But he was still bleeding, which meant his heart was beating. So I knew he was still alive. I shook off my already bloody jacket and tried to make a compress, tying his arm over the wound for extra pressure.

That was all I had time for.

CHAPTER 106

That had been it—two guards with nonworking guns. That had been the sum of security outside this door. Pietro had been sure McCallum was up here somewhere. Time to find out. I charged up the last staircase, took the knife out of my boot, and simply lifted the lock's latch on the door. A rat could have done it. A rat with thumbs, sure. But still. I was not impressed.

I flung the door open, immediately stepping in and to one side so my silhouette wouldn't be framed by the light outside. Iggy had taught me that.

And...no one seemed to notice me. It was a—TV station? People were rushing back and forth. On one screen I saw films of the morning's riots. On another I saw McCallum yapping as per usual. And in a chair, surrounded by three cameras, was McCallum. *Or was it?*

I moved closer, my knife dangling inconspicuously by my side. People were shouting at one another, but it was stuff like "Cut in the drone feed!" And "Patch him in live! Cut the numbers in half!"

McCallum was sitting in a chair, very still, his head nodding.

I stayed back in the shadows, trying to sort out what I was seeing. Right now no one was paying much attention to him. Printers were spitting out long sheets of paper. There was a wall with at least twelve vidscreens all playing different things... and then you had—McCallum.

How could this be the same person who railed against the public twenty-four hours a day? He seemed so...low energy? And this close, he looked much older than he did onscreen. Suddenly a harsh spotlight clicked on and he bolted straight up as if electrified. His face contorted and the cameras moved closer as he, like, *came to life* to spout his usual crap—ungrateful citizens, everyone had a role to play in this successful city, he was gonna lower the price of dope to show he meant well.

"Cut in with the rabbits!" someone yelled, and on a couple of the vidscreens, a family of rabbits started keeping their eyes on a suspicious new family in their neighborhood. Even tiny Fluffums was on to them, and she could barely hop yet.

The light turned off and McCallum sagged again.

This was so freaking bizarre and unexpected and crazytown that for a minute I stood there, just staring. Then, as I circled warily, staying in the dim half-light, I saw a tiny, transparent wire going from his shirt collar up to his ear. Someone was feeding him—lines? Instructions? Dope?

I for one wanted to know who was at the other end of that wire. The studio was chaos, paper churned out of the printers at an alarming rate, but no one was reading them. The light was out where McCallum sat, the video of the bunnies playing on a loop. It looked like they were going to stay with that for the time being. So, I stepped up to the man in the chair.

He hung forward limply, his head sagging onto his chest. Who *was* he? He was weirdly familiar, and not just as the asshole who ran his mouth all the time. Who. Was. He? For some reason I kept picturing him on the vidscreen in the big room at the Children's Home. I remembered a bunch of us watching... what was it? I gasped out loud when it hit me, but luckily everyone was too busy going batshit to care.

This guy—being McCallum—was *Major Panda*! I used to *love* Major Panda! He'd made up some fake animal that didn't exist, then called himself that. Major Panda. *McCallum,* asshole *supreme,* used to be *fun.* Now he was a meat puppet being fed lines. From who? That was the question. Because Major Panda didn't talk about lowering dope prices.

I ripped the earpiece out, the man in the chair barely raising his head as I did. And then I listened.

My mouth dropped open again. *Holy shit! Oh, my freaking sun! That's who is behind all this??*

Suddenly, the lights around Major Panda's chair came back on, fully exposing me. He sat up, whatever dope trip he was on ended by the flash of lights. I dropped the earpiece, opened my wings to their full capacity, swung in a big roundhouse, and kicked that dirty, rotten conspirator Major Panda senseless.

I bolted for the door, leaving a confused clot of aides to watch as I spread my wings, and sailed into the sky.

CHAPTER 107

Max

"There she is!" I yelled, pointing. The Flock and I were right below the gross clouds over the City of the Dead, looking for Phoenix. And, as the only flying creature larger than a vulture, she was easy to spot. Thank god she was flying and not somewhere on the ground.

In a tight vee, we dive-bombed to her level.

"Phoenix!" I shouted, and she looked up. Did she seem happy to see me? I couldn't tell. Her face was filthy, and tear-streaked.

"I'm so glad you're okay," I said. "I know your friend Clete…" Her face scrunched together, and I could see her fighting fresh tears. Now was not the time. "Anyway, I was so worried about you."

"I could use patching up," she said, and she looked it. She was covered with blood and bruises, one eye almost swollen shut, her lip split and puffy.

"Have you seen the vidscreens?" Nudge asked. "The feed is

frozen—McCallum's not saying a goddamn thing! Something happened!"

"I did that," Phoenix said, but not proudly. More, like, sad. Like a soldier at the end of a long battle. "I think my friend Pietro is dying, back there. He was the one who showed me where McCallum was broadcasting from."

"Dying, but not dead?" Nudge asked.

"I don't know." Phoenix seemed whipped, her head hanging low.

"Tell me where," Nudge said. "I'll go check him out."

"Thank you," Phoenix said gratefully. She gave Nudge directions, and Nudge took off, her caramel-brown wings smooth and powerful.

"So where've you been all this time?" Gazzy asked Phoenix as we flew south.

"Um, I was in the tunnels for a while, then in the basement of the Pater estate."

"What?" My heart dropped into my stomach. "We bombed that to smithereens! Is that why—why—I mean, were you there? Did you get bombed?"

My daughter looked at me. "No—I escaped by climbing up a chimney."

"Oh, thank god," Gazzy said, putting his hand over his heart. "I remember *seeing* the basement, after our second or third round."

"I must have just missed you guys," Phoenix said, sounding bemused.

"What'd you do to McCallum?" I asked her, and she told me.

"Reeeaaallly?" I asked, an idea popping into my mind. "I think we should be able to take care of that voice permanently!"

"I'm in!" Gazzy said.

"You got a *plan*, Max?" Iggy asked.

"Yep!" I lied. But I lied with confidence, as I poured on the speed.

CHAPTER 108

"Remember that place we tried to have the peace meeting at?" I asked Fang as we flew. He was matching me stroke for stroke, our wings just a few inches apart, as if we'd been flying together every day for the last ten years. I felt Phoenix watching us.

"Yeah?" Fang said.

"They didn't pick that at random," I said. "Those guys—all of 'em—knew that place well. *Especially* Giacomo Pater. I'll bet you a tattoo that he's hiding out there, watching his world implode."

"I bet you're right," Iggy said. "That place is probably full of fake walls and secret escape holes."

"It's been around forever," Phoenix said, actively listening. I liked that about her. It reminded me of me.

"You know something that could help us?" I asked.

She thought, two fingers pinching her lip, exactly the way Fang does when he's running his little brain hamsters especially hard. "It used to be on a subway line," she said. "I don't go there much because it's full of guys with guns. The subway's been shut down for . . . six years. But the tunnels are still there."

"Good to know," I said. "Okay, my *plan* is that me and Iggy will go through the front door, try to find Giacomo Pater. Gaz and Fang, run interference from above."

"Got it," Gazzy said, unsnapping his backpack so he could pull it around front, see what explosives he still had.

"I'll back you up on the ground," Phoenix said, all no-nonsense.

Of course I wanted her a thousand miles away, or at least back at Tetra, wherever she'd be safe. But she wasn't a stay-safe kind of kid. I was going to have to accept that, if I wanted her to let me keep calling her *my* kid.

"Let's do it!" I said and angled myself to rocket downward.

From above we saw at least twelve guards around the place, including three snipers on neighboring roofs.

"Ooh, ooh! Let me!" Gazzy said excitedly, pulling a tube out of his backpack. "I've been practicing and practicing!"

I nodded, and Gazzy put the forty-centimeter tube to his lips. Phoenix watched him, studying Gazzy as he judged *wind* speed, *our* speed, wind *direction*. Stuff any of us could do in a second. Stuff she hadn't learned yet.

He loaded it up, aimed, then blew as hard as he could. A dart hit a sniper's back, and he sank to his knees, probably still wondering what had hit him.

"Way to be!" I told Gaz.

"I've always said he was full of hot air!" Iggy said, which Gazzy let pass because he was aiming for the second sniper. He hit her in the back of her neck and she went down.

We weren't so lucky with the third one. He'd seen the other

two hit the deck and was scanning the skies. He spotted us and held up his rifle, looking enraged.

"It's an old gun!" Phoenix yelled. "It still works!"

Quickly Gazzy whipped out an IED and hurled it down. "So does this!"

The explosion made the rest of the Pater cadre flood out of the house like bats at dusk, but we were ready, armed, and skilled at chucking Gazzy's bombs as fast as snowballs. By the time my feet hit the ground, there was only one guy standing: Giacomo Pater.

He grabbed an old automatic rifle and sprayed a round of bullets at us. But there'd been a reason all those guns had been replaced—after decades of use, the dang things didn't shoot straight.

When Giacomo saw that he'd missed all of us from thirty meters away, he screamed in fury and threw the gun as hard as he could. Because *that* works. Sure. Throwing a fit should always be the last resort.

"Your term of service just expired, you piece of shit!" I yelled after him.

CHAPTER 109

Hawk

The Flock was ice under pressure. They just *knew* stuff. How to coordinate attacks, how to take out snipers. It was all of them, working together. A well-oiled machine.

"Go, go, go!" Max shouted, already pounding up the steps of the club. She pointed to the right and left as she ran, and Fang and Iggy took off, I guess to circle the building.

That left *me*, and I jumped up the stairs after Max. She yanked the door open—there were cowering servants inside—and tore through the building. I was fast on her heels, ready to go into battle with my mother. But we were finding...nothing. She threw a look at me, and I started back through the rooms, roaring orders, kicking guns away, scanning each room for hidden doorways, nooks, crannies, little hidey-holes, anything.

"Phoenix!" Max yelled, and I ran to the hallway. With one hand, she held a cook's assistant by the neck—I saw the pink marks her fingers were making. In her other hand she held one of Gazzy's bombs. This one had a *fuse,* and it was sparking and crackling. I tried to keep extreme panic and a *what the almighty hell* expression off my face.

Watching me, Max nudged the poor sap with her elbow. He made no sound but looked down at one of the carved panels of the hallway. Silently, Max raised her eyebrows at him.

Gulping, the guy flashed a glance at a wall sconce that was a fat baby in a tiny diaper holding a light bulb. Max shoved him away from her, strode forward, grabbed the wall sconce and pulled, all while I was trying not to shriek, "Get that thing away from me!" I'd seen what Gazzy's bombs could do to people.

Sure enough, the wooden paneling slid to one side, revealing an opening that I couldn't believe fat Giacomo Pater fit through. Max motioned to me, and I dropped to the floor and slid through without question. She followed behind, tossing the bomb back into the room just as the panel slid shut again, leaving us in darkness. Everyone screamed, there was a muffled *pluff!* sound, and Max turned on her shoulder lamp.

"Glitter bomb," she said, "Gazzy likes to throw a few of those into our packs in case we decide to throw a party."

Together, we doubled over and started crab-walking through the low tunnel. We came to a four-way intersection where we could almost stand, and I held up one hand.

"Gimme a sec," I whispered, closing my eyes. I hadn't been under here in ages, and it was dry—no convenient wet footprints to follow. Breathing in, I figured whether the air was colder or warmer, stale or staler, thick with factory fumes or full of street-cooking smells.

Then I smelled...Pietro. Pietro's clothes—the detergent.

I opened my eyes and smiled at Max, my mother: Giacomo's clothes would smell the same.

"This way," I said, and started heading down the tunnel.

"Faster to fly," Max said.

Confused, I slowly extended my wings, which were about half a meter too wide for this tunnel. I knew Max's wings were wider than mine.

Shaking her head, she demonstrated: straight ahead on the foreswing, then pull them in enough to push back hard, then pull in again to go straight on the foreswing. It was amazing—a way to *fly* through tunnels too narrow for regular flight!

But could I even do it? It seemed like the kind of thing that needed practice.

Max must have seen my question, because she gave me a quick hug—one tall, bony female to another. "I think you can do it," she said softly. "We gotta go!"

And with that, she turned, launched herself in the air, and *flew* through a tunnel *too narrow* to fly through.

No wonder she was kind of legendary.

And I'm kinda halfway glad she's my mom.

CHAPTER 110

I was right; it would take practice. I sucked at it. I wiped out so much that Max got way ahead. It was amazing how freaking fast and smooth she could fly through a tunnel too narrow to fly through. I needed a couple of months to practice.

She didn't come back to me, though once or twice at a cross tunnel she stopped, landed on her feet, and looked back. I waved her on, took another running jump, and tried again. There were times when I could do it for like four or five wing strokes and I'd get so psyched, surging ahead, and then I'd get too close to a wall and tumble to a humiliated, scraped-up halt.

I gathered myself up, took a running jump, and...flew right past a four-way tunnel cross. *Which way did she go?* Urgently I increased my speed, knowing that if I messed up, I could really do myself some damage. But I needed to find her, make sure she was on the right path.

I got the barest hint of Pater's scent a split second before an electrical wire, stretched taut across this tunnel, almost sliced me in half.

CHAPTER 111

I landed on the subway tunnel floor, breathing hard, adrenaline lighting up my fight-or-flight cells, scared to move—waiting for my guts to start spilling out onto the cold, dirty ground.

Shit, shit, shit. What happened? I glanced up, saw the wire, saw how it was tied tightly to old hooks on either side, about halfway up the curved wall. I started panting when I saw a bright red pool of blood seeping from where I lay. *What... what...*

"Hello, freak," said Giacomo Pater, coming out of the darkness to stand over me.

CHAPTER 112

"You know my son," he said, looking down at me. I had no energy left, felt my eyes rolling in their sockets as I tried to meet his gaze. My blood reached one of my hands, splayed out on the concrete. I was shocked at how warm it was, spreading past my fingers. Holy shit I was messed up. Where was Max?

"I *hate* that you know my son," Giacomo went on. "I'm going to make sure that you never see him again."

I wasn't sure Pietro was alive, but I said nothing. Probably not a good time to tell him that.

"*Mercenaries* think they can take my city from me? It would take so much more than your tiny, mosquito army."

The "mosquito army," the Flock, had destroyed his estate and a whole bunch more of the city, but I couldn't speak. My blood had almost reached Giacomo's shoe.

"You're going to die here, today," he said, like he was having a normal conversation. "And so is that other one. Today you get eliminated from my life. Then things go back to normal."

He reached into his pocket and took out a pistol.

I'd never been so scared in my entire life. Never had any idea that *anything* could hurt this much. I wanted to scream and swear and tell Giacomo Pater how evil he was, that he had no home, how much I hated him. But I was a trapped rat, scared stiff and too wounded to move. I was going to die now. Like Clete was dead. I clenched my teeth so hard to keep my lips from trembling. To hell with Giacomo Pater. The city was forever changed, and I'd had a hand in that. It would never go back to being the desolate hellhole it had been.

But...I would never fly above the clouds, never again feel the sun on my wings, my face. Never talk to Pietro again. Never see my mom and dad again.

Giacomo Pater pointed the gun at my head. If he monologued long enough, I would bleed to death, cheating him out of his kill shot. I was light-headed and felt sleepy. I moved one finger a bit to see if there was any forking way I could miraculously leap up and save myself. My body's feedback was like, No. Find some buckets for us to be carried in.

Oh, goddamnit. Max, Mom, this would be a good time for you to find me. Before it's too late. If it wasn't already too late. I closed my eyes.

A banshee wail, an unholy *shriek,* made me open them. I had no more than a second to see the white and brown jet streaking toward us.

Max! Max?

Giacomo Pater raised his pistol and fired it just as Max screeched to a halt. The bullet hit her somewhere—her whole body jerked.

I saw the surprise on her face and tried to scream. I tried to say *Mom* but couldn't.

Max's face looked like it was carved from stone. Then one long, strong wing whistled through the air and smashed into Giacomo just as he shot the pistol again.

His face crumpled like rubber as his neck snapped, the sound loud in the tunnel. His head flopped grotesquely to one side like a puppet's just as Max collapsed to the ground, her feathery warmth covering me. Her body limp.

Hot tears ran down my cheek, and I wished she'd never found me. Not this time, not ever.

EPILOGUE

"How long will it take them to rebuild?" Nudge asked.

"Forever," Gazzy said, tracing his fingers over the rough rock wall of this Tetran room. "They'll always be improving. I hope."

"I know that they've opened twenty new centers to help people get off dope," Iggy said.

"A new, real Children's Home has opened in what's left of the Paters' estate," Angel said. "Pietro has chosen a manager, and they already have fifteen kids there. Kids who were foraging in the streets."

"The people rallied against the rest of the Six," Gazzy reminded them. "I don't see how they could ever seize power again. I mean, I'm hoping the new City Council does a good job, but it might take a while."

Nudge looked over at Fang, whose dark eyes revealed nothing. He was rolling a small rubber ball back and forth in his hands, not speaking. He hadn't spoken much since it had happened. You don't just get over—

"I like it here," Iggy said. "Despite—"

"There's a lot to like about Tetra," Angel agreed as Calypso climbed into her lap. The four antennas on her back were now so long that holes needed to be cut into her shirts. "I miss Hawk," she said, and Angel nodded.

Rain stood up, holding out her hand to Calypso. "Come on, sweetie. I'll tell you a story."

Max came into the room, wearing the loose linen clothes that most Tetrans wore.

"Unh," she said, sitting down by Fang. "I feel like crap on a stick."

Fang put his arm around her and kissed her hair. "War is bad, honey."

"You were shot," Nudge pointed out. "Twice."

Max leaned over the table and put her head down on her arms. "Maybe some ice cream would help," she mumbled.

"I'll get you some ice cream," Angel said. "Again."

"Ice cream sounds good," a voice said from the doorway.

"Hawk!" Angel went over and gave her a gentle hug.

"You're up!" Iggy said. "You didn't say anything this morning."

"Wasn't sure I could do it," Hawk said.

Max looked at her daughter, this creature that she and Fang had made a lifetime ago. She looked like shit. And it was going to take a long time to remember to call her Hawk instead of Phoenix, which was *so much better.*

Max held out her hand. "Can you sit in a regular chair?"

"I'll try," Hawk said, gingerly making her way over. "I'm not real bendy these days."

"It'll get better," Fang promised.

"I still feel...like that was all so bad," Hawk said, carefully sitting.

"It was war," Iggy said. "It was necessary, to free those people and save the environment they live in, but war is always ugly. Always bloody. Always has too high a cost."

Hawk nodded soberly, then looked at Max and Fang. "Where will the next one be?"

"I don't know," Fang said. "But we'll find it."

"That's what's so horrible," Nudge said. "We always find it. *Always.*"

Hawk nodded again, not smiling. "And I'm always coming with you."

MORE EPILOGUE

Hawk

Turns out, I could eat ice cream without gagging. Two weeks of forced bed rest and recovering in the care center at Tetra had left me twitchy and anxious to be moving, but the Tetrans were determined, sneaky bastards. Every day they'd figured out how to keep me in bed, how to keep my mind occupied so I didn't go crazy.

"You were practically sliced in half," Ying had said disapprovingly, like it had been my fault somehow. "It took a hundred and forty stitches to put you back together, and that's not counting the part of your liver and part of your spleen that you lost."

"Hm," I said. Of course, they'd totally saved my life. No one had been more surprised than me when I'd opened my eyes and realized I was still alive.

For the first time I was being allowed to sleep in my own room, not at the care center. I sank gingerly onto the bed, telling myself that I would get under the covers in just a minute.

Then I felt eyes watching me and I turned my head to see Io, quivering with anticipation.

"Hi," she whispered. "Are you awake?"

My eyes were *open*, but whatever. I nodded. She scrambled up onto my bed, picking her way over my legs.

"They said I had to be so, so careful," she said, making her way up to my shoulder. She put one paw on me. "I'm going to help you get better! Look! My wings are so big now!"

She screwed up her face as if about to exert the supreme effort of popping her wings out, but I said, "Can I see them tomorrow? So tired."

"Sure!" she said and patted my arm until I caught on and moved it so she could snuggle up right next to me.

Her soft breathing calmed me down and I was about to drift off when I became aware that someone was coming toward me. In less than a second I was wide-awake, tensed, ready for fight or flight even in my pathetic condition.

"You two look cozy," Max said. "Room for one more?"

"Yeah." I tucked Io closer to me and she moved her paw over my chest. Max lay down on her other side and stroked the soft, thick fur.

"Oh, my god, she's like the size of Iggy's shoe under all this fur!" Max said.

"I know, it's weird," I agreed.

Max stretched her arm over Io and smoothed my mohawk down. She looked at me.

"If you say how cute I was as a baby, you're gonna have to leave," I said, setting some boundaries.

"Did I tell you how cute it was when you started to fly?" she asked solemnly.

"Yes."

"Did I tell you what your first word was?"

"You said it was *why*. Gazzy said it was *doughnut*. Fang said it was *no bath*."

Max snickered, then changed tactics. "What's it like having an amazing revolutionary for a mom?"

I knew she was expecting a jokey answer—we were kind of tiptoeing into anything deeper. But I used to see posters with her picture, or Maximum Ride on a T-shirt, and it had been like—seeing hope? The idea that someone even halfway like her could exist in the world...I had fantasized about her swooping in and saving me and the lab rats. That was before I even knew she had wings.

Now I understood that heroes were more complicated than that. Heroes could get hurt, be angry, sad, scared. That didn't make them less of a hero.

Max and Fang, my parents, were heroes.

Max had fallen asleep, waiting for my answer. She and Io were breathing in rhythm, both of their mouths open just a bit.

I reached out my hand and touched Max very softly.

"It's amazing," I whispered. "It's the best."

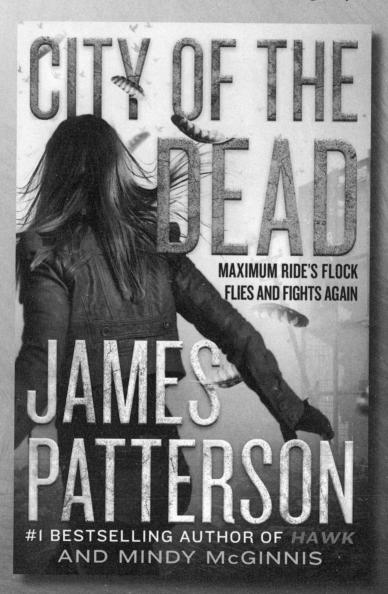

PROLOGUE

Who goes back to the city that tried to kill her? An idiot, that's who. But this idiot has wings, and I've spent most of my life learning how to fight. I guess that's supposed to be some sort of primal thing—fight or flight. There aren't a lot of people who learn how to do both at the same time. I'm one of them.

But I'm still an idiot.

Last time I saw Max—my mom—she told me that there will always be a war somewhere, and wherever that was, her and the Flock would be there to fight it. Given that she had two bullet holes in her at the time, the speech was pretty darn moving. I told her I'd be right there next to her, but that had lasted about as long as a pretty sunset...which in the City of the Dead means *not long*.

The pollution is better than it used to be, because the new Hope for Opes centers shut down the dope factories. But I still have to fly pretty high to get to clean air. That's where I am now—up. It's the only place I can get away from the Council, the people who are running the city now that McCallum and the Six Families are gone. Max and Fang—my dad—had me stay behind with my own little flock, kids from the Children's Home that I'd grown up with and looked out for. Calypso, Rain, and Moke.

But sometimes I even gotta get away from them, so I glide over here to the Marble Tower and watch the sunset, the warm rays getting choked out by the still-lingering smog. This is pretty much my own quiet time, and I can get kinda pissy if the Council needs me, or even my own group of orphan kids. The only person allowed up here with me is my trained raptor, Ridley.

Her head turns, eyes unblinking as her talons dig into my shoulder. She sees something she doesn't like, which means I probably won't like it, either. I follow her gaze, squinting in the dusk to see a fast-moving shadow tracing the edge of the Fallow Forest, which is just weird. Nobody goes in there. That place is overgrown and impossible to move through...plus I've heard more than a few scary stories about it. Not exactly bedtime stories either, because I didn't have a mom or dad to tell me those. More like nightmare stories about things that live in there.

Things like I'm seeing right now. I shift and Ridley moves with me, both of us extending our wings as we take off, cutting the distance between us and the shadow. In the last of the evening light I can see that it's a creature on all fours, back hunched, a tail zigzagging in the grass behind it. I dive for a closer look and it stands up on its back two legs—like a human. I hit the skids, letting an updraft grab my wings as Ridley lets out a distressed *caw*, right into my ear. She knows as well as I do—nothing and nobody goes into that dark, over-grown wreck of a woods. Nothing human, anyway.

Yep, like I said, I'm an idiot for agreeing to come back here.

But maybe Max and Fang are idiots, too. Because they didn't have to leave the City of the Dead to find the next war.

Looks like there's a new one brewing right below me.

CHAPTER 1

I've never been much of a morning person, and seeing the Council first thing doesn't improve my mood. The Council was formed after McCallum was overthrown, and the thug families of the Six went down with him. I know that bullets and bragging are no way to run a city, but I don't think that boring meetings at six in the morning are the way to go, either.

I'm yawning and have a knuckle in my eye when somebody says my name. I look up to find that every adult in the room is looking at me—and I don't know what the question was. Or even who asked it.

"Um..." I play for time, scanning faces, hoping one of them seems friendly.

They don't. Not a single person is glad I'm here. I bet they're all wishing I was Maximum Ride, the hybrid hero, sitting in this chair. Not her daughter, a gangly fifteen-year-old who was left behind to speak on her behalf...even though I never know what to say.

"Yes," I finally decide on a word to use. I'm trying to keep it positive.

"Yes," a woman with steely-gray hair repeats, looking over her glasses at me. "The question was, which vehicles should we be relying on? Gasoline, diesel, or electric-powered. And your answer is...yes?"

"Yes to all," I say, determined to stand my ground even though I don't know what I've put my foot in. "I mean, it's kind of dumb to want my feedback on that. I just fly everywhere." I spread out my wings to illustrate, and one of the men rolls his eyes before shuffling his papers.

"*Kind of dumb* or not," he says, "Langford is required to ask for your input, as you speak for the hybrid population."

Langford, that's the woman's name. I can never remember because I just mentally refer to them in my head by the nicknames I made up. Bad Haircut. Worse Breath. Really Big Gut. Of course, for all I know they might think of me as Bird Girl, so maybe I should shut it.

"I saw something go into the forest last night," I say. Everybody looks up, twelve pairs of eyes just boring into me. So much for shutting it. Oh, well. Go hard or go home. "It wasn't human," I add.

"Wasn't human?" Langford asks. "Could you be more specific?"

"Well..." I stretch my legs out, resting my black boots on the table. The man next to me pulls one of his papers out from underneath them. "I'm here to speak on behalf of the hybrids, right? Well, I think that's what I saw last night. Another type of hybrid."

There's a minor uproar. The guy beside me immediately launches into an argument with the woman to his right, saying that there's no proof that there are more hybrids. "She's just a science experiment gone wrong," he says, hooking his thumb back over his shoulder in my direction.

"We don't know that," another woman, one with long blond hair argues back. "The scientific exploration that created Maximum Ride and others like her was a secret, and could have been carried out in any number of places. We simply don't know what's out there."

I'd rather be referred to as an *exploration* than an *experiment,* but I don't have time to share my preferences. At the head of the table, Langford rises to her feet and slams down her sheaf of papers, bringing all the voices in the room to a screeching halt.

"Is this what happens when I don't bring coffee?" she asks, and the tension in the room evaporates into polite laughter.

"Now," she glances down at her notes. "I think we've agreed solar power is our best bet for the moment, but that some of the panels need repair. Holden, that's your area."

The guy I think of as Worse Breath nods. *Holden,* I remind myself. His name is Holden. Langford refers to her papers again.

"And as far as weapons resources go, we'll need to contact former members of the Six Families and see if any of them would be willing to share."

I snort. I don't mean to, but it slips out. I can't imagine my old friend Pietro, or any of the former bosses of the city, letting anyone know where their weapons cache is. Especially not the Council.

Langford ignores my snort, and clears her throat. "As for the question of, ah...a monster in the woods..."

Laugher erupts again, not as nice this time.

"Well...I think that speaks for all of us," Langford says, tossing me an apologetic look.

A familiar burn starts in my gut, making its way up to my throat, where I know some really nasty words are going to come out if I don't get a hold of myself. I'm fuming as the Council members get up and start streaming out the door. Max and Fang left me behind again, just for this. To be mocked by a bunch of people who couldn't win a knife fight if they had a gun. Nobody in here probably knows the first thing about pressure points, or how to choke someone out, either.

Why am I even here, in a boardroom at the top of a huge building? I belong down on the streets, getting my hands dirty and my face dirtier. My mom and dad made a mistake, asking me to be their stand-in for the Council. Nobody here takes me seriously. And no one is willing to listen.

"Hawk?" I look up from sulking to see that Langford has hung back. "Has anyone ever told you that you catch more flies with honey than vinegar?"

"Who the hell wants to catch flies when you can swat them?" I ask, and she gives me a smile.

"I'll see you at the next meeting, Hawk," she says, smacking my boots off the table as she leaves.

"If I bother to show up," I say under my breath, but then I spot a yellow square of paper on my boot. Langford must have stuck it there.

I'm about to crumple it up and leave it for trash when I see there's writing on it.

You're not wrong. There's something in the woods. I've seen it, too.

CHAPTER 2

Something is tickling my face and I swat it away.

"Not now, Ridley," I mumble, rolling back into my pillow. But the feather follows me, this time inching its way right up my nostrils.

"Hey!" I swat at it. Only after I manage to thump myself in the face do I hear a familiar laugh.

"Nice," I say, sitting up to see my mom perched at the foot of my bed, her wings unfurled. "There are better ways to wake someone up from a nap."

Maximum Ride fluffs herself, a few stray feathers falling. "Well I could just smack you around a little bit," she says. "It's not nice, but it's effective."

"Ha," I scoff, sitting up and pulling my sticky T-shirt away from my skin. I'd come back from the meeting in a crap mood, and fallen asleep in my clothes. "Effective like the Council, you mean? I don't know why you want me there. I'm just expected to sit and be quiet in the meetings. No one ever listens to what I have to say."

"And what's your tone like?" Max asks. "Do you have a weapon and are you threatening anyone when you speak?"

"Um…" I actually have to think about that one. There was an incident involving a switchblade and Holden that I'd rather not tell her about. But judging by the way her eyebrows go up, I'm guessing she already knows.

"Hawk," she sighs, coming to sit on the bed next to me. "I know you don't like being left behind—"

"Again," I cut her off. "Being left behind, *again*."

She goes on, ignoring me—just like everyone else.

"I talked it over with your dad, and Fang and I agree that having you with us right now is just too dangerous."

I pull a pillow onto my lap and wrap my arms around it. "What are you guys even doing?" I ask.

"We're trying to reform the prison that McCallum had me held in," she says, her eyes going dark at the memory.

"So why can't I be there, helping you?" I ask, but she shakes her head.

"No dice," she says. "It's not a friendly place, and I don't just mean the guards. There were so many factions fighting for control within the prison population, too. Right now, we're still trying to sort out who we can trust and who we can't." She pauses for a second, considering. "Also sorting out the death threats and trying to decide which ones actually mean it."

"You're getting death threats?" I ask. "But you're Maximum Ride! Everyone loves you!"

She pulls a face at that. "Not necessarily. McCallum did a good job of smearing my reputation—and your dad's—before we put him down. It'll take years to get everyone to believe we actually are the good guys."

I can't argue. Still, at least in a prison the bad guys are behind bars. As a kid, I lived on the streets without any kind of protection for a long time.

"I can take it," I say, shoving my chin out. "Let me come with you."

But Max just shakes her head and gets up, tucking her wings back in as she paces my room. There's plenty of space to do it in; the Council set aside the best suites near the top of this fancy hotel for themselves as soon as they came to power. As a representative, I got one, too. It's just about the only reason I keep showing up to meetings.

"Hawk, look at what you have here," she says, her thoughts following mine. "A warm bed, running water, clean sheets...and a great view." She goes to the window, her wings reflexively opening again at the sight of all that sky. They spread wide, lustrous and large. Maximum Ride is a breathtaking sight...but also kind of a punch in the gut when she's your mom. How am I supposed to live up to having superheroes as parents?

"Yeah, I'm spoiled," I say, looking past her wings to the view. "But I'm also bored."

"Bored isn't the worst thing," she says, turning back to me.

"What is?" I shoot back.

"Dead," she says.

I groan and fall back onto the bed. "Really? You're going to pull the parental concern card, after leaving me alone on the streets when I was five years old?"

"We've talked about that," she says, her voice hardening. "Fang and I thought someone was coming for you. We didn't mean for you to be alone."

"For ten years," I mutter.

"When are you going to stop punishing me for that!" she yells.

"When you stop treating me like a child!" I yell back.

She sighs, and walks over to my bed, her voice soft again. "Hawk, you *are* a child. You're my child. And I'm going to make up for all the protection I didn't give you then by taking care of you now. This is the place for you, here," she spreads her arms.

"I know you think the Council is boring, but you are fulfilling an important role…"

I put a pillow over my face to block her out. Her words are different, but it's the same conversation we've been having ever since McCallum fell from power. Both Max and Fang want to make the world a better place, and they'll go wherever they need to be in order to make that happen. Someday, I'll be by their side. But right now isn't *someday,* which boils down to this—I'm being left behind again. My mom is basically still saying the same thing she did the day they left.

You're not ready yet.

I was ready enough to fend for myself for ten years on the streets. Ready enough to take on members of the Chang family with only my fists. Ready to drop-kick McCallum and face down the head of the Pater family. But…none of that matters to Maximum Ride. She's still going to treat me as if I were an overfed baby, just like the Council does.

Except for Langford...the woman who slipped me the note. Her voice drones on but my mind wanders to Langford's words instead.

You're not wrong. There's something in the woods. I've seen it, too.

Sounds like there's someone who thinks I'm up to a challenge.

And I'm going to prove her right.

Read the rest of the action-packed sequel to **HAWK** in:

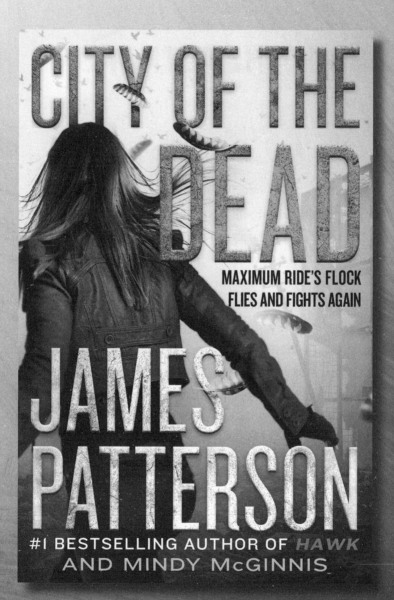

CITY OF THE DEAD

MAXIMUM RIDE'S FLOCK
FLIES AND FIGHTS AGAIN

JAMES PATTERSON

#1 BESTSELLING AUTHOR OF *HAWK*
AND MINDY McGINNIS

ABOUT THE AUTHORS

For his prodigious imagination and championship of literacy in America, **James Patterson** was awarded the 2019 National Humanities Medal, and he has also received the Literarian Award for Outstanding Service to the American Literary Community from the National Book Foundation. He holds the Guinness World Record for the most #1 *New York Times* bestsellers, including *Confessions of a Murder Suspect* and the Maximum Ride and Witch & Wizard series, and his books have sold more than 400 million copies worldwide. A tireless champion of the power of books and reading, Patterson created a children's book imprint, JIMMY Patterson, whose mission is simple: "We want every kid who finishes a JIMMY Book to say, 'PLEASE GIVE ME ANOTHER BOOK.'" He has donated more than three million books to students and soldiers and funds over four hundred Teacher and Writer Education Scholarships at twenty-one colleges and universities. He also supports 40,000 school libraries and has donated millions of dollars to independent bookstores. Patterson invests proceeds from the sales of JIMMY Patterson Books in pro-reading initiatives.

Gabrielle Charbonnet is the coauthor of *Sundays at Tiffany's*, *Crazy House,* and *Witch & Wizard* with James Patterson, and she has written many other books for young readers. She lives in South Carolina with her husband and a lot of pets.

JIMMY PATTERSON BOOKS
FOR YOUNG ADULT READERS

James Patterson Presents

Stalking Jack the Ripper by Kerri Maniscalco

Hunting Prince Dracula by Kerri Maniscalco

Escaping from Houdini by Kerri Maniscalco

Becoming the Dark Prince by Kerri Maniscalco

Capturing the Devil by Kerri Maniscalco

Kingdom of the Wicked by Kerri Maniscalco

Kingdom of the Cursed by Kerri Maniscalco

Gunslinger Girl by Lyndsay Ely

Twelve Steps to Normal by Farrah Penn

Campfire by Shawn Sarles

When We Were Lost by Kevin Wignall

Swipe Right for Murder by Derek Milman

Once & Future by A. R. Capetta and Cory McCarthy

Sword in the Stars by A. R. Capetta and Cory McCarthy

Girls of Paper and Fire by Natasha Ngan

Girls of Storm and Shadow by Natasha Ngan

Girls of Fate and Fury by Natasha Ngan

You're Next by Kylie Schachte

Daughter of Sparta by Claire M. Andrews

It Ends in Fire by Andrew Shvarts

Tides of Mutiny by Rebecca Rode

Freewater by Amina Luqman Dawson

Hopepunk by Preston Norton

Confessions

Confessions of a Murder Suspect

Confessions: The Private School Murders

Confessions: The Paris Mysteries

Confessions: The Murder of an Angel

Crazy House

Crazy House

The Fall of Crazy House

Maximum Ride

The Angel Experiment

School's Out—Forever

Saving the World and Other Extreme Sports

The Final Warning

MAX

FANG

ANGEL

Nevermore

Maximum Ride Forever

Hawk

City of the Dead

Witch & Wizard

Witch & Wizard

The Gift

The Fire

The Kiss

The Lost

Cradle and All

First Love

Homeroom Diaries

Med Head

Sophia, Princess Among Beasts

The Injustice

For exclusives, trailers, and other information,
visit jimmypatterson.org.